M000235482

"What the hell was that? out. Nothing. I glanc The taxi driver lies on the road behind us, his head attached to his body by bloody strands of muscle. His eyes stare blankly after his car. "What the fuck?" I'm suddenly nauseous, made worse by the road kill stench, and light-headed from the abrupt unrealness of the taxi cab driver lying on the road, practically decapitated. My sweaty hands slide on the vinyl seats and I wipe them on my pants.

"Hey!" Filled with a sense of dread, I turn to see who's driving. A woman's face reflects in the rearview mirror and I think: she's dead. The realization zips through my mind, exploding like a Fourth of July firework. The driver is a dead woman in her mid-twenties. Maybe she's not dead. But her skin is that odd shade of dead, pale blue that you see in all the zombie movies.

I look over where the gravedigger had been digging. He's face down on the ground and it looks like the coffin lid is open.

I glance back at the driver. It's definitely a young woman. My curiosity is stronger than my good sense to flee and I lean forward. My big mistake. The driver's head turns slowly on a stiff neck.

Your neck would be stiff too if you were dead in a box in the ground for—

I gasp and throw myself back. Her dead-doll eyes tremble and stare through me. The lips, devoid of color, form a wordless sigh. The make-up covering the bullet hole in her forehead is gone, leaving a blackish-red circle filled with thick ooze. A fly crawls around the circle searching for lunch. But it's not until I hear her speak, that I realize I'm in a shitload of trouble.

"Rick."

Copyright © 2019 by xxx
ISBN 978-1-950565-42-9
All rights reserved. No part of this book may be used or reproduced in any manner
whatsoever without written permission except in the case of brief
quotations embodied in critical articles and reviews
For information address Crossroad Press at 141 Brayden Dr., Hertford, NC 27944
A Macabre Ink Production -Macabre Ink is an imprint of Crossroad Press.
www.crossroadpress.com

First edition

FOREVER WILL YOU SUFFER

BY GARY FRANK

1.

Mount Moriah Cemetery is Hell on Earth. It's treeless and broiling hot from the ferocious July sun, which sears everything, including me. The two headstones—among hundreds—draw tears that blur the world like a Monet painting.

MARI ANNE SUMMERS
BELOVED MOTHER, WIFE
1940–1996

ALLISON BETH SUMMERS
BELOVED DAUGHTER, SISTER
1976–1996

I've come out here for eight years on the anniversary of the car accident, and it still hurts so damned much. The therapists all said it would take time, but so far, no good.

My father doesn't come any more. Five years ago, he met Marilyn, a woman in her thirties, and remarried. For the first time since Mom and Allison died, he was getting on with his life. I thought I'd be happy for him, but after Marilyn convinced him to put us in his past, I'm pissed that he doesn't show.

I kneel before the headstones and look at each of them, as if my mother and Allison sit here, hanging out. A blank space for my father waits to the left of my mother's name, while to the right, a blank space waits next to Allison's name.

"Another year," I say. "I'm still in New York." I glance at my mother's headstone. "And I still can't keep a girlfriend very long." There's comfort in this monologue; this cemetery is a sacred place, and even though I know their souls are gone, it still feels right to talk to them here. "I have my gigs and my job at the bookstore." Looking around the cemetery, I wish things were different. "I miss you guys so much."

The man who slammed head on into them at sixty miles an hour didn't die. Mr. Walker couldn't explain what happened, though he said he didn't do anything wrong. Bullshit. Was the car possessed? He said that he was driving along and then the car took off on him. Serene Southern Drive turned into a collision scene so brutal that they had to pick pieces of bark from Allison's skull and—it was just real fucking bad.

My mother and Allison had been driving to the supermarket for groceries. The seatbelts had been released seconds before the accident. The police said the two belts hadn't even fully retracted. What the hell happened? The only answer my father and I received was that it was a malfunction. They hadn't gotten them completely on yet. Who expects a sixty-seven-year old man to suddenly play hot rod chicken?

"Sometimes I think about getting the old band together in honor of the two of you and doing tributes and making you proud of me. I think it's just so I can see Katarina again. But after all that happened, I know it's a bad idea." I sigh and shake my head. "You don't need to hear this shit. Yeah, I've been cursing a lot lately. Better than punching people, right?" I rise, looking from one headstone to the other. "I just wanted to say hi and ask you to give Grandma and Grandpa my love." I glance up at the sky as if my grandparents are looking down on me.

Is there an afterlife? Do we reincarnate for another go round or just get tossed in a box to become worm food? I like to think there's something more waiting for me at the end of my life, but I can't say what. Maybe I'll see my grandparents, my mother and Allison; maybe I'll see New York City one more time.

"See you guys soon." I don't actually mean it, but I say it to everyone I know.

A tentative touch brushes my arm. I turn, half expecting to see Allison with her teenage girl smile that melted all the boys' hearts.

A hot wind abruptly kicks up.

"Take care, Rick," a woman's voice whispers like a breeze.

But no one's here, just my anger, loneliness, and me. Fifty yards away, a man in shorts and a T-shirt digs at a fresh grave. He shimmers like a mirage in the retched heat. He stops and stares at me. Goosebumps break out on my skin and I shudder for no reason. Why be scared of a gravedigger? A growing pile of dark earth obscures him as he continues digging. There should be a police officer present if the body is being exhumed. I shudder again. It's just my imagination running away with me.

"Take care."

The heat must be messing with me; I usually don't hear people's voices trickle through my brain. I place a stone on the top of each headstone and offer a prayer of safekeeping; I'm not a religious man, but for family, it feels right.

I head back to the old, dirty taxi waiting on the narrow road that winds through the cemetery, tossing a look back toward the gravedigger. I'm annoyed that my nerves are getting the better of me when I should be somber and peaceful. The memories of my life before the accident are good and that's what I always hold on to when I go home.

The breeze swirls up from the ground, sighing with desperate loneliness that sends a chill through me. I imagine that a sigh so terribly alone should be reserved for very old widows, widowers or …

Knock it off, Summers. It's bright daylight in the middle of July. The dead don't come out this time of day, only at night when it's not this blisteringly hot. Maybe they're smarter than we are.

As I climb back into the cab, the driver's door closes. I'm lost in memories of summer vacations, family barbeques, friends and parties that leave me empty and sad. I stare up the hill at the two headstones and even though I don't want to leave, the cab's meter is running, and I don't want to sit here much longer. The trip back to the city shouldn't take more than a half hour, though I'm in no rush to get back to my apartment. It's going to be hellish with useless fans barely pushing suffocating air around.

"I'm ready," I say, and the cab pulls forward. "Back to the city."

I start sweating almost immediately. Then I get a strong whiff of rotten meat, like road kill.

"Wanna turn the A/C on?" I stare at my mother's and sister's headstones, then others dotting the green grass. Something thumps against the driver's side of the car and the back-tire rolls over it.

"What the hell was that?" I move to the window and peer out. Nothing. I glance out the back of the car.

The taxi driver lies on the road behind us, his head attached to his body by bloody strands of muscle. His eyes stare blankly after his car. "What the fuck?" I'm suddenly nauseous, made worse by the road kill stench, and light-headed from the abrupt unrealness of the taxi cab driver lying on the road, practically decapitated. My sweaty hands slide on the vinyl seats and I wipe them on my pants.

"Hey!" Filled with a sense of dread, I turn to see who's driving. A woman's face reflects in the rearview mirror and I think: *she's dead.* The realization zips through my mind, exploding like a Fourth of July firework. The driver is a dead woman in her mid-twenties. *Maybe she's not dead.* But her skin is that odd shade of dead, pale blue that you see in all the zombie movies.

I look over where the gravedigger had been digging. He's face down on the ground and it looks like the coffin lid is open.

I glance back at the driver. It's definitely a young woman. My curiosity is stronger than my good sense to flee and I lean forward. My big mistake. The driver's head turns slowly on a stiff neck.

Your neck would be stiff too if you were dead in a box in the ground for—

I gasp and throw myself back. Her dead-doll eyes tremble and stare through me. The lips, devoid of color, form a wordless sigh. The make-up covering the bullet hole in her forehead is gone, leaving a blackish-red circle filled with thick ooze. A fly crawls around the circle searching for lunch. But it's not until I hear her speak, that I realize I'm in a shitload of trouble.

"*Rick.*"

My heart thuds in my ears. My breath is so unsteady that if I try talking, I'll stutter. But my mind's not working to speak.

What would I say anyway? Please stop, I'd like to get out now? Yeah, like that happens in all the horror movies.

I don't know how the dead girl got out of the grave, nor do I care, but I'm not staying. I grab the passenger side door handle, but the lock descends into the door and all I can do is jiggle the damned thing.

Okay, Rick, stay calm. Stay calm? I can't catch a good breath. The heat's unbearable, tortured by the smell of the dead woman that isn't dead, but driving the cab. I roll the window down, but no one's around to help me. I glance back at the once-pretty, but now hideous driver, then stick my head out the window to breathe. The heat slams against my face, but at least it's better than the stench inside the cab. I draw in a deep breath, grateful for the cleaner air.

The front passenger window rolls down. Reflected in the side mirror, the dead girl leans over. She's pretty but for the damned bullet hole in her head. "Rick," she says, "It is Rick this time, right?"

I don't answer; I have no idea what she's talking about.

"Pull your head in before it gets ripped off."

Her eyes quake in their sockets; the irises trembles very quickly from side to side.

"I'll take my chances out here, thank you." I look at anything but her because when I do, chills run through my body and I want to scream and vomit.

"I can't afford you getting hurt." Her words come slowly from a thick tongue that hasn't spoken since before the bullet sank into her brain.

"You may not be aware of this, but you're dead and you're stinking up the car!"

"Deal with it, Rick." The woman pulls the taxi over, gets out and opens the driver's side back door. She reaches in and her hand tightens around my ankle. I gasp in pain from her strong, icy touch.

"Let me go!" Panic sets in and I kick at her, but she avoids me.

"We have plans." Her other hand grabs my bare leg. She yanks me back in with strength belied by her thin body. "Now sit still." She slams the back door, gets in the front seat and we're off.

I sit up and rub my leg, trying to get some warmth and feeling again. "What do you want from me? Where are we going?" The stench twists my stomach and even breathing through my mouth is bad. The stink of decay sticks to my tongue and forces its way down my throat. If I pass out, it'll be a blessing. Maybe then my heart will stop jackhammering in my chest. "What are you?"

She just laughs.

The smell intensifies and I sit as far from her and as close to the window as I can, trying to breathe in any air that isn't tainted with death. It's no use and the nausea wins. Holding my breath only lasts a few seconds and the next breath I take is like swallowing thick bile. I squeeze my eyes shut and half my breakfast forces its way out from between my teeth.

"That is really gross," the woman says.

"And you're a ravishing beauty." I wipe my mouth with the back of my hand and try to breathe through clenched teeth in hopes of keeping the rest of my eggs and ham down.

"Why, thank you."

With my eyes closed, I focus on Kerri and the breath exercises we've done together. *Yeah, that's it, breathe slow and deep, ignore the smell of—forget it, this isn't working at all. I might as well just—*

"Oh, Rick, did you make a mess back there?" The woman sighs angrily. "Now the car's gonna stink."

"Right. As if it didn't reek before." I keep my feet away from the mess on the car floor. "What do you want from me?" No matter how hard I try to keep my voice steady, it trembles badly. My hands shake and my heart does a staccato beat like a prog-metal double bass drum riff.

"You'll see. We're going to a familiar … haunt." The woman turns her head and her mouth stretches in a rictus grin.

Suddenly, the radio snaps on. "Truckin'" by the Grateful Dead rolls out of the front speakers.

I jump and gasp.

"How apropos. It has indeed been a long strange trip." She

chuckles dryly. "I could really use a drink. Judith hasn't talked much in the last few days."

"Judith?"

"This body belonged to Judith Baxter until her husband put a bullet through her brain because his dinner wasn't hot enough. Men are such bastards. For you though, I am death, come to claim you and your beloved once again."

"My ...? I don't have a beloved."

"Yes, Rick, you do."

I try the door handle more aggressively, but to no avail. "Let me out of here!" The handle jiggles, but nothing more. I roll both back windows down, hoping the hot breeze will pull some of the stench out. Either it's lessened or I'm getting used to it.

"Where are we going?" I demand of the dead woman, but she says nothing and all that answers me is the Dead's Bob Weir singing how cities across the country are really all on the same street. *Okay, Rick, it's time for a plan.* The taxi slows as we approach the cemetery gates. *I can fit through the window. Better than staying in the cab ride to Hell.*

As soon as the taxi comes to a stop, I try throwing myself out, but I'm not as fluid as I'd hoped and instead of floating out the window, I get my upper torso out first, then push off the seat with my feet. Suddenly the window rolls up, pressing into my stomach. I gasp and try pulling myself back in.

"All I ask is that you sit still," Ex-Judith Baxter says. "We have somewhere special to go. But you can't do that, can you?"

The window rolls up, cutting into my stomach. I wince and groan in pain.

"What is it?" Judith asks. "A little pain? How high do you think the window can go before you suffer bodily harm? Another two inches? Three?"

The edge of the window cuts painfully into my stomach. "Let me go." Tears spring from my eyes.

"What do you think'll happen? The window's not sharp enough to pierce flesh, so that leaves internal injuries. If the window closes too much, something inside you will rupture or snap. You may not die, but you will be damned uncomfortable. By that point, of course, you'll be useless to me so I might

as well let the window keep rolling up until the dull glass rup-
tures the rest of your organs and your body breaks in two."

"Open the fucking window!" The pressure worsens as the
window creeps up. My back is pressed against the window
frame, wrenching my spine. "Okay! I'll come in!" Sweat drips
in my eyes, blinding me. Tiny little white dots blossom in my
vision. My heart thuds like war drums in my brain. The pain
rolls in waves to my feet and my head.

"Hm. Do you think your spine would crack in two, paralyz-
ing you before the window cuts through you?"

I imagine what she said is about to happen any minute. How
much longer until my spine snaps? The pain in my back intensifies; it takes my breath away until I'm suffocating and drowning
in the thick heat. "All right! Let me go!"

"What?"

I feel close to being crushed as the glass inches higher. "I'll
do what you want."

"That's real good of you." Her sarcasm drips like the sweat
down my back.

Suddenly the pressure of the window draws back, and I take
a deep breath, afraid at any moment residual pain will cause
something to pop, like my spleen, and it'll be all over. I fall back
in the car and stay on my side, praying the pain in my back subsides quickly. "God damn it!" I shout, pissed, more than anything else. My spine is sore and no matter how I move, it hurts.
At least lying down I can't see the dead woman. That makes me
feel somewhat like the universe isn't totally fucking me.

Maybe someone did this as a practical joke. The woman's
really alive but made up to look that way. Right, and for a practical joke I'd love to smell like death, too.

My friend, Dallas Richards, once said that in the face of the
incredible or unbelievable, it's easier to go by the theory that
such things can't be, than to accept the evidence and facts that
are in front of you. He's right.

I don't have any more escape plans. The door's locked
and the windows are set to kill. The stench lessened and
that's about all I'm thankful for. Whoever this woman
is, she has my attention. All I can do is stay calm and

enjoy the ride and the music. Mitch Ryder sings about the Devil in a blue dress and I think, no, today, she's in a green summer dress.

After ten minutes or so, the pain in my back's subsided, though it still hurts. I sit up and look out at the passing scenery, as the taxi speeds along Route 3, heading away from New York, and jumps on Route 17 North. The stench is all but gone, and since I agreed to behave, Ex-Judith hasn't tried killing me.

I've attempted conversation, but she's silent and I get this sinking sensation because I know where we're headed.

We take the Route 4 fly-over too fast, heading west in the direction of Fair Lawn, the town where I grew up and fell in love with Katarina Petrovska. I wonder how she's doing: did she ever kick the drugs, or did they kick her to death?

Katarina was part of the old band, TwistaLime, a bunch of addicts. Drugs, sex, porn, alcohol. You name it, we could addict ourselves to it. Yet, even wasted we were a good band, playing gigs at local bars, dreaming of bigger things. It wasn't until friends started dying that the whole thing fell apart. What a damned shame.

Ex-Judith speeds onto the Broadway exit off Route 4, then slows and stops at the red light by McDonald's. Flies race into the cab, swarming around her, but she doesn't wave them away. When they land on her face, she lets them crawl. She suddenly catches one and slowly pushes her fingers into her mouth, chewing on the fat fly.

I shudder and turn away, about to retch again.

She accelerates and takes the turn I hoped she wouldn't take, the one that leads to Kat's house. Maybe this is just a short cut to somewhere else. But the dead woman stops the cab exactly there, behind a teal Corolla.

"We're here. Get out." She slides the shifter into *Park* and stares at the house. She suddenly spasms, choking on something—her tongue? The fly? Her body flails around, arms swinging like a marionette's, jerked back and forth, up and down. "She's not here. Shit. Shit. Shit." When the spasms finally subsided, she turned to me. "Get out of the car, go in that house, and stay there. I have to go find the bitch."

I grab the handle and the door miraculously opens. *Wonderful. Of all places for the damned thing to finally work.* I throw myself out and slam the door.

"I have to find her!" Her head jerks toward the open passenger window and her dead eyes narrow and her gaze is pure hatred. "I will bring her. Don't even think of leaving. I have pets that will hunt you down." She makes a gesture in the air with her index and middle fingers together.

The car accelerates away with "Crawling" by Linkin Park blaring over the tinny cab speakers.

2.

I stare after the taxi as it screeches onto Southern Drive and speeds out of sight. "Just a joke. That's all it was. Someone's twisted idea of a prank."

Staring at the front door, memories come like the first winds of a hurricane: the stormy nights when Kat's fire consumed me and the dream-like weekends of drugs, sex, and band practice. Trash had his porn magazines and news of the latest X-rated movie stars and his plans to meet and sleep with them. Nettles was nowhere near as pathetic: he stuck with hard liquor, usually whiskey or bourbon, sometimes just vodka. Veronica, the British cutie who let razorblades dance on her arms, always had slash marks on her wrists and the haunted look of quiet desperation in her eyes. Those were the good old days of Hell. I blink and they're gone.

"Rich? Rich Summers? Is that you?" Dave Dawson, the neighborhood militant, stands where the three-foot tall bushes end at the sidewalk. He's wearing a "Get 'er Done" hat with camouflage shorts and a faded "Kill 'em all! Let God sort them out!" T-shirt that's too small for his beer gut. "How's it goin'?" His face is set in that *Don't fuck with me* sort of way he always had.

"It's Rick and I'm fine." I despised him when I was wasted, and I don't like him now. Back in the Days of Haze (Kerri's phrase for the years I spent wasted with Kat) Dawson and his son, Dave Jr., watched us like we were criminals. Dave Jr. used to stand in the yard and stare at Kat and Veronica, making rude noises until his father called him in.

We never saw Dawson's wife, Elaine, outside. We knew she was there because we occasionally saw her staring at us through the windows of their house, but she never came out. Then one day an ambulance came and took her away and that was the end of Elaine Dawson.

Memories run through my mind like mini-movies of someone else's past.

Dave Dawson grins at me like the wolf that finally got the sheep. *What if he has Kat in his basement and Dave Jr.'s doing whatever he wants to her?*

Stop. Dawson and his family might be crackers, but that was going a little too far. But I still glance over at his basement window.

"What happened to ya?" he asks. His features used to be sharper, but he's in his fifties now, and age and beer have rounded his face out a lot. His eyes are still dark and even from this distance, I feel like his gaze bores through my eyes to root around in my brain.

"I moved to the city."

"Got away from that weird chick and her family, huh?" He hasn't changed a bit.

"Yup."

"Don't think nobody's home." He shakes his head. "No. Well, since you left, the father split and then the mother flipped out. The girl had her mother institutionalized or something. She's been livin' pretty much alone in the house, except when her sister comes by." He nods, agreeing with his own words. "She left in a hurry a couple of hours ago. Went off somewhere with her drug-addict sister." His face freezes in thought and then he shrugs and says, "The family's fucked up. People comin' and goin' at all hours of the night. Fightin' and screamin' and that girl sleepin' with whoever the breeze blows in. It just ain't right."

"No, I suppose it's not." No matter what Kat's been doing, Dawson has no right talking about her that way. I open my mouth to express what I think of him.

"Katarina's a beautiful girl." Dave Jr., now in his late teens, steps up next to his father. He must've been watching and listening since I got out of the cab. He looks like a thinner, younger version of his father, and hardly good looking by any stretch of the imagination. "Woman is hot."

Dave Sr. pats his son's shoulder as if giving fatherly approval. Then he looks at me. "Y'all be careful, there's strange goings on with that family."

"Thanks." I offered my best fake smile.

The two of them stand there as I turn to the house and walk to the porch.

The Petrovska house is a modified Cape that hunkers one house from the corner of two quiet side streets a couple of blocks off Broadway. The house reeks of memories and I wish to God I wasn't here. The two-car garage, set back on the right side of the house, was where TwistaLime played during endless summer parties and where, in the winter, we practiced until our fingers grew too numb to feel our instruments.

Katarina's black Mitsubishi Eclipse sits in the driveway. The license plate reads, *Kat's Car,* and it, complete with the tags, was a birthday gift from her father. It has a few scratches and dents since I saw it last; Kat was never the best driver.

The lawn is smaller than I remember, but drugs'll do that to you. Three-foot tall bushes still line either side of the property, though they look worn out and tired.

What am I doing here?

Ex-Judith thought it was important to drive me back to this nightmare. I should just call for a taxi ride back to New York, instead of getting involved in this nonsense again. But a part of me wants to see Kat one more time, to know she's doing well. Then I'll go home.

I walk up the stairs to the porch. The door stands open and I glance back at the Corolla. I don't remember any of our friends driving one, but that was years ago. I doubt it's Kat's sister's car. Nikki was too much of a bitch to settle for something so average. A Spyder or GT3000 perhaps, but nothing as droll as a Corolla.

I reach for the handle of the screen door when a woman appears. Her angry energy slams into me. "Can I help you?" She's beautiful with a dark copper mane and the face of a goddess. Her white T-shirt, tucked into snug jeans, is cut deep and a long chain—with a unicorn pendant—hangs into her cleavage. It's hard not to stare. She's got that "I'm beautiful" attitude about her; it's written on her face. "Hey! Stop staring."

"Where is she?" I open the door, but she doesn't move. I walk in anyway, nearly knocking her over.

"Hey! You can't just walk in here! Who are you?" She takes a step back, though not too far. "You're … Oh my God." She scrutinizes me.

"Where is she?" I try moving past her, but she blocks my way.

"You're Rick Summers, aren't you?" Her jaw hangs open and her eyes are too wide.

"Yes, I am, as a matter of fact and—"

She slaps me as hard as she can. I see it in her eyes the second before her hand connects.

"Ow." She shakes her hand. "That hurt."

"No fucking kidding." I touch the spot that stings and radiates heat. "What the hell did you do that for?"

"You broke her heart, you bastard."

"And who are you again?" My cheek hurts, but at least the initial shock's faded.

"I'm a … a friend."

"A friend, huh? And that makes it all right for you to hit people?"

She snorts. "You deserve it after what you did to her."

"Oh, don't make Kat out to be the innocent princess here. We were all pretty stupid back then."

"Sure, but she didn't walk out on you, did she? She didn't up and disappear without a word, did she?"

She has me there. "All right. Whatever. Where is she?"

"Why should I tell you where she is? What are you even doing here?"

"A dead woman dropped me off. Seems she's looking for Kat as well."

"What?" The woman backs up and gives a quick glance to the portable phone. "What do you want? Why are you here?"

"I just told you. A—"

"A dead woman dropped you off. I heard you. Do you listen to the shit you're making up?"

I frown, trying to seem tough and angry, but all I pull off is angry. "Where's Kat? Just tell me where she is, because she just put me through hell, and I want to know why."

"I'm not telling you anything." She grabs the portable phone. "She told me all about you and how you treated her. You have ten seconds to tell me why you're here or I'm calling 9-1-1. Your choice. And I want the truth, not some bullshit about a dead woman."

She has to be difficult. I'm in no mood for this. "Put the damned phone down and just tell me where Katarina is. That's all you have to do, and I'll be out of here."

She looks me over and shakes her head. "I don't think so." She holds up the phone and presses one button with her thumb. "I asked you nicely and now we'll do it the hard—"

I grab the phone and press the hang-up button. "Stop being a pain in the ass and tell me where Katarina is."

"Screw you." She tries grabbing the phone from me. "I don't know who you think you are, but—"

I keep the phone out of her reach. "I told you the truth. I was paying my respects to my mother and sister and when I got back in the cab to go home, this woman, who looked real dead, drove me here. She wouldn't tell me why or what the point was. I figure Kat put this woman up to this and I want to know why."

The woman stares at me, her mouth wide open, but no words come out.

"Close your mouth before you start attracting flies."

"You're crazy." She shakes her head. "You've got some reason for coming here, and now that you find Kat's not here, you're making up some bullshit to sound like it's all some mistake. But you know what, Rick? Kat's not here and I'm not telling you where she is. You don't deserve to see her again." She grabs the phone and walks away.

"Who the hell are you?" I follow her into the kitchen, and memories come back in flashes of alcohol, drugs, sex on the floor, vomit, blackouts, and …

"Why should I tell you?" she asks. "You're a real prick,

hollering at me like that." She stops in the kitchen and turns to face me.

I nearly collide with her but stop short.

"If you don't leave right now, I'm calling the police."

"On what charges?"

"You don't live here, do you?"

She shakes her head. "No, but I have a key. Did I invite you in?"

"You're going to say I forced my way in and attacked you?"

"There's a stranger in the house harassing me."

"Just tell me where Kat is, and I'll leave! What the hell's wrong with you?"

"What's wrong with me? My ... Katarina's disappeared. Someone's stalking her. Whoever it is could have her right now and she could be ..." She shakes her head. "No, she's still alive. I know she is." She looks suspiciously at me. "No one knows who it is and ... No. I'm not telling you anything until you tell me what you're doing here."

"I told you already, but you don't want to believe me. Fine. I don't believe the whole thing myself, but, against my will, here I am." I fight the urge to care about Kat. I don't want anything to do with her. But five years ago, I loved her, and a part of me still does. "What's this about a stalker?"

"I don't trust you." She presses that damned button again. "Get out of here."

"What are you doing?" I step back from the table, hoping she'll take this as a sign that I'm not here to harm her.

"Calling the police. I'm not taking any chances. If you're not the stalker, you can tell the police and then you have nothing to worry about. If you are the stalker, then—"

"I don't know anything about a stalker."

"Hello?" the phone says in a female voice.

I say, "If Kat's being stalked by someone, I want to know. Someone's stalked her before and hurt her bad."

"Hello?" the phone says again. "Anyone there?"

"How do I know that you're not that someone?" the woman in front of me asks. "Maybe you want her back, maybe you want to hurt her for what you think she did to you."

"I have no reason to hurt Kat. I've been living in New York the last five years and I don't get out here except once a year to visit my mother and sister."

The woman holding the phone clicks the line off. "Okay. Fine. I still don't believe you, but—"

"Sure, now that you left the line open long enough for the police to trace the call, I'm sure you're fine." I take a cigarette from my shirt pocket, light it, and head to the door. "You don't want to tell me where Kat is, that's fine. She's being stalked again, I want to help, but you seem to be on some crusade and I'm not waiting until the police get here. They'll never believe how I got here, and I have better things to do than hang around with you and the police." I throw the screen door open and step outside into the ridiculously hot day. "See ya." Pissed that I let this woman get to me, I take out my cell phone, intent on calling a cab to take me home. It will be more expensive than I'd planned, but at least I'll be away from here.

I can probably catch a bus that goes to New York, so I start walking toward Broadway. As I walk, I tell that part of me that still loves Kat, too bad, I hope she's alive, but I won't be a sucker again. The chaos still looms like a mad beast around this house and this family, and I've grown up and out of any desire to be a part of it. The hell with everybody, I'm out of here. I look around the old neighborhood, wondering if anyone else still lives here. Of course they do. People are like weeds. Once they were in, it was hard to get them out.

"Wait!"

I glance back at the woman in the doorway. She waves the phone. "Let's talk. I'm sorry."

I almost tell her too damned bad, too damned late, but I don't. I keep my silence and wait to hear her truce.

"I called them off." She looks over at Dawson's house, and then waves me back, holding the screen door open. "Let's try this again."

I toss the half-smoked cigarette into the street and blow out a stream of smoke. *Well, Rick, here goes nothing.* I step inside and walk past her as the screen door closes with a hiss and a bang.

"I called off the police." She closes the front door. "You reek of smoke."

I shrug. "One of the hazards of smoking."

"It's disgusting." She stalks back into the kitchen. "My name is Meggan and I'm a … friend of Kat's."

I open the refrigerator in search of something to drink. "A … friend, huh?"

"Yeah, a friend. She's still got a few, you know. Just because you split doesn't mean all her friends did."

I pull out a bottle of hard apple cider and grab an opener from the closest drawer. Nothing's changed here.

"Do you mind? It's not like you live here."

I take a long drink and it feels good going down. "You gonna call the cops on me again?"

"No."

"Kat's still got friends, huh? Anybody from the band?"

"No. She doesn't see them anymore. She's got other friends. Ones that care about her and don't run out when things get tough."

"Well, Meg, the band *was* most of her friends. A couple of the others died of drug overdoses. In case she forgot to tell you, that's why I split. Kat thought she was invincible, untouchable, and immortal. She could do drugs and get as fucked up as she wanted, and in the morning everything would be fine." I take another drink. "But Meg, I saw Margo when she thought she could fly, and I saw Mitch when he thought he could outrun a train and I swore to myself I'd clean my shit up before I tried dancing with trains or flying without wings."

"How noble of you. Good for you. Now you're perfect, huh? Clean off the drugs and life is just excellent for you, right?" Her glare is venomous.

There's something Meg's not telling me, so I decide to step out on a limb. "You've got to be sleeping with Kat. You're way too damned self-righteous and pissed off to just be Kat's friend."

Her jaw clenches and she tries killing me with her icy stare. No, this is beyond icy, this is downright freezing. "Don't you dare presume what my relationship is with Katarina. And stop calling me Meg. My name's Meggan."

"Sure, *Meggan*. Whatever you say." I take another drink and toss the cap in the garbage can. This one will be done soon enough. Luckily, I had noticed a few more in the fridge. If this conversation keeps up like this, I'll need them. I had sworn off drugs, but if the day keeps going like this, I may have to take up drinking. "I know Kat's bi. Don't pretend to be so self-righteous."

"Don't patronize me." Her voice has that frosty quality that's real freaking endearing. "I don't need your shit."

"And I don't need yours, either. I've had a bitch of a day and your scintillating personality is just piling more shit on." I'm about to say something brilliant, when a moaning breeze rises throughout the house as if the place is in pain.

"What is that?" Meggan covers her ears.

"I have no—"

Just as abruptly, the sound stops.

"Okay. That was weird." She drops her hands from her ears. "Sounded like the house groaned."

Something rattles over our heads like metal nails spilling across a wood floor.

"What was that?" I look up at the ceiling. "Someone up there?"

"No."

"You sure Kat's not here?" I glance at Meggan.

She nods. "I've checked the entire house. She's not here."

The nails roll across the floor, moving over our heads toward the back of the house.

"That sounds more like some kind of animal," Meggan says.

"A raccoon? Kat keeping strange pets?"

Meggan frowns and gives me a *don't be ridiculous* look. "We should get out of here."

We should. It's what sane people would do. Except I've never claimed to be sane and I wonder if Kat has been hiding and kicked something over that spilled across the floor. Right. And the moaning was … what?

"Why don't we check?" I walk through the house, listening for more movement, but it's quiet. At the stairs I pause, waiting for the nails to roll again. Silence. Halfway up, I stop again. Was I ready to deal with some kind of wild animal?

"What's wrong?" Meggan whispers behind me.

"Nothing." I look up the stairs to the second-floor landing. I try to stay calm, but I still feel my chest tighten with each breath. Why am I even doing this?

Somewhere above us, a wall or ceiling gives way and something heavy thumps to the floor and then chitters madly, more like a drill on the fritz than anything alive.

"Rick?" Meggan asks in a quick, hushed voice. "We should really go. Now."

The hairs on the back of my neck rise like a sixth sense. I grab the banister for strength and head up to the second floor.

Every bedroom door is closed and there isn't a sound coming from behind any of them. Meggan comes and stands beside me. "What do we do now?"

"Throw all the doors open and let the sun shine in." But I don't move. My subconscious seems to know better and shouts at me to flee this place instead getting to the bottom of the mystery.

"Well?" Meggan asks.

"I'm waiting for any more noise so I know which door to go to."

"I thought you were just gonna open them all?"

"Spontaneous poor judgment. Happens to me all the time."

"Are we just going to stand here and wait?"

"You can open every door if you'd like, but—"

"Kat said you were many things, but not a wuss."

"Hey, look, I'm usually gung-ho to kick ass, but this is not the usual. Something is definitely wrong here."

"Maybe it has to do with the way you left Kat."

"Knock it off."

A door closes downstairs.

"Kat must be home," Meggan says.

I expect Meggan to head downstairs, but she doesn't move.

"So?" I ask. "Why don't you go see her?"

"I …"

"Yeah, right. Me, too. Do you hear that?"

"Hear what?"

"Sounds like someone's dragging a heavy bag or something

downstairs." The sensation of wrongness grows stronger, as if something invisible approaches us. If there was a cat here, it'd probably be hissing right about now. I wipe my palms on my shorts and take a deep breath to calm down. No use. A sense of dread permeates everything and keeps my heart racing.

Nails roll above us. They scrabble toward the back of the house.

"What is it?" Meggan steps away from me, staring up at the ceiling.

The house remains silent as if it's holding its breath. Then, one by one, metal drops rain down above us, moving from the back of the house, over our heads. Plaster explodes in Kat's bedroom. We hesitate and then I hurry to the bedroom door. Meggan shoves passed me and pushes the it open.

A blur of motion scuttles up the wall and disappears into a ragged hole in the ceiling. I move to the far corner of the bedroom and stare up into darkness. The nails race across the ceiling headed for the back of the house. I cautiously move under the hole, hoping that the thing doesn't come back. Ragged pieces of plasterboard hang down from the hole. White powder and chunks of ceiling cover the floor.

"What the hell was that?" Meggan screams as she hugs herself and stares at the ragged hole in the ceiling. "What in the name of God was that?"

I shake my head. "I don't know." A sheet of paper lies folded on Kat's bed and I pick it up it.

"What are you doing?" Meggan stalks across the room and tries to grab it from me. "Give me that!"

"Did you leave it?"

"No, but—"

"Then you have nothing to worry about." I unfold the white paper and read the ornate script.

"Dear Katarina,

You are very beautiful, unlike any woman I've ever known. Even after all these centuries have passed, and I have seen so many beautiful women from faraway places and exotic lands, you are by far the

*most precious to me. Each night that we've shared is magical and full
of wonder and excitement. You move me as no other woman has in all
the years I've lived.*

*Time, as you know, my Katarina, means very little to one who is
neither dead, nor alive. The feel of your skin under my hand brings me
such peace, that this un-life I live is spared the loneliness and emptiness
I knew before I met you. Being inside you, feeling you around me, is
worth the empty centuries I've lived.*

*But tonight, my precious, will be unlike anything you have known,
for tonight I come to your dreams with companions, gentle loving
spirits who wish to share in your beauty and the bounty that is your
unbridled passion."*

I laugh. *Who is this idiot?* Sounds like he's read one too many
Harlequin romances.

"What is it?" Meggan tries to see over my shoulder, but I
need to finish this uninterrupted. Besides, Meggan's gonna go
ballistic when she reads this.

"Wait, I'm almost done." I read on.

*"We will bring you to such heights of ecstasy that no mortal being
will ever be able to satisfy you again. But fear not, my Katarina, for we
shall come as often as you wish us to and you will never be alone, and
you will never need another lover.*

*I know how eager you are to satisfy me and how you anticipate my
arrival. But after tonight, you will spend the days aching for our return
and I can only offer this consolation to you: Each night we will come to
you and fulfill all your wildest dreams and desires.*

All my love, passion, and desire is for you,

Eduardo"

Meggan yanks the paper from my hands. I should leave
before she reads the entire letter, but if that thing comes back, I
don't want Meggan—pain in the ass that she is—alone in here.

"What the fuck?" she says.

"We've got to go." I take her arm and try pulling her from the room. "Take it with you."

She pulls away from me, walks toward the hallway, reading the letter. Forget about the blur that shot into the ceiling, this is gonna freak her out worse. Her breath shortens as her eyes scan the page. Her brow furrows. Her mouth opens. There's something fascinating about watching her: Study of a woman on the edge and going over. She reaches the last line, closes her eyes and calms her breathing.

"I don't understand what this is," she says quietly. "Who left this? Why would someone leave this?" Her voice fills with anger. "Who the hell is Eduardo? Who's he planning to bring with him?" She rips the page to shreds. "He's coming tonight with his buddies? Fine. I'll be here and when he gets here, I'm gonna kick his damned ass!" Storming out of the room, Meggan heads to the stairs.

The thing scuttles above the ceiling like it's following Meggan. I toss one last look at the hole and leave the room, closing the door on the way out.

Meggan's already halfway down the stairs when I remember someone, or something came in and slammed the door. It could still be in the house. "Meggan! Wait!" But she's not listening.

In the kitchen, she's rummaging through drawers until she hefts one of the biggest butcher knives I've ever seen. She looks at me with steely resolve. "Someone's fucking with Kat. Eduardo wants to drop by and screw around? He wants to be a ghost? I'll help him with that!"

How do I argue this point? If I'd ever found out someone was pulling this kind of crap when Kat and I were together, I'd have reacted pretty much the same.

"Kat told me she was having these dreams where a ghost came to her at night and told her some crap about being trapped in this world because he vowed to never leave his love. She started taking sleeping pills so she wouldn't remember them, but she said they got more vivid, more real."

"A little too real."

"It's bullshit. He's raping her whenever he feels like it." She wields the knife, checking the balance. Her eyes are captivated by the light reflecting off the blade. I've seen the look before in movies when the barbarian finds the perfect sword to skewer his archrival.

"I'll stay with you."

She looks up at me in surprise. "I thought you wanted to go home?"

"This changes things. Besides, there's some weird shi—"

Something crashes in the basement. Meggan jumps, almost dropping the knife. "I wonder if Eduardo is already here." She gazes at me. "Let's go check the basement."

She follows me to the closed basement door, and I wonder why the woman with the mini-sword isn't in front. Slamming doors, moving shadows, groans: sounds like this house has gotten haunted since last I was here. I always thought if a house was haunted it was always haunted. Dallas and I talk about this sort of shit all the time. He once told me violent, emotional events could actually start a haunting. So, what's happened here in the five years I was away?

He used to be a paranormal investigator when he lived out in Kansas. Since he's moved to the City, he doesn't hide his fascination with the supernatural, metaphysical, and all things strange. Because of this, most people avoid him. But we're like brothers and I enjoy our conversations. He should be here experiencing this madness.

I open the basement door without thinking. Even though we've talked about ghosts and their kin and how most just make a lot of noise, I don't want to give myself a chance to remember Poltergeist or Amityville Horror. No thanks. I'm sure it's just some kind of raccoon or squirrel or—

The living, evil, brain-sucking, flesh-munching, rip your spleen out zombies from Hell

—some other rodent that knocked something over.

The smell that drifts up from the basement is more than mold or mildew. It reminds me of the smell the instant after I've lit matches, but a lot stronger. Even at the top of the stairs it's nearly overpowering. But a basement in suburban New Jersey shouldn't smell like that. The stink freezes me to the spot and my throat is suddenly dry.

"What's that stench?" Meggan asks, close behind me. "Oh, God, it reeks."

Her voice grounds me and I flip the basement light switch on, expecting to see some vagrant run away from the light. No such thing. As a matter of fact, nothing happens but a new smell wafts up from the darkness.

"It's piss." I hesitate as a quick, heavy chill shudders through me.

"Someone peed in the basement? Why?"

I stop on the first step and look back at Meggan. "How am I supposed to know?" It must be an animal. This neighborhood is too nice for people to break in and urinate in their neighbor's basement.

"It was rhetorical. I didn't expect an answer."

I head downstairs breathing through my mouth, taking the steps slowly so nothing jumps out at me. Why the hell am I doing this when I should be fleeing this place and heading home? Oh, yeah. Katarina Petrovska. I've done crazier shit for that woman.

Half way down the stairs I stop. My imagination kicks in and I picture some undead thing waiting in the dark, its body reeking of decay, its breath hot and nauseating. When I get close enough, all I'll see are red eyes and white fangs the moment before it tears me to pieces. I just hope I'm dead before it starts eating my liver. It would really suck to be alive for that.

"Why'd you stop?" Meggan asks.

"Nothing." I take another step and a new stench hits me like a wall of fog. This is thicker than the urine and much more overpowering.

"Oh, gross, it smells like rotten vegetables," Meggan says.

The air grows warm and moist and the stench fills my mouth. It has a taste of wet, dark earth and I spit, afraid worms will abruptly grow on my tongue.

"I can't do this," Meggan says. "I'm choking. I can't breathe."

"Give me your knife." I hold my hand out.

But she ignores me and heads back up the stairs, leaving me alone with my fears and half a dozen steps left to go. "Thank you!"

She's the smart one, but I don't want to look like a wuss, driven out of the house because someone left—

undead, eyeball chewing, razor-clawed, fanged, drooling zombies

—vegetables to rot.

I swallow, half expecting my throat to fill with earth, like being buried alive. Suddenly a drumbeat grows out of the silence until I can't hear anything but the bi-dum, bi-dum, bi-dum. The sound forces itself into my brain, growing louder and faster. The drumbeat deafens me. Bi-dum, bi-dum, bi-dum.

I try to move but my hand, damp with sweat, clutches the banister and I can't let go. I feel feverish and I'm breathing too hard. The drumbeat's my heart, pounding like a motherfucker.

Opening my mouth to breathe, a squirming thing drops on my tongue. I spit out nothing.

Go back upstairs, Rick, this is fucking bad karma here. My hand won't let go of the banister and my feet won't move.

In the brief moment the basement light sparks bright before it dies, something hobbles toward the stairs. Wheezing breath drifts up and then the smell of shit and dead things, like road-kill in the middle of the summer, assails us. I back up the stairs; I don't care what it is, I'm not going down and saying hello. Fuck that.

Whatever's down there starts sniffing, taking short, fast breaths.

I've got half a dozen steps above and behind me. Something heavy makes the bottom stair creak. It's coming. Its stink precedes it and chokes me. Does it know I'm here? If I cough will it find me? I back up the stairs until I nearly fall over in the hall-way. The thing in the basement is still sniffing, coming up the stairs. I slam the door and look around for Meggan.

"What was down there?" Meggan asks. "It smells awful and it's getting worse."

"Some kind of creature and it smells like it took a crap on

itself." I jump to my feet and come into the kitchen. "I'm out of here. If you want to stay, you're more than welcome, but I don't want to be here when whatever it is comes upstairs."

"How did it get down there?"

I shrug. "I don't know, front door?"

"Let me just call Kat." She pulls out her cell phone and dials Kat's number.

"You can call her outside. We need to go before that thing comes up here." I pull her toward the front door as Meggan puts the phone to her ear.

"Kat, this is Meggan. Wherever you are, don't come home. Something … happened here. Give me a call and I'll explain everything. I'll be at my apartment with—just give me a call. Take care wherever you are. Bye." She folds up the cell phone and shoves it in her pocketbook. "Let's go."

I turn to the front door. An icy breeze slips past me and I shiver. "What the fuck?"

"What is it?"

The wall next to me shifts, turning to a thick column of sand. A million grains speed ahead of me, curve in front of me and meld with the adjacent wall. It solidifies, bleeding a dark brown until the color spreads quickly down the hall and all around us. The walls change from bland white to dark wood paneling.

"Oh my God." Meggan backs away from the hallway. "What's happening?"

A heavy footstep falls on the basement stairs.

"Rick? What's happening?"

The walls of the kitchen change from friendly, sunny yellow, bleaching into a bland flower pattern of lifeless blue and mold green.

The house changes itself, creating walls and destroying others. The colors of the walls run and melt together until they become filthy white with dark patches.

Another footfall hits the stairs.

"We've got to get out of here!"

"No kidding!" I barely hear her over my own thudding heartbeat. I don't want to walk into a new wall and become part of the house, but I don't want to stand here doing nothing.

The white Formica countertop ripples until it changes to wood, stained deeply with dark splotches. I don't want to even guess what they are. The hanging utensils start swinging, pots and pans crashing into each other. Meggan holds her ears against the cacophony of steel on steel.

Yup, Rick, we're fucked big time. I grab Meggan's wrist and she screams. I pull her out of the kitchen, headed for the hallway that now bends to the right instead of straight to the front door.

The house shudders as more footfalls come quicker from the basement. The thing is coming for us.

The hallway is hotter than the kitchen, and with no lighting, the wood paneling is almost black.

"What's happening?" Meggan screams.

We're trapped in the Amityville Horror, waiting for Rod Steiger to come running in to save us. Father Delaney, where are you now?

A new wall materializes and cuts across the hallway, blocking our way. I stop abruptly, trying to keep from slamming into it.

"Shit." I turn around, ready to head back. A door, halfway down the hall, opens toward us. It's the basement door. I pull Meggan behind me as if that'll stop the thing from getting to her.

The stench of rotting meat precedes the creature itself. My head grows heavy and I hold on to consciousness to keep from passing out.

"I don't want to die," Meggan whispers behind me.

"I had other plans myself." I have to joke. My heart's a jackhammer. An adrenalin rush stronger than any drug trip I've ever been on surges through me.

The door closes slowly, and the thing is silhouetted in the hallway. It laughs, then cackles. "Welcome home." Its laughter echoes through the house as it turns amorphous and rushes at us, a black mass spreading across the hall like death itself, opening its arms to embrace us in one final gesture of kindness. It shrieks as its body loses shape until it floats, wraith-like, above the floor.

Meggan screams as the thing passes through us, bringing a wind so cold that it feels like the temperature drops to freezing. I shiver and my teeth chatter. I immediately turn around and hug Meggan, searching for any warmth and hoping to calm her down. She grabs me, not a hug per se, but more of a clutching for dear life movement. Her screams subside to sobs. I take a deep breath, hoping my heart calms to its usual rhythm. The chill dissipates until the temperature is back to normal.

"Let me go." Meggan pulls away from me. *"Please."*

I suddenly realize how hard I have her and back away. "I'm sorry."

We look around at what had been Kat's house, but is now an ancient, decaying structure from some time a century ago.

"This place looks ... old," Meggan says.

"It feels old."

"I don't understand what happened. Why did that thing say, 'welcome home'?"

I shrug. "I've no idea but we should find a way out of this place before something else happens."

She nods.

A new room opens to our right, dark with a musty smell. Something sits in a chair breathing wet and heavy, watching us. This is not the way to go.

"Let's go back to the kitchen." I take Meggan by the arm and guide her away from the dark room. "We can go out the back door."

"If it's still there."

The kitchen has completely remodeled itself into something out of the distant past with old, stained wood counters and cabinets. The floors are loose wood boards, not the linoleum I've known for years. The table is a simple slab of wood with four sturdy legs and the chairs are just as plain.

Meggan steps hesitantly into the kitchen. "I feel like I've stepped back in time."

I follow her in, looking around the room. The wooden ceiling is broken by ragged holes leading up into darkness. The filthy white walls are covered with splotches of black that reminds me of a news article on killer mold I saw on TV. "It looks like no one's been here for years. Wherever here is."

At the back door, I reach for the iron knob, but what I see outside freezes me.

Meggan glances out the back door. "Oh my God."

The backyard stretches further than it should, and that dilapidated barn shouldn't be there. The houses that once stood behind Kat's are gone, replaced by farmland. Next to the barn is an old, rusty plow.

"Somehow we've moved back in time," I say.

"How is that possible?"

"I don't know, but I can't think of any other explanation." Right next to me, a narrow door stands ajar with a cramped stairway leading up.

Someone upstairs cries out.

I reach for the door's rusted iron handle.

"Rick, I don't think it's a good idea we go up there."

A sense of familiarity draws me toward the stairway.

"Rick? What if we should stay down here or get out of this house altogether? I don't like this place." She looks around and hugs herself. "We should leave."

I stare at the door's handle. If we've shifted through time, I shouldn't interfere with anything. It could mess up the time stream and then—damn, this isn't an Isaac Asimov book, for Chrissake. I grab the handle and pull the door open.

"Rick, please."

I don't look back. That sensation grows stronger. This is more than déjà vu, more like a memory.

As I climb the stairs of the hallway that probably leads to the third floor where the servants lived, I try to be as quiet as possible, but the stairs are old and creak with each step I take.

The hallway reeks of mustiness from the walls and the worn carpet on the stairs. As I reach the mid-point of the claustrophobic stairway, the stink of sweat, sex, and rot ooze down and around me, clinging to my skin and clothes. I take a breath through my mouth and taste the stench. My stomach flips and I have to concentrate on breathing to keep from vomiting.

In the room above me a little girl demands to be left alone. The other person, a man, laughs and—

The next stair betrays me, groaning like a banshee, and I freeze, listening in case someone heard me.

"Stop it!" the man shouts and there's a hard smack of flesh on flesh. The girl grunts and cries louder. "Stay still." A mattress squeals and two feet hit the floor. "I swear," he says, loud enough for me to hear, "if it's one of those damned slaves, I'm gonna carve their eyes out and shove them down their throat!"

Why always bad shit? Why can't this be some gang of gorgeous, desperate women hoping for some release to their tensions? Why does it always have to be ...?

Above me, an immense shadow falls on the stairs and the mixed reek of alcohol and sweat pours off him like a thick cloud.

"Who's there?" he shouts.

I try to say my name, but I squeak. Squeak, for fuck's sake! Not cough or whisper, but fucking squeak! That'll put the fear of God into a man! "Rick," I finally get out. "It's Rick."

"Rick who? You a new servant?"

"No." I try to see his face, but the light's coming from behind him. I make out his large body and something long (and probably sharp) in his hand.

"What are you doing here?"

"Making a mistake. I was looking for someone, but they're obviously not here. I'll be leaving." My hands feel clammy and my palms are slick on the banister.

"How do you know they're not up here? Have you checked?"

"I'm sure they're not."

He looks over his shoulder.

"I think they are," he says. "Maybe you should come up here and see."

"Rick!" Meggan whispers behind me.

I glance back at her, annoyed that she didn't listen to me. "Get downstairs! Now!"

"The girl you're looking for, what's she look like?" he asks.

"I never said I was looking for a girl." My heart skips a beat. For a second, I believe he has Katarina. How do I know he isn't Eduardo? This can't be him. This isn't even my time. "I'm sure it's not her."

"You come up here or I'm gonna come down and get you."

"Wait here," I say over my shoulder.

"You're not going up there." Meggan steps closer to me.

"Just wait here."

"I'm coming with you."

"You coming up, boy?" he shouts.

"Yeah, I am." I take a step up. I've handled tough jackasses before. Another step. When the band was together, we had all kinds of shitheads messing with us. Another step, creaking badly under my weight. We kicked ass and I was right there in the thick of things. I've climbed enough stairs to see an obese naked man standing by a decrepit bed, holding a machete. I've handled freaks before. He's naked. Fear squeezes the courage out of me with each stair I climb, making each step more hesitant.

"That's right, boy. You come right up here and see if she's the one you're looking for."

I can handle this. I can handle this. I can—

Rick, the guy's freakin' naked with a machete. Do you remember anyone like that at a show?

—run the other way! But my feet drag up, one step, then another as if I've been here, as if I know this place and need to be here.

The man laughs and backs away from the stairs. I know that laugh, but I can't place it. I take each stair slowly, ready to flee back down if he moves toward me. No, he's gonna wait until I'm in the room, then block off my escape. I can't let him, but I've got to know who *she* is.

As he backs up, the sun falls on him. He's not one of the servants. He's a rugged man, probably from working out in the fields. He's built like a wall with a bit of fat and thick graying hair on his torso and legs. His hands are big, and he holds the knife tightly.

His face is wicked. Though there's nothing outwardly wrong with his looks—he's too handsome—his eyes are wild like a caged animal's.

I stop three stairs from the top.

"Uncle William, please!" A young girl, maybe twelve or thirteen, is curled on a wooden bed with a beat-up mattress that's too thin to offer much comfort. Her wrists are strapped to the bed's wood headboard. She's naked with long red welts on her back from a strap and streaks of blood on her thighs.

"Shut up, Abigail!" He turns to me. "Who are you?"

The room is sparsely furnished with two beds, a scratched wooden dresser with a broken leg, and a low chest that looks like a coffin with its lid cracked off its hinges. A bowl of water rests on the floor by the bed the girl is tied to, and a damp, filthy rag is crumpled at the girl's feet. The wood floor is barely covered by a frayed rug and old tattered curtains flutter by a ghost breeze. The mustiness is thick, mixed with the stink of sweat and sex and filth.

"Who are you?" he asks again.

I want to say something tough, to scare him. But he's holding the knife and I can't think of anything to say.

At least I know his name, if nothing else. "My name is Rick." I keep my voice as steady as possible. "I'm looking for a friend and she's not here."

"That's all well and good, Rick, but we have ourselves a little problem here." He glances down at Abigail. "We were busy before you showed up and now that you're here and you know about this, I'm not letting you leave. I can't afford to have you telling anyone what you've seen. I'm sorry I have to do this, but—" He glances over my shoulder. "What have we here?"

Behind me a stair creaks. *Meggan. Great.*

"Oh God," Meggan says.

I shake my head. This is what I was trying to avoid.

"Well, aren't you something to look at?" Uncle William asks. "Come up here."

"Get downstairs, Meggan," I say.

Abigail sobs loud enough that I can't hear myself think.

"We can't just leave her here," Meggan says.

"Meg, this isn't our time. We can't do anything that'll change the events of—"

"I don't care! I can't leave her like that."

I glance at Uncle William's knife. I can leave her.

"What are you talking about?" Uncle William asks. "What's all this nonsense about time?" He leans down the stairs. "Come on up, Meg, and tell me what events you think you're here to change."

She hesitates behind me. I feel her tremble, wanting to do something.

"Back down the stairs," I say. "There's nothing we can do."

"Don't leave me here!" the girl shouts.

"Come save her." Uncle William grins like a wolf.

The house shudders and a breath comes like the house is sighing.

Uncle William's grin disappears. "What was that?"

"She's coming." Abigail smiles.

"Who's coming?" Meggan asks.

"Auntie Jean," Abigail says. "She's coming to save me."

As if Abigail speaking her name summons her, the curtains flap madly, and the drawers in the dresser jump out at once, scattering old clothing across the floor. The bed jumps up and down like an excited dog. A strong wind ruffles Uncle William's hair and pushes him back against the wall, even as he leans into it and tries moving toward the bed.

But I don't feel the wind at all.

"Meggan, get downstairs!" I give her a shove, but she's transfixed by the scene playing out before us and doesn't move.

"Damn you, girl!" Uncle William brings the blade up and approaches the bed. "The Devil has you, child!"

The sun grows brighter until William's shadow falls thickly across the floor, almost reaching to the doorway.

Abigail sits up on the bed, her wrists straining at the leather strap biting into her skin. All her attention is focused on Auntie Jean's arrival. When William hesitates, she cackles. "She's here!"

William's shadow suddenly reaches out, grabs my arm, pulls me into the room, and slams me against the wall. My arm goes numb from its brief, chilling grasp.

The door slams shut in Meggan's face.

"She's come!" Abigail shouts with glee.

"I'll kill you!" Uncle William screams into the wind. He raises the knife, its foot-long blade shining in the sunlight, blinding me.

I shield my eyes in time to see the blade turn in his hand. The shadow seems to clutch the weapon now, bringing it to bear on Uncle William. His eyes go wide with terror.

"Abigail, no!" he shouts.

The wind presses me against the wall; even if I want to help him—which I don't—I'm held fast.

Abigail climbs to her knees and watches in rapt fascination as Uncle William's shadow forces the blade around.

The girl grins wickedly at him. If this is how things had gone—whenever this happened—then I'm not going to stop him. Whatever he was doing to her, he deserves what he's about to—

Uncle William screams as the shadow hand plunges the machete into his guts, ripping him open to his throat. He tries holding himself together, but there's too much of him spilling out to have any affect. I turn away as the nauseating stench of blood and guts fills the air and intensifies. Darkness reaches out and grabs me. The last sound I hear before I pass out is Uncle William choking and Abigail giggling.

3.

I open my eyes and stare at a ceiling crossed with thick, dark wood beams. This isn't Kat's house. It stinks from piss and worse smells that all mingle together to form one indefinable stench. Where the hell am I?

"Ah, Herr Schwartz, you are awake," someone says. He speaks German, but I understand him. Overhead, a bright light is turned on, blinding me. At the edge of my vision, two men come toward the bed I'm strapped to. "How are you feeling today?" They're nothing but blurry shadows and I feel nauseous and sleepy. I must be drugged or something.

"Who are you?" I ask. This is way bad.

One of them laughs. "You know who we are. You know why you are here. Are you ready to tell us what we want to know?"

"And what's that?" I shiver from the chill in the air and from their voices. A dream-like familiarity frames this moment like I've lived this before but with no memory of having been here.

They're silent for a moment before the other one says, "Must be the drugs." He leans over and shouts, "You are here, Herr Schwartz, to tell us where you hid those Jews."

I was right. This is way bad. "What Jews?" This is no memory. It's some whacked out dream with no basis in reality. It'll play itself out and I'll wake up, hopefully back in my Manhattan shithole. Why does it feel so real, like this is actually happening? What if this isn't a dream? But I was in Kat's house. No, I was upstairs with Uncle William, Abigail, and Auntie Jean somewhere in time. How the fuck did I get here? Maybe I should just play along in case this isn't just a dream.

"Herr Schwartz," the first one says, "your son phoned and

told us you were hiding Jews. Now, why don't you save yourself and tell us what we want to know. Oh, come now, don't look surprised. Hitler Youth has no patience for dissenters."

Hitler Youth? If this isn't a dream, I am really fucked. "I don't know what you're talking about. I don't know anything about hiding Jews."

"That is what you said this morning before we took your leg. You screamed quite a bit, but you didn't tell us what we need to know."

I try to look down, but a strap crosses over my neck. I have minimum range of motion. I'm not sure if I can feel my leg, but I've heard it said that even after an appendage is cut off, you still believe it's there. I may not be able to feel my legs, but I can definitely hear my heart racing. This is a dream and any moment I'll wake up in Kat's house for real and—

"You will tell us, Herr Schwartz, or do we have to get Heinrich again?"

"Please, I don't know what you think I've done. There's been some kind of mistake!"

"Yes, Herr Schwartz, the only mistake is the one you made harboring Jews. Heinrich!" He sighs and leans closer to me. "I do not want to do this," he whispers. His breath is hot and foul. "Tell me where you hid the Jews and I'll tell Heinrich to leave."

"But I don't know anything!" I try the restraints; they have little give to them. "I swear, if I knew anything, I'd tell you, but I don't!"

The second man leans over me. "Let me explain something to you. We will keep asking the same question and if you continue to keep silent, we will take your other leg, your arms, and when those are gone, we will take your testicles, your penis, your ears and yes, Herr Schwartz, we will even take your lips. You will not die, but you will know pain like you never have before. All we are asking is what you did with a family of Jews. A simple question that needs a simple answer."

"I killed them."

The two men laugh.

"Your son has sworn allegiance to the Hitler Youth. Can you think of a reason why he would lie to us?"

"He's never liked me." *Talk quick, Rick.* "He has hated both his mother and I since he was young. In school, all his friends were going on holiday, but he had to stay behind because he was sick. He was furious at us and has despised us ever since. That is why he's lied to you!"

"That is a good story, but before we came in here, he signed an affidavit that says he's spoken the truth. Shall we bring him in here for you?"

"Listen. Fine. I was only trying to save them, but I will talk now. At least I will have one leg."

The two men lean closer.

"In … in the basement there's a floorboard that's loose. There's a room underneath. That's where they are." I hope this saves me or wakes me up.

The two men stand back and while they confer with each other, a third man joins them. He holds something thick and long with a jagged—

"You are lying to us, Herr Schwartz. Heinrich, take his other leg!"

"No!" I fight against the restraints to no avail.

The third man turns and bends over me. A sharp pain hits my leg as the saw rips through my clothes.

"Slowly, Heinrich," the first man says. "Do it slowly and we will listen for him to tell us what we want to … Ah, Fraulein Fox, how good of you to drop by! Herr Schwartz was just about to tell us where he's hidden the Jews your husband's been looking for."

I try to crane my neck, but the restraints are too tight.

"It looks like you're about to cut his leg off," Fraulein Fox says.

"Only to get the truth."

The woman comes to my side, no more than a soft, fuzzy blur. "This is Herman Schwartz?" Her voice is cigarette husky, in a sensual way. "You are sure?"

"Of course we are sure! We went to his house and picked him up ourselves! Why would you ask such a thing?"

"Because this isn't his day to die." She stands and the sound of three gunshots fill the room. She turns back to the bed and starts undoing the restraints. "I must hurry. It will be hard to move you, but we've got to get you out of here." Her hands are cool where they touch my skin and she smells of roses.

When the straps are gone, she helps me off the table. I'm still half blind and I almost lose my balance trying to stand on both feet.

"I'm afraid you've only got one leg, Herr Schwartz, but it is still better than what they had in store for you." She doesn't look at me. "We have to get you out of here." She helps me away from the bright light, into a dimmer room. "This is a rear door. There's a van waiting out back."

"Thank you, Fraulein," I say. "You saved my life. But what did you mean that it is not my day to die?"

"It seems I have a habit of doing this."

"What do you—"

She shoves me forward and I flail wildly, reaching out for her, for anything to keep from falling, but there's nothing to grab onto and I tumble down. I brace myself for the floor's impact, but it never comes. Instead, I keep falling with her last words trailing after me.

"Remember Athens."

4.

Faces and scenes appear before me and whip past leaving colored streams behind them. Some look familiar and others hold a familiarity I can't place, like a dream just out of reach. A sense of time, stretching out before and behind me, dazzles me, fills my eyes with sweeping colors that swirl and melt together until all these images and faces become one long streak of vibrant reds, greens, yellows, and blues.

I feel like I'm moving at warp speed and I pray that I wind up in my own time. Hell, as long as I don't wind up back in Naziland, I'll be very happy. Freefalling, comforted that I've left the interrogators, I'm still afraid of where my dreamself's gonna wind up next. Past, future, the right time? I hope I—

I hit something soft, slide sideways and hit the ground hard, face down.

"Shit." I run my fingers through low-pile carpet and automatically assume this is a good place, because I never thought Hell or any of its derivatives would have wall-to-wall carpeting. I open my eyes and look around. I'm on the floor next to the bed in Kat's room. So, it's a toss-up about carpeting in Hell. I stand on shaky legs and look at myself to make sure I'm complete, but I don't have the strength to stay upright.

I sit on Kat's bed, close my eyes and I'm back there again, but this time it is only the memory. My stomach tightens from the fear and I have to retch. I get to my feet, almost fall, and rush to the bathroom, heedless of what century the house is in. Falling in front of the toilet, I puke my guts up until there's nothing left, then rest back against the bathtub and close my eyes.

Okay, Rick, what the fuck is going on here? I can't stop shaking and suddenly I'm crying, tears streaming down my face. I hear the interrogator's voice echo in my head, "Where are the Jews!" and I squeeze my eyes shut, trying to fill my head with anything but the smell of that room, thick with blood, sweat, and urine. I hum songs, picture having wild sex with Kerri, think about fleeing from this fucking house with Meggan, and pretending none of this ever happened.

But it's no use. Those images, voices, and sensations of the Nazi torture chamber fiercely insinuate themselves in my psyche. What the hell was that all about? I certainly wasn't alive to be in Nazi Germany, but that felt too real to just be a dream, more like deja vu.

I shake my head and hesitantly stand on legs that are no stronger than they were before, but I have to get out of here. I don't want to spend any more time in this house with all the ghosts of memories loitering there. No thanks. Besides, I've got to find Meggan. I cautiously move out of the bathroom, using the tub ledge, the sink, and then the doorknob for support. Thankfully, the house has returned to New Jersey, circa 2004.

In the bathroom doorway, I realize how wiped out I am and how damned dry my mouth is. I'd rather collapse in a pathetic heap and just take a nap, but I can't. Too much weird is not good for the soul; at least not this kind of weird.

I head downstairs, waiting for Meggan to show up, all the while wondering what happened to her. I shouldn't give a damn about her, but she really isn't a half-bad person.

The Nazi dream assaults me again. Heinrich over my body with his bloody saw, ready to take my other leg, the interrogators screaming at me, my son in the Hitler Youth, calling the police on me, dinner with Inga and Alec, my son, interrupted by a knock on the door. "Come with us, Herr Schwartz, we need ..."

My head spins and I almost lose my grip on the banister. *Oh no! Not Nazi Germany again! Please!* My foot slips off the carpeted stair. I start sliding, twisting around, falling. I grab for the railing, not wanting to fall into the stinking torture chamber again, somehow knowing that if I fall again, I won't get out.

I clutch the banister and catch myself before I tumble down

the last third of the stairs. My heart's hammering in my chest. Half the images that scratch and claw at my sanity I didn't experience in that room. Where the hell are they coming from?

Then I remember Dallas and I talking about reincarnation. Are these past life scenes? I was never quite into the idea that we keep coming back until we learn all the lessons we need to. As a matter of fact, I never gave Death and God a whole lot of thought. Spirituality and Divinity, yes. Death and God, no. Go figure.

Right now, however, I'm giving all that a lot of thought, both to negate the images of life in Germany flooding my head and to open a dialogue with the hereafter in case my ticket's about to be punched.

I take a deep breath and sit on the stairs. My heart slows, so it's not trying to pound its way out of my body, just kicking in my chest.

What if all that was a past life flashback? I want to say it was all a dream, but what I experienced was too real. Those were powerful images, complete with sensations and emotions. This wasn't just some random dream image floating through my subconscious, but a scene from a memory. I should write that down; it sounds like a great song title.

The house is quiet, not quite calm, but peaceful enough that I can get something to drink before I leave. I stand cautiously, making my way down the stairs with more hesitation than I've done before.

In the kitchen, I open the refrigerator and grab a bottle of Mike's Hard Lemonade hidden behind a diet orange soda. Why would anyone want to drink diet orange soda? I tried it once and it turned my stomach. I open the bottle and take a long swallow. The clock on the wall catches my eye. It's nearly seven. How long was I in dreamland for? Damn, it's late and it's still quiet. Even though all the strange shit's happened, I feel safe enough to give Kerri a quick call. Then I'm definitely out of here.

I pick up the phone and dial her number. Kerri Hunter is my boss at the Turned Page Bookstore in Greenwich Village. I've been there for every day of the five years I've lived in the city. Between the bookstore and my gigs in local clubs, it's enough to pay rent on a real cheap studio not far from the store.

Kerri and I met while the band was still together. We had a show at the Baggot Inn in the Village and between sets, while the rest of the band members were feeding their addictions, Kerri came up to me and pulled me over to an empty table. She had incredible insight, and at some point in our conversation made me wonder about staying with the band and their addictions.

"You're killing yourself," she had said. "And for what?"

That's all she had to say. After that I never looked at the band the same way. Within months I realized I had to get out. I talked to Kerri often and she convinced me to come to the city and work at her store. She knew someone who knew someone who could get me a cheap place to live. Less than a year later I moved to New York.

"Hello," Kerri says. There's no question in her word, just a simple greeting that all's well and she's confident that everything's okay in the world, which makes me feel terribly guilty for calling her. I almost hang up, but she says "Hello" again and I don't want her to think this is a prank.

I steady my breath, which I realize is too fast and sharp. "It's me."

"Rick? Where are you? What's going on? You sound terrible."

"I'm in New Jersey. At Kat's house."

"Why?" Her voice turns tense. She knows my history with Kat as we talk about our lives all the time.

"It's a long, unbelievable story and truth to tell I'm a little unnerved by what's happened."

"What is it, hon?"

We have an intimate relationship and if it wasn't for Tina, the art major who loves painting Kerri—literally, head to toe—Kerri and I could be something, should be something. But Kerri's too wound up with Tina to notice my heart on my sleeve. We play games of innuendo and get all hot and bothered, but we never consummate our game. Not yet, anyhow.

"Some weird shit's going on here." I tell her everything, from meeting Ex-Judith up to the Nazi interrogation. I know I'm dumping a truckload of crap on her, but once I start talking, it all comes out.

"Okay," she says slowly, taking it all in. Does she think I'm crazy? We've known each other too long for that, but I can't believe she believes everything I've said. "You think the house ... moved through time?"

"I think this house somehow shifted in time, back to—I don't know—centuries ago. I'm scared, Kerri. You know me. I'm not like this."

"No, you're not." Her voice has lost some of that confidence as if my admitting fright has cracked her image of me as strong and indefatigable. "I'd leave, but not without Meggan."

"Something's wrong with this house like someone's opened a door to a real cold place and let in a foul draft." I wait for her to say something that'll make everything better. Kerri's usually not at a loss for words no matter what the situation is. Her silence makes me shiver. "Kerri?" My voice comes out in a hushed tone.

"Rick, you should get out of there. I don't care if Katarina's missing or not. I don't care that Meggan's upset. I care about you and I don't like the fact that you're in that house alone and all that shit's happening. What if the house shifts again and stays wherever it lands? I don't ..." She pauses.

"What?"

Kerri whispers, "I don't want to lose you." I hear the tears in her voice and feel my own tears force their way up through my eyes. "Come over here, Rick. I've got some wine and we can watch a movie or something. Just get out of that house."

The idea of relaxing with Kerri and a movie seems absolutely unreal. When did real life and insanity trade places? I consider her offer. I could call a taxi and be at Kerri's place in less than an hour. Maybe that would be more intelligent than staying here and waiting for Satan's daughter to make her next appearance.

What about Kat? I can't just leave her to the stalker again. Can I? I've already walked out on her once. Should I go two for two and leave, or stay to absolve my guilt? I could just wait outside for Meggan. Then if the house disappears, I'll still be in present day New Jersey.

Kerri doesn't seem real, just a disembodied voice on the

other end of the phone. If I hang up, she'll be gone, and I'll still be here with all this crap. I should just nod my head and tell her I'll be right over.

I glance at the glass doors that lead to the backyard, about to tell Kerri I'll be there in less than an hour, when I realize someone's outside in the dark, staring at me. The sensation that someone's walking on my grave grips me. I hear a woman calling my name, but I ignore her, trying to make out any features on the person outside.

The sunlight's faded too much to see anything more than a silhouette, but I know it's not Meggan, nor is it Kat. It might be Eduardo; the figure is tall enough to be a man, but some instinct screams that this isn't a man or a woman or anything human. Its gaze tears through my eyes into my head. What's it looking for?

Images—memories?—flash through my mind. They seem like a photomontage of a travel journal. Places I've never been to—Greece, England and Russia—fade in for a few seconds and then fade out. Yet they feel familiar, as if they're memories.

Somewhere far away a woman calls my voice over and over. Something slips from my hand and thunks on the floor. The thing outside draws me closer and I hesitatingly move toward the glass doors, never taking my eyes from its form that looks like a hulking man in rags and tattered cloak.

Beads of cold sweat break out on my forehead and my hands tremble. I don't want to go any closer, but I'm powerless as if the thing is somehow pulling me forward. More images assault me: orgies in slaughterhouses, ending in bloody massacres as knives dissect human flesh, slicing through muscles to skewer hearts and lungs. I glimpse acts of sexual depravity so terrible— men and women raped with swords, drowned in oil and set alight and then disemboweled—that my mind forces the scenes into dark corners of my imagination.

Through all of this, five people stay in a close circle, staring grimly at each other and the horror around them. Another one stands a distance off, grinning wickedly, gazing with cold malice at all of this. I know them all. Their eyes reflect a familiarity I know, and it chills me to my heart.

Then new images spring to life in my mind's eye. A man and two women dressed in what seems to be colonial garb. Names drift through my mind: Sarah, Thomas, Abigail. Sarah is my lover, Abigail longs to be. My lover collapses next to me, her skin drying up and flaking from her bones. The other woman laughs until her eyes go wide and then red rope marks blossom around her throat. She gags, scratching at her skin and as her face turns red, then blue, she points accusingly at me. She opens her mouth to speak, but instead of words, blood pours from her lips, soaking her clothes, spilling to the ground. Through bubbles of blood, she speaks one sentence: Forever will I remember, and forever will you suffer.

I shudder and blink the images away. "What the hell?" My hand is freezing on the glass door, pressed up against another hand, but this one more hideous than any mutilation I've ever seen. One finger is missing, while two others look as if they're being eaten away by rot. The palm is covered with pus filled blisters, some which have broken and smear the glass door with yellow filth.

While my heart hammers in my chest, I'm paralyzed with fear even as my brain screams to run. I step away from the glass doors and my legs give out. My head spins and as the darkness of unconsciousness swallows me, two words blow through my head like an autumn wind: Remember Athens.

"Rick?" A voice whispers through my head. "Rick?"

"Remember," I mumble.

"You must leave this house," the frighteningly familiar voice says. "Now."

My eyes snap open and I'm abruptly conscious. I look around but I'm alone, enveloped in the scent of flowers like the perfume Dad gave Mom. The same perfume that scented her casket the last time I saw her.

"Leave." The one word echoes in the kitchen until it fades away.

"Mom?" I know it's ridiculous to think she's here, but the scent of her perfume is real strong, as if she just left the room. I feel the pain of missing her grip me tightly and tears distort my vision. They race down my cheek and the only thing that keeps me from coming completely unglued is the fucking telephone that won't stop ringing. Don't they have an answering machine in this house anymore?

I get up off the cold kitchen floor and pick up the phone, ready to give hell to the person at the other end. It's probably some damned telemarketer trying to sell me a subscription to *Time* or something. "Hello?" I suddenly remember dropping the phone, but not hanging it up.

"What happened to you?" It's Kerri. "One minute we're talking and then next nothing, like you disappeared. I almost called the police, Rick. What happened?"

"I'm not sure. I thought I …" The phrase passes through my head: Forever will I remember; forever will you suffer. What's it mean?

Muddy footprints track from the glass doors into the kitchen. They're misshapen as if the person had bloated feet. Whatever that thing was, it got in. I shudder when I realize it could still be in here and I don't know where Meggan is.

"Kerri, I can't talk right now." My own voice is drowned out by my jackhammer heart, threatening to explode out of my chest.

"What do you mean you can't talk now? Rick, I'm scared for you. Please come back to Manhattan."

I hate to do this. "Kerri, I've got to go. I'll call you as soon as I can. Don't worry, I'll take care of myself and I'll be home as soon as possible."

"Rick, wait."

"I love you." I click the portable off and suddenly realize what I just said.

My throat goes dry. My head swims and I feel like I'm either going to vomit or pass out. I glance back at the window where I know the filthy yellow streaks are. Did that thing get in here while I was out cold? And if it did, what did it do? Is it still here? And where the fuck is Meggan? What will that thing do to her if it—

The phone rings.

I grab the phone and click the "Talk" button. "Hello?"

"Did you say you love me?"

I roll my eyes because this is the last thing I want to get into right now. "Yes, I did."

"Jesus, Rick. What the fuck am I supposed to say? You want me to tell you I love you, too? You know, I'm trying to deal with our little game at the store and trying to keep my feelings in check. Then you call and tell me all this shit's going on and I get scared for you. That's not enough. You have to tell me you love me?"

"I'm sorry I said I love you. I'm just ... it's just ..."

"Just what?" Kerri's tone starts to aggravate me.

"Kerri, listen to me—"

"Rick, I don't know what you want from me."

"I don't want anything," I say. "I mean—Kerri something really fucked up is happening here and though I'd love to hang on the phone and talk, I have to help Meggan and we have to get out of here. I'll call you as soon as I can."

Kerri's silent, either angry, scared, or confused. Probably all three.

"I'll call you," I say again, and reluctantly press the disconnect button. "God, that sucked." I glance around the kitchen and listen for any shuffling, walking, chewing (chewing?). But the house is silent, which is worse than if there was a deafening racket going on. At least I could find that or stay away from it. Silence means that it might be lurking in the dark and I could walk right into the thing.

Okay, Rick. Let's get a hold on ourselves because we can't afford to go to pieces right now. Not until we find Meggan and get the fuck out of here. Okay. Right. Find Meggan.

I grab the bigger of the steak knives, hoping that the thing from outside isn't in here with us. I leave the kitchen for the darkness of the hallway. Why didn't we turn every light on when we had the chance? Now the shadows move. And the darkness breathes. And my hands are sweaty and my heart beats too fast. The only thing that would make matters worse is if—

The kitchen light flickers out, plunging the house into complete darkness. *Flashlight, Rick, that would've been a good idea.* But I don't know where they are, and of course the moon is hiding as well as if it's afraid to shine its light down on this house. I freeze, listening again, straining to hear anything, but I might as well be deaf for all the noise in this house.

Something breathes.

Somewhere, someone's crying very softly.

Something breathes again.

Darth Vader's in the house.

Someone's playing a huge bass drum. Very quickly. Oh. It's my heart beating. I clutch the knife tighter, close my eyes and take a deep breath. When I open my eyes, the darkness is marginally lighter than when I had my eyes shut. The breathing hasn't grown louder or quieter. I don't know what that means, but I think it's a good thing. I slowly head to the living room, keeping my fingers on the wall so I know where to turn. I want to reach out in front of me to make sure I don't hit a wall, but I'm too afraid my hand is going to touch that thing that stood outside. I remember the yellow smears on the window and my stomach turns.

The crying is definitely coming from the living room.

"Meggan!" I whisper as loud as I dare, praying it is her and not that witch kid, Abigail, or Auntie Jean for that matter. Shit. What if it is Auntie Jean and she—

"Rick?" Meggan says.

I rush in her direction, and in my stupidity to get to her, forget about the coffee table in the middle of the room. I slam my shin against the hard, wooden edge and spin around, trip over my feet and fall in front of the couch. Luckily, I dropped the knife so I wouldn't fall on it. At the moment, while that slow, heavy breathing fills the room, I wish I still had a tight grasp on it.

"Motherfucker." The pain radiates up and down my leg and I sit on the floor gently rubbing the sore spot. I turn to the couch and barely make out Meggan curled in a ball, sobbing. "Meggan, it's Rick. What happened?"

"I can't … I can't talk." She starts sobbing again. This isn't good. We should get out of this house before something worse happens. If that thing from outside is in here, we could be in deep trouble.

I wonder what happened to Meggan. My own experience in

Germany was pretty bad, but luckily that woman saved me. If she hadn't, would I have felt the pain of my leg being cut off? I shudder at the thought.

"We have to get out of here."

In the light from outside, her eyes shine with tears and fear. "I'm really scared, Rick. The dreams were so real, and I couldn't stop them. It was like I was there, living it like a memory."

"I know, Meggan. We'll talk about it later. Okay? Right now, we've got to hold it together and get out of here."

"What's that?" She points behind me and when I look back, I understand the cliché of blood running cold.

In the dim light coming in from outside, I see muddy footprints, spaced three feet apart that come into this room, then head back to the basement door, made, I'm sure, by the thing from the backyard.

"Okay," I say over the mad pounding of my heart. "We've got to get out of here right now."

She's about to say something but catches her breath. "Do you hear that?"

Chick-chick-chick.

"What is that?" I glance around the room.

Chick-chick-chick.

Like a leaky faucet. Or claws on a wood floor.

I remember the thing outside touching my mind and the sights I saw as if they were memories long buried in the blackest depths of my brain. And what did it mean by "Remember Athens"? What if that thing is inside, leaving trails of yellow pus wherever it touches? Fucking gross.

"Listen." Meggan sits up.

The chick-ing sound stops. Is it my imagination or is someone humming? I glance at Meggan and her wide-eyed gaze is already staring at me. I'm not imagining it. Someone, somewhere in the house, is humming.

"What the hell is going on?" Meggan whispers.

"I don't know." I wish I had a cigarette. "Maybe it's Eduardo."

"It's coming from upstairs." Her eyes are wet with fear. "I want to get out of here." Tears streak down her face. "Please?"

"Sure." I help her to her feet and as we start across the living room the voice becomes clear. It sounds like a young girl humming a slow, dirge-like song. Not a happy song one would expect a young girl to be singing, but something dark and intensely sad. Then the lights flicker on and off several times. Meggan gasps and abruptly stops. "I don't like this, Rick."

I glance around, expecting hands to come out of the walls and grab at us. I pull her quickly to the front door, but as I reach for the knob, the lock clicks open, and the door knob turns on its own.

"Maybe it's Kat." Meggan looks at me. She doesn't believe her words.

"Maybe it's the guy."

"Then who's upstairs?"

"If it was Kat, she wouldn't be coming in that slow."

"If she's stoned ..."

The door opens too slow, as if whoever is pushing it open doesn't want anyone to know they're here.

"Get in the kitchen!" I shove Meggan. "Find a knife or something. Anything!" We move into the kitchen and I shut the light off. We hide on our knees by the cabinets. Unless they come in here, they can't see us. I contemplate going out the back door, but that thing could be out there, and I don't want to run into that in the dark.

"Hello?" the man at the door quietly asks. "Hello?" When no one answers, he says, "She must be asleep upstairs. Come on."

It's Kat's father.

"You sure you wanna do this?" Dave Dawson Sr. asks.

"I told her I was a ghost and tonight I was bringing more of my friends with me to experience the living."

Dave laughs. "You are really something, Chuck!"

"Quiet, Dad!" Dave Jr. chides his father. A regular circus. I can just hear the tag line now. "This is Chuck. He's convinced his estranged daughter that he's a ghost from the past so that he can sleep with her. One night he brought his neighbor and his son over for a little ghost gang-bang. Now today, we've got Chuck, his neighbor, his son and the daughter and they're ready to go at it, here on the Jerry Sprin—"

Downstairs in the basement something crashes to the floor and I know it's that thing from outside. I don't know which is worse, Chuck and his friend or the creature prowling in the basement.

Meggan and I stare at each other. That same look of fear in her eyes intensifies, making her eyes shine. "What was that?"

"Something in the basement."

"Something? Don't you mean ...?"

"No." I imagine the ragged hulk rummaging around in the dark cellar. "Some thing."

"Like before?" There's fear in Meggan's gaze.

"I hope not."

"You hear that?" Dave Sr. asks. "Is someone else here?"

"No," Chuck says.

"That car out there belongs to that chick," Dave Sr. says. "The one that Kat's been hanging around with."

"What other chick?" Chuck asks.

"I don't know her name. She's been hanging around your daughter an awful lot. I think there's something going on with the two of them."

"Like they're lesbos?" Dave Jr. blurts.

"Just like Lesbos," Dave Sr. responds.

"My daughter's no les ... she's not ... never mind. I know exactly who you're talking about."

Meggan scowls at me. I'm glad we're not armed. At least for the moment.

Chuck says, "Meggan fucked Kat up real good. If she's here, we'll get two for one!"

They all laugh.

That's what you think. I rummage through my mind for an easy plan and it makes me feel better. Something tangible and straightforward is much more preferable to the mind-probing monstrosity in the basement that's Ex-Judith, daughter of Satan.

"What are we gonna do?" Meggan asks. "My cell phone's in my pocketbook by the couch in the living room."

I have mine, but calling the police isn't the first thing I think to do. "Don't worry about the cell phone. Let's go say hello to Mr. Petrovska." I start to get up, but Meggan grabs my arm.

"Wait a minute!" Her voice is tense and clipped but hushed so they (hopefully) won't hear us. "I don't think we should just stroll right up to them and say hello. I don't want to wind up as their plaything. We need another plan. What if we wait until they go upstairs and then sneak out? We can call the police from outside."

"That's a better plan then anything I could think of." My head is still cloudy from the thing's prying through my brain and it's hard to think as clearly as I need to.

"Good. Besides, I don't want to be schmoozing it up with Kat's dad and have whatever's in the basement come up to say hello."

"Safety in numbers," I remind her.

She nods in the direction of the living room. "Not those numbers."

I agree and we wait. They'll go upstairs and—

"I think I'll get something to drink first," Kat's father says. "I could go for a beer. How about you, Dave?" His voice grows louder.

"We're screwed," Meggan whispers.

"Sure," Dawson says. "If we're gonna wait for you, might as well get me one, too."

"You got it." He turns the light on in the kitchen and stares at us. "What the hell are you two doing here?"

We quickly get to our feet.

"Looking for mice," I say. I've always hated this man because of the power he had and apparently still has over his daughter. It repulses me and I want to punch him in the face.

"Rich." Dawson comes into the kitchen followed by his son.

"Rick," I correct. I look at Chuck. "Strange finding you here."

"I used to live here." His voice takes on that authoritative quality parents get when they reprimand their children. He straightens up and stares at me with such hatred. "Rick Summers. The boy who broke my daughter's heart and got her hooked on drugs. Nice to see you again." Like a cobra, his fist shoots out, catching me hard in the stomach. I double over and fall to the floor, trying to breathe.

Meggan kneels next to me. Her hand on my arm is warm

and comforting. My chest tightens with rage and when I look up, I'm ready to kill him.

"What are the two of you doing here?" His eyes come to rest on Meggan. "And you." He pulls her to her feet. "You turned my daughter into a lesbian!"

"Is that why you come here and rape her?"

"Where is she?" Chuck says coolly, ignoring her remark.

"Don't know," Meggan says matter-of-factly. "Do you know where she is?"

"Don't get smart with me," Chuck says.

"Are you really a lesbo?" Dave Jr. asks.

"Loves pie," Dave Sr. says, then looks at Meggan. "Don't you?"

Her eyes narrow to slits. "Fuck you."

Chuck backhands her hard across the face. "Don't you ever talk to my friends that way!"

Her head snaps back and she almost falls. I grab her and steady her. She quickly wipes tears from her face.

"Gonna cry now?" Chuck asks.

She trembles and her hands curl into fists. "Let go, Rick."

"Don't, Meggan," I say. "Just relax. We're going to walk out, okay?"

Her body sags in my arms, but I don't let go. Not yet. I want to see what Chuck does next before I let her at him.

"Well," Chuck says, glaring at Meggan, "seeing as how Kat's not here and you are, and I would hate to disappoint my friend—"

"I don't think that's a good idea." I move in front of Meggan, but she pushes me over, so we stand next to each other.

Chuck shakes his head. "You're not going to cooperate, are you, Rick? That's fine. Dave, you and Dave Jr. take Rick downstairs and tie him up so no matter how loud he shouts and screams we won't hear him. In the meantime, I'll take Meggan upstairs and tie her down to the bed."

"You really don't want to do this," Meggan says.

"Oh, yes I do," Chuck says.

Dave Sr. takes a pistol from behind his back. "Thought there'd be trouble here."

"All right, Dad!" Dave Jr. cheers.

Chuck grins. "Well, that certainly straightens things out!" He nods at me. "Now, go downstairs like a good boy, and when we're done upstairs someone may come down and untie you. That is, unless we're too exhausted!" He leers at Meggan.

I shake my head. "I'm going to say this one more time. Don't make a mistake you're gonna regret."

"Seems Dave's got the gun, Rick," Chuck says, "so I don't see us as the ones making any mistakes. You, on the other hand, could make one that'll cost dearly."

Behind Chuck, Dave cocks the pistol and aims it at my face.

Chuck nods. "I wouldn't want Meggan getting hurt because you wanted to play hero. Just go with Dave and his son and everything'll be just fine."

"It's okay, Rick," Meggan says. "I can handle him."

Chuck laughs. "Oh, I hope so!"

Dave Sr. waves the gun and with resolve to act soon, I go to the basement door. *But, Rick, that thing's down there. You know, the one that ripped through your mind and showed you such horror you'll never sleep without a light on for as long as you live? Remember that? It's down there and waiting to show you such wonders!*

As my hand tightens on the basement doorknob, I realize this is the part in every horror movie where the audience screams at the idiot not to go down into the cold darkness. About five minutes later, he usually gets his head ripped off or his intestines pulled out through his mouth. Maybe it's not the nightmare from the backyard that's down there. Maybe it's—

—something far worse—

—just a raccoon that got in and he's frightened and trying to find a way out. I open the door and hesitate. The blackness of the basement is palpable. Cool air, tainted with the stench of rot, drifts up at us. I don't want to go down there.

"What the fuck?" Dave Sr. asks behind me. "Something die down there? Chuck, what you been keeping down there?"

"Nothing," Chuck says. "Just get down there and tie him up."

I turn back to Dave Sr. "Something bad is down there. You can tie me up in the kitchen, but I'm not going down there."

"Summers, stop being a fucking girl and get downstairs."
Dawson waves the gun at me.

"Listen to me. Strange shit's been happening to me since this
morning and I don't feel like running into a hungry, undead
psycho with a meat cleaver who hasn't eaten anyone in a week."

"Since when did you turn into a pussy?" Dave Sr. asks. He
shakes his head, pushes ahead of me and switches the light on.

For a second nothing happens and then the light flickers on.
That's unusual. Never happened like that before.

"Nothing down there. Probably some raccoon or possum
got in and knocked something over. What a fucking girl! Let's
go, Summers, we haven't got all night."

I glance at Meggan, then at Chuck and shake my head. "Bad
idea. Believe me."

"Just get downstairs." Chuck drags Meggan into the living
room.

Dave Jr. shoves me toward the stairs. "Hurry up, Summers.
I wanna fuck the lesbian!"

I almost turn around and punch him in the face, but that's
not part of my plan. I don't really have a plan. But punching him
now would ruin whatever I will think of. I just imagine him
screaming in a pool of boiling oil.

Down in the basement, Dave Sr. turns the lights on. The
place is just as I remember it, except our instruments aren't here.
The floor is covered in wall-to-wall thick brown carpet. Against
the near wall is a dry bar with four stools and to the left is the
old leather sofa where our friends used to sit and listen to us
play. I'm touched by a moment of nostalgia. We had some real
good times down here.

"Something wrong with you?" Dave Sr. asks.

I shake my head. At the far end of the basement are the slatted doors to the laundry area. One of the doors stands ajar and
thick darkness leaks out onto the carpeting. I can just make out
a smear of something on the open door. A smear of pus from a
blistered hand. Oh fuck, it's down here with us.

Dave Sr. pulls a bar stool over and sets it in the middle of
the room. "Here you go, Rick. One nice, comfy seat for you." He
looks around. "No TV?" He shrugs. "Guess I can't put the game

on for you. But that's okay. I don't want you to have any distractions from thinking about what we're doing to your friend upstairs." He looks at his son and nods at the laundry room. "Go in there and see if you can find any rope or twine or something to tie him up with."

Dave Jr. nods. A shame Dave Sr. doesn't keep looking at him, because it could be the last time that he sees his son. The same smell from the cab, though not as strong, permeates the basement. I'd run up the stairs, but I don't want Dawson shooting me in the back.

Dawson glances at me, smiling and waving the pistol again. "I want you to be able to imagine your friend naked, on her hands and knees, Chuck behind her, me in front of her. He's giving it to her up the a—"

The lights go out. The darkness doesn't just happen, but explodes around us, rising and swarming like a living thing. Something shuffles behind me, in the laundry room. Dave Jr. gives a muffled cry, and then silence.

"Dave! What are you doing in there?"

The darkness fills in quick and complete and I can't see him or anything else around me. The air grows cool. I want to run screaming like a little girl, but I don't want to run smack into something warm and gelatinous or cold and leathery. So I stand like a statue, praying for God to make the lights go on before—

A sound like hundreds of nails spilling across the ceiling fills the room, coming from the far end and sweeping overhead.

"What the fuck is that?" Dave Sr. asks. "Dave! Where are you? Chuck? What's going on up there?"

The nails come back around, racing to the far end of the basement and then spill down to the floor. I imagine hundreds of rats with razor-sharp claws running in the walls. The first beady red eyes I see is my sign to run upstairs and my acknowledgement that it's okay to scream like a little boy because something really fucked up is happening and I deserve the scream.

"Chuck! What the hell are you doing up there!"

No one answers.

"Dave! Chuck! Rick!"

"Stop screaming!" I shout back. "You'll wake the dea—"

Dave Jr. screams and it's worse than the scream of a little girl. It's the scream of someone being torn apart.

"Dave!" Dave Sr. runs toward his son's screams. I run in the opposite direction, straight to the stairs; I've been here so many times, it's easy for me to find them. I pray whatever it is stays in the laundry room. I take the first stair too quickly and stumble, slamming my knee against the next stair up. "Shit!" I grab for the railing, but I miss, and I sit down hard on the bottom stair. This is no time for relaxing.

"Dave?" Dawson calls. "Where ... what the fuck?" His screams come in short, loud bursts like he's drawing in breath between each scream. "What are you? No! Please! Rick! God help me!"

No way I'm going back there. I try shutting out his pleas, mumbling the serenity prayer as fast as I can, chanting it over and over, picturing the words until nothing exists, but "God, grant me the serenity to get the fuck out of here!" I turn to go up the stairs, and gaze down to the other end of the basement at the absolute worst possible moment. In that brief second, I have before scaling the stairs two or three at a time, the lights flicker back on. The basement is empty and tomb-like silent. The Dawsons are gone in body and in voice. Something catches my eye and I pause, long enough to see the doors. They're bleeding. Dark blackish liquid spills from the slats on the nice, clean carpet. My mind conjures a horrific image and as I flee up the stairs it stays with me. The doors have turned to razors and something slid Dave and his son up and down them like a cheese grater. I know if I look closer, I'll see strips of flesh on the slats.

I chant the serenity prayer again, hoping to clear my mind. I come to the top of the stairs, throw the door open, and run right into Meggan. We both scream and fall, twisting away from each other.

When she realizes it's me, she hits me. "Stupid fuck!"

I stand and pull her with me to the door. "You have the keys?" I don't care where Chuck is at the moment. My only concern is getting out of the house.

"They're in the kitchen on the counter."

The sound of the rats in the walls is all around us as she pulls me back to the kitchen.

I glance around, waiting for one of the walls to crack and whatever it is to come out at us. I let her go, hoping she can find her keys.

"Fuck," she says. "I left them right here when I came in." She looks down at the clean counter, then at me. "Did you take them?"

"Of course not."

Something very heavy thumps on the floor above us.

"Where's Kat's father?" I ask.

"Lying at the bottom of the stairs. I convinced him to leave me alone." She darts around the kitchen, looking at all the flat places. "Okay. This isn't funny."

Whatever thumped overhead pulls itself across the floor.

"My, Uncle William, you're sure heavy when you're dead," a girl's voice comes down from above us. It's Abigail and hopefully not Auntie Jean.

"Now would be a good time to find your keys."

A stain begins spreading from the center of the ceiling, expanding across the white plaster. It's age and time. The plaster remolds itself into warped wood until the entire ceiling is dark timber. Then time spills down the walls. The house is shifting in time from the top down. "Find those fucking keys!"

"I'm looking!" She pauses and closes her eyes. "I came in, closed the door, and put my keys down—"

The rats in the walls intensify their attempt at getting out. Do they smell our hot blood and crave a taste?

The tops of the walls spontaneously grow decay, the white turning a dull brown with darker streaks.

Abigail laughs as she jumps down one stair at a time. "Auntie Jean, do you think that man we saw before would like to play with us?"

"Oh, I think he would, Abby!" A woman, with a voice like leather, cackles.

"Can I bring Uncle William with me?" Abigail asks. "Should I push him down the stairs?"

"No," Auntie Jean says. He'll make too much of a mess.

His guts would certainly spill out and that would be yucky. Leave him here and when we find your friend, we'll bring him upstairs. In the meantime, give Uncle William to me." She drags the body away from the stairs. Her footsteps make the house shake. How big is she?

Meggan looks frantically around the kitchen then heads back to the front door. "Where did I put them?"

I rush into the kitchen and look under and over every surface, praying the keys will just materialize. Something huge slams against a wall upstairs and the house shudders.

"He's mighty heavy," Auntie Jean shouts.

"Rick!" Meggan screams.

The past consumes the walls, turning the white semi-gloss to filthy white with spatters of dark brown that could be blood.

"Oh, fuck. Meggan, find your damned keys!"

"I—" Her voice is drowned out as a wall explodes above us. Something has definitely broken through from one room to the next. I pray it's not a support wall, or the whole house is gonna come down real soon. Auntie Jean cackles madly above us.

Cracks form across the ceiling, racing from the kitchen outward in all directions. I don't care if Meggan's found her keys or not, we're getting the fuck out of here.

I rush into the living room to find her standing there holding her keys. For an insane moment, I imagine her ready to say, "Come on, Rick, we'll be late for the show!", but she says. "Let's go!"

"Wait!" Abigail shouts.

I don't want to wait. I don't want to look back. I grab Meggan's hand and we run like hell (maybe that's not the best word to use) out of the house. I pull her to the car, and she spins from my grasp and unlocks her door, sliding into the driver's seat. She starts the car, leans over and unlocks the passenger door. As I jump in, something catches my eye; a blur of motion to my left, but when I look, it's gone. I slam the door and the Corolla screeches away from the curb.

5.

"What the fuck happened in there?" Meggan pants, catching her breath, staring at the road ahead of us.

"I don't know."

"I heard Dawson screaming for his son."

"Something was in the laundry area and got both of them. Thankfully, it was before they tied me up, or else I'd be burgers right now. Before I came upstairs, the lights came back on and I saw blood all over the doors. I don't even want to imagine what it looks like in there."

"Jesus."

My adrenaline makes me shake and I stare straight ahead out the window, hoping for calmness to settle over me. I don't need any more of this twisted shit I just lived through—thank you, God. "All right, it's time to go home now. I've had quite enough. You can just drop me at the local bus stop, and I'll find my way back to the city. Thank you very much. It's been nice meeting you, but there's no reason to put up with any more of this supernatural bullshit."

"We're going back to my apartment," Meggan says with a steady voice that surprises me. Maybe whatever she lived through wasn't as bad as what I experienced. Then again, she could be holding herself together with a piece of tape and a handful of spit.

"Why? Give me one good reason to—"

She pulls over, puts the car in *Park* and glances at me with tears in her eyes. "I need your help. Kat's gone and I don't know where she is. I can't find her on my own. I don't like you, but you're all I've got. So … Do you want me to drop you off at a bus stop?"

I sigh, trying to come up with a plan to find Kat and go home at the same time. Nothing. "No." *God save me.* I wonder what she went through while I was in Germany.

"Thank you." She pulls away from the curb and accelerates a bit too fast. I don't say anything. The sooner we put miles between us, that house, and whatever is haunting it, the better. "You can stay at my apartment. I'm sure Ariana won't mind."

"Roommate?"

She nods. "And a good friend, too." She looks at me. "How do you think the house kept shifting?"

"I have no idea. When we first pulled up to the house, Satan's daughter did some kind of spell. Maybe that's what did it. The best I can tell, the house shifted in time from the top down. The ceiling changed. The walls changed."

"What if ... Rick, what if somehow the inside of the house shifts back in time, but the outside stays in the now and Auntie Jean gets out?"

"I don't even want to think about it." I have no idea what Auntie Jean is to consider what she can do.

That look of fear is back in her eyes. Yes, Meg, life's completely out of control right now and I'm not sure how we'll get it back again. "When we get to your apartment, I have to call my friend, Dallas. He's into all this supernatural shit. He should know what to do."

"Ariana thinks all that stuff is crap."

"He doesn't take kindly to people who think the supernatural is bullshit. He's going to want to come out here first thing in the morning. The sooner we resolve all of this, the better."

6.

Meggan lives in the upstairs apartment of a two-family house in Ridgewood.

"What do you do for a living? This is some art collection you've got." I look around at the paintings on the wall and the bronze sculptures on the end tables to either side of a leather sofa. The three paintings are copies of impressionists, Monet and Renoir, I believe. The sculptures might be Rodin, but I can't place them. "They must pay you awfully well."

"I work in advertising." She locks the front door and comes up the stairs. "It pays all right. Ariana loves art, too. Some of this is hers."

The living room opens into a small dining room with a smaller kitchen next to it. A hallway leads off the living room to two bedrooms and the bathroom.

Meggan drops her keys on the dinette table. "I need a quick shower. We should order food. I'm starving." She walks into the kitchen. "Pizza okay?"

"That's fine."

She orders a pie, adding my request for sausage and hers for pepperoni, gives them the address, and hangs up. She gets two bottles of Heineken from the refrigerator and hands me one. "I really need to take a shower and wash the smell of that house off me. Make yourself at home." She digs in her pocketbook and pulls out a twenty. "I'm buying, but I want change."

"Sure." I take the money and she heads to the bedroom.

I pop the top off the bottle and take a long, refreshing swig. After all I've been through today, getting drunk doesn't seem like such a bad idea. Of course, no matter how drunk Meggan gets, we'll be in two beds. Damn, she's beautiful.

I pick up the portable phone and dial Dallas's number. It rings five times before he picks it up.

"Go," he says.

"It's Rick. I need your help."

"What's wrong? Where are you? You sound like you've been through hell."

"I'm still in New Jersey. You're not going to believe this." I tell him everything that's happened to me since meeting Ex-Judith, including Meggan, Kat's disappearance, the stalker, and the whole episode with Uncle William, Abigail, and Auntie Jean.

"Sounds like I should be there," Dallas says.

I go on about the Nazis, the thing in the backyard and the visions with the man and two women from the colonial days. I tell him the phrase that sticks in my mind: Forever will I remember, and forever will you suffer.

"What do you think it means?" Dallas asks.

"Someone remembers something I don't and I'm going to suffer for it. If I didn't know any better, I'd say I hurt someone and now they're going to get me back."

"Yeah, but who? The colonial chick? The jilted one? I don't think she's around anymore, unless ..."

"Unless what?"

"I don't want to say anything on the phone." Silence and then, "Damn, I'm missing all the fun out there."

"That's why I want you to come out here. Kat's still missing, the stalker is still out there, and I know you thrive on this kind of shit."

"Sounds supernatural."

"Oh, yeah. No doubt. If you'd seen the things I did today, you'd think so, too."

"All right. I'll call in sick tomorrow and catch a bus to—where?"

"Ridgewood." I give him the address, then tell him I'll have Meggan call with directions. "One more thing. Go to my apartment and get me some clothes. I really wasn't planning on an overnight trip and I need something else to wear."

"We're good to go," he says. "I'll see you tomorrow morning."

We hang up and I sit down on the couch. A few minutes to catch my breath and then I'll—

The doorbell rings.

"I got it." I go to the door, half expecting Kat to be standing there, but it is the pizza guy. I pay him, adding a generous tip, and take the pizza to the kitchen table. Meggan comes out of the bathroom, dressed in a T-shirt and shorts. Her hair hangs in damp copper ringlets. She looks even sexier than she did before.

"Something wrong?"

"No, why?"

"You're staring at me."

"You're beautiful."

She blushes with a warm smile. "Thanks." She reaches for the stack of paper plates on top of the refrigerator and when she does her T-shirt clings tightly to her, exposing her flat stomach and snugly outlining her breasts.

"I've got to move them somewhere else." She turns with plates and I glance at my hands to look away before she catches me again. She puts them on the table and stares at me. "Jesus, Rick, you look like shit."

"Thanks. After what I've been through, it's no surprise." I take another swig of beer and sigh.

"What happened to you?" She cuts a slice and passes it to me on a plate.

I tell her what happened from the moment the door slammed in her face right up to the conversation with Kerri. I don't mention the monster in the backyard because I'm still not sure what happened. I finish off the first slice and wash it down with the last of the beer. "There's something about that phrase, 'forever will I remember, forever will you suffer'. The woman in that vision said it and it's stuck in my head."

"Want another one?" She's already at the refrigerator, pulling two more beers out. "I think we'll need these." She places them down on the table. "What do you think it means?"

"I don't know, but I think it's significant." I pop the top off the next beer and take a swig. "What happened to you?"

She stares at the pizza on her plate and frowns.

"You don't have to talk about it if you don't want to. I figured while we were sharing our nightmare—"

"Something happened in that house." Her voice is low and frightened.

"I know. I saw …"

"You didn't see anything." She shivers. Her voice trembles. Her eyes stare at the top of the pizza box, but her gaze is further away.

"Meggan, you don't have to say anything else."

"After the door slammed shut, I fell down the stairs and I don't know how long I laid there. I guess I was unconscious or something." She slams down the rest of her beer and snaps the top off the second. "I woke up. I was sitting in a chair in a living room, but not Kat's house. I felt like I was in the south. I don't know how or why." She sips slowly. "I was part of this family and we all sat around looking at each other. There was my mother, well, not my real mother, but this dream mother, two brothers and another sister. At first, my father wasn't there, but then he came in." She frowns and her hand grips the bottle tightly. "He was soaked in blood. His clothes, his hair. His hands and face were splattered with red. We were all horrified. He had a huge knife tucked into his belt and a shotgun in his hand. He grinned a lot and then he put the barrel up to my mother's head." She shudders. "He pulled the trigger. He kept laughing. He turned the gun on my one brother and shot him, blew a hole in his chest." Her voice changes, slowing, taking on a slight southern drawl and speaking as if she were uneducated. "We was all screamin' then. But that weren't the worst of it." She stares at the pizza and sips her beer like she's at a party. "No. The worst is when he made Billy … made Billy … Oh, Jesus. He made Becky take her clothes off—my sister for Christ's sake— and made Billy do it. You know what I mean?" She gazes at me, but to her I'm not there. "He raped her. And then Daddy put the gun up to Billy's back and Billy started cryin'. Daddy called him a God-damned sinner for fuckin' his sister and Billy knew better than to talk back so he just apologized and tried getting' away from Daddy and Becky, but he was stuck between them." Tears stream down Meggan's face, but she's oblivious to the here and now. "He pulled the trigger." She nods and sips from the bottle. "Shattered Billy's spine and blew a hole in Becky you could see through. I was yellin' and screamin', but when he turned to me with that demon look in his eyes, I shut up right away. But it didn't matter. He had the devil in him. He threw the gun away and took the hunting knife from his belt. 'I'm gonna carve you up', he said over and over. 'Carve, carve, carve.'"

"Meggan, you don't—"

"He came at me. I ran for my life. What else could I do?" Then she grins like she's just heard the best joke. "But I found Mother's knitting needles. He never saw them. I grabbed them right before he tackled me. He climbed on top of me and laughed. He brought his face close to mine and said, 'I'm gonna cut you the fuck up, Sally! But I'm gonna do it real slow so you feel every inch of the blade cuttin' you open like the pig you are!' He laughed. I was so afraid, but Jesus gave me the sense of mind to drive Momma's knitting needles as hard as I could into his ears. I kept ramming them in as hard as I could. There was blood and yellow juice comin' outta his head, but I kept fucking him with those needles until he dropped the knife and his screamin' stopped and he collapsed. I think even after, I kept driving those needles in until I felt them scrape together inside his head. There was brains on those needles for certain and then ... I ..." Meggan sways in her chair, her eyes fluttering, rolling back in her sockets. "Oh my God." She breaks down and collapses in tears. She cries hysterically, huge sobs shuddering through her body.

I try getting close to her, but she throws the chair back and grabs the knife she used to cut the pizza. Suddenly the cheese and bread and tomato look like brain matter and I don't need another piece.

"Don't fucking touch me! I know who you are, you fucking bastard! You're him! You've come back to finish what you started and I'm not going to let you! Get out of here or so help me I'll kill you!"

"Meggan, it's me, Rick, Katarina's ex-jerk. Put the knife down."

She waves the knife at me. "I thought I killed you, but

somehow you survived and now you think I'm just going to do what you tell me? So you can rape me again?"

"That wasn't me, Meggan, that was—"

"Stop calling me Meggan! My name's Sally! Don't you remember it? You should, you were fucking moaning it all those times you ... I should just kill you!" She grips the knife's handle tighter until her knuckles are white as bone. "I'm going to kill you before you have the chance to do anything."

She's lost it. Wherever she was after we got separated, she's there again. Luckily, I left Heinrich and the Nazis back where they belong. Meggan's in whatever dream she was forced to live. I don't know if I can reason with her, but I can hope that she's in such a fragile state she won't put up much of a fight. "Meggan! It's Rick! It's me! I'm not who you think I am!"

"Oh, I know who you are! You tried killin' me before and now you wants ta try again, but I'm not lettin' you! I'll kill you again, you bastard!"

"Look!" I hold my hands open to her. "I don't have a knife. I'm not here to do anything. Look at me, Sally. I'm not here to hurt you. I just want to help you. I know you had to kill your daddy because he was a bad man, but that's all over and you're safe. I just want to help you." I let my voice take on a touch of the south and use the name she thinks she is called. Why make more trouble than I've already got?

"Why?" She waves the knife in the air. "Why would you want to help me now after what you did?"

"Because I know you're hurtin' and I want to help you get through it. That's all."

"All right," she says quietly and lowers the knife. "If you want to help me, that's fine." She stares down at the floor. "I don't know what came over me." She chuckles. "I guess it's from everything that's happened today." Her voice still has that southern accent, but I want to believe she's back to herself.

"I know. We've been through a lot. Just put the knife down on the table and we'll talk. Okay?"

She glances up at me as she comes closer. "I'm sorry." She's still Sally. "So very sorry." She lunges at me, knife swinging through the air.

"Fuck!" I duck under her swing and grab her around the waist.

She brings her arm back, hoping to backhand me across my face with the knife. I grab her wrist and hold tight until she winces and the knife clatters to the floor. "Meggan! It's Rick!"

She turns into me and starts pounding me with her fists. But her hands grow weak as heavy sobs shake her body. Finally, she collapses against my chest and cries. I lead her to the couch, hoping she's back to Meggan again. When she falls into a fitful sleep, I go back to the kitchen, pick up the knife and place it on the table, then drop into one of the chairs and drink my beer. What next?

"Where am I?" Meggan sits up. "What am I doing on the couch?" She rubs her forehead. "What a fucking headache." She stands and shuffles to the bathroom.

I maintain my seat, finishing my second beer and debating a third. I have to keep my wits in case Sally decides she wants to try skewering me again.

Meggan comes in and stares at the kitchen table as if seeing it for the first time. "What did I do? I remember starting to tell you what happened to me at Kat's house and then I woke up on the couch."

I tell her what she said and did, but she doesn't remember any of it. All she says is, "Shit." She sits down at the table and grabs a cold slice from the box. "I'm sorry, Rick. I don't know what happened to me." She puts the slice down and looks at me with tears in her eyes. "I've never felt so scared or out of control before. I still feel—I don't know—like I left a part of me back there or maybe I brought something back with me. Does that make any sense?" Her eyes plead with me for some truth she can grasp because what both of us have gone through is pure madness.

"It makes perfect sense." I want to reach over and touch her arm to emphasize my point, but I decide better of it. "I want to bring Dallas to the house tomorrow."

"Why?"

"Because he knows this shit. He used to live in Kansas with these guys that did paranormal investigations. He's done this before. He'll know what's going on."

"And what about Kat's father?" She finishes the slice and pushes back from the kitchen table. "I didn't kill him. What do you think he's going to do? Think he'll wait until Kat comes home?"

"I don't know."

"What if the house shifts while you and Dallas are there?" She slides the pizza box in the refrigerator and pulls out a bottle of wine. "Interested?"

"I'll take another beer." I take the two empty bottles to the sink and line them up on the counter. "I don't know, Meggan." I don't have an answer, not even something witty and smart.

She pulls a Heineken out and hands it to me. She finds a wine glass and we move the party to the living room.

We sit next to each other on the couch and she unscrews the cap from the wine bottle.

"Would you call Dallas and give him directions so he can get here? He's coming in the morning."

"Give me his number." She picks up the phone and as I give her the number, she dials. After a brief introduction as Kat's friend, she gives him directions from the Ridgewood Bus Depot, which is only a five-minute walk from the apartment, then hangs up.

I pour her glass almost to the rim and set the bottle down.

"Thanks." She places the bottle on a magazine and throws a couple of coasters out in front of us, and then she settles back with her wineglass. "Well, what are we going to do now? If Kat goes back to the house, she could be in serious danger. But I don't know where she is to warn her."

"No kidding." I down half my beer, feeling the creeps sinking into my soul. "Meggan, when you were in that dream, did it feel like a dream or more like a memory?"

"What do you mean? It was just a dream." Meggan finishes her first glass and pours another.

I finish the rest of the bottle. "Do you mind?" I hold the bottle up.

"No, go ahead. There's two sixes worth."

"Thanks." I've got a slight buzz and when I stand, I wait

for the room to tilt back to normal and then I make the beer bottle line one longer and grab another from the refrigerator. "When I was in Germany, the experience felt more like reliving a memory than a dream."

"That's ridiculous. I've never been to the south and I know that's never happened to me." She looks away from me. "Jesus, it's never happened to me." She quickly sips her wine and frowns at me. "I don't think you were alive when the Nazis were in Germany. Were you? You certainly don't look that old."

I laugh. "That's true."

"Then it was just some dream."

"Sure." I nod and take a gulp from the bottle. I wish I could say with complete certainty that what I experienced was a dream, but the feelings were too strong and everything so vivid, the pain included. If it wasn't a dream, then what was it? Like Meggan said, I wasn't alive in Germany during the Nazi occupation.

Maybe I had been. Dallas has talked about past lives before, but we never decided whether such a thing existed or not. A friend of his had said that any past life experiences we have now are really genetic echoes from our ancestors and not our own true memories.

But as far as I know, I didn't have any relatives that lived anywhere near Germany during World War II. Maybe I did. Maybe that "dream" was some kind of subconscious genetic echo buried in my DNA. Right, and it's just coincidence that Meggan and I both had experiences like we did at the same time.

"What about reincarnation?" I ask.

She shakes her head. "No such thing."

"What? You think you live, you die. That's it?"

She shrugs. "I don't know." She takes another drink. "When we die, we're judged and then we either go to Heaven or Hell depending on how we lived our lives and how virtuous we were. If we sin, we have to ask forgiveness and hopefully God forgives us."

"A one-time deal, then. Born, live, die, judged and either favor or penalty. Period."

"What about you, Rick? Obviously, you don't think too much of God's judgment after the life you've lived and what you've done."

I laugh and ignore her dig. "I can't believe all this is just for one lifetime. What about kids that die? That's it for them?"

Meggan shrugs. "Maybe God calls them back early."

"For what? No, there's more than that. I think we live more than one life to learn certain lessons like humility and kindness and we keep coming back until we get it right."

"What are you saying? That your dream of Nazi Germany was a past life?" She takes a fast gulp of wine. "And the dream I had was something I really experienced in the past? What was I supposed to learn that lifetime? How to watch everyone I love die? How to kill? Bullshit, Rick." Closing her eyes, she squeezes them, and tears slip down her cheeks. "Just Heaven and Hell. That's all."

"I'm sorry. I didn't mean to upset you."

"Sure. Fine." She wipes her eyes and sips her wine.

"You think you'll see all your relatives that've passed on?"

"What's with you? Why the hundred questions?"

"I'm just making conversation to get my mind off what we experienced." I shrugged. "Maybe we'll find out that reincarnation is real, and you'll have to reassess everything you believe."

"Please." She frowns at me. "I don't think so."

I take a long drink from the bottle, remembering the images that creature showed me, especially the last and that phrase that still haunts me: Forever will I remember, and forever will you suffer. "After I woke up from Naziland, I went into the kitchen. Something was standing outside in the backyard."

"Don't you mean someone?"

"No. I mean some *thing*. I was drawn to it and it showed me images like a movie. Most of them were jumbled and pretty damned horrific. But one stood out as a scene from a memory. I was with two women. I was in love with one of them, but they both loved me. The one I loved, collapsed dead and the other woman said something as she was dying. She said that forever she will remember and forever I will suffer."

"What are you thinking? That somehow this woman from

your dream is causing all this?" She gives me that "you're out of your freaking mind" look and drinks half her wine.

"I'm just saying that I've got this weird feeling that this ... dream is relevant. That's all. When Dallas gets here, we'll sort everything out." I know Meggan's not buying this and there's no point in continuing this conversation.

She notices my beer bottle is almost empty. "Want another?"

I stare at the bottle, wanting something stronger. "Do you have any Southern Comfort and 7-Up?"

She gets up and walks to the kitchen. Her shorts are a little tight. She's got a great—

"I have both actually. What mix?"

"50-50," I say to her perfect ass.

She pulls a bottle of Southern Comfort from one of the kitchen cabinets and a 2-liter bottle of 7-Up from the refrigerator. "What do you think happened to Kat's father? I didn't kill him. He's still alive." She pours an even mix into the glass and leaves the bottles on the counter.

She doesn't want to discuss reincarnation for whatever reason and though I'd love to push the issue, I'll talk to Dallas tomorrow. "Maybe whatever's in the house got him. Then we don't have to worry about him at all. Maybe all that noise upstairs was him being thrown around."

She returns with the glass, hands it to me and picks up her own. "Wouldn't that be nice?" She holds her glass up. "Here's to monsters slaying monsters."

I raise my glass to her toast, and we drink to supernature setting things right. The SoCo and Seven is hot going down and pleasantly warms my insides.

"What if he's not dead?" Meggan asks. "What if he got out and he finds her. He's crazy enough to kidnap her, maybe even—"

"Meggan, right now we have to find Kat, wherever she is. Her father can wait."

"Rick, he's molesting his daughter whenever he damned well feels like it. How can you just sit there and be okay with that?"

"I never said I was okay with it. But we need to sit down

with Kat first and explain all this to her and let her decide what she wants to do about him. It is her father."

"Have you grown that cold? She was your lover. How can you be so calm about this?"

"I know." I can't think of anything else to say that won't be a repeat of all I've said already, so I take a long drink. "What were you doing at Kat's house?"

"We were supposed to get together this afternoon and when I came to pick her up, she was gone. Nothing like this has ever happened before."

"I really need a cigarette."

"Go outside. You're not smoking in here."

I don't want to leave her. I don't want to be alone. Everything that's happened today has rattled me more than I want to admit. I thought I'd seen it all when the band was together, from fans trying to have sex with Kat on stage, to gay fans making gestures at all of us. Drunk fans are easy enough to throw off stage.

But the supernatural—dead women, ghosts, and monsters—are more than I want to deal with. If only I didn't care so much for Kat, I could be out of here and safely in Kerri's arms (at least) or her bed (at best). But I never exorcized this particular demon completely, and now it's back to haunt me. Fucking great. I down the SoCo and Seven, hoping it'll cancel out all the pain, memories and jagged edges, but it can't. Nothing can.

"We should call the police on Kat's father and get him locked up." Meggan refills her wineglass. Half the bottle is empty.

"And tell them what? While we were in the house snooping around, her father and his friends came in? Doesn't that make us trespassers?"

"I have a key. Besides, Kat got a restraining order against her father because he freaked about our relationship and Kat thought he was going to hurt her. He'd be breaking the court order and we could have him arrested."

"You two are lovers, aren't you?" The words drop out of my mouth before I know what I'm saying.

She looks at me and sips her wine. "And if we are, so what?" Before I can answer, she says. "Yes. Kat and I are lovers. You had your chance with her. You messed it up. If you think you're going to try some kind of reconciliation, forget it. She's over you, end of story."

"I'm hardly looking for any kind of reconciliation. As long as she's happy, that's what's important."

"Well, she's not. Nikki won't leave her alone and Kat's got no willpower to stay clean. I'm trying to help her stay clean, but Kat doesn't realize how much it hurts me when she pulls this shit."

"Same old Kat. She hasn't changed a bit."

"That's not fair. She has. You left and she hit bottom. She stayed there for a long time; I didn't think she'd make it out. But I helped her find a way to help herself and she stuck with it for a while." She sips her wine and stares into space. "It's a shame she couldn't stick with it."

"Why do you stay?"

Meggan shrugs. "I love her. She makes me happy. It's Nikki. If she'd leave Kat alone, then I think Kat would straighten herself out. I've tried talking to Nikki, but she doesn't listen."

"Nikki's always been a drug addict, just doing enough to get fucked up, but not enough to try flying, and she loves getting high with Kat."

Meggan nods and drains her glass. "Damn." She pours another, careful not to spill any. "Yeah, Nikki keeps coming around." She sets the bottle down and takes a fast drink. "You know what she says? When she does drugs, God comes to her and gives her the best orgasms she's ever had."

"Isn't that sacrilegious or something?"

Meggan shakes her head and sighs. "Believe that shit?" She takes a quick gulp. "This is what I have to deal with. She drags Kat down so she won't be alone when she gets stoned, and Kat goes along with her. She says, it's her sister, how can she say no? I say it's easy: no. But she doesn't, and then she tells me not to feel bad." She looks away from me. "But I'm not giving up on her. I can't." Meggan smiles and it gives me the warm fuzzies. She's quite beautiful. She finishes another glass of wine and places it down on the table. Her eyes glitter with pain and tears, and when she closes them, fat drops roll down her cheeks.

"I'm scared," she announces. "I don't understand what

happened at the house, and this stalker thing is freaking me out. I feel like my grip on reality is slipping and I don't know how to get it back." She refills her glass and stares at the pale pink wine. "I can't do this by myself and the only person I really trust and love is missing." She covers her eyes and cries.

I put my glass down and move closer to her.

"No." She puts her hand up between us. "Don't." She wipes her eyes. "I'll be all right." She sips her wine a little too quickly, then eyes my empty glass. "Want another?"

"I'll just have some wine."

She pours the end of the bottle into my glass. "Luckily, I have another." She stands slowly and staggers into the kitchen. "I don't usually drink a lot, but today deserves it. Right?" She comes back in with another bottle of wine, the bottle of Southern Comfort and a 2-liter of 7-Up. "You can have some of the 7-Up, but I have to leave some for Ariana. It's all she drinks. But I do have another bottle of Southern Comfort if you want it straight." She shrugs and places the bottles down on the coffee table. "Can you open the wine?"

I open the bottle, leaving the cork next to it.

"Can I ask you something?" She drinks down half her glass and closes her eyes, swaying slightly. "I'm getting a little fucked up here. I'm sorry. I usually don't get like this."

"Don't worry about it." I sip the wine, an abruptly bitter taste after the SoCo and Seven.

"Do you miss her?"

I gaze at her for a moment, wondering if she needs to know if I'll be competition when Kat shows up. I almost say "no" to allay her fears, but then I decide to keep to the truth for both our sakes. If she's afraid of me, too bad. "Yeah. I miss her, sometimes worse than others. Once I got clean, I realized my feelings weren't just because of my addiction. They were genuine. After that, I fought with myself to call or stay away. What good would calling her do?" I take a long drink and then a deep breath. A sensation rises from my gut and spreads out, overwhelming me. I look away from Meggan so hopefully she won't see the tears building in my eyes.

"You still love her."

I can't figure out what to say that will be anywhere close to the truth. I still love her. But I can't rescue her. She's got to go the road on her own. I can be there to help her along, but—

"She still loves you, too." I glance at Meggan. "I know I said she's over you. She says that. I know she's lying. She doesn't say she still loves you, but I can tell from the look in her eyes every time she talks about you and yes, she still talks about you. She may be calling you a shit and some other nasty things, but her eyes say something completely different. She's set up a wall of anger so she won't have to deal with her feelings for you, but it's better for her than missing you all the time. When she started cleaning up her act, she expected the feelings to go away, but they only got stronger. Seems the drugs were masking her deep feelings. She thought you two were soulmates." It's her turn to look away. "She still does."

"I thought you said she was over me."

She keeps her face turned away. "I said it because I'm pissed at you and I wish she was over you. But she's not and I have to deal with sitting on the couch next to her soulmate, wondering where she is and when she comes back if she'll stay with me or leave."

"Oh." I want to say something like, "It's okay, Meg, I don't feel anything for her anymore." Lie. "Don't worry, I'm over her". Lie. "I've got someone else". Not a lie, but not true. I don't know what Kerri and I are. Everything I think to say would only be a lie, but maybe right now I should lie, if for no other reason than to make Meggan feel better. Fuck that. Why should I make her feel better when I don't? I certainly didn't need to know Kat thinks we're soulmates. What the hell made Meggan say that in the first place?

"'Oh'? That's all you can say? No snappy comebacks? I'm surprised. I thought you'd have something ironic or sarcastic to say."

"No, sorry. Nothing sparkling to take the edge off of things. Thanks though, for telling me how Kat feels. I really need to know this." I hope she catches the dripping sarcasm. I finish the wine and make another SoCo and Seven. I let the hot drink slide down my throat, aware at how fucked up I can get if I let myself. I'd rather be clear headed tomorrow when Dallas and I go to Kat's house.

"Fuck with the 'oh' shit, Rick. Say something." She slams down the last of her wine and I expect her to break the glass on the edge of the table and threaten me. But she doesn't. "Tell me you're deeply in love with someone and you've got no intentions of ever coming back to Katarina."

"She's all yours, Meggan. I've got no one I'm serious with, but stepping backward isn't my thing. What Kat and I had will never be again and it probably isn't a good idea for us to try."

"Can you tell her that?" She looks up at the clock. "Where is she?"

"She's probably out with her sister getting stoned. Why don't you call Nikki's number?"

"I tried before, but she didn't answer, and I left a message." She gets up, swaying slightly and staggers into the dining area. "I'll try again. What the fuck, right?" She pulls half her pocket-book out, tossing it on the table. "Shit. I know it's . . here it is." She punches in Nikki's number and waits. "It's ringing." She stares at me and as the phone keeps ringing, she frowns. "Nikki, this is Meggan. I'm looking for Kat. If she's there with you, please call me back. Thanks." She clicks the phone off. "See?" She comes back in and practically falls onto the couch. Her voice takes on a weary tone. "I try, Rick. I really do. But Kat's Kat and she does what she wants." She wipes tears from her eyes and stares at the clock. "I should really get some sleep. I have to work tomorrow." She sees the way I look at her. "I'll be okay. We'll talk more tomorrow. You're right. There's not much we can do until we know where Kat is, but I hate this feeling of not being able to do a damned thing. I'm sorry. I didn't mean to … never mind." She slowly stands. "I hope you don't mind sleeping on the sofa, but we're not exactly set up for company." She pulls a pillow and an old blanket from the linen closet and tosses them to me. "Good night."

After she closes the door, I go to the bathroom, "borrow" some Listerine I have no intentions of returning and rub tooth-paste over my teeth. I rinse my mouth; shut all the lights, annoyed at how many damned light switches there are for such a small apartment. I turn back and realize I've no light to see my way to where the coffee table is, but I move slowly until I find the couch and lie down.

I stare at the ceiling and the first person that drifts into my mind is Kerri. I really told her I loved her, didn't I? Damn. I know Kerri and she's not going to let that go any time soon. We've had almost five years of tense innuendo floating between us and now this. Does she feel the same? She was really caught up in being confused and afraid for me that she never said how she feels. Of course, she's with Tina now, so I really shouldn't have told her I loved her. It was just the heat of the moment and the fear of never seeing her again. Yeah, that's it, that's the answer.

I roll over to face the back of the couch, close my eyes, and imagine I'm home in my apartment, and all of this is some crazy dream.

"There he is!"

"Murderer!"

I start to roll over when hands grab me and pull me off the couch.

"What the hell?" I'm not in Meggan's apartment any more. I'm in an old house. Men reach for me, while women stand off to one side of the room, weeping. The men wear long coats and frilled shirts, short pants with leggings, pilgrim shoes, and three-cornered hats.

"Who are you?" I ask, but the men are all in a frenzy.

"Thomas Corwin, you are guilty of murder!"

"To the pillory with him!"

"Execute him!"

The women wail unconsoled.

"Wait!" I shout. "I didn't do anything!"

"Murderer!"

Someone spins me around and I'm face to face with an older man in his late fifties. His black hair is streaked gray and his face reflects a hard life. But his dark eyes are sharp, and they search my face. "Thomas. What have you done?"

"I haven't done anything. And my name isn't Thomas, it's Rick." I look at him, but there's no understanding on his face. "I was just trying to get some rest and ..."

The room falls silent. Even the women's cries are quieter.

"After what you've done?" someone asks.

"It's the madness," another man says. "He's been gripped with it."

"It's more than madness." The crowd parts for a tall man with graying hair, piercing eyes, and a strong face. He walks with authority and his eyes sweep the crowd as if making sure they all know he is superior to them.

"No, Magistrate." A man close to me shakes his head. "No."

When the Magistrate turns his hawkish gaze to the man, he backs away, head lowered. "I meant no offense."

"You are just unschooled, Mr. Beecham." The Magistrate turns his dark eyes to me. "Thomas Corwin. I thought better of you than this."

"What are you talking about? My name's Rick." I look around at the faces of strangers. "Where am I? This isn't Meggan's apartment. I was ..."

One of the men looks at me, then to the Magistrate. "You don't think—"

"I know what it is. I have seen it before." He comes closer and stares into my eyes, then nods. "Yes. It is as I feared." He backs away and looks at the men gathered. "The pillory will do nothing for him. He will learn no lessons from it. There is only one punishment for him. Death."

I swallow. My throat's gone dry. I suddenly feel cold as if all my blood's just left my body.

"No!" The crowd parts for a panicked young woman in her mid-twenties. Golden hair streams out behind her as she rushes through the crowd. "No!"

"Elizabeth, please!" another woman shouts.

"Please, Magistrate," Elizabeth says. "There must be another way." She comes to the Magistrate's side and touches his arm. "Please, do not condemn him to death. He ... he is gripped by the Fever and doesn't know himself."

"And who are you that knows the Fever so well?" the Magistrate asks.

An older man steps forward and gently moves Elizabeth back. "She is my daughter."

"And Thomas is your son!" Elizabeth pulls herself away from her father.

"Mr. Corwin." The Magistrate nods. "Have you ever seen your son like this?"

Mr. Corwin—my father?—shakes his head. "Never."

The Magistrate turns to the gathered crowd. "Then I put it to you that Thomas Corwin has come under the influence of the agents of darkness."

There are loud gasps in the crowd, both men and women.

He glances at me, then back to the people gathered. "His actions, though his own, were not directed by a mind of his own."

More gasps.

"No," a woman mumbles.

The Magistrate goes on. "He has been tainted." He suddenly turns and points at me. "I put to you that Thomas Corwin has consorted with the Devil and has given his soul over to Lucifer!"

"What?" I shout.

"God save us!" someone yells.

"What the he … I don't understand what's going on." I look from face to face, but they quickly turn away before meeting my gaze. "Anybody? Hello!" Only Elizabeth meets my stare. "What's happening."

She comes next to me. "Do you not remember anything?"

I shake my head. "I was trying to fall asleep on the couch in Meggan's apartment and the next thing I knew, these men were grabbing me." Which leads me to believe this is all a dream, albeit a very detailed dream. I smell pipe tobacco and perfumes, candles burning, and an odd mustiness like the aroma of an old bookstore, and something else like spoiled meat. It underlies every other scent in the room, and I wonder if anyone else smells it. No one seems to be alarmed by it, so maybe it's just my dream-imagination.

"What?" She looks at me as if I'm insane. "I don't understand what you're trying to say. What's 'Meggan' and 'apartment'? I don't know these words."

"Where am I?"

She frowns at me. "You are in Sarah's house."

"Sarah who?"

She stares at me. "What happened to you?"

I take a deep breath. Around me, the men are shouting over what to do with me. The women have renewed their wailing. A man—Mr. Corwin—stares at me as if he doesn't know me, which is good because I have no idea who he is.

"Thomas?" Elizabeth says. "You don't remember what happened to Sarah?"

Then I remember those images that filled my mind when that thing stood at the glass doors in Kat's kitchen. Within that storm of scenes and emotions, one scene in particular stands out now. One man and two women in colonial clothing, very much like this ensemble of screaming lunatics.

"Leave him in the pillory until he dies!"

"The stocks!"

"Hang him!"

"He's a witch! Burn him!"

"Oh, Thomas," Mr. Corwin says. "What have you done?"

"Nothing." I turn to Elizabeth.

"Your sister is the only one who stands by your side," Corwin says. "Have you subdued her will so that she does the bidding of ..." He turns away. "Damn you."

"I haven't done a thing!" But he's not listening. No one is. Except Elizabeth. "Tell me what's happened."

Her eyes are wet with fear and she hesitates. "They found Sarah ... murdered in the back room and you sleeping in here. All the doors were locked from the inside, meaning you're the only person who was here when she was murdered."

"How was she murdered?"

She looks at the crowd around us, but not before I see tears in her eyes.

"Elizabeth, tell me how she was murdered."

She stares at the walls.

"Her throat was torn open." Mr. Corwin stares down at his hands, refusing to look at me. "Her body was ravaged." His hands turn to fists. "Why, Thomas? Why did you do this to her?"

"I didn't do anything to her. I was just—"

"Stop it! Stop lying! I'm your father, dammit!" Corwin stares into my eyes. "Tell me the truth and I'll talk to the Magistrate. If you won't talk to me, there is very little I can do for you."

"Elizabeth." I turn her to face me. "I need to know something and it's going to sound really strange."

"Leave her be, Thomas. She's been through enough."

"Mr.—Dad—I need to know something. It's very important."

"Dad?" Corwin asks. "You will call me Father."

Elizabeth shoots him an angry glance. "What is it, Thomas?"

"Is there ...?" Suddenly I can't find the words to ask. "Another woman?"

"What do you mean?" Elizabeth asks.

"Thomas, you're troubling your sister. Stop it."

"Another woman. Another woman that loves me."

Elizabeth's eyes go wide. Her mouth opens as if to speak, but she doesn't say a thing.

"What? What's her name?"

"Thomas!" Corwin grabs my arm. "Stop it! You're frightening her!"

"A ..."

"Abigail?" I ask.

Her jaw clenches and her eyes water.

"What do you know?"

"Jacob," Corwin says to the man next to him. "Take Elizabeth, find my wife and bring them both home."

He nods and waits for my "sister".

"What do you know?" I ask.

She shakes her head furiously. "Nothing. I swear."

"It's Abigail, isn't it?"

"Thomas! Stop it!" Corwin steps between Elizabeth and me. "Leave her be. You have more important things to worry about than whether some woman loves you or not."

Forever will I remember. Forever will you suffer.

"Jacob, take her." Corwin stares at me. "You should be ashamed of yourself." He shakes his head. "My own son. Guilty of ... of murder. Why?" He frowns. "What could have driven you to murder Sarah? She loved you and you loved her. What did she do to you that was so terrible you murdered her?"

"Nothing. She didn't do anything. I didn't—"

"Silence!" the Magistrate shouts over the noise of the crowd. He turns to me. "Thomas Corwin, you will spend the night in the pillory and in the morning, you will be executed for the murder of Sarah Goodman."

"What about a trial?" I ask. "Don't you have to try me first to find out if I'm guilty?"

The Magistrate laughs. "There will be a trial while you stand in the pillory and you will be found guilty of murder and in the morning you will be hanged."

"He didn't do it!" Elizabeth shouts from across the room. She fights her way free of Jacob.

Everyone turns to look at her.

"Then who did it, child?" the Magistrate asks. "He was alone in a locked house. Explain yourself."

"I ... I cannot." She breaks down and cries.

"God save us," Corwin mumbles.

"Then we will proceed." The Magistrate glances back at me. "Take him to the pillory. The council will convene immediately to discuss the fate of Thomas William Corwin."

"Wait!" I shout.

Several of the younger, stronger men come at me, anger in their eyes. I feel like I should know them, but I don't know why.

"Come, Thomas," one of the men says. "Give us a reason to beat you."

The rest of the crowd—older men and women—back away, giving the men a wide berth.

"I really don't want to fight any of you. I'll come peacefully." I glance at them, young men in their twenties, eager to release some of the pent-up anger that fills this room like a fog. I can understand their feelings. This looks like a small community and one of their own had been murdered. These people want a killer. Unfortunately, I'm not it.

"Sorry to hear that," the man says. "I was really looking forward to making you bleed." He stares at me as if daring me to hit him. But that would be playing into his hands and I don't want to do that. I figure if I lay one hand on him, all his buddies will join in on the ass kicking and I'm in no mood. "You have no idea who I am, do you?"

I shake my head. "No."

"You courted Sarah for almost a year. You've come to our house for dinner. We've gone fishing together and you don't know who I am. How is that possible?" He comes closer, keeping several feet away and walks in a slow circle around me. "Explain that, Thomas. Explain how you don't know me."

This is going to get ugly. "I know you, I just can't remember who you are."

He raises an eyebrow and keeps circling me like a vulture waiting for the right moment to strike. "Now you are mocking me."

"Hardly. Something very traumatic happened tonight and I'm not myself."

"He's consorted with the Devil, Samuel," one of his friends says, and laughs.

"Do not joke about such things," Samuel says.

"I'm not possessed."

"But you admit you're not in your right mind," Samuel says.

"No." I shake my head. "I'm not."

Samuel looks over and around me. "Magistrate."

The man breaks his conversation and turns to us. "What is it?"

"Thomas says he's not in his right mind. Perhaps he should be remanded to the madhouse." Samuel nods at me. "I'm sure Mr. Corwin would prefer his son be alive than executed."

"A good purgative might help cure him!" one of Samuel's friends says, and they all laugh.

"Or perhaps an emetic," another says. "That'll get the Devil out of him!"

The Magistrate takes two steps and backhands the man hard. "Do not mock the Devil!" He glares at the other men. "His ways are wicked and subtle and while you mock him, he works his evil upon your heart, soul, and mind!" He grits his teeth and shakes his head. "I pray to God you learn to keep your mouths shut before the Devil makes his home under your tongues." He turns to me and then looks at Mr. Corwin. "If it be the Devil possess him, only an exorcism will cure him. If it be madness that has gripped him, Eastham House might be able to help."

"You want to put my son in with the insane?" Corwin asks incredulously. "No, I will not have it."

"Mr. Corwin, I want you to know that the only other option is a trial and certainly an execution. I would have to write to England for a priest to come to perform an exorcism and I don't think the people of Sloterdam want to wait that long."

The two men stare at each other. The stench of spoiled meat grows stronger as if someone just walked into the house wearing rotten beef. I need to wake up now.

"Thomas!" a girl calls. "Thomas?"

I look over the crowd and through it to catch a glimpse of the woman calling my name. My name? My name's Rick. Isn't it?

Thomas?" A young woman in her late teens or early twenties pushes through the crowd and stops short before me. "Who are you?"

"What?" I've never seen her before in my life.

"Who are you? What are you doing here?"

"What? I'm ... I don't know. I ..."

Someone shoves me from behind and I fall toward the girl. I reach out for her, but she backs away.

"What the fuck do you think you're doing? Meggan?"

I hit the floor—carpeted in a low pile—and open my eyes. I quickly roll over and look up at a woman with long red-bronze hair that tumbles over and past her shoulders. She's got a face that some men might consider average, but to me she's fairly beautiful. No pouting lips or long, seductive eyelashes, but her face has that elfin quality, and in the dark her eyes seem to shine on their own. I shiver, suddenly afraid this is Abigail grown up, and I'm lying here with no weapons.

She drops a backpack on the floor by the end of the couch. "Who the hell are you?" she says louder. "How'd you get in here?"

I sit down on the couch, holding my head. The smell of the dream still fills my nose and it's unpleasant. I look at the woman staring at me.

Meggan dashes into the living room with a broom in her hand, ready for anything. "What's going on?" She sees the two of us staring at each other. She smirks and it's good to see she's trying out smiles. "Ariana, this is Rick. Rick, Ariana. I didn't think you were coming home tonight."

"Where'd you think I'd sleep?" She has some kind of accent, maybe English or Irish and it reminds me of Elizabeth. "Bennett's? Not after tonight!" She looks at me with her ice blue eyes and a chill runs down my spine. Something very familiar clings to her. "Now, what are you doing here?"

"Ari," Meggan says. "What happened with Bennett?"

"His dick is too small. I like a man with inches, not millimeters."

"Ari." Meggan throws a look at me that says, "Here she is, my roommate, the sexually unrepressed, free speech advocate".

"Look, Meg, we were supposed to go out to dinner tonight and at the last minute he changes his mind and just wants to get a fast bite to eat. We're at this diner and this girl comes over. She can't be more than eighteen and says, 'Hi hon, what's up?' The bitch looks at me and says, 'Who's she? Your sister?' Then while Bennett is trying to speak, she says, 'I thought you were coming over and we were gonna spend the whole night fucking'."

"Ari, no, she didn't say that," Meggan says sympathetically.

"Fucking asshole." She looks at me. "Fucking men." She looks back at Meggan. "Maybe you do have the right idea." She frowns and continues. "Then Bennett gets up and runs out with the little cunt following him. Now I've got our dinner bill and no way home. Luckily, the waitress took sympathy on me and let me go with half the bill and gave me a ride back to Bennett's so I could get my car."

"What a jerk."

I nod in agreement.

Ariana looks at me, then says to Meggan, "You're not switching sides, are you?"

Meggan bursts out laughing. "Hardly! I went over to Kat's house and when I got there, she was gone, and he was there. Some weird stuff happened. And we came here. He's staying until we find Kat."

"Where is she?"

"I don't know," Meggan says slowly.

"So, what's Rich got to do with this?"

"It's Rick," I say. "I used to be … Kat's my ex and someone dropped me off at her house without telling me why."

Ariana stares at me for too long and only says, "Hm." The moment breaks, and she shrugs. "I'm going to bed." With that, she disappears in her room and Meggan goes back to hers.

I lay back down on the couch, thinking about Elizabeth, Abigail, Sarah, and ghosts, but as soon as my head hits the pillow, I'm falling into dreamland, half wondering where Kat is and how we're going to find her.

Katarina stands before me, as beautiful as I remember her, in a graveyard as dead leaves swirl around us. It's an overcast November afternoon and I pull my coat tighter to cut the chill. The air is crisp with a hint of winter coming. The trees are bare of leaves and a thick fog creeps in around us with the scent of dry ice.

"Katarina," I say.

Her eyes look beyond me until I call her name again and then she focuses on me. She shrugs her coat off her shoulders, and it slides down her arm, falling into a leather puddle at her feet.

Katarina's sweater is a dark green angora that slides off her left shoulder, exposing bone white skin. "Here," she whispers.

The wind blows her black hair across her face. In one graceful movement, she slides her sweater over her head and a sudden gust of wind sweeps it away. As it floats on the air, it turns brown and breaks apart into dead leaves. "Here." She unclips her bra, letting it fall. Her eyes water with an infinite sadness. "Rick." Her hands reach for me and I take a slow step toward her. "Here." She sits on her knees. She runs her hands through the green blades. Tears roll from her emerald eyes and fall from her chin to her breasts. "It's no good." Her hands claw at the grass, yanking up clumps of earth. "Rick."

"I'm here." I keep moving closer to her, walking as if in a funeral procession.

She raises the dirt and grass over her head, digging her fingers into the soft earth and it showers down on her, flecks of dirt in her hair, on her upraised face. Blades of grass on her neck leave slight trails of blood as they skim down her skin.

"Katarina?" I can't move. My feet are buried in the ground.

Her eyes snap open and burn into me. She rises and with each step she takes, I feel vines crawl up my legs, encircle my hands and my arms, and pin them against my sides.

"Why?" I ask.

"You know," she says playfully. She stops in front of me and unbuttons her jeans. "You know." They slide down her legs and she steps out of them.

"I don't know, Kat. Please, tell me."

She slides her thumbs under the elastic of her red panties. "You know, Rick." She pushes them down her thighs, over her knees, letting them fall silently to the grass. "Am I not beautiful?" Her hair is full of grass blades like a green crown.

"You are." My dream body reacts to her nakedness.

"Do you not desire me?"

"I do."

"This is for you." She bends and yanks more grass from the ground. "You, my lover." She lets the grass fall over her chest and where the blades touch her skin, thin lines of blood appear.

"Stop it."

"Does it pain you to see me bleed?"

"Yes."

She moves closer and the aroma of rich earth envelopes me. With her crown of grass, she's an Earth Goddess and her blood is the blood of the planet. I watch her and now the scent of blood mixes with the earth, making me slightly dizzy. Across her skin, tiny cuts drip blood, leaving trails of red down her body. "I don't believe you." She takes a blade of grass between her fingers and glides it between her breasts. Blood wells up in small drops, running down her skin.

"Stop it."

"What about you?" She opens my coat and shirt. "What about Rick?" She touches my chest with the blade of grass, and it feels like a knife. "Will it pain me to see you bleed?" She runs the blade down my chest, and I wince at the pain as a drop of blood trickles down my stomach. "No." She shrugs. "Nothing."

"Katarina, please." The November chill makes the cut sting.

"Maybe deeper? Maybe another one?" Her fingernails find the cut and press into my skin.

I cry out as her nails sink into my chest. The pain becomes white hot. "Please! Stop!"

"Did you?"

Deeper.

"What?"

"Did you stop?"

"What're you talking about?"

"When you ... walked ..." Icy fingers push into the wound and tears stream down my face.

"Please, Katarina!"

"Out ..."

Her fingers slide in and the pain overwhelms me. I scream, praying for an end to this torture.

"On ..."

She forces her hand in, her fingers brushing my ribs.

"Me!" Blood pours down her arm as she reaches into my body and draws out my heart, still beating. Veins and arteries pulse blood through the dripping organ.

"Please ..." I feel an aching emptiness in my chest and the world swims away from me.

"You took my heart, Rick. Now I take yours." I watch her hand tighten and her arm muscles knot. "Can you go on?" With all her strength she pulls hard and suddenly blood sprays over her naked body. She laughs, holding my heart, pumping blood down her wrist on to the green grass as I fall backward, free from the roots. Falling. Falling. Fall ...

I wake up screaming. I can't breathe.

"What's wrong?" Meggan runs into the living room with Ariana close behind her. "What is it? What's wrong?"

"Shit!" I clutch my chest, making sure there are no holes. Under my skin my heart is beating furiously, and I take deep breaths, hoping to calm it before it explodes.

"What happened?" Ariana asks.

"Rick?" Meggan sits down on the couch next to me. "Dreams?"
When Ariana kneels at my side, I smell the scent of flowers.
I look at Meggan. "Nightmare. Bad. Real bad."

"Are you okay?"

The portable phone rings. I almost reach for it, but Meggan grabs it first.

"Yes," she says. "Everything's okay. A friend of mine is staying, and he just had a bad dream. I'm sorry that he woke you. No, he's not twelve. I said I was sorry. I know you have to get up for work tomorrow. I do, too. No, he's just staying for tonight. Yes, I understand. Don't worry, he'll be gone. Thank you. You, too." She clicks the phone off and leaves it on the coffee table. "What an asshole." She glances at me. "Are you all right?"

I stand on weak knees and promptly sit down again. "Yeah." I nod for effect.

"No, you're not," Meg says. "Tell me what happened."

"Not now." I stare at Ariana like she's a stranger that I should know. "I think I'll go for a walk." The half empty glass of SoCo&7 sits on the table waiting for me. Should I refill it? I've already drunk too much and a another might put me over the edge. On the other hand, that might be the best thing for me. On the third hand, the last thing I want is a killer headache along with a hangover. On the fourth hand, do I really give a shit right now? Yes, of course I do.

I still feel Kat's dead-cold fingers in my chest, and I shiver. Drink or walk? What'll help the most? Glancing at Ariana, I wonder if she'd like some company for the rest of the night. Probably not. Maybe some other time.

I stand, making sure I'm not going to fall over drunk, and when I'm sure I'm stable, I head to the front door. "I'll be right back." I try a smile, but it fades too quickly.

"Don't you want the keys?" Meggan asks. "We're not planning to stay up waiting for you."

"Oh. Yeah. The keys."

"I'll get them." Meg goes to the kitchen and rummages through her pocketbook.

"Are you okay, Rick?" Ariana takes my hand and stares into my eyes.

I look at her until Meggan says, "Here they are." Instead of giving them to me, she heads to her bedroom.

I want to ask what she's doing, but Ariana's gaze holds me frozen. "Your heart is very heavy. You may've cleared out some room for yourself, but your demons are waiting for you."

"What?" I ask.

"Come on," Meggan says behind Ariana. "I've got the keys." She's dressed in jogging shorts, sneakers and a sleeveless sweatshirt, hastily zippered halfway. "I'm coming with you." To Ariana, she says, "Don't wait up. We won't be long."

Ariana places my hand down and backs away from me taking the scent of flowers with her. "All right." She stares into my eyes. "Is everything okay?"

"I don't know." I tear my eyes from her gaze and follow Meggan down the stairs and out of the apartment.

7.

The night is barely cooler than the day. The only sound is the soft chirping of crickets and grasshoppers. Occasionally, a bird or bat flies across the night, calling to friends and relatives.

Meggan pulls the door closed behind her and we start walking.

"You wanted to talk, but not in front of Ariana. I could see it on your face. You said you had a bad nightmare. Katarina was in it."

"What makes you say that?"

"Just a wild guess."

"Yeah. She was in it." I take a deep breath and it feels good to be out of the apartment. We walk slowly like a couple out enjoying the late night. "Katarina ripped my heart out." I tell her the dream, every detail I remember, down to the way my heart looked in Kat's hand and the determined ferocity on her face as she tore my heart out.

"Wow," Meg says. "Sounds like you're afraid to see her. A lot of guilt and regrets. Are you?"

"I didn't think so." I stare at the street in front of us, unsure of what to say or even what I feel. "I feel bad for what I did. We had so many Kodak moments and so much shit. No matter how I feel for her now, I'm not going back. Does that make you feel better?"

"I don't know. Kat still believes what she believes."

"And she always will."

We walk for a while, neither one of us wanting to break the quiet of the night and whatever reverie we're in. Finally, she says, "There's a park a little ways from here if you don't want to rush back to the house. I mean, we're not supposed to go there after dark, but who'll know?"

"Sure."

As we walk, she says, "I'm sorry about the way I treated you this afternoon. I was just really upset about Kat not being home and no note. That's not like her."

"Don't worry, I'll get over it."

We walk in awkward silence for a while.

"When Dallas comes over tomorrow, we'll take a cab to Kat's house."

"I'm not going back there, Rick."

When I look at her, her fingers toy with the zipper on her sweatshirt. Her arm muscles are well defined white skin and shadows under the light from the quarter moon.

I expect her to say why, but she doesn't. I decide to push it. "Why not?"

She laughs. "Are you crazy? You want to go back there? You said to me at one point, what if the house shifts in time and doesn't come back? Well, now I'm asking you. What happens if you're in there and it shifts somewhere else and doesn't come back? Then what?"

"I guess I get to live an entirely different life than I had planned."

"That's not funny."

"Are you concerned about my safety?"

"You were concerned about mine. It's the least I can do."

"Thanks." There is a very fine line between bravery and foolishness and going back to Kat's house definitely crosses that line. But I know Dallas is going to want to see the house.

The park in front of us is small with a winding path that does a little circle. At the back on the far left is a swing set and a slide illuminated by a single overhead lamp.

"I don't think you're going to solve anything by going back to Kat's house," Meggan says.

"I'm sure Dallas is gonna wanna see it."

"So the two of you can get shifted in time and ..."

"And what?" I turn to Meggan, but she's gone. Poof.

Disappeared. Yeah. Fucking poof. "Shit. Meggan?" I turn in a circle, but she's gone. Where? Was she ever here? Am I still dreaming?

A sound, like the long gasp of the dying, floats over the empty park, echoes across the grass and surrounds me. A chill trickles down my spine as another gasp, almost intelligible, slides across the park from all directions.

I look back to make sure the road and sidewalk are still there. They're not. A dark field stretches out where the cars and houses should be.

The shriek of rusty metal draws my attention to the swings. They're moving in unison as if two people swing together. I wouldn't feel as freaked if there were actually humans in them, but they're empty.

My heart beats loudly, thumping in my chest and my throat's parched. After being scared shitless as much as I've been lately, I think I'd be used to this, but I'm not; it's so damned abrupt.

"Meggan!"

Children's laughter comes from the swings. One starts swinging with more force, higher and higher. The laughter turns to screams. "Stop it! Stop it!" Someone else starts laughing, a woman who is as invisible as the children.

I shake my head. "Okay, Rick, this is just some kind of ..."

Mist, white and nebulous, grows from the ground by the swings like a slow, chaotic tornado trying to cut loose from its moorings. The hot July night starts getting cooler as a gentle breeze picks up from the direction of the swings, blowing the mist like a sheet in the wind.

My first thought is that some kind of gateway is about to open, spewing forth demons and all kinds of hellish things. But when it detaches from the spot and begins moving in my direction, a brand new fear sets in that this is some apparition that means to do me no good.

A sigh rolls across the field as if someone just took their last breath. The mist seems to shiver and glitter in the moonlight. Where'd the moon come from? Wasn't it a new moon when Meggan and I left the house?

The mist slithers, occasionally rising up like a snake

checking the ground in front of it. Before the blanket of living white, the air turns cold and gooseflesh rises on my arms. I back away, but the field behind me offers no shelter or anywhere to run. The wraith-like mist undulates in my direction, carrying the scent of mustiness and flowers. Not beautiful live flowers, but dead flowers that reek of the breath of decay and death. I back away out of instinct, ready to run.

The fog moves faster, shimmering, as if reflecting ice within itself.

I take three steps back, turn to run and trip over my own stupid feet. I crawl as fast as I can, but I feel the first tendrils of chilled air reaching for me. The hairs on the back of my neck stand on edge. *Don't look back, don't look back, don't look ...*

I look over my shoulder and see nothing but the white glittering mist growing before me, rising up to swallow me.

"Rick," it whispers. "*We're waiting for you.*" It comes closer, obliterating the world around me, until I'm wrapped in white fog. "*Down here in the cold, wet darkness we're waiting for you to come home.*" Cold, moist fingers touch me, caress my arms, press against my skin. Wet tongues lick my neck and I shriek, crawling away from this nightmare but the fog closes around me.

"*You have no choice.*" A man-shaped shadow slithers through the whiteness, coming at me, reaching out for me. The fog thickens, elongates, and more shadows move forward. Another, slightly smaller, reaches for the man and holds him.

"*Leave this place!*" a woman says from within the fog. "*This is not for you! Rick! You must not give up! No matter what you see, believe there is hope! Rick! Rick! Are you ...?*"

"... okay? Rick? Are you okay?" Meggan kneels next to me, her hand on my arm and deep concern on her face. "We were walking, and you suddenly collapsed. Are you all right? Should I call an ambulance?"

"No." I look around. I'm lying on the grass in the park. The swings are still. The night is calm hot and clear. With no sign of fog anywhere. "I'm fine." I glance down at myself for no good reason, if only to affirm I'm in one piece.

"What happened to you?"

I stand with her help. "Thanks. I'm not sure." I tell her what happened, trying to make sense of it as I go, but nothing's clear.

"What about the people? Did you know them?"

"One woman's voice sounded like my mother's. It was the same woman from Mount Moriah cemetery that told me to take care." I start walking back to Meggan's apartment with Meggan following close behind.

She stops. "But isn't she ...?"

I keep walking. I don't want to be out in the night any more. I'd rather be under a sheet on Meggan's couch. At least if the dead come to get me, I'll pull the sheet over my head so they won't find me. Hell, it always worked when I was a kid. "Yes, Meggan, she is. It was all good yesterday and now I'm talking to the fucking dead. This doesn't happen to people in real life!" I turn back and look at her. At first it seems like the mist is back and swirling around Meggan, but it's just the play of the white street light. "It's not bad enough that the dead seem to hang around me, but I wonder if maybe the dead are after her as well. Meggan, I've seen things that have scared the fuck out of me and truthfully, I don't know what to do or how to start resolving any of this."

"We have to find Katarina. No matter what else is happening, we have to find her and make sure she's safe. Then we can worry about everything else." She wipes tears away and stares at me for a long time. "I wish I knew where she was. She's never disappeared like this before. I'm afraid for her, especially with that stalker around." She takes a step and then she's in my arms. "I'm scared."

We stand on the sidewalk holding each other, both of us scared for Katarina. God only knows what she's gotten herself into. I ask the Divine Spirit to take care of her, to make sure she stays safe until we can find her.

"Do you think she's okay?" Meggan asks.

"I'm sure she's okay. Katarina knows how to take care of herself." I don't smile like I want to. I barely believe my own words, but I have to say them. They're the only words that make sense to say.

"I hope so. I don't know what I'd do if anything happened to her." Meggan looks at me and in the light of the streetlights, her eyes are wet with fear. "I love her, Rick."

"I know."

Meggan breaks our embrace and she starts walking.

Back at the house, I follow her upstairs.

Meggan says, "I need sleep." She drops her keys in her pocketbook and with a "Good night," she disappears into her bedroom and closes the door.

8.

I open my eyes, blink, and realize Ariana's staring at me. "Yes?"
"You look real familiar, but I can't place where I know you from." She sits in the chair next to the couch, slowly sipping from a mug, wearing an electric-blue, silk babydoll that comes down just to mid-thigh. The straps are thin, showing off a pair of well-defined shoulders. "I doubt I know you, but something about you is very familiar." She stretches her bare legs out on the coffee table. "You have any idea what that is?"

I tear my gaze away from her perfect legs and go through the litany of jobs I had, cafes and bars we've played in, and then she runs down her list. We have nothing in common, but I still swear I know her.

I swing my legs off the couch and sit up. "You have any orange juice?"

"Sure." She gets up.

I watch her walk into the kitchen. "Is Meggan still here?"

"No. She left for work."

"What time is it?" I glance at the clock on the wall and it says ten o'clock. "Is it really ten?"

"Sure is." Ariana comes in smiling and hands me the glass. I drink it slowly, letting the bits of pulp swim over my tongue. I never drank coffee, so I don't know that caffeine jolt. But orange juice works just fine for me in the morning.

"Thanks." I look for the phone. "I better call work and find out if everything's okay there."

"Here." She hands me the portable and I dial the number.

She sits down, places the mug on the coffee table and stretches; her whole body seems to rise and it's a wonderful thing to behold.

"Hello?" someone says, and I realize it's Isabelle at the other end of the phone.

"Isa, it's Rick. How're you?"

"My dearest Richard! It is good to hear your voice! When Kerri had heard no word from you, we began to worry. But now I shall find her for you! One moment, my dear!"

Isa and I have always played this way, like we're in some real bad, melodramatic war movie. I have no idea how it got started, or if there's anything to our verbal play, but it's charming and we both get off on it.

Ariana returns to her relaxed pose with her ankles crossed on the coffee table.

I drink my orange juice, staring over the rim of my glass at her long, very womanly legs.

"Well, look who's on the phone," Kerri says.

"I'm not going to be in today, but I'll be there tomorrow." I picture her in her usual black and violet. Miniskirt, black stockings, black Doc Martens, lace blouse and violet vest. If the light catches her just right, one can see the shimmer of violet in her dyed-black hair. She's elfin, only five two or three, and her sexuality is a tangible energy that floats around her like an erotic aura. I figure sooner or later we'll wind up in bed. It'll most likely be later though with her seeing Tina.

"Rick, please tell me you're not still at Kat's house."

"I'm not. I'm at Meggan's apartment. Dallas is coming by and—"

"Rick, I need you."

"I love when you say that."

"At the store."

"My gothic goddess, how long can you hide your true desire for me?"

"Until you get down on your knees and ki ... yes, Jeffrey, all those piles. Now what was I saying?"

"Your true desire for me?" I look up at Ariana watching me.

"Ah, yes. When you get down on your knees, grovel for a while, and kiss my ass."

"Any plans for tonight?"

"Tina. We're not getting on real well. Maybe some other time."

"Good luck with Tina, then. I hope everything works out for you guys." My evil, selfish, lustful side hopes things don't work out, that way I can have her for myself.

"Thanks. Rick, please be careful. I don't have a good feeling about you being there."

"It's just because I'm not coming in." I smile, hoping she'll hear the grin in my voice.

"It's more than that, Rick. I don't know. It's just a feeling I have. I want you in here tomorrow, okay?"

I sip my orange juice. "Sure will."

"Rick, I've been having this dream, a nightmare. We're both in it and someone else is and they're trying to kill you."

A shiver slides up my spine. "Do you know who the someone else is?"

"No. She keeps speaking in some foreign language I can't understand. I think you should just come back to New York."

"I can't. I have to do this."

"Rick." There's a moment of silence. "Be careful. All right?"

"Never fear, I'll be there."

We say goodbye and hang up. I click the "Off" button and place the phone back on the receiver, feeling bad about not working today. But more than that, I feel terrible about putting Kerri through all this. Yeah, she's got Tina, but Kerri and I have something that she and Tina never will.

What about her dream? What does it mean to her? To me? And who's this third person? Abigail, who else? The sense of foreboding eases when I tell myself everything's fine, and if nothing else Kerri's safe in the city.

"Your gothic goddess?" Ariana says with a grin.

"It's a long story."

"I'm sure it is. If you're not working, what are you doing today?"

"My friend Dallas is coming by and we're going to Kat's house."

"Why? Hoping to see Katarina again?"

"Not quite." I remember what Meggan said about Ariana's take on the supernatural. Do I tread carefully or just go ahead with what I'm thinking? I don't want to scare her away. Nothing ruins the chance of hot sex faster than frightening the potential woman in question.

"Some strange things happened there last night and being Dallas is into strange, I thought we'd go over there."

"Strange like how?"

"Strange like …"

"What?" She glances at me in such a way that my heart thumps in my chest.

"You are incredibly gorgeous." The words slip out of my mouth before I can keep my lust in check. I chalk it up to tension and let it go.

She blushes and a subtle smile plays with the corners of her mouth. "Thanks."

"And you have the cutest smile I've ever seen."

"Cuter than your gothic goddess?"

Almost. "Yes."

"Wow, that's something."

This is not getting me any closer to finding Kat or getting naked with Ariana. At this point I don't know which is more important. Finding Kat would certainly make Meggan happy. But who cares what makes Meggan happy? Don't be such a shit, Summers. You're thinking with your—

"You'll have to do better."

"Better than what?"

She pulls her legs back slowly and stands up. "I'm not that easy." She grins and heads to her bedroom. The soft click of the lock tells me we're finished for now. But in that brief instant that she slowly brought her legs up, her nightshirt slid up her thighs and I couldn't look away from the black thong she had on.

As I sit drinking my orange juice, I spy a box of Chocolate Frosted Pop-Tarts. The breakfast of champions. In the middle of my covert operation to remove a package without being heard, Ariana walks in and I almost drop the box. "Mind if I have one?"

"They're Meggan's. Go ahead. I thought you might want to take a shower, so I left towels in the bathroom for you." She places her mug in the sink. "You were saying something about the strangeness at Kat's house that you and your friend—what was his name? Dallas?—were going to check out." She turns to me with her light brown eyes sparkling.

"Some strange noises, flickering lights, and other paranormal activities."

"You believe in that crap? Ghosts and UFOs?" She laughs. "Tell me Dallas isn't it this as well."

"We both are."

She says, "hm," and walks back to her bedroom.

9.

I shower and get dressed, eager for Dallas to get here with some new clothes. The Pop-Tart and orange juice should hold me for now. Before I decide what to do next, the doorbell rings. I head downstairs and open the door. Dallas nods and hands me a plastic bag with a change of clothing. He's wearing his reflective shades so he won't be recognized. "Welcome." I open the screen door and he comes in.

He's tall and thin, and stands slightly bent with long, dark hair and watery blue eyes. I think he stands that way because he's very self-conscious of his height. Not only is he a ghost hunter, but he's also a conspiracy theorist who believes aliens and the government are performing some sort of mass hypnosis experiment on the general public. He usually keeps to himself and hardly anyone talks to him but me, because most people find him too eccentric.

I close the door and head back upstairs. "Make yourself comfy. I'm gonna change."

"Sure."

A quick change into new shorts and faded blue T-shirt and I'm ready to go.

Dallas sits in the chair. "So, when do we leave for Kat's house? Has Kat even shown up yet?"

"No, not as far as I know. She could be at the house, but she hasn't called."

Ariana comes out of her bedroom, her hair pulled back in a ponytail. "I'm taking a quick shower."

I introduce the two of them and after she says, "Nice to meet you," she returns to her bedroom.

"Seems nice enough," Dallas says. "What's the situation?"

I explain everything that happened yesterday in more detail, from the car ride to our arrival here.

"Sounds like someone's playing a joke on you," Ariana says, standing by the stairs.

"Weren't you taking a shower?" I ask.

"Yes, but your story sounded intriguing. I thought I'd listen."

"And you think it's nothing?" Dallas asks.

"As opposed to what?" Ariana comes into the living room, her gaze taking both of us in. "Someone's out to scare you."

"But the smell, and everything that happened at the house—"

"I'm sure you can find a spray or something that reeks," Ariana says. "As far as the house, whoever set you up rigged the house. Meggan and the others were just unlucky enough to stumble onto it." She glances at me. "I'm sorry, it's really ghosts and demons, right?"

"Have you ever had any kind of paranormal experiences?" Dallas's tone comes from dealing with the arrogant and ignorant.

She stares at him. "No." But something in her eyes shows a glint of fear.

"Then you have no basis of fact to approach this conversation, do you?"

"There's no such thing as ghosts."

"Really?" Dallas sighs. "I spent ten years as a ghost hunter and—"

"A ghost hunter?" Ariana laughs. "You're not serious, are you? Was this in the Twilight Zone or the house where Casper lives?"

Dallas nods and grins; he loves this stuff. "No, actually it was in a house where a seven-year-old girl took a gardening trowel and hacked her mother and father to pieces and when she was asked why she did it, she said the ghost of Lizzie Borden told her to. That was the evening after a ten year old boy eviscerated his father, and his excuse was his dead grandfather told him to assume the mantle of the family."

"Stop it," Ariana says coolly.

"That was two weeks before we went into a house that was

reported haunted and nearly the entire team was killed by the spirit of a mass murderer." Dallas's voice gets louder, angrier.

"Stop it!" Ariana demands.

"And that was exactly three years before we went into another house that turned out to be a vortex from Hell and Sheila had her head ripped off, and Jeffrey had his guts ripped out from what the tenant told us was a mildly annoying ghost. Guess what? It wasn't. It was a fucking demon. Don't you dare pretend that you have any idea what ghost hunting is about unless you've been there!"

If looks could kill, they'd both be dead. Ariana stalks off to her room and slams the door hard enough that the windows rattle.

"Sorry," I say. "I should've warned you about her."

"She's got a lot of nerve making jokes like that."

Dallas never told me what happened that made him quit the ghost hunting business, but if it was anything like the demon, I can understand. "She doesn't understand."

Ariana's bedroom door opens, and she steps out, but before going into the bathroom, she looks at us and says, "I don't know what to tell you."

"Because you can't come up with anything reasonable," Dallas says. "Can you?"

She shoots him an angry stare. "Just because I can't come up with a reasonable explanation for what Rick and Meggan experienced, doesn't mean there isn't one." She shakes her head. I expect her to laugh, but something dark creeps across her face as if she's remembering something.

"You know what," Dallas says, "Rick called me here to help him and if you don't mind, we need to discuss how we're going to proceed."

"Call the police," Ariana says. "Have her arrested for stalking or whatever it is she's doing and that'll be that."

"I hope that's all it takes," Dallas says. "I hope she's nothing more than just some wacko stalker and I hope you're right. As a matter of fact, if you are right and this proves to be nothing but some wild charade, I'll buy you a drink and we'll celebrate. But if I'm right and she's more than that ..." He lets the statement hang. A shiver slides down my back and I hope Ariana's right and this is nothing but some twisted fan with an obsession. Dallas turns to me. "We should check Kat's house for any body parts and blood."

Ariana laughs. "And when you find fake blood, then what?"

"What do you suggest?" Dallas asks, his voice clipped and tense.

"Find Kat and ask her what's going on." Ariana looks at each of us as if we're simpletons, unable to understand the simplest plan. "And I'll be waiting for that drink."

Her idea would make perfect sense if half the things that had happened hadn't. But after the shifting house and the thing in the backyard, her idea has no basis in reality.

"Okay." Dallas sits back in the chair. "We'll go to Kat's house and see what's there. If there's nothing, we'll pursue your idea. If we find anything otherwise, we'll plan from there."

"I'll come with you," Ariana says.

Dallas rolls his eyes. "No, you won't."

"Why? Afraid I'll mess up your fantasy?" She smiles.

Dallas laughs. "Beautiful, just beautiful."

"Thanks." She stands and offers me a grin that says a thousand words. If only I knew which thousand words those were. She heads to the bathroom to shower.

"What's wrong with her?" Dallas asks.

"I'm sorry. Ariana doesn't believe in the supernatural. I just didn't realize how strong her convictions were."

"I wonder what happened to her?"

"What makes you think anything did?"

"It's not that she doesn't believe, it's that she's afraid."

I shake my head as if that'll clear the confusion rising in my brain. "Why do you say that?"

"When I was doing paranormal investigations, I found that a number of people, after experiencing something supernatural, denied the experience and then vehemently refused to accept anything supernatural after that. If something happened to someone when they were very young, it's possible that therapists along the way tried to convince the person that what they experienced was really just either a natural phenomenon or, in the case of some women, claiming they were molested by ghosts or demons, that it was Dad, a boyfriend, a male relative, or even their husbands. Psychology isn't exactly open-minded about the paranormal."

"What are you saying? Something happened to Ariana and now she's refusing to accept anything supernatural?"

The bathroom door opens and Ariana, a robe tight around her curvaceous body, slips into her bedroom, closing the door behind her.

Dallas lowers his voice and says, "It's possible that she had some kind of paranormal experience and if she sought therapy, they probably told her it was something perfectly normal, convincing her that it wasn't anything outside of the ordinary. Most people think that it's better to hold on to a belief than to acknowledge that belief isn't true, even if they're confronted by facts that indicate otherwise."

"Like demons."

"Exactly. And ghosts. Most people hold that ghosts don't exist and even if they're confronted by one, they'll still hold on to that belief. It's pure denial. You know what that's like when you've believed something and then you're confronted with facts that contradict your beliefs."

"Yeah." I remember Kat and my drug addiction and the load of crap beliefs I dearly held on to in hopes of maintaining my twisted life. Thank God I gave those beliefs up. My life is a lot better now. Fucking ha.

Ten minutes later the doorbell rings again.

"Oh shit," Ariana says, dashing out of her bedroom wearing baggy shorts and a tank top. "Damn, damn, damn!" She grabs the wall and skids on the wood floor. She hurries down the stairs and opens the door. "I am real sorry!"

"It's all right," a woman says.

"A friend of Meggan's stayed over and I'm completely out of sync. Come in."

Ariana comes up the stairs with an older, attractive woman following her. "Beth, this is Rick and Dallas. Rick and Dallas, Beth." She turns to the woman. "Just sit. I'll be dressed in a second."

"Don't worry. We've got plenty of time." Beth's long blond hair is pulled in a ponytail and I guess her to be in her early to mid-forties. She's dressed in a crinkly white skirt and a blue tank top with a floral pattern across her chest. Her sandals have low heels and her toenails are painted the same light pink as her fingernails.

"Just let me change." Ariana disappears into her bedroom.

Beth glances at the couch, still covered with the sheet I used as my blanket. Dallas offers her the chair and drops down on the sofa, oblivious of the sheet.

"Thanks." She smiles, making herself comfy. "I don't remember Meggan ever mentioning you before." Her smile is warm and generous.

"That would be because we just met yesterday." I fold the blanket as best I can.

"You two just met yesterday?" I can tell by the tone of her voice that she's intrigued and curious. She sits forward to hear the tale.

I drop back on the couch. "I wound up at my ex-girlfriend's house. Meggan was there, but Kat was not. We had some problems at the house, and she let me stay here last night."

"I see." She nods slowly and I imagine she's formulating her own theories about my use of the word "friend". That's fine. What do I care?

"I'll be ready in a minute." Ariana darts out of the bedroom into the bathroom and closes the door.

"She's really something," Beth says.

When I look back at her, she's eyes me, as if sizing me up for something, a suit or a woman.

She leans across the arm of the chair. She's about to conspire with me. "She's very sweet, but she keeps picking the wrong men."

I lean closer to her. "I've heard."

"Are you single?"

I almost laugh. "Yes." Kerri's smiling face floats through my mind, but there's always Tina.

"You seem like a nice guy."

And you seem like a great matchmaker. I didn't see any rings on Beth's finger; she could be angling for her own desires. "I've been told as much. Others don't necessarily agree."

"Looks can be deceiving," Dallas chimes in with a grin.

"Like my friends, for example."

She laughs. "Isn't that what friends are for?"

"Ready to go?" Ariana comes out of the bathroom in a light blue, sleeveless dress that shows off her toned arms and legs.

"Pardon me." She stands like a cat uncurling from the chair and strolls to the bathroom, closing the door behind her.

"She's nice, isn't she?" Ariana straightens her dress, smoothing it out over her very womanly curves. "We've known each other for years. She was my yoga teacher back when—"

A thousand steel nails roll over our heads.

"Fuck," I say.

"What was that?" Ariana stares at the ceiling. "Damn it. I wonder if there are squirrels in the attic."

"Didn't you say you heard something like that at the house?" Dallas gets up and walks around the room.

"Yes, and it wasn't good." My stomach twists and my throat tightens. "We have to get out of here. Now." I knock on the bathroom door. "I'm sorry, Beth, but there's an emergency out here and we really need to get out of the apartment."

Ariana glances back at me. "Why?" She stands under the swing-down hatch to the upstairs crawl space. "What is that noise?"

"Doesn't matter," I say. "We're getting out of here." I start toward the stairs, but Ariana and Dallas stand under the attic hatch door, staring at it like they're debating getting boxes down. "Guys. Let's go."

"We don't keep anything up there." Ariana stares up at the trap door with the two-foot pull string hanging down. "Sometimes squirrels or raccoons get in, so we don't want to leave anything they can eat into."

The nails spill across the living room ceiling.

"That doesn't sound like an animal," she says.

Dallas shakes his head. "That's not a good sound."

"It's not a good sound," I say, ready to descend the stairs. "Can we go now? We'll call the police once we're outside."

"What is that noise?" Beth asks from the bathroom.

"I don't know," Ariana says. "Wait in there a minute." She looks at me. "Wanna see what's up there?"

"No. We should get out of here." I don't want to know what's up there. *Let it stay there,* I think. *Let it go away.* But Ariana watches me, and I don't want to come off like a wimp.

The nails spill around up there, coming back toward the door.

"Rick's right," Dallas says. "We should leave the apartment and call the police."

"The police? Oh, for God's sake," Ariana says. "It's probably just a squirrel!" Her hand reaches for the pull rope.

Beth opens the bathroom door. "What's going on out here?"

Ariana pulls on the cord. "Just a squirrel."

"Wait!" I grab her wrist.

"Don't!" Dallas shouts.

The nails head for the crack of light.

"Let go, Ariana!" I pull her wrist, but the hatch comes down. "Let go!"

"What's wrong?" Beth says, stepping out of the bathroom.

"Rick, let go of me!" Ariana tries pulling away.

Beth screams. "What the hell ...?"

A blur of hairy legs and serrated claws swings down from the opening and crashes into Beth. The force drives her back into the bathroom and before any of us can move, the door slams shut.

One second of silence. Two. Th—

Beth screams. Ariana, Dallas, and I rush the door and throw our weight against it at the same time. It cracks but doesn't open.

"Help me!" Beth screams. "Please!" No more words come, just terrified screams ripped from her throat. Something keeps slamming against the bathroom door, rattling the knob and hinges and any moment I expect to see Beth's bloody head crash through the wood.

"Open the door!" I shout. The three of us push against it. The door doesn't open, but it cracks a little more.

"Why doesn't the door open!" Ariana's in tears. "Beth! Open the damned door!"

Cries of agony mix with screams of terror until Beth's voice is raw. Then nothing but silence. We look at each other and I—the brave or stupid one—gently push the door. This time it creaks open. Someone's splattered the bathroom with bright red paint. That has to be what covers the walls. Then I see Beth. Or what's left of her.

"Oh my God!" Ariana turns away and retches.

"Jesus Christ." Dallas backs away and starts gagging.

I stand there, my stomach sending the orange juice and Pop-Tart straight back up my throat.

It's a horror movie set, I tell myself over and over in hopes of keeping my food down. But my mind can't deny the truth, and even when I shut my eyes I still see it in vivid color. Bloody pieces that might be a hand or fingers stick to the shower curtain while strands of muscle are flung over the shower curtain rod like brown string cheese. Her face is ripped to shreds and her nose is gone as are her eyes. Remnants of her brain ooze out her eye sockets. Her torso, clean of skin, but covered in shredded muscle, lies in the bathtub with one arm flung over the side as if she's taking a bath. Her wrist is slit, and the fingers of this hand have been chewed down to the knuckles. Her intestines have been pulled from her body and left, half chewed, in the tub next to her. Her legs are bent back, snapped at the pelvis and also picked clean of skin. Her heart, still connected to veins and arteries, weakly pumps blood onto the slick, red tile floor, soaking bits of her brain and skull that's been cracked open. On the mirror, in blood, are two words: Found you.

The thick stink of blood mixed with the stench of carnage is inescapable, and I take one step, fall to my knees and vomit.

I keep my eyes closed, reach for the bathroom door and slam it shut. My heart pounds in my chest and sweat pours down my back. But at least I'm not vomiting any more.

"We're getting out of here," I say, still down on my knees.

"What's happening?" Ariana screams.

"Dallas, get her out of here. I'll be right behind you."

He makes a noise, I guess, in agreement.

"Dallas, find her keys. We're going to lock this place up and call the police."

He makes the same noise.

I feel my heartbeat calming and I'm grateful it's not going to burst out of my chest.

"No!" Ariana shouts. "Get away from me! Beth!"

Please, I think, *let that be Dallas and not that fucking thing again.*

"We have to get out of here," Dallas says.

"Beth!"

"Get her out!" I scream back. "Knock her the fuck out if you have to!" I tell myself everything is okay right now. The bathroom door is closed, and we can get out of here and lock this place up. I slowly stand on shaky legs and open my eyes. But for the spatters of vomit, the place looks fine. The hatch door to the attic is open about six inches, but I don't hear anything up there.

Dallas and Ariana aren't in the living room, but I hear her sobbing. They're in the kitchen. When I walk in, Ariana is curled in a fetal position in the corner of the room.

"Ariana, we've got to go," I say.

"No!"

"Come on, honey. Let's go outside." I kneel next to her. "Come on."

Her eyes are wide, her breath is too short and quick. She's in shock. Just as suddenly, her whole body sags and she weeps.

"Rick," Dallas says behind me.

"What?" I look over my shoulder at Dallas staring at something in the living room. Then I hear the nails.

"It's still here," Dallas says.

"Help me get Ariana out of here." I turn back to her. "Ariana, we're leaving now and—"

"Don't leave me!" She shakes her head furiously. "No. Don't."

"I'm not." I offer her my hand. "I'm not leaving without you, but we've got to get out of here." I'd sooner crawl up next to her and call it quits, but there's too much at stake for that.

She stares at my hand, but pulls herself away from me. "Beth?"

"Beth … Beth's not here, Ari. If you take my hand, we can leave now. Okay?" Over my shoulder, to Dallas, I say, "What's it doing?"

"Nothing," he replies. "It's just sitting on the railing by the door."

"On the railing? Shit. How the hell are we gonna get out of here?"

"A window?" Dallas comes back into the kitchen.

"Great idea." I glance out the kitchen window, two stories up. Jumping isn't an option. "Call the police and tell them what's going on."

Dallas nods and makes the call.

"Ariana?" I kneel next to her. She stares off into space. "Ari?"

"Rick?" Dallas says. "They want to talk to Ariana."

"She's in no condition to talk."

Dallas repeats what I said. "No, she's in shock. Fine. Thank you." He hangs up. "They're sending a car. We have to get out."

"Great." I look at Ariana. "Ari, we need to go outside, and I need you with me."

She glances at me. "I have to wait for Beth. We're going to a luncheon today."

Dallas kneels by us. "Ariana? We're going outside. I'm going to help you up and then we're heading out. We can't stay here. The police are coming, and they'll take care of Beth."

She looks from me to Dallas. "But the luncheon—"

"Don't worry about the luncheon right now," Dallas says. "Let's just get outside and then we'll discuss the luncheon."

She nods slowly. Dallas helps her stand. "Wait here with Rick. Okay?"

"What ...?" She suddenly looks frightened.

"Wait." He lets go of her and heads into the living room. I wish I could help, but Ariana leans against me, staring after Dallas.

"Where's Beth?" she asks. "Beth?"

"Ari."

She glances at me with a confused look on her face. "Dallas said we had to get outside. Why are we still standing here?"

"Because he told us to wait."

She pulls away from me and before I can grab her arm, she's in the living room. "Oh my God."

I follow behind her.

What looks like a cross between a spider and a lobster sits clutching the railing with serrated claws. It's at least two feet long, if not longer, with too many jointed legs. It moves like a tarantula. Its hair is bloody with bits of Beth matted into its fur. It seems to stare at Dallas with two quivering eyestalks.

Dallas stands five feet from it.

"What are you doing, man?" I ask.

"Trying to decide what it is."

"Decide what it is? Dallas, that thing just ..." I remember Ariana's in the room, still in shock. "Hold on, Dallas. Don't do anything stupid." As if standing five feet from this thing is smart. I go back into the kitchen and rifle through the drawers until I find a butcher's knife with a ten-inch blade. It's not as big as the one at Kat's house, but at least it's something. Of course, if this thing is as fast as the one Meggan and I saw, there's no way I'm gonna kill it, but maybe I can get it far enough away from the railing that we can get out.

Back in the living room, Dallas is a step closer.

I stand next to Ariana in case the thing leaps at us, I can—hopefully—fend it off with the knife. "Dallas. Stop moving. I have a knife. We can—"

"Stay back. It doesn't seem to be doing anything but watching me."

"Yeah, just like the second before it attacked Beth."

Ariana tenses next to me and she gasps.

I turn to her. "Ariana ..."

She grabs the knife and stalks toward the spider-lobster thing. It turns to face her.

"Ariana, get back!" Dallas shouts.

"Ariana, don't!" I take two steps before the thing crouches back and launches itself at her.

Ariana screams.

It leaps straight at her.

She reacts from instinct and throws her arms up in front of her face, dropping the knife.

The thing crashes into her, sending her sprawling backward. She falls and slams her head against the wood floor, crying out in pain. The thing clings to her, its claws snagged in her dress. She tries wrestling it off, but it flails its long legs, slicing her arms.

I grab the knife and try stabbing at it, but its foot-long legs thrash wildly. I can't get close enough. Dallas tries moving in to kick at the thing, but again, those fucking legs whirl and slice the air with serrated claws.

"What the fuck are we gonna do?" I ask.

"Help me!" Ariana screams.

The spider-lobster moves closer to her face with slow, tarantula-like movements, but still keeps a dozen other legs in motion.

Blood drips down Ariana's arms from numerous cuts and though she tries valiantly to get out from under the thing, she's fighting a losing battle.

It raises its two front, mantis-like arms, slowly stretching them up to Ariana's throat.

I slice at the legs, but they move too fast and even when I cut one off, another seems to take its place so that I can't get close enough to stab at it.

It crawls up to her chest, stretching those two claws out until they hover over Ariana's eyes.

"Help me!"

It lays one claw down on her cheek and slowly draws it along her skin, leaving a trail of blood like tears that drip down her face.

I have to take a chance, even if I get cut. If I don't, Ariana's blind at the very least, dead at worst. I turn the knife blade down and take a deep breath. I have to judge this perfectly or I'll have done the spider-lobster's bidding.

As if it reads my mind, it flattens itself out along Ariana's body, stretching out to cover her from neck to waist. But its legs have stopped flailing. They're stretched out around her in a monstrous embrace. If I stab at the thing, will it rip her open? Do I have a choice? The two front claws still dance menacingly in the air over her face. If I stab it, it could thrust those claws right into her eyes.

"Do something!" Ariana shouts.

I look for Dallas, but he's gone. "Dallas?"

"Rick! Get this fucking thing off me!"

"All right!" It doesn't seem to be doing anything, like it's waiting for us to make the next move. Where the fuck is Dallas? I could really use his help. I look around the room for anything to give me inspiration before the spider thing grows tired of waiting.

Dallas hurries back from Ariana's bedroom with a sword in his hand. "Give me the knife. Take this." He holds the sword out and grabs the knife from me. "Wait for me to give you the signal."

I stare at the three-foot long sword, wondering what she's doing with it and then we switch weapons. "And then what?"

He shrugs. "Use it."

"What?" I watch him go over to Ariana and stand by her head. "What are you doing?"

"Get over here," he says.

"Do it!" Ariana shouts.

For fuck's sake. I grip the sword tightly and approach Ariana and the spider-lobster.

Dallas looks at me. "Ready?" He quickly glances down at the knife and the creature.

"Sure. What the fuck, right?"

"What the fuck." Kneeling, Dallas stares at the thing. "On your mark."

The thing freezes, its two claws half a foot over Ariana's face.

"Get set."

"What are you doing?" Ariana screams.

"Go." He lashes out with the knife and hacks off the two front legs, then slashes at the eyestalks, blinding the thing. It raises itself up and suddenly its legs are flailing again.

Flipping the sword blade down, I plunge it straight through the thick bulk of the monstrosity. Its legs thrash madly, blindly at the sword. I stop my momentum before skewering Ariana. Her eyes are wide with fright. Oh my God; I didn't stop in time. I thought I stopped in time, but I—

"Get this fucking thing off me!"

I try pushing the creature off her, but it keeps flailing its legs to get a hold of her as she squirms away from it. Long, sharp legs catch on her dress. One leg slices her arm, another slices across her chest, causing a ribbon of dark red to blossom. Grunting, she tries moving away from its deadly claws.

I drag the sword to my left, while Ariana rolls to my right. The sharp, serrated claws lose their ability to clutch onto her and soon she's out from under it. Dallas tries to help her, but she pushes him away. Her breath comes fast and tears streak down her face. Where the thing cut her, blood soaks her dress. In several places it is torn and frayed. "OhmyGodohmyGod." She watches the thing at the end of the sword.

The spider-lobster's legs move slower and slower until they stop. The thing is still.

10.

"Jesus Christ!"

Two police officers stand at the top of the stairs. One has a gun pointed—hopefully—at the spider-lobster thing.

"What is that?" he asks.

"Dead, I hope." I stare at him, the sword still in my hand.

"Drop the sword and move away from it."

"Sure." I let go and it clatters loudly.

"Now back away." The officer trains his gun on me.

"Wait a minute." I shake my head.

"Just back away."

"But I didn't—"

"Just do it!"

I take a couple of steps back.

Two EMT's come up and stand behind the officers.

"What's that stench?" the male EMT asks.

"Smells like a slaughterhouse." The other EMT is a woman. She heads to the bathroom where blood pools at the door and pushes the door open. "Oh God."

The second police officer glances in the bathroom. "Holy shit!" He covers his mouth, gags, and runs down the stairs.

"Dammit." The officer keeps his gun pointed at me as he lifts his radio. "This is Walker, I need back up to secure the scene at 151 Dobson."

His radio crackles. "Understood. Sending back up."

He takes a deep breath and looks at Dallas and Ariana. "Are you two all right?"

Dallas nods.

"Oh …" Ariana's eyes roll back in her head and she collapses.

The two EMTs are at her side.

I take a step forward, wanting to help any way I can.

"Don't move!" The officer grips the gun tightly.

"But ..." I look at him, then back at Ariana.

"She'll be fine," the officer says. He looks at Dallas. "I want you out of here. The EMT's will take care of her."

Dallas nods and heads down the stairs.

The officer takes handcuffs out and turns back to me. "I'm going to ask you to let me put these on and then we're going out to the car."

"Handcuffs? For what?"

"For your own safety."

I debate arguing. It's not like I killed Beth. But this isn't the time to put up a fuss. I hold my hands out to him.

"Behind your back."

I comply and then he leads me down the stairs to his squad car. The other officer leans against the car breathing deeply.

"Back seat." The officer behind me unlocks the back door and holds it open for me. I climb in as best I can with my hands cuffed behind me. He closes the door and walks away.

Fucking great.

Several more cop cars show up, one pulling in behind the one I'm in, the other in front as if they want to make sure I don't steal the car. The officers get out and confer with the first officers on the scene. They disperse, three going in the house and the rest walking around the outside.

Other cars arrive. The crime scene people have arrived, with photographers and specialists who will find out we had nothing to do with Beth's murder.

I glance over at the ambulance parked across the street. Ariana sits on the back step of the rig and Dallas stands next to her. The female EMT checks Ariana and says something to Dallas. He nods and smiles politely.

The male EMT joins her as does Walker, the police officer that brought me down. Though the front window is open, the back one isn't. I can't make out any of their conversation.

Dallas helps Ariana stand and they walk to one of the other cruisers. The EMTs climb into the ambulance and leave. What more can they do? The two officers join Dallas and Ariana and they talk for a bit before they split up. Dallas and Officer Walker head to one car, the second officer stays with Ariana. The questioning begins as one of the newer officers on the scene strings up yellow police tape around the property. Wait until Meggan hears about this. Better yet, wait until her landlord sees this.

I lean back, trying to get comfortable, but that's not happening. Not with my hands cuffed behind me. Does he really think I did this? Hey, go back inside and look at what's left of Beth and then you tell me that I took a sword and did that! It doesn't matter. Ariana and Dallas will explain everything and by the time he gets to me, I'll tell him what he's already heard.

More police cars pull up. People come out of their houses to watch the show. Wonderful. How many police officers do they need to secure the scene? Then again, given the condition Beth's in, I'm sure they don't want to take any chances. They all go over to Officer Walker, talk for a bit, and head off to the house.

A Ford Taurus Wagon pulls up where the ambulance had been and a guy in a suit gets out and looks around. Officer Walker goes over to the guy and they talk for a bit before the guy heads into the house and the officer goes back to questioning Dallas. Probably the medical examiner or the coroner.

I expect any moment that Ex-Judith is going to get in the car and drive us away, back to Kat's house. Wouldn't that be just fine? Stealing a police car, leaving the scene of the crime, kidnapping, and I'm sure there'll be some assault as well. Of course, by the time the police arrive at Kat's, Ex-Judith will be gone and there I'll be, stuck in cuffs in the back of the car.

No matter what, I hope this doesn't land me in jail. I can't afford to lose time with Abigail on the loose and spider-lobster things attacking us and Katarina still missing. I can only hope that Ariana and Dallas have similar stories. Yeah. Right. I've a bad feeling their stories will not be anywhere close. I should have faith in Dallas. He knows better than to get into the whole supernatural realm with the police. Especially since Ariana's going to be saying "I'm not sure" and "I don't know" an awful lot. A feral raccoon or a really pissed off mutant squirrel. I chuckle and close my eyes. *Where the hell are you, Katarina?*

It's unpleasantly warm in the car, but there isn't much I can do but sit and sweat. What the hell was that thing? Where did it come from? Is this the same one I saw in Kat's bedroom or another one? Too many unanswered questions and I'm stuck here waiting to be interrogated.

I glance at Walker talking to Dallas. Should we bring the police in? Into what? A haunted house? Officer, we're having past life problems. Can you have some officers posted inside the Petrovska house in case it shifts back in time? Oh, yeah. They'll go for that.

Walker flips his pad over, nods at Dallas, and comes over to the car. Finally! He opens the door and gets in. "Hot in here."

"Yup."

"Sorry about that. We don't get situations like this often, so when we do it's absolute chaos."

"I can imagine."

"I've talked to Mr. Richards and I've spoken with Officer Kaufmann about what Ms. Hopkins said. Now I'm here to ask you a few questions and hopefully get to the bottom of all this."

"I'm all for that." I try getting comfortable, but the cuffs keep digging into my back. "Is there any way you can take these cuffs off?"

"Right after I finish my questions."

I roll my eyes and sigh. "Sure."

"Let's start easy. Name?"

"Rick Summers."

"And where do you live, Mr. Summers?"

"Greenwich Village."

"What were you doing in New Jersey?"

"Visiting my sister and mother at the cemetery."

"George Washington?"

Why's he mentioning him? "I'm sorry?"

"George Washington Cemetery."

"No. Mount Moriah in Fairview."

"Fairview? How'd you get to Ridgewood?"

I stare out the window at Dallas and Ariana. He hands her his cell phone. Probably calling Meggan. "I ... uh ... took a taxi ride to Fair Lawn." I'm gonna have to lie because I doubt he's gonna buy the whole Ex-Judith story line.

"Why? Got family there?"

"Ex-girlfriend." Leave it at that.

"Still talk to her?"

"Haven't seen her in five years. Thought I'd surprise her."

"How did you wind up in Ridgewood?"

"I met her current love interest. I had nowhere to stay, so we came back here, and I slept on the couch." This all sounds very innocuous. Amazing how easy it is to tone down the truth.

"Couldn't you have taken a bus back to the city?"

"It was late, and she offered me the couch."

"She? Your ex?"

"No, Meggan, my ex's current love interest." I let a smile slip across my lips.

"I see. This would be Ariana's roommate?"

"Exactly."

"Did you notice anything strange last night?"

I'd rather avoid the whole incident at Kat's house. Though we heard the nails there, I don't want to get into explaining the supernatural elements of our time at Kat's. I'd rather keep the focus on this morning. "No. Meggan and I stayed up talking, wondering where Katarina is."

"She's missing?"

Oh, crap. "We figure she's with her sister. She does this a lot."

"But you don't know for certain."

"No."

"I want you to give me a full description of what this woman looks like."

I really don't want the police involved in this. They're only going to get in our way and cause us more trouble than it's worth. But I can't exactly argue with him. "Actually, you'd be better off talking to Meggan. She's seen her more recently."

"Do you know how I can get in touch with Meggan?"

"I believe Ariana just called her. She should be home soon."

"When she arrives, I'll have one of my officers talk to her. So this morning you woke up, and then what?"

I skip the bit about the chocolate Pop-Tarts and my whole discussion with Dallas. "My friend Dallas came by and then—"

"Why?" Walker looks over the front seat at me. "Why'd Dallas come to see you?"

"Because." I have to tell the truth, as I'm sure Dallas did. "Because he used to be a paranormal investigator. Something happened at my ex-girlfriend's house that I thought he should see."

"Such as what?"

I want to avoid this whole discussion, but Officer Walker seems intent on pursuing this angle. Ah, well, the truth shall set me free. "I believe the house is haunted by the spirit of a young girl, and Dallas used to look into these things."

"What makes you say the house is haunted?"

"Doors slamming. Shadows. Screams. Visions. That sort of thing."

"Did you call the police?"

"No."

"Why not?"

"Because I figured it would be more trouble explaining what happened than it was worth."

"A woman is dead, Mr. Summers. I guess you figure it's worth explaining what happened now that a woman's been murdered."

I don't say anything. Suddenly, it all seems real stupid. Why didn't we call the police immediately? Maybe then, Chuck would be under arrest, the Dawsons wouldn't be dead. Shit. Someone's going to wonder where they went, and I'll be implicated in that incident as well.

I can't worry about that now. More's coming out than I really wanted to talk about. I look out at Dallas and Ariana talking. This shouldn't be happening. None of this. Beth should be alive and happy and trying to fix Ariana up with eligible men. Dallas and I should be in New York.

If we'd called the police last night, would that have changed anything? We would've spent the night at the police station and that thing would never have made it to Meggan's apartment. I close my eyes and shake my head.

"Mr. Summers? What happened this morning?"

I look at Officer Walker. "We heard a noise. It came from

the attic. We went to see if a raccoon got trapped and when we opened the attic door, something dropped out and got into the bathroom. The door slammed and we couldn't get it open. When the door opened again … well … that's it."

"You couldn't get the door open?"

"No." I shake my head. "The three of us leaned on it, but it wouldn't open until…"

"Until what?"

"Until Beth's screaming stopped. After she was dead."

"Then the door opened."

"Yes."

"How do you explain that?"

"I don't. Would you believe me if I told you that whatever that thing was didn't want us helping Beth and somehow kept the door locked until it was too late?"

Frustration is written on his face. He probably got the same thing from Dallas. "Right now I don't know what to believe." He jots down more notes on his pad. "No one actually saw the thing attack her?"

"No. We couldn't get the damned door open." The moment comes back with incredible clarity, except now the memory is overlaid with the view of what was happening in the bathroom. "Jesus."

"Is that when you called the police?"

I nod. "We were about to leave. Ariana was in shock and I was trying to calm her down enough so we could get out and then the thing appeared again. It blocked the stairway, keeping us from leaving."

"It blocked your way out? You mean it was just in your way."

"No. It blocked our way. It didn't want us leaving."

"You're suggesting it was intelligent and purposely kept you from getting out. Why?"

I shrug as best as I can in handcuffs. "Someone sent it after us."

"What? Mr. Summers, what's going on here is all very strange. Bad enough there's been a murder, but to hear that the killer is some kind of—I don't know what it is—is just a little unbelievable."

"Do you think one of us did it with the sword?"

He doesn't nod or shake his head. He rubs his eyes and takes a deep, tired breath.

"You can't seriously believe one of us did that, do you?"

"This is a police investigation, Mr. Summers. We found you holding the sword when we got there and a dead woman in the bathroom."

"But I was trying to—"

"You are very fortunate that we have that creature. That whatever it is, is the only thing keeping you out of jail. Do you have any idea where it came from? What it was doing in the attic?" He keeps writing.

"No." Is there any point in getting into Abigail and the whole stalker thing? "I think someone sent it after me."

He pauses and looks at me. "Excuse me?"

"Someone is stalking Katarina and me. I don't know who they are, but five years ago we were doing a show—we were in a band together—and after the show, this fan caught Katarina in the bathroom and raped her."

"Was this ever reported?"

"No. No one ever saw what the guy looked like."

"Not very smart."

"Yeah, well, whoever it was disappeared. He'd been sending her shit and all of a sudden it just stopped. I don't know how or why, but he disappeared. That was over five years ago. When I met Meggan yesterday, she told me someone was stalking Kat and I think it's the same person."

"And they're stalking you as well?"

"I don't know why, but yes, I think they are."

Meggan pulls up across the street in front of Dallas and Ariana. She gets out and looks around.

"That's Meggan."

Officer Walker rolls the passenger window down and calls Officer Kaufmann over. "Ben, the woman who just arrived is Meggan Reynolds. She lives here. Mr. Summers told me that a mutual friend has disappeared. Have Ms. Reynolds give you a description of Katarina Petrovska, her sister, and then ask her what she knows about this stalker."

Officer Kaufmann nods and heads over to the Corolla before Meggan can talk to Dallas and Ariana.

Walker turns back to me. "Let's see if I've got everything." He reiterates my story from the notes he took. He's thorough, missing nothing.

When he's done, I say, "Yup."

"What would you say killed the woman in the bathroom?"

I remember something Dallas once said to me. *Believers are far and few between.* "I don't know what it was, but it's dead and in your trunk."

He sighs again. "Christ. All right. That's about it. I just need a phone number, your address, and where you're staying."

I give him my cell number and my address in the Village. "And I have no idea where I'm staying. I was planning to go home today, but that's not happening."

"I would really prefer if you stay in the area in case we need to ask any more questions."

"Sure." I look at Officer Kaufmann talking with Meggan. "Any idea when we'll be able to get back into the apartment?"

"When the investigation's completed."

I look at Officer Walker, knowing he can't give me an answer. I guess after the questioning's over, we'll figure out something, most likely a hotel. I vaguely remember Dallas telling me his sister lives out here somewhere, but I don't want to bring all this shit to anyone else's place. No one else is dying because of Abigail.

"I'll take the cuffs off. You're free to go." Officer Walker gets out of the car and comes around to open my door. He reaches behind my back and unlocks the cuffs.

Now I understand why people rub their wrists after they get the cuffs taken off.

"Take care of yourself. If anything else happens, you call me immediately."

"I hope I won't have to." The truth is, I have no intentions of calling him. I can't afford to have the police getting messed up in all this while I'm trying to stop Abigail.

I head over to where Dallas and Ariana talk. Meggan is still being questioned.

"How'd it go?" Dallas asks.

I shrug. "If all our answers match, I guess we win." I look back at Officer Walker heading into the house. "I don't think he was too crazy about the answers I gave him, but if they jived with what the two of you said, we're clean." I turn to Ariana. "Somehow, I don't think you gave quite the same explanation as Dallas or me, but as long as it was close, that should be fine."

"What the hell is that supposed to mean? What if I didn't join in your little fantasy?" Ariana gives me that whole "if looks could kill" gaze.

"I can't imagine you told the police something so radically different from what Dallas and I said that they're going to arrest me for what happened in there."

She says nothing, but scrutinizes me very carefully as if searching for something.

"What's with the sword?" I ask. "You don't strike me as the type to keep weapons around."

"Ever hear of the SCA?" Her gaze softens, but her tone is still sharp.

"Society for Creative Anachronism," Dallas says.

Ariana nods. "And I also do medieval re-enactments like renaissance fairs."

"Hm." I try to look sufficiently impressed, but she shakes her head and walks away.

Meggan joins us with a sour look on her face. "Why did they ask me about Kat and Nikki?"

"Because I accidentally told Officer Walker that Kat's disappeared. I really didn't want to, but I did. I couldn't tell him what Kat looks like. That's why he had one of his officers ask you."

"I thought we weren't bringing the police into this," Meggan says.

"We're not. But if the police can find Kat and keep her safe from her Nikki, the stalker and her father, then that's a plus." Then I remember what Dawson said about Kat's mother. "What happened to Kat's mother?"

Meggan rolls her eyes. "She had a nervous breakdown and went down to South Carolina to stay with her sister."

"Okay. I'm sure there's more to that and maybe someday

after all this is over, we can sit down with some hard alcohol and laugh about it."

"Someday," Meggan mumbles, staring off into space. She suddenly looks at me. "Shit. My landlord's not going to be happy about this." She pulls her cell phone from her pocketbook and dials. Taking a deep breath, she glances at the house, then turns to me. "Hi, Mr. Barker, this is Meggan Reynolds, your upstairs tenant. Something's happened at the house. A murder. And … yes, someone's been killed. A friend of Ariana's. Well, the police are here trying to figure that out. Not really. Ariana and a couple of friends. Yes, they did. Yes, Rick's right here. All right." She cups her hand over the phone and holds it out to me. "He wants to talk to you."

Great. I take the phone. "This is Rick."

"First, who are you and second, what the hell happened?"

Hell, indeed. "I'm a friend of Meggan's."

"Was that you screaming last night?"

"Yeah."

"Meggan said it was a bad dream."

"It was."

"What were you doing sleeping over?"

No one expects the Spanish Inquisition. "Mr. Barker, it's a very long story and the police are here right now. I'd be more than happy to tell you about it—"

"Just tell me one thing."

"What?"

"Did you sleep with either one of them?"

I stare at Meggan, knowing what I want to say, but knowing it probably isn't a good idea.

"No, I didn't."

"Didn't what?" Meggan asks.

"Nothing."

"What?" Mr. Barker says.

"I was just talking to Meggan."

"What the hell happened?"

"We heard this noise—"

"Who's we?"

"Ariana, myself and my friend, Dallas, and—"

"Who's Dallas?"

"He's a friend of mine. He came out here to help me with something."

"Did he stay over as well?"

"No."

"Go on."

"Something came out of the attic and attacked Ariana's friend, Beth."

"Out of the attic? There's nothing up there."

"Well, there was."

Meggan taps my shoulder and I know it's time to go. On the other end of the phone Mr. Barker is rambling on about something. "I've gotta go." I click the phone off and hand it back to Meggan. "What's wrong?"

"What the hell are we going to do now? We can't get back in there, can we?"

"Not until they're finished," Dallas says.

"And how long do you think that's going to be?" Meggan asks.

Dallas shrugs. "A few hours, a couple of days."

"Barker's gonna freakin' flip."

I nod in agreement.

"You know, it's a good thing that creature didn't get away," Dallas says. "Otherwise, there'd be no way to prove what happened."

"I find it damned near impossible to believe that after they see what's left of Beth, they would think one of us did that."

"People are capable of doing some pretty wicked and gruesome things. Serial killers torture, mutilate, dismember their victims, sometimes while they're still alive."

"We're not serial killers, Dallas."

He nods. "We know that. The police don't."

I look over at Ariana standing a few feet away. She stares at their apartment with her arms folded. "Ariana? How are you?"

She gazes at me. "What the hell is happening?"

"I don't know, but we're safe right now." I walk over to her so the neighbors standing on their porches and front steps don't hear me.

"For right now?" Her voice wavers. "What do you mean 'for right now'?"

I look into her hazel eyes, shot through with gold. "Ariana, something supernatural is going on here. Whatever you want to believe is fine by me. But I know what I saw, and I know what Meggan and I experienced and all I can say is it wasn't explainable."

"Please, Rick, don't do this. I can't take it."

I sigh, wanting all of this to go away, but knowing it's all just started. Whatever that thing was, it came from Kat's house. That blur I saw when I got into Meggan's car last night must've been that thing hitching a ride to keep an eye on me. Ex-Judith said she'd find me if I left and I can only imagine the spider-lobster was her way of keeping track of me. But we've killed it. I wonder what she's going to do next.

Dallas joins us, Meggan coming behind him. "What next, Rick?"

I stare at the house, going over what I think I know. "If this creature was Abigail's way of keeping track of me, what else is out there watching?" I expect Ariana to make a crack about Abigail, but when I look at her, she's silent, wiping her eyes.

"The question," Dallas says, "is what Abigail has to do with anything. All she said to you was not to leave Kat's house, but she didn't say why."

"No." I wish I had a cigarette. "Then when we got to the house, she started shaking and saying 'She's not here' over and over. Obviously, she was talking about Kat."

"But why? What's her deal? And where did she conjure that thing from, and can she do it again? Or summon something worse?"

Ariana frowns, looking annoyed. "What do you mean that she conjured that thing? Like a witch?"

"Something like that."

She scowls at him.

"You saw it, Ariana," Dallas says. "What was it?"

"I don't know." She walks across the street as if she doesn't want to be with us.

"She's got to get a grip," Dallas says. "I don't care what she believed before today, but you can't deny what just happened was supernatural."

"She can. Something's up with her. I don't know what, but I'm gonna find out."

Dallas shrugs. "Who knows with her?"

"The truth is out there."

"Okay. Now what?" Meggan asks.

"Kat's house," Dallas says.

"I think I've changed my mind about going." Meggan turns to him. "It's a bad idea."

I step into the conversation. "That was the plan."

Meggan whirls to face me. "No. I've reconsidered. What if that house decides to shift back to God knows where."

"Not this again," Ariana shouts a bit too loudly.

A lot of people around us—most of them as a matter of fact—stare at us and whisper or, if they're alone, just shake their heads. Yes, people, we're the freaks your parents warned you about.

Meggan steps closer to her. "Ari, please—"

"Don't 'Ari' me," Ariana says.

"Fine. Something happened in that house and I'm not going back."

"It was all staged." Ariana looks from Meggan to me. "Why don't you believe that?"

"Okay," Meggan says. "Maybe it was staged. Maybe you're right and I just dreamed it all."

I shake my head. "Bullshit, Meggan. You know exactly what happened."

She gazes at me with something akin to loathing. "Don't be such a fuck, Rick."

I throw my hands up and walk away. People are watching us, watching the little freak show play out and I hope they're all amused by the spectacle. I turn back. "Dallas." I wave him over.

He strolls across the street, nodding and smiling at the gawkers. When he's next to me, he folds his long thin arms across his chest. "Okay, Rick. I know we're friends and all, but you've gotta cut Meggan some slack, bud. She knows what's going on, but she has to protect Ariana."

"From what?"

"From us, from herself, from the truth." Dallas shrugs. "It doesn't matter. Something supernatural is taking place with you—probably you and Kat—at its center, and I want to know what it is and hopefully stop it before anyone else dies."

"Have you ever encountered anything like this?"

"What? Angry spirits? Sure." He grins. "Not too often, thank God, but a couple of times."

"What did you do?"

"Whatever we had to do to banish or exorcize them."

"Did it work? All the time?"

"Mostly they left on their own once they realized they had to move on. A few didn't and that didn't work out as well as we'd hoped." He frowns and slowly shakes his head. "But I'll tell you something, Rick, I don't think that's what's happening here. This is more than an angry spirit stuck in the house. Houses shifting in time is more than a minor paranormal event, bud. Something major is happening here."

"Then I'll have Meggan drop us off at Kat's house."

Dallas shakes his head. "We still don't know what that thing was doing in Meggan's apartment. The best plan is to stick together, go to Kat's house, and see what's happening there. And I agree. No Meggan or Ariana. It's too dangerous."

"I don't mind telling you I'm a little scared of the house jumping in time and staying there." I remember the last time it jumped and what I had to deal with. What if Abigail and Auntie Jean are still there? Well, then at least Dallas can reason with them and tell them it's time to move on. That's assuming we go back to their time.

"Understandable, and hopefully it won't happen. But you never know. Those are the risks you take."

"The risks I take for what?"

"Solving this mystery."

"I'm real glad I got out of bed yesterday."

"You breathe, you risk." Dallas heads back to the two women and I follow. "I think it's best if you two make other plans. Meggan can drop us off at the house, but—"

"I'm going," Meggan says.

"Why?" I can't figure her out. One minute it's yes, then the next it's no and now, yes again.

"I need to prove to myself that this wasn't just some charade."

It's probably about proving to Ariana that this shit is real.

"I don't like it," Ariana says. "But I've nowhere else to go right now."

"I don't like the two of you coming along when we don't know what we're facing," Dallas asks.

"I've already faced it." Meggan heads to her car.

Ariana looks like a deer caught in the headlights of an 18-wheeler coming around a downhill curve in the middle of winter. Dallas's smile is grim but determined. And me? I need a fucking cigarette.

Once the house is secured and no more spider-lobster things are found, most of the police leave. The gawkers still linger, and I wish another spider creature would pop out of nowhere and scare the bejeezus out of them. But that's not going to happen.

"I can't believe Beth's ..." Ariana says.

"I can't believe I'm doing this." Meggan unlocks the Corolla and we pile in.

"You can wait outside," I say.

Meggan doesn't say anything and I don't blame her. She's been very adamant about not going back to that house and here we are getting in her car for the ride over. I'd rather not go either, but we have to try to find some clue to what's happening, and Kat's house—as usual—is a nexus for the weird.

"And what's this trip going to prove?" Ariana asks.

Meggan glances at me and says cautiously, "That something ... supernatural is happening there."

Ariana sighs. I'm sure she didn't want to get into this now. "We've had this conversation before, Meg. There's absolutely no proof that any of that stuff is real."

"No proof?" Dallas laughs. "There's plenty of documented proof."

Meggan says, "You weren't there, Ari. You don't know the coldness in the rooms, the sound of nails scraping and rolling across the ceiling, the screams from the basement, the thumping from upstairs like something huge was pulling itself across the floor."

"Meggan, you weren't thinking rationally. Kat's disappeared and things happened at that house. But I doubt any of it is so out there that a rational explanation can't be found."

"See what I mean?" I say to Meggan.

"How do you justify your rationale?" Dallas asks. "You heard the nails today and you saw what made them."

"I don't know what I saw," Ariana says. "But we're not talking about today, we're talking about yesterday at Katarina's house."

I nod at Meggan, aiming my thumb at Ariana. "I need to go back to the house with Dallas so he can help us find answers. All I need to do is find one piece of evidence that supports what I'm saying and ..."

"And what?" Ariana asks. "Is that going to prove something paranormal happened in the house?"

"You don't give up, do you?" Dallas asks.

"I'm sorry. I don't buy into any of that stuff. Anything can be rationally explained."

I turn to look at her. "Rationally explain what happened today."

She stares at me, biting her lower lip. "I can't explain it, but that doesn't mean there isn't a rational explanation."

Dallas laughs.

I almost feel sorry for Ariana, but she had it coming.

"What if Kat's father's there?" Meggan asks.

"Then he can tell us what he what he experienced last night," I say.

"What difference does it make?" Meggan starts the car and pulls away from the curb. "We both know what we saw there."

"What do you think you'll find?" Ariana asks.

I hesitate to answer because I don't want to get into a discussion with her on things she can't explain and refuses to accept. "I have no idea. Two bodies, maybe three."

"Think whatever it was got Kat's father?" Meggan asks.

I turn the air conditioner on. "Depends how hard you hit him. If Abigail and Auntie Jean ever made it down, he was the first thing they would come across."

"I hope they killed him." Meggan's fingers tighten on the steering wheel.

"I wonder if we'll meet Abigail and her aunt," Dallas says.

"I hope not." I roll the window down until the air conditioning kicks in.

Dallas says, "Yeah, well, we have to figure that they didn't kill him and he's not at the house any more. Now that he knows Kat's not there, he's probably out looking for her."

Meggan glances at me, fear for Kat reflecting in her eyes.

11.

The car ride's quicker than I would've liked and before I have time to formulate a plan, Meggan pulls up in front of Kat's house. I always like having a plan when I head into trouble, though I doubt today will be anything like last night. Besides, we can roll the shades up, push the curtains back and let the sun shine in so it's not as dark as last night.

"Plan?" Dallas asks.

"Walk around the house and see what there is to see." I look around to see if Dawson and his son are anywhere to be seen. From what I heard last night, they should be missing at the least, found torn apart, at worst. "Stay together and listen. The first sound of nails across the ceiling and we get out."

"I'm all for that," Dallas says.

"Mm." I think Ariana agrees.

"I don't even know what I'm doing here." Meggan looks at the house and winces. "I hope he's not here."

"If he is, he's probably dead," I say.

Meggan blinks at me. "That's comforting."

We get out of the car and stare at the house. I expect Dawson to swagger out of his house and lay some shit down about the people who live here being fucked up, and to stay away from them.

"Thank God it's daylight out," Meggan says. "I want to be out of here before the sun sets."

We all agree to that.

Ariana looks at me with a pained expression. "Why do you believe?"

"I have no reason not to. I've always believed that there's

more to this world than just what we can see, and Dallas has given me plenty of reasons to believe."

She looks over the car at him. "Was he really a ghostbuster?" She tries to smile but it's more of a wince.

"I wouldn't tell him that, but he did paranormal investigations for a while."

Meggan and Dallas head up the front walk with Ariana and I following.

I study her until she looks back at me. "I don't think you're as much a disbeliever as you claim you are."

"And I don't think you're as much a believer as you let on to be."

"What does that mean?"

"You want to believe all this mumbo jumbo, but you don't. Not enough proof for you to believe." She puts her hand on my arm. "Tell me something, Rick. Last night, did you really think it was some kind of monster attacking the Dawsons? What did you think was happening?"

"I don't know. Given the taxi ride over with that thing driving, I didn't—"

"Stop." Ariana lets her hand fall. "I really think you were distraught at the cemetery and thought you—"

"Forget it." I look at Meggan. "You have the keys? Let's go."

"Why won't you listen to me?" Ariana asks behind me.

I turn too quick and almost collide with her. She gasps, stops short, and I have to grab her arm to keep her from falling. "How can you stand there and make things up when you weren't even there? You think you know my mental state at the cemetery, but what if I've come to peace with what happened to my mother and sister and I wasn't distraught at all?" Pure bullshit, because I'm not at peace, but I'm not about to tell her.

"Are you at peace with yourself?"

"Stop being my God-damned therapist." I turn away from her and collide with Meggan. "What are you doing?"

"Fools and paranormal investigators first." She steps out of the way and offers us the open door.

"We need to say a protection prayer first," Dallas says.

"What?" Meggan asks. "Why?"

He looks at her as if she's a child. "Because we want to be protected from whatever spirits—good or bad—are in the house."

"Oh. Okay."

"Repeat after me." Dallas clears his throat. "God, protect us with Your Light so we are safe from those that would do us harm."

We, in turn, repeat his prayer.

"We're in." Dallas leads the way into the silent house, but not before leaning close to me. "I think she likes you."

I shake my head. "Agent Richards, you may be good at the paranormal, but please, stay away from the love connection."

We both laugh.

"Glad you guys think this is funny." Meggan follows close behind us, looking nervously around. "This isn't some school field trip, you know."

"I always went with the buddy system in the haunted houses." I shrug.

Meggan shoots me a "give me a fucking break" look. She's patented those. "What are we looking for?"

"Anything that would indicate something other than the ordinary happened here last night," Dallas says.

Ariana comes in and closes the door with a thick finality like this is the beginning of the end.

"That didn't sound good," Meggan says.

"Nothing sounds good in this house." I walk into the living room and open the shades. There's no sign of Kat's father where Meggan says she left him, but then again, Abigail and Auntie Jean were coming down the stairs when we fled, so who knows what happened. "We should check upstairs first and then the basement. Maybe Kat came home and she's sleeping."

Meggan smirks. "And we'll just scare the crap out of her by trouncing into her room."

"What do you suggest?" I ask.

She opens her mouth to shout Kat's name, but Dallas quickly covers her mouth with his hand. "No shouting. If anything else is here, we don't want to alert it to our presence."

"I'd say slamming the front door gave us away," Ariana says.

"Let's go." I take the lead and start up the stairs with the others behind me.

"Shouldn't we have weapons or something?" Meggan whispers.

"They won't help," Dallas says. "If you see anything out of the ordinary, say so. This is a fantastic opportunity to study the supernatural."

"How about if we just scream and run?" Meggan asks.

"If we treat them with respect and caution, they won't come after us. If we just watch, they may not even notice we're here."

"That's comforting," Meggan says.

All the doors are closed on the second floor and I try to remember if we had left any open. I thought we had, but Kat's father could've closed them, or Abigail could be here waiting for us.

"I want to see if Kat's here." Meggan heads over to the door to Kat's bedroom.

"Wait!" Dallas is three steps behind her.

"What?" She turns as the door opens.

Ariana screams.

Meggan looks into the room and screams.

"Holy shit!" Dallas comes up behind Meggan and politely moves her out of the way. He looks down at the floor and stands at the threshold of the room, but doesn't go in. "Rick, look at this."

I come up behind him and stare into the room. A chill, cold as winter, blossoms up my spine.

"Wow!" Dallas stops short. "Time flux!"

What had been Kat's room is half the size and bare, with a wood floor. A small dresser hunkers in the far corner and a bed—more like the cheapest cot I've ever seen—rests along one wall. A chair is on its side in the middle of the floor. The only sound is the creaking coming from the rope tied up at the ceiling.

"Oh my God."

"Rick?" Dallas looks at me.

"It's Elizabeth."

"Who?"

I cross the threshold and step into the room without thinking. The sensation is like walking through a wall of plastic wrap. It grows taut at first, but then lets me through, making a slight popping sound as I move into the room.

"Ri ..."

She's dressed a little differently than she was in my vision, or nightmare, or whatever it was, but the clothing style is the same. She's in her late teens, maybe early twenties. What a damned shame. I walk around her, making sure not to touch the body. Still, some unseen hand makes her slowly spin, as if she's keeping an eye on me.

"Look at this room!" Dallas says, stepping through the plastic wrap barrier. "Somehow it's displaced the real room and joined into our time."

"This is the woman from my dream. She was the only who didn't believe I killed Sarah. She knew something, but she was too afraid to say anything."

I stare at her, unsure of what I feel. It was only last night in—what I thought was—a dream that she tried saving me from execution and now here she is. Dead. Why? What made her do this?

"Her name's Elizabeth. She was my sister." I look at her gentle face, now swollen and tinged blue, and feel incredibly sad. But that whole thing last night in Sarah's house was just a dream. If it was, how is it that I'm standing here looking at her? I glance around at tiny-framed drawings hanging on the wall with the name "Eliza" scrawled at the bottom corner. She was a wonderful artist. One drawing catches my eye. Just above her name it says, "Thomas and Sarah...in Love". I shudder, remembering the angry mob accusing me of killing Sarah. None of this makes sense.

"Buddy, you okay?"

I stare at Dallas as if he's the illusionary stranger. "Fine." I turn away from the pictures and Elizabeth. Sun comes into the room from two windows, one facing the side yard, the other facing the street.

"This is amazing!" Dallas says. "I've never seen anything like this."

I look out the front window, down into the yard. Twenty-first century Fair Lawn's disappeared, replaced by a narrow dirt road. Across the way is a barn with old farm equipment stacked next to it. Of course, it's not old because the world outside is no longer now, but then. A carriage with a horse comes past the front of the house, slowing as if to stop, but continuing on. I wonder what it would be like to step outside and live in this world. But that's completely idiotic and pointless. There's too much to do in my own time. I start to turn away when a young girl appears out in the yard, maybe in her late teens, and stares up at me. It's Abigail. "Dallas, look outside."

He comes over, but when he looks, the girl's disappeared. "What?"

"There was a girl outside; it was Abigail."

"Dude, we better get back to our time before we get stuck here. I'd love to stay and check things out, but we've got the basement to investigate."

Suddenly, a strong wind howls through the room, pushing us back. Dallas says something, but the gale force ripping through the room shreds his words. Elizabeth hangs like a broken doll, unaffected, and her slow twirling mesmerizes me.

Dallas grabs my arm and pulls me toward the doorway, but the force of the wind is strong and taking a step becomes nearly impossible.

Dallas shouts something, but the words are torn away the second he speaks them. He points to the doorway where Ariana and Meggan are in the hallway. But they're becoming blurry, fading into a swirling mass of whiteness.

His grip on my arm slips and he stumbles forward, falling into the whiteness and through it. He turns around and urges me on, but the wind buffets me so hard it's an effort to stand.

I lean into the impossible wind, now screaming like a banshee. I've never heard a banshee before, but I imagine this is what one would sound like.

The wind hits me, shoving me until I back into Elizabeth. "Fuck!" New strength courses through me and I lean into the wind, taking one step, then another, then—

Behind me a little girl laughs. "Won't you stay and play with me?" How do I hear her? Meggan, Ariana, and Dallas wave me on, screaming at the tops of their lungs, but all I hear is the screaming wind and the laughing girl. "Stay and play with me. Please?"

I never look back, because if I do something bad's going to happen. Maybe I'll see her skin slide off her skull, or she'll actually be one of those spider-lobster things, or I'll look into the face of Death itself.

"Please stay," the little girl says. Then she touches me. Her fingers are icy cold. "Stay with me!"

She's no longer a cute little girl pleading for a playmate. She's the fucking devil's daughter.

Throwing myself forward, I fall across the threshold, landing where Dallas had fallen seconds ago.

"What the hell was that?" I stand and make sure I'm in one piece. When I look back at the room, it's Kat's room again.

"Temporal displacement," Dallas says. "As surely as the room dropped in, it had to go back to wherever it belonged." He shakes his head at me. "Another few seconds and we'd be reading about you in history books."

I shiver, staring into the room. "What caused it?"

"Ah," Dallas says. "Good question."

"Just like yesterday," Meggan says.

The voice of the little girl is still in my head. "Did any of you see a girl in the room right before I jumped?"

Ariana nods. "Yeah, but all I saw was her silhouette. The room was too cloudy to really see any detail."

Meggan agrees with her as does Dallas.

"I could hear her." I turn back to the three of them. "She asked me to stay and play with her. I couldn't hear any of you over the wind, but I heard her clear as day."

"Was it the same girl you saw out the window?" Dallas asks.

"Yes. It was Abigail."

"The girl from yesterday?" Meggan asks.

"The same."

Dallas frowns, staring at the floor. "Abigail's hanging around here." He looks at me. "Sorry. Bad choice of words. It is possible that Abigail loved Thomas enough that when she died her love for him kept her stuck here in this house, unable to move on. Were there ever any spectral encounters before this?"

"Not that I know of." I shake my head. "Unless they've started since I left. But you know, when I got here it felt like a door had opened."

"Somehow that woman who drove you here is connected to all this. I hope she comes back. Maybe we can get some answers from her." Dallas heads down the stairs with the three of us following.

"I doubt it. Ex-Judith wasn't exactly the most talkative woman I've met."

Dallas sighs. "Let's see what we can find in the basement. From what you said, it should be quite a mess."

"Maybe you guys should go down there," Meggan says. "We'll wait in the kitchen."

"No." In the kitchen, I take a couple of the bigger steak knives from the countertop knife holder. "We should all stay together in case the house shifts again. I don't want the two of you trapped somewhere without us." I hand one knife to Dallas and keep the other.

"Flashlights?" Dallas asks.

I open the lower cabinets under the sink and find a stash of three. Dallas gets one, Meggan gets one, and I keep the third.

"What about me?" Ariana asks.

"You stay between me and Meggan. Dallas is leading this little adventure."

Dallas nods. "Ready?"

Meggan frowns. "As ready as I'll ever be."

We walk to the basement door and pause there. I listen for any sounds out of the ordinary, but the house is silent as if it's waiting for a storm to arrive. No slamming doors, nothing crashing in the basement, no ...

"Do you feel that?" Meggan asks.

I do. "It feels like a cloud of cold."

"Cold spots are pretty common paranormal activity," Dallas says. "But it also has a ... a darkness, an evilness about it that's very strong."

"I don't think we should go down there," Ariana says.

"We have to." Dallas opens the basement door and flicks the lights on. He turns back to us. "It may get colder, and you may want to run, but we have to stay together. If anybody feels the desire to flee, say so. If we have to, we'll come back up, but otherwise we should check out what's happening down there."

"Sure," I say.

Meggan and Ariana aren't very eager to agree, but they do.

I grip my flashlight and knife a bit tighter as Dallas starts down the stairs. Unfortunately, I've seen too many horror movies, and this is where the people in the audience shake their heads and go, "Stupid people". Yup, that's us. Of course, we won't be killed outright. No, this'll be the slow, bloody gore fest some people live for. Hadn't the laundry room doors been turned into a human grater? Sure, but I was delirious and scared shitless so what could I have seen? Just my imagination running away with me.

The stairs creak under us. I don't know about Dallas, Meggan, or Ariana, but my heart races like a jackhammer and I can't hear anything over the thudding and rushing of blood in my ears. Now I understand what Dallas meant about wanting to flee. Gooseflesh breaks out on my arms as the air grows colder with each creaking step I take.

"What's happening?" Ariana whispers.

"We're getting closer," Dallas says.

"To what?" Meggan asks.

"I don't ..."

The air suddenly turns warmer, returning to its usual temperature.

"It's gone," Dallas glances back at us.

"What is?" Meggan asks.

"Back up." Dallas shines his flashlight three stairs behind Meggan. "See if it's still cold."

"Why?" she asks. "I like it warmer."

Dallas frowns. "Just take two steps back."

She does.

"Anything?" He points the flashlight back at her face.

She shakes her head.

"Let's go." At the bottom of the stairs, Dallas looks around. "What next?"

"To the laundry room."

He finds the light switch that illuminates the basement. The chair they planned to tie me to is on its side, but otherwise nothing's been moved or changed. There isn't even a drop of blood by the slatted doors, nor is there any indication someone was grated.

"No blood," Dallas says.

"I know what I saw."

Ariana folds her arms. "I told you, Rick, you were pretty upset after what the Dawsons did." She looks like she's almost in "Gloat" mode, that "I told you so" attitude she seems to enjoy.

"Then explain the screaming."

She shrugs. "Maybe the kid was afraid of the dark and something fell on him."

"I'm sure. Just like you've got a rational explanation for what happened upstairs, right?"

"As I said before, just because I can't give you a rational explanation, doesn't mean one doesn't exist."

"You still won't admit there are things beyond us?"

"There are things, explainable things, beyond us. Black holes, quasars, spontaneous combustion, and—"

"I'm afraid of spontaneous combustion," I say.

The three of them look at me.

"I am."

"You're just making fun of me." Ariana frowns at me.

"No, actually, I am afraid to just explode into flames."

"Since when?"

"Since he learned it could happen," Dallas says.

"No shit!" Ariana grins at me, almost laughing.

"All right, it's not that funny."

"Oh, yes it is!" Ariana's hand brushes my arm. "Wait, you're afraid one day you're gonna wake up and just go boom? Ashes of Rick everywhere. Wow."

As the three of them head to the laundry room, I wonder what I did to deserve her and all the rest of this nonsense.

At the doors, Dallas turns to me. "This is where you said …"

"Yeah, I know." I look around, checking the floor. "Where's the freaking blood?" Gathering my courage, I pull one of the doors open and quickly turn the light on. The laundry room runs the side of the house, long and narrow. At this end is Kat's father's tool bench and work area. The washing machine and dryer are at the far end of the room.

"Looks clean in here," Dallas says.

"You're not helping my cause."

"Where are the body parts you promised?" Ariana asks.

I look at her and frown. "What are you so gung-ho about?"

"You promised proof of the supernatural." She looks around the room. "I don't see anything."

"Actually," Dallas says, "the lack of evidence is hurting your cause, not me."

"Thank you, Agent Richards." I make my way down to the other end, with Dallas, Meggan, and Ariana behind me. The walls are clean, the floor's clean. This makes no sense. Of course, Ariana could be right and this whole thing was staged. But why? Why now? Was Kat the one behind this? Maybe it was her charming sister, Nikki. I could imagine the two of them, stoned off their asses, coming up with this elaborate hoax to piss the crap out of me.

That image of the two of them, wasted and conspiring, gets my pulse racing and that old anger starts burning through my veins again. My chest tightens; my teeth are clenched. Taking a deep breath, and closing my eyes, I shove the image from my head.

"Rick." Dallas's voice is way too serious.

I open my eyes.

He kneels in front of the washing machine. "Check this out."

I don't have to bend down to see the red smears on the floor like fingers dragged on the concrete. The streaks end at a small rug under the appliances.

The two women come up behind us and stare at the red streaks.

"Help me move the washing machine." Together we roll it over a few inches, enough to lift the edge of the rug.

"There's a door under here," Dallas says. A glimpse of wood shows from under the rug. "Let's check it out."

"I told you I wasn't dreaming." I glance back at Ariana, staring innocently at me.

"Red smears don't mean bodies," she says.

We shove the washing machine to the side and take the rug up. A wooden two foot by two foot door is recessed into the floor, and suddenly the truth of the streaks is obvious.

Dallas brushes his fingertips over the dried marks. "It looks like someone with bloody hands was trying to keep themselves from being dragged down. The streaks are definitely fingers. Whether they're Dawson's or his son's, it's hard to tell."

"What do you think of that?" I ask.

Ariana is silent, staring wide-eyed at the door.

"I think further examination is required," Dallas says.

The handle is recessed and when I pull on it the heavy door moves an inch.

"Let me help." Dallas gets his long, thin fingers into the handle and the two of us pull the door up. The overwhelming stench of damp earth and rot comes like a speeding passenger train, nearly knocking us over. "Jesus."

"Oh, gross." Meggan turns away, holding her hand over her nose and mouth.

"It's disgusting." Ariana backs up, also using her hand to keep from breathing the foul air.

"Holy shit! What the hell died down there?" I regret almost every word I just said. Around a door into the black earth is no place to use the words "hell" or "died". Nope. Nosiree Bob.

We look at each other, neither one of us brave enough to take command.

"Well," Dallas says. "Now what?"

"Two go down, two stay up here." I glance down into the hole. It is as black as pitch. "The two going down both have flashlights and weapons of some sort." I pull my cell out and check the battery: half power left. I should be fine.

"Too bad the police confiscated Ariana's sword. That would sure come in handy."

"We'll have to make do with what's down here. There are plenty of tools we can use as weapons." I draw the butcher knife from my belt. "I'll hold on to this." I turn to the two women. "Who's joining me?"

They look at each other.

"I'm not," Ariana says.

"Me neither." Meggan nods at Dallas. "The two of you can go down there."

"You're both okay with being up here by yourselves?" I look at Meggan. "What if Kat's father comes back? What if Abigail comes down here?"

"Meggan, we'll be fine," Ariana says.

"Maybe Rick's right," Meggan looks at her roommate. "Maybe it would be better if one of us went down there with him."

Ariana groans in frustration and rolls her eyes. "Fine. I'll go." She looks around the room and picks up a hammer. "I'm sure I won't need any more than this."

I point over by the dryer. "Grab that baseball bat over there, would you?"

She looks at me like I'm nuts, but that's okay because anyone who'd drop down into a black hole in the earth can't be too sane.

"Here." She hands it to me. I tuck the knife back in my belt.

I feel better with a large, hard piece of wood in my hands that I can swing at a distance instead of something close range like the knife. I hand Ariana a flashlight. "I think we're set."

"Okay. What's the plan?" Dallas asks.

I stare down into the blackness. "I'm not sure. Maybe we'll find some clue as to what's going on around here."

"I wish I was going down there." He grins.

"Tell you what. If we see anything that looks like your type, I'll come back and you can go down there."

"Deal."

"Maybe we'll find parts of Dawson or his son down there." I glance at Ariana. "I don't want to be down there too long or wandering miles away. Just a short stroll to see what we can see."

"How will you know you've gone far enough?" Dallas asks. "What if there's something there and it's just out of reach of the flashlights and you decide to come back?"

"Don't worry, Dallas, if something's down there, I'm sure we'll find it."

Dallas nods. "Good luck."

An old wooden ladder descends into the darkness that seems thicker than it should be. When I shine the flashlight down the hole, the light doesn't reveal the ground. I don't say anything because I don't want Ariana changing her mind. I drop the baseball bat down, waiting to hear the thunk of it hitting the floor. It makes a soft noise like the floor's just dirt. At least I know there is a floor down there. I swing around and climb down with Ariana a couple of steps above me.

"What do you see?" Dallas asks.

At the bottom of the ladder I pick up my baseball bat and look around, shining the light in all directions. The basement light, a faint square on the ground, offers little illumination.

I look up at him. "A brick wall and a tunnel that runs away from the house. Not much more than that. No sounds. But it smells like ..."

—*the bathroom after we got in and found what was left of Beth*—

"... It's just musty."

"No it's not," Ariana says. "It smells really bad down here."

"Any signs of life or death?"

"Nice, Dallas," Ariana says.

"Sorry." He pokes his head into the hole. "Wow. Sure is dark down there!"

"I wonder what this was?" Ariana asks when she's reaches the bottom of the ladder.

I play the light over the earthen walls and the dirt ceiling waiting for something to happen. This would be about when Abigail should make an appearance. "Nothing important or they would've braced the walls and ceiling with wood." No memories, images, or ghosts come to me.

"Nothing important to us," Dallas says. "But it may've been something very important years ago."

"Right." I take the lead, but Ariana moves next to me.

"We stay side by side, this way nothing'll happen to one of us that the other won't know about."

"What are you afraid of?"

"Nothing."

"That's bullshit. What do you think happened upstairs?"

"I don't know. I told you that before."

"Any kind of guess?"

"You just want me to say it was some kind of supernatural phenomenon."

I put my hand on her arm and stop her. "I want you to say what you thought it was."

Her eyes glisten in the flashlight's beam.

She gently pulls away. "I don't know what happened." She starts walking ahead of me.

"What happened to side by side?"

"Keep up."

Ahead of us, the air is cooler, and the light seems to have a hard time penetrating the utter pitch blackness. The dark feels alive, moving over us like a cool, damp mist.

"I wish I had a sweater," Ariana says. "It's cold down here."

"I didn't think it would be—"

"Did you hear something?"

I strain to listen.

"Sounds like a little girl crying," Ariana says.

"It's Abigail." My skin crawls. Images flash through my mind. Uncle William slicing himself open. Elizabeth hanged in her bedroom. The girl outside the window, her eyes filled with hate and amusement. The sound of a body dragged across the floor as Abigail and Auntie Jean talk. "I'm not going that way."

"What? Why not? If a girl's lost down here, we should find her. Her parents are probably worried sick."

"Her parents are dead."

"Rick, you're being ridiculous." Oblivious to my pleas, she starts to rush into the darkness.

I grab her arm, spinning her around. "Listen to me. You may not believe in the supernatural, but I've seen a little girl and she's not very innocent. I watched her summon a … a … I don't know—something—and saw it force a man to cut himself open. I don't know what you want to call it, but the word supernatural is just fine by me."

She yanks her arm away from my grasp and when she speaks her voice is hard and cold. "I don't know what you saw or what's gotten into you, but there's a girl crying ahead of us and I'm going to help her. If you want to go back, you go ahead, but I'm not leaving her here."

"Since when have you become so courageous?"

She frowns. "Since I heard a girl crying." She turns away and heads in the direction of the girl. She may be ignorant and arrogant, but I won't let her walk into trouble on her own. "Wait a minute." I catch up to her.

"Decided to act like a grownup?"

"What the hell's that supposed to mean?"

"Instead of acting like a child."

I catch her arm again and turn her to face me a little more forcefully than I mean to. "Who the fuck do you think you are? Were you here yesterday when a little girl made a man's shadow take a butcher knife and slice him open? No, you weren't. You weren't in the room upstairs when that same girl stood outside the window and her eyes froze my blood. You weren't in that room when she asked me to play with her. I know who she is. I've seen what she can do. I don't think it's wise to find her."

She looks at me and slowly nods. "You don't know if this is the same girl or not and I'm not going to stand here while she's crying just because of whatever it is you experienced." She gently pulls away from me. "Wait here if you want. I don't care."

She walks about ten feet until her flashlight beam catches a girl, maybe five or six, sitting on the floor dressed in a ragged, dark dress. When she cries, her body shakes with each sob. "It is a girl!" Ariana hurries to her side. Does she notice her flashlight beam's dimming and the temperature dropping unnaturally as we get closer to the child?

By the time I join them, her flashlight is completely useless and mine's fading. In the dim light, I see my breath coming in short, white plumes that disappear quickly. I check my cell again. No signal, no power.

"Hello," Ariana says, kneeling next to her. "What are you doing down here?"

I aim my flashlight at the girl's face, trying to see if it's the same girl from before, but her face is unrecognizable under all the dirt and grime.

"It looks like you haven't had a bath in days," Ariana says.

"I'm lost," she whispers between sobs. "I was playing in my basement and I found this door and I went through and now I'm lost." Her accent is unmistakably European, probably English.

"Why don't you come back with us and we'll bring you home?" Ariana asks.

We're almost completely in darkness.

"What's your name?"

"Abigail."

The little hairs on the back of my neck rise. I try to keep calm, but the memory of Uncle William succumbing to his own butcher's knife plays over in my mind's eye like a movie. "We have to get out of here."

"Rick, what's wrong with you?" Ariana looks down at the girl. "Can't you see she's frightened?"

I think we're the ones who should be frightened. I smile at her. "How did you get down here?"

"Rick," Ariana says, "she just said she was playing and wandered down here. Why are you being like this?"

"Do you remember me?" I ask the girl.

Abigail shakes her head.

"Why would she remember you?"

It's not worth repeating what I've already told Ariana; she doesn't get it. Then again, this could be happening before Uncle William ties Abigail to the bed. "Why don't we get you out of here." *That's it, just be nice to her and everything'll be just fine. We're all friends, no Auntie Jean to show up and murder us.*

"That's better." Ariana slides the hammer into her belt. She holds out her hand and the little girl takes it and climbs to her feet. Abigail looks at me and offers her other hand. I take it with some hesitancy. How soon will it be until Auntie Jean shows up again? Hopefully, as long as we're nice to her, Auntie Jean will stay wherever she is.

I hold the flashlight and bat in one hand, and she places her hand in mine. She giggles with some secret joke. My flashlight goes dead. We're cast into pitch blackness. The light from the trap door leading to Kat's basement is gone as well. Has the house shifted in time again? If we do find a way up, we could be walking right into God knows what. What if this is moments before Uncle William finds her and drags her upstairs? Would he kill us first? But how could he if I met him afterward? Time is freakin' tricky.

"What happened to our flashlights?" Ariana asks. "And when did it get so cold down here?"

Even though Ariana will probably go off on me for being some kind of fruit cake, I tell her what I think. "This girl somehow drained the power from these flashlights and I also noticed—"

"Rick you're being ridiculous. She's just lost."

"Let's head back. We're not that far and the tunnel's straight." I don't see the light from the trap door, but I'm sure it's back there. "Just stay close together and ..."

Abigail laughs.

I look down at the little girl. Somehow, her eyes reflect like a cat's at night. She blinks and looks away.

"What's funny, Abigail?" Ariana asks.

"Oh, nothing." Her hand changes. The fingers elongate and the palm widens.

"What ...?" Ariana gasps.

Abigail's hand tightens on mine; I can't pull away.

"What's happening?" Ariana asks.

The girl's giggle deepens as if she's maturing as we walk. But her skin grows colder by the second. Her body changes as well. It feels as if I'm holding hands with someone my height, as opposed to a little girl.

"Abigail?" Ariana says. "What are you doing?"

The girl grows silent. Her skin becomes clammy and damp, but not sweaty damp, more slick, like oil damp as if I'm holding a fish in my hand.

I try to pull away in revulsion, but her grip's too tight.

"Abigail!" Ariana shouts. "Let go!"

It's a terrifying woman's laugh that echoes through the tunnel. She's no longer a girl, but something less human than a woman.

Suddenly Abigail lets go of my hand and Ariana screams.

I shake my flashlight, flick the switch on and off, but we're still in pitch darkness. The temperature drops even further, and an icy chill pushes me back. I shove the flashlight in my jeans pocket and grip the baseball bat, bringing it up to swing, but in the complete darkness I'm afraid to hit Ariana. How could this be happening after we said that Prayer of Protection at the front door, unless it only covers the house itself and not sub-basements that connect directly to Hell?

Can't worry about it now. "Ariana!" I shout. As soon as I hear her, I'm swinging to take Abigail—or whatever she is—down.

"Help me!" Ariana is further away from me than I thought, but just how far is impossible to tell.

I take a step in the direction where I think she is. "Ariana!"

"Please!" she cries.

I have to be close to the wall. I reach out to touch Abigail, hopefully to pull her away from Ariana. If I can see those glowing eyes, I'm swinging big time. My hand touches some*thing*. The skin is cold and moist with way too much give. My fingers sink into the soft flesh and I yank my hand back in disgust. I take the end of the bat and shove it at whatever it is in front of me. It grunts.

"Ariana, duck!" I step back, wind up and swing. The crack of wood meeting bone startles me. I expect Abigail to grunt or scream or cry out, but nothing.

"Help me! It's pulling me into the wall and she ..." Ariana moans in pain.

"Ariana!" I wind up to swing again. I had to do some kind of damage to the creature. Maybe another shot will—

"Oh, God, she's ... she's trying to ... help me ..."

The ghastly woman-thing laughs, cutting off anything else Ariana says.

Then I feel a deep, resonating hum coming from further down the tunnel.

What used to be Abigail gasps and screams in a voice that's more a warped chorus than a single voice, "No!"

The hum grows louder and takes on the tone of men chanting, like the throaty rumble of monks in prayer.

"No!" Abigail screams.

The flashlight comes to life, casting a dull beam up to the ceiling. I take it from my pocket, pointing it at the wall where

Abigail and Ariana are. I fear the worst. Abigail's ripped Ariana's throat out, and she's covered in blood as she slips lifelessly to the floor. Maybe Abigail's ripped her eyes out and ...

The beam plays over what had been a little girl but is now a young woman in her late teens, dressed like a peasant. Behind her, dark arms come out of the dirt wall, and ... no, they're not coming out of the wall—it's some kind of man-like thing with its arms around Ariana. She barely struggles against the sinewy arms holding her. The creature's face is gaunt and leathery with yellow eyes that glare at me with intense hatred.

Abigail spins in my direction, her filthy face a mask of fear and insanity. Her eyes still glow with that cat-like light.

The chanting grows clearer and her head jerks toward the sound. "No! You cannot do this to me!"

The skin on her upper arm cracks open, drooling thick, black blood.

"No!"

Another hole appears in her thigh as if something stabs her with a sharp stick. The wound spills dark blood down her leg.

"Please!" Abigail drops to her knees in supplication. "Please, I beg of you!"

The chanting changes, takes on a melodic quality. The sound is clear and pure, like the voices of angels.

More holes, no bigger than a pen would make, explode on her skin. She screams as more blood, blacker than the darkness, spills down her body.

The beam of my flashlight brightens with each wound that opens on the woman.

She glances at me and I stare at her pitiful, terrified face. Her skin darkens and begins to flake and the stench of burning flesh fills the tunnel. The voices grow louder and with each peak of their chanting, another hole breaks through Abigail's flesh.

I look past Abigail at Ariana. The brown leather man leers at me, his hands roaming over Ariana's slumped body. It pulls her up and gropes her, offering a smile filled with crooked, rotting teeth. Then the thing backs up, moving into the earth wall, taking Ariana with him.

I step around what's left of Abigail, raise the bat and swing at the brown man's head. I half expect it to throw Ariana at me, to take the brunt of the attack, but it doesn't. Its head collapses like a rotten melon and it falls backward into the earthen wall. Ariana slips from its grasp and crumples to the floor.

I swing again, smashing what remains of its head into pulp; it won't be getting up any time soon. Of course, it may be one of those undead things and doesn't need its head to murder someone, but I hope it's not and it stays down and dead.

Ariana curls into a fetal position, pressing herself against the tunnel wall. Her flashlight sits at her side, its beam projected down in to the darkness.

Something stirs further down the tunnel, moving in our direction.

"Oh, fuck." I watch in amazement and terror. It's a force of crackling, dark energy without substance, but solid enough that I can't see through it.

"Please!" Abigail is covered in her own blood. Most of her skin is black and cracking off. She crumples to the floor, weeping.

The force moves at us. I hurry across the tunnel and grab Ariana. She screams and pulls away from me, but I hold her tightly and drag her to her feet. "Let's go!" I pull her in the direction of the ladder and make the mistake of looking over my shoulder. The energy-filled darkness sweeps through the tunnel, slamming into us with hurricane winds. Ariana and I are torn apart from the force of the howling winds. I hit the dirt wall hard, getting a mouth full of earth. The flashlight spins out of my hand, whipped by the winds, and disappears, into the thick blackness.

I reach for the wall to anchor myself, but it crumbles in my hand and I'm torn away and slammed against the opposite wall, causing the packed earth to explode around me. I hunch over and shut my eyes to avoid being blinded by the loose dirt stinging me like sand in a hurricane.

From the heart of the living darkness come deafening wails and cries. I cover my ears, but it's no use. The cacophony of voices rises up in a wail of agony and despair, presses down on me until my own scream joins theirs. I press my eyes closed, refusing to open them because I know I'll be blinded by—

the sight of living death

—the wind-whipped earth.

Something crashes into me, knocking me back against the wall and tangles itself in my arms. I trip, the thing landing on top of me, pinning me down. Pieces break off between my fingers when I push it aside. It reeks like charred flesh, clogging my nostrils until I roll to the side and dry heave. The thing clings to me for dear life. I shove it off and my hand cracks its surface, sinking into warm, thick liquid.

"Oh, fuck. No, no, no." I yank my hand back and try crawling away from what's left of Abigail, but it seems to grasp me, clawing its way closer to my face. "No!" I kick at it, but its fingers dig into my arms and it pulls itself up my chest.

"Thomas," it whispers. "Thomas, my love." I don't understand how I hear her voice over the howling storm, but I do, and it freezes my blood.

"Get away from me!"

"I want to kiss you," it whispers.

"No fucking way!"

"Look at me, Thomas. I love you."

"No!" But curiosity is stronger than my will to keep my eyes shut. I open them and stare at what's left of Abigail. Her face is a patchwork of charred flesh. More blackened skin strips away, revealing her gray-white skull, devoid of eyes lost somewhere in the storm or burned away from the chanting. The lipless mouth attempts a smile, but it's just teeth, jawbone, and bits of flesh and muscle. Her warm stinking breath washes over me, and I turn my head and vomit again.

"Kiss me."

I punch and kick at Abigail until finally the foul winds sweep her away from me, taking her back to whatever hell it came from.

A sharp sound, like the air being sucked out of a vacuum slams through the tunnel, and suddenly the living dark disappears with the wind.

I lay there, pressed up against the wall, staring into the dark, afraid to move, afraid to breathe, afraid to call out, afraid to not get up and run back to the ladder, head up and right out the front door. Let whoever wants to follow me or not.

In the silence, someone sobs, and it takes me a few minutes to realize it's me.

Someone else is crying as well.

Even though I'd love to stay right here and never move again, I've got to get Ariana out of here. "Ariana?"

No one answers, and for a second, I imagine it's Abigail crying, and Ariana's gone, taken by the living dark.

"Ariana!"

"No, please, not again!" It is Ariana. "Stay away from me!"

"Ariana! It's over! It's me, Rick!"

"Oh, God."

I crawl toward her sobs until I think I'm close enough to touch her. "Ariana?" This close I smell her, a mix of sweat and a sweet, flowery scent, probably her deodorant, and earth.

She reaches out, touches my arm and then throws herself at me, wrapping her arms around me. She keeps moaning, "Oh, God," over and over. I hug her tightly, refusing to let go. I start laughing and crying at once, relieved at finding Ariana and that, for now, the nightmare's over. Or is it? I glance in either direction, hoping to see a square of light that would be the trap door. But darkness stretches as far as I can see. "Ariana? Do you have your flashlight?"

She hugs me tighter until it hurts. "Don't let them take me! Please, don't let them take me!"

"I won't, Ariana, I'm right here. I won't let them take you."

"But you can't stop them, you can't! Look what happened to Eddie and Mom and Dad!"

"What happened?"

"They're ..." She goes hysterical again and all I can do is hold her and try soothing her. Who's Eddie? I wonder if Meggan knows.

"Where are they, Ariana? What happened to Eddie and to Mom and Dad?" I should have a therapist down here for this. I could send her over the edge.

Her voice gets very small, like a little girl's. "They're sleeping, but they're white and cold. Can you wake them up?" She shakes her head furiously. "Oh, God, they're dead! And Eddie!"

"How'd it happen?"

"The therapists told me is was carbon monoxide poison and somehow I'd managed to survive because of where my bedroom was." Her voice changes to a whisper. "But I know what happened. I saw them in my dreams. They tried to get me, but I hid, and they didn't find me. I tried to warn mommy and daddy and Eddie, but they wouldn't listen, and they came and …"

"Who're they, Ariana?"

"I don't know."

"Were they people?"

"No. They were … *things*. Shadows of men. They were bent and twisted like trees and they came in through the walls and stole the breath from Mommy and Daddy and Eddie and they came for me, but I hid and they didn't find me, but they're here again and …" She gasps. "Do you feel it? Resonations. It's like …" She goes slack in my arms.

"Ariana? Oh, great." Resonations. What did she mean by that? Dallas said that children who experience the supernatural can, with the help of therapists, deny the reality and come to believe what the therapists tell them they should believe. It sounds like the case here. That would explain her vehement skepticism and her refusal to accept the supernatural.

I shift around, resting my back against the wall with her head in my lap. I glance down at her, wondering what she went through that night she found her parents dead.

It's impossible to tell how many minutes have gone by when the scent of lavender and frankincense drifts over me. I know that fragrance all too well. I can't see Katarina, but in five years I never forgot her scent. She loved burning frankincense to ward off the dark spirits and she always seemed to have the fragrance of lavender about her. I wonder how she's here and then I figure it's probably my own imagination conjuring her. I remember the nightmare and shudder; hopefully, she's not here to rip my heart out.

"Mind if I sit?"

"No, by all means. Pull up a spot of dirt."

"Thanks."

"How the hell are you?"

"Fine."

"What are you doing down here?"

"Just walking along and my feet brought me here."

"Where've you been these days? I've missed you." I smile at the woman I loved more than anyone else in my life. "Are you real?"

She laughs. "Where is that light coming from?"

"What light?" I try to see what she does, but there's nothing, only blackness in either direction. "Kat? I don't see any light."

"Damn. Maybe I'm dead and that's the light of Heaven."

"What? You're not dead. Are you?"

"Oh. Maybe I'm somewhere else and that's the light at the end of the tunnel. It's coming for me."

"Kat? What's happening?"

"Don't take this away from me!"

"Take what away from you?"

"I'm not finished yet. Where've you been?"

"At your house. Some really weird shit's been happening. Since you disappeared, Meggan's been worried sick and—"

"She's beautiful. I love her."

"I know. We've been really worried about you."

"I'm sorry."

"Where have you been?"

"What's Ariana doing here?"

"Kat, your house is possessed." There's too much to explain and so many questions to ask. But I'd rather do it with Meggan and Dallas in the kitchen with a couple of beers or something. Not down here in this cold, dark tunnel.

"What's she doing here?"

"Why are you getting angry?"

"She shouldn't be here. She should be ... should be ... oh. I don't know. Do you know what Ariana means? I'll tell you. It's Greek for Holy."

I glance down at the woman in my lap. I look back into the darkness at Kat. "You still haven't told me where you've been."

"None of your fucking business."

"My, we're nasty."

"Do you love her?"

"No, and it's none of your fucking business." I think about Kerri, and Kerri and Tina, and if I want to start something with Ariana, I have every right to.

"You do. Are you going to leave her, too?"

"Don't start that shit. I suppose maybe, but I've got too much baggage with me. Truth is, Kat, my ex-dear, I haven't been the same since we split up. Fucked up, brought down, kicked in, tossed out, but never falling in or brought up or settled down."

"I love your tears. They make you very fragile."

"God, I miss you, Kat."

I glance at Ariana and run my hand through her hair, brushing it off her face, away from her eyes. Then I look up, but I know Kat, or my figment has disappeared. Tears run down my face. Where are you, Kat?

"Miss who?" Ariana says.

"Jesus, you scared me."

"Who were you talking to?"

"How much did you hear?"

She falls silent.

"We've got to get out of here. Problem is, I don't know where the flashlights are, and I don't know which direction is back to the trap door."

Her weight disappears. "You're right. I don't see anything."

"Are you okay?"

"I'm sorry about that before when I was hysterical. I just … never mind."

"Go on."

"Thank you for saving me." She reaches out and somehow finds my cheek with her fingers. "Let's get out of here." She stands up. "Do you have a lighter or matches?"

"Are you sure you're okay?"

Her hand touches my shoulder. "There you are. I'm a little shaky, but I think I can make it."

"So? Any matches?"

I check my pockets. Wallet, change, guitar picks. "Lost my lighter."

"We can walk arm's length from each other and maybe, if we're lucky, one of us will kick a flashlight."

I stand up, holding her arm and bracing myself against the wind-ravaged wall. "Pick a direction."

"This way."

"Very fucking funny. I can't see you. Left or right?"

"I'm facing you."

"Okay. Which way?"

"Give me your hand."

I hold my hand out and in a moment her fingers brush mine. She takes my hand and points with it. "That way."

I turn and we touch each other's shoulders, then move apart and start walking.

"Are you going to ask me to rationalize what just happened?" she asks after a short silence.

"No."

"Why not?"

"Would you?"

"No."

"Someone can explain it, just not you."

"Everything has an explanation," she says. "I don't know everything."

"There's another reason you don't want to believe any of this weird shit."

"What's that?"

"Who's Eddie?" Maybe this isn't a good time to bring up her dead parents. I should stick with the "Hero" angle and play that up. There'll be plenty of time to deal with Eddie, her parents, and what killed them later.

"Eddie was my brother." Her voice is too quiet.

"I'm sorry. Let's go back to the "You saved my life" bit. That—"

"Forget what I said. It's not that important."

"You mean about me saving your life?"

"No. I mean about my brother and my parents. Forget about it."

"Oh." I can be a real ass sometimes. "Sorry."

When we stop talking, the silence is ominous and after

walking for what seems like ten minutes, Ariana says, "Stop. We should try the other way. We're not getting anywhere."

"Maybe we'll find something in another ten feet."

"Or twenty or thirty," she says. "We could be walking in the right direction and turning around will get us completely lost. But without a flashlight, we have no way of knowing where we're going. I'm open for suggestions."

"If we had two sticks, we could rub them together and—"

"Behold. Fire. Nice, Rick. Any other scintillating ideas?"

"We can forget about surfacing and start a new civilization down here."

She's silent.

"Are you thinking about it?"

"You're sweet, but not that sweet."

We decide to head back in the other direction, but after a while that proves useless as well. Ariana sighs. "How far did that wind storm blow us?"

"Maybe we're just not anywhere near the house," I say.

"Wasn't there a brick wall by the ladder?"

"Sure was."

"Then why aren't we finding it?"

I shrug. "Wish I knew. If we're back in time, then maybe that brick wall didn't exist."

"Back in time?"

"Oh, I'm sorry, you don't believe in that stuff."

"How are we going to get out of here?"

"Pick a direction and we'll keep walking."

"Until what?"

"Until we find light." I don't want to doubt our ability to get back to Kat's house, but we've walked what seems like a mile and we're no closer to the ladder and the trap door than when we started. Of course, Dallas could've closed the door when the winds started, and the ladder could be two inches from us or half a foot away from where we stopped last time. How far should we go?

I decide on another tactic. "Dallas!"

No reply.

"Meggan!"

"Damn," Ariana says. "How far can we be from the basement?"

I wish we had a flashlight. This darkness makes me paranoid. Any second now, I expect Abigail to reappear and try to kill us.

"Let's walk the other way and see if we can find the ladder."

"We can do this for hours."

"Maybe even days. Got a better idea?"

"Keep going this way. The tunnel has to lead to something."

"Yeah, a dead end."

"Okay. Fine. We'll turn around and walk back." Her voice gets further away; she's already walking. "Probably be down here for days."

I catch up to her. "Try to be a little optimistic."

"Yeah." Then she's silent.

I wonder what Dallas and Meggan are up to, if they're just hanging out waiting for us, or has the house shifted in time and they're trying to stay alive. A cool breeze flows through the tunnel, and somewhere down in the darkness, voices like a September wind through the trees, call out as if they're in pain. They sound like children, or women. The wind carries the voices, whips down the tunnel until the cries of despair surrounds us and deafens me. They scream for release from their torment and buried deep within those terrible wails is laughter, sinister and insane. A woman cackles at their pleading.

"What is that?" Ariana asks.

"I don't know." I hold my hands over my ears but it's no good; their voices claw through my fingers and into my brain. Who are they? What torture do they suffer that their pain doesn't end? And who the fuck is laughing like a mad hyena?

Then the screaming subsides, and a faint light approaches me as if someone's carrying a lantern down by their knees.

"Hello?" Ariana calls.

"Who's there?" It's a woman's voice that calls softly.

"Meggan?" Ariana asks.

"Elizabeth?" I almost ask, "Aren't you dead?" But I don't. Time around here is very unstable. The image of Elizabeth slowly swinging at the end of the rope slams into my mind, blue and cold, hanging from the rafter of her bedroom. Why did she do it? What would've caused such despair to make her kill herself?

"Thomas? Is that you?"

"I … yes, it's me."

"Thomas?" Ariana asks. "What's she talking about? Rick? Hello?"

"Thomas, you've got to get out of here! They're coming for you!" The light grows brighter until I can make out a woman's figure.

"What happened?" I ask.

"You escaped Eastham House." She comes closer and now I can just make out her facial features; it is Elizabeth. "Don't you remember? You fled a day ago. They've been looking everywhere for you."

"Rick? What is she talking about?" Ariana is illuminated by Elizabeth's lantern.

"Elizabeth, do you see anyone with me?" I ask.

"No. Who would be with you?" Elizabeth stares at me as if I am truly insane. "Please, Thomas, you have to remember."

"Why doesn't she see me?" Ariana asks.

"I don't know, Ari."

"Who's Ari?" Elizabeth asks.

"Never mind, Elizabeth." Of course, I don't remember any of this, except from the dream when my "father" refused to incarcerate me. "The last thing I remember was being taken from Sarah's house. Dad didn't want me going to Eastham. I don't remember him changing his mind. What happened?"

"Rick …" Ariana's curious, but I need to understand what's happening or what happened centuries ago.

"Just … wait a minute. Elizabeth, what happened?"

"Dad? Who's Dad? You really aren't in your right mind. Mother convinced Father to send you there. At least she'd be able to visit you. Father argued that he didn't want his good name ruined because of what you'd done. Execution would've been simple and easy. But Mother refused and eventually talked him into agreeing with her."

"And here I am, hiding out after escaping from Eastham House."

She nods.

"What's Eastham house?" Ariana asks.

I turn to Ariana. "Listen to me. Let me finish here and then I'll explain everything." To Elizabeth, I say, "What happened, Elizabeth?"

"Who do you speak with?" She gasps and her eyes go wide. "You do consort with the Devil!"

"No, I don't. It's the Fever. Please, Elizabeth, just tell me what happened."

She holds the candlelit lantern up and stares at me. Her dark eyes are wet with fear and uncertainty. "You were alone in the house with her. You were found unconscious on the floor near her ... what was left of her body." Elizabeth starts crying. "What more is there to tell?"

"You can tell me how Abigail is involved in all of this. What do you know?"

She turns away. "I don't know anything."

"Then why won't you face your own brother?"

"Your ... she's your sister?" Ariana shakes her head.

Elizabeth spins around, glaring at me. "You don't under-stand, Thomas, the townsfolk are coming! They won't send you back to Eastham House now. They'll drag you to the gallows and ... You must leave now! Hurry!"

"Elizabeth, help me to understand. I don't quite remember what happened. I know I was alone with Sarah, but then I don't remember anything until all those people came in."

"You poor man. I wish there were time to take you back to Eastham. They can do so much for you there." She places a warm hand on my shoulder, and I flinch away. "Why do you jump so?"

"I didn't ... I don't know." I didn't expect to feel her at all. I expected her hand to go right through me and that I would feel something cold, not warm skin.

"What is it? Why do you act this way?"

"I ... I'm not ... I'm sorry. I don't understand what's happening."

"Why did you flee from Eastham House?"

As if I can offer any kind of answer to her. "Because they

tortured me in there, bled the answers out of me with leeches."
I shake my head. "No thanks."

"That's gross," Ariana says.

"But they will hang you, Thomas! Surely the leeches are better than death!"

"Tell me about Abigail. I know she's involved in this somehow. Just tell me how."

"I ..."

"Elizabeth, if you know anything about Abigail, you must
tell everyone and absolve me of Sarah's murder."

"Tell him," Ariana says. "Then we can get out of here."

"I cannot! I'm sorry, but—"

"Even to save the life of your own brother?"

"Don't make me do this!" She backs away from me and
starts crying.

Is this secret what drove her to hang herself? What if I
helped her prevent her suicide? Could I? I suppose that depends
on if she's a ghost or this is really the past. "You can tell me,
Elizabeth. It's all right."

"No, I cannot, Thomas. It's too terrible."

"If you tell me, you'll feel better."

"I appreciate your desire to ease my ills, but I must handle
this on my own."

"Sure." This conversation is all well and good, but it's not
getting me any closer to leaving this tunnel.

"She's not cooperating, Rick," Ariana hugs herself. "Just ask
her how to get out of this tunnel. I really don't want to stay here."

"I'm getting to that," I say.

"Getting to what?" Elizabeth asks.

"I need your help getting out of here. I seem to have gotten
myself lost and I don't know which way to go. If what you say is
true and the townspeople are looking for me, then help me get
out of here and I will hide somewhere until I can discover who
really murdered Sarah." I'm sure Abigail had something to do
with this, but I'd rather get out of this tunnel and back to my
time than stand here and debate with Elizabeth. If somehow, I
am back in the past, then those people are real, and I can't afford
to get stuck here.

"I ... I cannot help you."

"What?" I stare at her in disbelief. "You have to! You just told me that I had to get out of here and now you won't help me? I don't understand."

Ariana sighs. "What is wrong with her?"

Elizabeth steps back and cries. "I can't help you. I know ... but I cannot say."

"What about ... what about witchcraft?"

She gasps. "No!" She shakes her head furiously. "No!"

"Elizabeth, please. What do you know?"

"Don't make me do this!" She drops the lantern and runs off, crying and screaming. She will hang herself soon, taking her secret to the grave. What a shame.

The lantern lies on its side, barely shedding light on the floor and wall. Why didn't it disappear when she left? The lantern doesn't belong in this time; it belongs back wherever Elizabeth's from.

"What the hell was that all about?" Ariana asks. "And why was she dressed like that?" She walks over and reaches for it. The light winks out and the handle crumbles in her hand. It ages centuries in seconds.

"What? I don't understand. Rick?"

The darkness settles in around us and we're no closer to getting out of here than we were before, but I do have a head full of things to discuss with Dallas, based on what Elizabeth said. "She was my sister in what I can only guess was the past life I lived when Abigail first showed up. Sarah was murdered and I was blamed, but Elizabeth knew something. She hanged herself and never told anyone."

"What? I ... I don't know what to say."

"You're at a loss for words? I'm astounded."

"Was she really there?"

"I don't know. You saw her, didn't you?"

"Yeah, but ... yeah, I did."

"Come on."

"Where are we going?"

"Let me think. I have to forget about Eliza, Abigail, and Sarah and figure out how to get out of here. The tunnel runs from the basement out in a straight line. The front of the house faces west. This tunnel runs north, away from the house. All I need is a compass to figure out which way is north, and I've got it made. If only my parents had let me be a Boy Scout, I'd be prepared for shit like this. But I don't even own a compass, for fuck's sake. Elizabeth went that way. That's the way we're going."

"But she was a … a … I don't know. What was she?"

"A figment of our imaginations. Let's go." I reach for Ariana's hand, find it and hold it.

"What are you doing?" She gently pulls her hand away, but I don't let go.

"Walking this way and taking you with me. This is the easiest way to keep track of each other. Stop fighting me." I continue in the direction Eliza went. "As soon as we find the ladder, I'll let you go." If this was a tunnel back then, maybe Elizabeth knew the way out. Of course, things could've changed since then and the reality is that we could be walking toward a dead end, but what the f …

I kick something solid, like a body, but it doesn't move. "Shit." My heart thuds in my chest. If only I had my lighter, I wouldn't be so damned jumpy. But in the darkness, a dead body could be a patient zombie.

"What is it?" Ariana asks. "What's wrong?"

"There's a body here."

"Dead?"

"It's not moving."

"Who is it?"

"How am I supposed to know? I kick it again. "It's too big to be a child. It could be Dawson or Kat's father. I should check him for matches." Sure, and just when I'm reaching down, he'll suddenly lunge at me and take a huge bite out of my arm. No, thank you. I'd rather stay in the dark.

"But there wasn't anybody when we came down."

"I know that." Did that wicked wind blow it here, or have we been walking in the wrong direction? If that's the case, Ariana was right, and we should go back the other way. I close my eyes and sigh, wishing this whole thing were just a dream, that I was still in my crappy apartment in the Village and far away from here. But I know it's not. Somehow, I have to figure out a way back to the house.

"Rick."

"I know. We should go back the other way."

"Rick."

"What?"

"Look."

I open my eyes and stare at a vague shimmer, not more than three feet high and two feet wide hovering above the floor in the direction I intended to go. Is this the sign I wanted to see? Probably not, but at the same time I'm drawn to it.

The smear of opaque white glitters like an undulating fog of ice, stretching and taking form and reminds me of the mist in the park. Slight curves and a gentle outline make me think of a woman's body, but this isn't human, nor is it a woman. If anything, it's a mockery of human form created by—

"*Rick.*"

"Uh. Yes?"

"*I'm ... trying to re ... you ... ut ... hard.*"

"Who are you?" My insides go cold and a sweeping chill grips me, shaking me, bringing tears to my eyes. "Who are you?" My voice shakes with rage and emptiness.

"*Oh, my child, I—*"

"Stop it! You're not ... You can't be!"

"*Why won't you ... ieve me? It's M ... Rick. I lo ... ou.*"

"Please, stop." I can't see for the tears in my eyes.

"Oh my God," Ariana whispers behind me.

"*... op her. Bef ... e kills aga ... Rick.*"

Oh, fuck.

"*It was h ... She got in ... hea ... made us ... ake off ... sea ... elts. Rick, you've ... ot to stop ... r.*" The glittering form seems to shrink back in the direction I intended to walk until it disappears altogether, leaving us in complete darkness again. I'm thankful that Ariana doesn't see my tears.

I piece words together. My hands clench into fists. Is this new truth possible?

"Rick?" Ariana asks quietly. "What was that?"

"That was a spirit and please don't argue right now."

"Are you all right?"

"No, I'm not."

"Did you understand any of that?"

"Yes." I turn to her, even though she can't see me. "What did that shimmer look like to you?"

"A woman."

I tremble from rage and the freshly re-opened wound of their passing that I've been trying to heal for eight years. "My mother and sister were killed in a car accident. Since yesterday at the cemetery my mother's been trying to reach me, to tell me to be careful and something else. I think I just learned what the other thing was."

"What's that?"

My chest tightens and the words come with difficulty. "Abigail killed my mother and sister."

"You said they died in a car accident."

"They did. I believe she was trying to tell me that Abigail somehow caused it."

Ariana's silent. I don't care. It's better than listening to her argue. I know what I saw, felt, and heard; it was my mother. How could Abigail have anything to do with their deaths? She said something that sounded like Abigail got in their heads and made them release their seatbelts. How? Why would she kill them? Up until yesterday, I'd never even heard of Abigail. Why's she going after my family? I wonder if Dad and Marilynn are still alive.

I have to stop this woman before anyone else dies. But how? I don't even know what she looks like or where to find her. I take a deep breath, trying to get my heart to slow down before I'm totally consumed by rage and do something stupid. I unclench my fists and force myself to focus on getting out of the tunnel. Once we're out, maybe the four of us can come up with some sort of plan.

Something creaks in the ceiling behind us. I turn and watch a crack of light grow wider until a silhouette blocks most of it.

"Hey, Rick!" Dallas calls. "You down here!"

I quickly wipe any residual tears away. "We're coming."

"Meggan's on the phone with Katarina."

Oh, for fuck's sake. No peace at all.

We get to the bottom of the ladder and I stare up at Dallas's smiling face.

"What happened to the two of you?" Dallas asks.

Ariana glances at me as if I have the answer.

"It's a long story." I offer the ladder to Ariana and she takes it, helped up the last few rungs by Dallas. I climb quickly, not wanting to be down here anymore.

In the laundry room, Meggan's on her cell phone. She paces back and forth in front of the doors, occasionally staring at the wall of tools.

"Welcome back to the land of the living." Dallas closes the trap door and moves the rug back over. He turns and looks us over. "You guys are a mess! What happened down there?"

"I'm not completely sure. We met that little girl again, the one from the bedroom upstairs." I glance at Ariana, waiting for her to say something, but she walks away, staring at the floor. "I hope she's all right. She experienced some bad shit down there."

Dallas nods. "Like what?"

"I don't know. It was pitch black. Hopefully she'll be okay, and she'll talk about it later." I tell him what we experienced. I'm glad to have this chance to go over everything so that I don't have to listen to Meggan on the phone with Kat. If I'm lucky, Meggan will go off to meet her lover, and the three of us can go somewhere else. I don't want to stay in this house any longer than I have to, but I would like to at least clean up.

"All I know," Dallas says, "is a real strong wind kicked up and I had to close the door, or we would've been sucked down there."

"It wasn't much fun down there in it, believe me." I glance at Meggan and when she looks at me, her gaze is very serious, almost sad.

"What do you think Abigail wants?" Dallas asks.

"I don't know. I think Abigail had Sarah murdered somehow. Jealousy?" I shrug. "Elizabeth, in the two times I've met her, was very scared. She knew something and hanged herself for whatever guilt she carried. I think she knew what Abigail was planning to do."

"But what about now?" Dallas asks. "Abigail seems to have some desires on you."

"But what?" We look at each other for a long time.

"That's the question," Dallas says. "Isn't it?" He looks pensive and then says, "Reincarnation."

"What?" I ask.

Ariana shakes her head. "No, that's absurd."

Dallas glances at her. "After everything you experienced down there—"

"I don't know what I experienced," Ariana says, a bit too angry. "I don't want to talk about it."

"You do know what you experienced," Dallas says. "You just don't want to admit it to yourself."

Ariana gives him her patented death stare. "I'm going upstairs to wash up." She leaves the laundry room and heads upstairs.

"I don't think she should be alone in this house." Dallas says.

"None of us should be." I follow him to the laundry room doors where Meggan's still chatting with Katarina.

She looks at me with hard eyes and mouths the word "wait".

I sigh as best I can to let Meggan know I'm not happy. "Dallas, go follow Ariana, I'll be right up."

He looks at Meggan, then back at me and nods. "We're not done talking about what happened down there."

"No, we're not." I stand there, hoping that she notices my intense, glaring stare.

"I know, hon," Meggan says into her phone. "I wasn't planning for things to go like this either, but some strange things are happening here. Yes, we can meet anywhere you want. The Cliffside Diner? Where's that? In Oakland? Is that where you are? Oh. And you're not going to tell me where she lives, are you? I didn't think so." She gazes at me. "Kat, listen, I know Nikki's your sister, but maybe you should come stay with Ariana and me instead. Because I love you and I don't like it when you get fucked up. No, Kat, I'm not trying to tell you what to do, it's just

… oh. All right. We'll see you at the diner in about a half hour. Fine. I love you, too. Bye." She folds the phone and slips it in her pocket. When she looks up at me, tears well in her eyes. "Well, it looks like we're going to the Cliffside Diner in Oakland to meet up with Kat. She said she'll explain everything."

"Who's we? The four of us?"

"No. Just you, me, and Kat." She looks me over. "You're a mess."

"Of course. We were down in a tunnel where the walls came apart pretty easily."

"Kat wants to see you." Meggan doesn't look pleased with this new arrangement. The frown on her face speaks volumes.

The Devil's got many faces and Hell comes in a variety of flavors. This is one of them.

"No. I don't think so. I've no reason to see her."

"I wasn't going to tell her you were here, but then I realized Kat has to make the decision for herself. What kind of trust would I be showing if I didn't tell her you were here?"

"Oh." Now I understand the frown. This is the moment Meggan's been dreading since I showed up yesterday. Who will Kat pick? Does it matter? I'd rather wait for Kerri, thank you, or Ariana, or be alone. Let the past stay there and don't bother me. But that's not how it's going to go. It's God's plan, not mine. "Remember when I told you about that woman driving me to Kat's house? She said something about wanting Kat and I together. Maybe this isn't a real good idea."

"I think you're just afraid to see her and you're reaching for excuses."

"I think you weren't in the car and you really don't know what you're talking about."

"We're going. End of story." She heads out of the laundry room and back upstairs.

I follow close behind, not wanting to be alone in the basement. "Dallas and Ariana can come along. They've got nowhere else to go."

"Kat said—"

"I don't give a fuck what Kat said. We're all going together because we're not leaving Dallas and Ariana here and there's nowhere else for them to go."

"We can drop them off at the apartment, Ariana can get her car and head to a hotel. We'll meet them." Her tone is hard and cold. She wants this to be what Kat wants. How noble. Tough shit.

"No. Dallas and Ariana can come along." Truth is, I want Dallas there for moral support, and Ariana's pretty face will be a welcome sight from the memories I've shoved down since I left New Jersey. They'll be back, I'm sure.

Meggan turns on the stairs, her gaze filled with ice. "Why can't you do this? Why do you have to have other people there? What is it, Rick, you don't want to be alone with us? Are you afraid of Kat?"

"I'm not afraid of Kat at all. I told you, that dead woman said she wanted the two of us together and I can't imagine it's for a photo shoot. Something bad's going to happen if we're together and that woman shows up."

Meggan sighs and continues up the stairs.

In the living room, Dallas and Ariana sit in silence, and when we join them, they look at us expectantly.

"Guys," Ariana says. "I don't want to be any problem here." She cleans up nicely and as soon as this conversation is over, I'm going to do the same.

"Neither do I," Dallas says.

Meggan and I are in a glare-off to see who's going to give in first.

"You're coming with us," I say.

"We are going alone," Meggan shoots back.

"What if we're together, the three of us, and Ex-Judith shows up? Are you ready to handle her?"

"Handle who?" Meggan asks. "A dead woman? Please Rick, just admit you're afraid to face Kat."

"No, Meggan, this has nothing to do with Kat. It has to do with being afraid of some lunatic woman that—"

"Has no idea where we're going."

"No, Meggan, just like she had no idea I was at the cemetery, or at your apartment. That thing came from Kat's house and somehow followed us to your apartment. Why? Maybe to keep an eye on me? To make sure I didn't find Katarina?"

"That's ridiculous," Meggan says.

"Of course it is. It's easier to believe that I'm just afraid of Kat. That makes you feel better, doesn't it? Makes you feel that you've got no competition for Kat's love. Well, guess what? You don't. I've no interest in Kat. Oh, I'm sure those old feelings will come back, but the past is over and done. Period. Katarina's all yours."

"Can we get out of here?" Ariana asks.

Meggan and I look at her.

"You okay?" Meggan asks.

"We just should leave this place." She looks around the room and hugs herself. "I don't like it here."

"What do you feel?" Dallas asks. "Are you cold?"

"I ... yes."

"Let's get out of here," Meggan says.

"Wait," Dallas says. This is what he does, what he lives for.

"For what?" Meggan asks.

"Something's happening and I want to see what it is."

"I don't." Meggan digs through her pocketbook for her keys. "I was here last night, and I saw all I want to."

"I'm with Meggan," Ariana says.

A door slams shut upstairs.

"Well," I say, "we know it's not Kat."

Dallas turns to me. "Come upstairs with me."

"Are you nuts? I appreciate you wanting to understand what's happening, but after last night—"

Upstairs, another door slams shut.

"Come on." Dallas starts for the stairs, then turns back and waits for me.

"We'll meet you guys outside." Meggan finds her keys and heads to the front door.

She never makes it.

A wall appears out of nowhere and Meggan crashes into it. She grunts and stumbles backward. Ariana catches her, helps her up.

"Holy cow," Dallas says slowly.

Around us, the house shifts back through time.

"Is this what happened yesterday?" Dallas asks.

"Yeah." I look around, feeling the creeps sinking into my bones.

"Can we get out?" Ariana asks.

"Not unless you want to be trapped wherever the house stops."

The house changes from its present form, losing walls, plaster changing to wood, windows shrinking, glass becoming warped and thick.

"Holy shit," Dallas says.

"What's happening?" Ariana's eyes dart from the paintings disappearing to the carpeting shredding away under our feet. A rug, stained, frayed, and worn weaves itself together across the living room floor.

"I've never seen anything like this," Dallas says. "The house is literally deconstructing itself from the present house to something in the past."

"Just like the bedroom." I hold my breath, waiting for the changes to stop, for the house to settle in a time.

When the shifting ceases, the house is completely different, early colonial from what I know of history. What had been the living room, hallway, and dining room is now one big room. A wall grows over the archway to the stairs, obliterating any trace of them. A dark hallway leads to the back of the house and from that hallway comes a small sound, but one that sends dark shivers down my back. It's the sound of something scratching at the wood.

The four of us look at each other.

"Outside's gotta be safer than in here," Ariana says.

"The house has shifted in time," I say. "If we go outside now and the house shifts back to 2004, we're seriously screwed."

"What do you suggest we do?" Tears fill Ariana's eyes and stream down her face.

I wish I had an answer.

Meggan goes over and consoles Ariana.

"Oh, I didn't know anyone was here."

As one, we look at a man in his late twenties. By his clothes he's a man of God, a preacher or minister, though his clothes are disheveled, and his skin is dirty as if he hasn't bathed in days.

"Can I help you, folks?" He looks us over, his eyes lingering a bit too long on Meggan and Ariana. "You are dressed strangely. Where you folks from?"

"Around here," Dallas says. "And you are?"

"My name is Reverend Paul Brown." He extends his hand to Dallas and then to me. When I shake it, his skin is soft and cool. His handshake is weak, as if his hand is boneless. I introduce the four of us and then he says, "You say you're from around here, but no one I've seen dresses like that." He leers at the two women. "And you have odd names."

"We're … uh … from across the river." Dallas nods for effect.

"I see." He frowns. "Well, I'm a little busy right now, so I'm gonna have to ask you good folk to leave."

"We can't really do that," I say.

He looks at me and for the briefest instant his gaze is filled with rage that softens, but not fast enough. "Why is that?"

"We live here," Meggan says.

Reverend Brown shakes his head. "I'd tend to doubt that. I know the family who lives here and—"

"Master sir, I was just … oh." A young boy around nine or ten comes up behind the reverend. He's naked with a collar around his neck. Smears of blood cover his genitals.

"What did I tell you about coming out here?" Brown turns the boy around and pushes him toward the back of the house. The boy's back is badly scratched and there's more blood on his backside.

"Who are you?" Meggan asks.

He glances at her and smirks. "I told you. I'm Reverend—"

"What are you doing to that boy?" Meggan asks.

"None of your business." He looks at each of us. "Now, I've asked you nicely to leave. I may be a man of the cloth, but I know how to fight. I was school champion when I was twelve."

The look on Meggan's face is one of pure disgust. "You are no man of the cloth. You're nothing but a predator."

"It's not me. It's this house." He waves his hand around. "This house is a predator. It draws you in and makes you see the Light." His voice gets loud and harsh. "And I have seen the

Light!" He draws a long, hooked blade from behind his back. He must've tucked it down the back of his pants when he heard us.

"We don't want any trouble," I say, getting Meggan and Ariana behind me.

"Then you should just leave. Now." He crooks his head to the side as if listening to something. "What?" He turns his gaze back to me. "Oh. He will, will he? Well I can't let that happen." His eyes grow hard and his face goes blank. "She says you're gonna go out and tell everyone what I'm doing."

"I don't know what you're doing," I say. "Who's 'she'?"

His laugh is an unpleasant sound, almost a bark. "Oh, yes, you do. I saw it in your eyes when the boy walked in here. You know exactly what I'm doing. And I can't let you walk out of here and tell everyone. I'm well respected here." He grips the blade tighter until his knuckles are white. He gnashes his teeth. "I won't let you ruin everything I've built." He stalks toward us, erratically swinging the blade in short, sharp arcs.

"Head to the basement!" I shove them where I know the stairs are.

"There's no way down!" Meggan says.

"What?" I take a quick look over my shoulder at a blank wall.

"No stairs," Brown says. "Never was a basement." He comes at us, the blade held tight in his hand.

"Spread out." I shove Dallas to my left and Meggan to my right. "You want me?" I say to Reverend Brown. "Here I am." I've dealt with punks with blades back when the band was together. He might be older and the blade a little different, but I still know how to deal with his kind.

He leers at me, swinging the blade, switching it from one hand to the other. "Think I'm a stupid man?" He chuckles insanely. "She knows better." He nods. "Oh, yes, she does."

"Who's she?" I ask.

"The mistress of the house. The house's *soul!*" He fakes attacking me and shifts, turning in Ariana's direction. He lunges at her, but I tackle him from behind. I grab for his wrist, but before I can, he kicks me in the stomach and shoves me back.

He gets up and faces Dallas and me. He stands between the two of us and the two women. "And the Mistress tells me what to do here." His eyes are wild, like the soul and mind behind them are free from the constraints of sanity.

He spins around, the blade at arm's length, keeping us from getting to him. He laughs like he knows the greatest joke in the universe, and it's on us. He's probably right because we're stuck somewhen in time and I don't know if the house plans on returning. Meanwhile, Reverend Whacko is making like a top and none of us can get close enough to tackle him.

Dallas glances at me and I shake my head, hoping that dissuades him from doing whatever he thought to do.

"Reverend!" I call out.

He jerks to a stop and holds the blade out in front of him, ready to swing at any second. "You wish to confess? To repent?"

"How about this," I say. "You let us go, we won't say a word to anyone. As a matter of fact, we'll leave here altogether, and you'll never see us again."

He grins and slowly shakes his head. "I wish I could believe you, but I know better. I've seen how it happens and it's not pretty. Someone does something a little peculiar and then the community brings the wrath of the Almighty down upon them. I'm not ready to take that kind of fall."

"But aren't you here to do His work?" Ariana asks.

He screams and throws himself at her. Before any of us can move, he has her pinned to the wall, the blade at her throat, shouting, "Down on your knees!"

"Reverend, she meant no offense," Dallas says.

"Sometimes the ignorant need to be taught a lesson they won't soon forget!" Brown shouts. "Kneel before me!"

Ariana slides down the wall until she's on her knees. Tears spill down her face. *"Please."*

"It was just a misunderstanding." I take a step closer to him. "She just doesn't know. That's all."

Dallas moves forward as well. Meggan stands deer-in-the-headlights still.

"I know what you're trying to do." Brown shakes his head. "I know your kind. You think you can talk me into letting down

my guard long enough that you can rescue her. But it's you that
doesn't understand." He presses Ariana back until her head
rests against the wall. "Blasphemers and sinners. They're all
alike. They never understand what the Light is like, what the
Word actually means."

"Then tell us." I take another step forward, closing the distance to half the room. I pray I can keep him talking before he
assaults Ariana. Back here in old New Jersey, I doubt they've got
the medical facilities to keep her alive if he does anything to her.
"She'd learn better if you told us. Hurting her won't help."

"The wicked only understand pain, blood, and fire. The
Mistress told me so."

"What else did she tell you?" I ask.

"She told me you'd be coming here and that I should look
upon you as blasphemers and treat you accordingly."

"Her name's Abigail, isn't it?" I ask, knowing I'm treading
dangerous waters.

He freezes. Good thing, bad thing; I can't tell.

He gazes at the floor and slowly shakes his head. "The
wicked will know the name of She who is Mistress, and you
will know them by the dangerous words they speak. Only in
blood will they be purified and healed. Lead them, she told me,
to the Light." He brings the blade to Ariana's neck. "You will
not come near me or I will kill her."

That makes me stop. Dallas does the same.

He hovers over Ariana. "I will, upon her skin, place the
mark so that all will know that she is wicked and ignorant of
the Truth." He cuts her shirt open. "What is this?" He stares at
her bra. "I have seen the like, but nothing this ..." He reaches
out and touches her bra, rubbing his hand over her breast. "It's
... what?" He cocks his head again.

If I rush him, he could kill her or turn and kill me or kill
both of us. If I do nothing, he's going to hurt her badly. I need a
plan, something to ...

The house shifts again. This time the wood is recovered,
becoming more modern. Thank God. Back to 2004 and Reverend
Brown will just stay back there and wonder whatever happened
to us. Maybe he'll get God and stop listening to the witch. Maybe

he'll … Why isn't he disappearing? When the house shifted before, anyone from back then disappeared and remained back in the time they belonged. So, why's he still here?

He slides the blade under her bra, completely oblivious to his surroundings, and slices it open.

Ariana whimpers as tears flow down her face.

"I'm not going to kill you," Brown says softly. "But you must understand, you have to bear the mark of the wicked so that all may know you."

"How are you still here?" I ask. "You should've stayed back in the past where you belong!"

"I belong in all times." His voice changes, growing slightly higher and smoother. "I travel where I wish." His clothes disintegrate to dust, his flesh tans to brown, and his whole body contorts. All fat disappears and his skin grows taut over his muscle and bone.

I gasp. It's the same creature that attacked Ariana down in the tunnel.

The skin on his back takes on the texture of leather, with swirling symbols carved into his flesh from his shoulders to his waist. "I am timeless, for She has seen to it!" Its voice is like shifting sand.

"Those are magic symbols on your back," Dallas says. "What do they mean?"

"They are her brand," it whispers. "Now, upon this fragile skin, I carve the symbols of Dominion. She will be indebted to the Mistress for eternity." He brings the blade to Ariana's throat.

"No!" I rush forward and grab the creature by its bony shoulders. I try pulling it away from her, but it's like moving stone. "Dallas!"

He comes to my side and together we try moving the creature, but to no avail.

"I will do what I must." It presses the blade against her flesh.

Ariana cries out as the blade breaks her skin, drawing a streak of blood.

"Stop it!" Meggan screams.

Suddenly, Dallas lets go and leaves the room.

"Dallas!" I reach down and grab its wrist, trying to pull it away from Ariana, but no matter how hard I pull at the cool, leathery arm it does no good. The cut is perfect with a gentle sweep from above Ariana's breastbone curving down under her left breast.

She groans and struggles to move away from the blade, but the creature has her pinned against the wall so she can't get away. It stops the curve and then comes back about an inch from the end of the line and begins a cross cut.

Ariana cries as her skin slices open under the blade's pressure. But the creature is careful not to cut any deeper than a layer or two of flesh.

I make a two-handed fist and swing at the creature's head. My hands hit the hard, leathery skin with some force, but do little more than make the creature twitch as if I was a gnat. My hands ache from the force of the blow.

Dallas comes back with a handful of butcher knives. "Look out." He takes a medium-size knife and plunges it into the creature's shoulder. It hisses at him but continues carving Ariana's flesh. Without waiting for a reaction, Dallas jabs another knife, this one a little bigger, into the creature's back.

The thing pauses, turns, and hisses again at Dallas. It brings the blade up and slashes at his knees. He falls back as the blade slices air. But he drops the other knives and they scatter on the floor. The creature returns to its work, bringing the blade down gently and opening up another line of skin from the sweeping curves midpoint down to her navel.

"Do something!" Meggan screams. She rushes at the creature. It never looks up. Instead, it swings its arm out and trips Meggan. She goes sprawling, almost slicing her hands on the fallen knives.

The air thickens with the stink of Ariana's blood.

I pick up one of the bigger butcher knives and look for the best place to stab it. At the top of its neck, several symbols scroll together, and where they meet, I plunge the knife in as deep as I can. That did it. It drops the blade, arches its back, and leans to its side.

Hot, fetid air explodes from the wound as if the thing is made of gas and not bones and sinewy muscle. It deflates, falling away from Ariana until it crumples and turns to sand.

Meggan crawls to Ariana. Dallas runs into the kitchen and returns with damp towels that he gives to Meggan. Taking them, she gently wipes the blood from Ariana. I stare at the pile of sand. Abigail knows how to get to me, to us, no matter where we are. What's gonna happen when we meet up with Kat? What's Abigail got planned for us then?

I stare at Ariana, innocent and suffering because of me. She grimaces and winces as Meggan cleans her cuts.

Meggan looks at Dallas and me. "Go to the bathroom and see if you can find any gauze or bandages."

"Sure." We hurry to the bathroom. "What do you make of that?"

Dallas Shrugs. "Time transference? Something from back then travels to the present? Never heard of such a thing."

"But we went back there, so why not?"

"First of all, time travel in and of itself is unheard of. How this house is shifting through time is beyond me. I've dealt with the paranormal, not the absolute fantastic."

In the bathroom, I open the medicine cabinet and find aspirin, band-aids (useless to me), toothpaste and toothbrushes. For a moment I stare at this accumulation of normalcy and wonder when it all slipped away. The mundanity shocks me. It all looks ridiculous in the face of what's been happening that I want to laugh at the dental floss, the Bic Disposable razors, and Pepto Bismol.

"I found some gauze," Dallas says behind me. He pulls a couple of boxes out from under the cabinet next to the bathtub. "This should do."

Back in the living room, Ariana is lying on the couch with towels covering her wounds and her breasts.

"Oh, thanks." Meggan takes one box of gauze and unravels it. "The cuts are superficial. The worst was the pain. Whatever that thing was doing, it was careful not to cut too deep."

"Just enough to raise the wound so that the symbol would be noticeable." Dallas puts the other box down on the arm of the couch.

Meggan glances at me. "What the hell was that?"

"I don't know." I think to say, exactly that, but figure it won't help.

"We need a place to go," Dallas says, sitting down in one of the chairs. "A base where we can plan what to do next."

Meggan sets to work wrapping the gauze around Ariana's chest. "Let me know if this is too tight."

"It's fine," she mumbles.

I sit down across from the couch and stare at Ariana. I feel terrible. Why did we come here in the first place? Dallas wanted a feel for the place. Now, Ariana has a partial symbol carved into her skin. It kept talking about the Mistress and how Ariana would soon be the Mistress's slave. What the hell does Abigail want? If she would only show herself and explain why she's doing what she's doing, then at least we'd have a chance of getting out of this alive.

Fuck it. I should just go back to New York. If something bad's going to happen when Kat and I are together, then it behooves us to keep apart. Meggan and Ariana can go to see her while Dallas and I go back to the city where it's safe.

Meggan turns back to Ariana. "Why don't we get you to a hospital?"

Ariana shakes her head. "I'm all right. It just stings."

Meggan says to me, "We should bring Ariana and Dallas to the hospital and then meet up with Kat."

"Really," Ariana says. "I'll be fine."

"Call an ambulance," Dallas says, and I'll go with her."

I can't see her wounds but taking her to the hospital would be for the best. "If her cuts get infected by that blade, you'll be better off in a hospital." I look around for the crescent blade, but all that's next to the large pile of sand is a small pile of wood dust and rust. So much for holding on to the knife.

"No, I'm ..." She goes to sit up, winces and lies down again.

"Let me get you something to wear." Meggan heads upstairs and I follow close behind. "Why are you following me?"

"None of us should be alone in this house."

She walks into Kat's room and goes straight for the low dresser. "We should call an ambulance."

"And wait where? In this house?" I shake my head. "No way.

We could bring her outside and bring a chair with us."

"Agreed. I can drive them to Valley Hospital." She yanks a black T-shirt—a staple in Kat's wardrobe—out of the drawer. "I hope this fits."

"I'm sorry Ariana got hurt, but there was no way any of us could've known that would happen. We were already on our way out when the house shifted."

The look in her eyes is pure hostility. "We never should've come back here in the first place. The only reason we're here is because *your friend* had to come and experience the house for himself. I hope he's happy now and he enjoyed the experience." She grabs a bra from next to the T-shirts, slams the dresser drawer and storms out of the room.

"The two of you didn't have to come along, but you felt the need to prove Ariana wrong." I follow her and she suddenly turns. Her eyes are filled with rage.

"Why don't you and your friend go back to New York before someone gets killed?"

"You said before that Kat—"

"You know what, Rick, maybe Kat's life is more important than watching the two of you reminisce."

I take a deep breath, listening to several thousand thoughts fighting for supremacy in hopes that one of them will trickle down to my mouth and fall out. "Fine. Take Ariana to the hospital and then go see Kat. Dallas and I will go back to the city, and that'll be the end of that. Nice meeting you, nice knowing you, but it's time to call this over."

The rage disappears from her eyes and the anger on her face dissipates. "Are you serious? Even though Kat said she wants to see you, you're willing to leave?"

"Yes. Because you're right. No one else has to get hurt because of me. It would be better and safer for you and Kat if I just left."

"You know she's not going to be happy."

"Better alive and miserable than dead. I don't understand what all this is about with Abigail, Thomas, and Sarah. All I know is that something happened sometime in the past and it's as if Abigail is still trying to get revenge."

"That's ridiculous."

"Are you willing to bet Kat's life on how ridiculous it is?"

"No. You're right. It's better this way."

"For you, too. Don't look so down. It's not like you wanted Kat and I to see each other." I pass her and head down the stairs. "We should get out of this house before something else happens."

"Agreed." She follows me down.

At the foot of the stairs I stop, my heart suddenly kicking in my chest. Meggan almost collides with me.

"What—" She stops next to me and gasps.

Ariana, still topless, straddles Dallas with one of the bigger butcher knives pointed down at his throat. "Ah, there you are. Glad you could join us." Her eyes tremble slightly as she stares at me just like ex-Judith's did.

"Ariana," Meggan says. "What are you doing?"

"See, there's your mistake." The woman laughs.

The tone of her voice is different, but I know it from yesterday's joy ride to Kat's house. "Judith, what do you want?"

She grins wickedly. "Not Judith. Abigail."

"What?" Meggan asks. "But—"

"What do you want?" I ask. "Why are you doing this?"

"Here's what's going to happen." She rests the knife's point on Dallas's Adam's apple. "You two are going to meet Katarina like you're supposed to. Dallas and Ariana can go wherever they want. If you don't meet up with Katarina, they will die. Is that simple enough for you?" She looks at Meggan then back at me. "Now, you'll get in Meggan's nice Corolla and go to Harriman Park. Follow Seven Lakes Drive to the Rangers' station, take the circle around to the left and follow the narrow road. You'll find Katarina waiting there for you."

"We're supposed to meet her at the diner," I say, as if that even matters.

"I've changed your plans," Ariana/Abigail says. "Harriman State Park."

"Why are you doing this?" I ask.

Ariana's grin is terrifying in its wickedness. "Because, my

dear, Thomas, the cycle is coming to fruition once again and I will not be denied."

"Thomas?" Meggan asks. "His name's Rick. Ariana, what's wrong with you?"

She called me Thomas. Like Elizabeth did. I'll ponder it later. I turn my fiercest gaze on Ariana/Abigail. "Get out of her head!"

"I can crush her soul with a thought, Rick. Don't push your luck. The only reason I'm leaving her alive is because she's easy to manipulate and I may want to stay in her for a while. Now, be on your way before Dallas gets a tracheotomy." She slowly spins the knife on his throat. "Meggan, hand me those clothes."

She hands the T-shirt and bra over.

"Thanks."

"We're going." I give Ariana/Abigail one more blazing stare. "Dallas, take care and I'll see you soon."

Ariana laughs. "Foolishly optimistic!"

"Take care, Rick," Dallas whispers.

I open the front door and a sudden chill wraps around me. It doesn't come from outside, but behind me. And as it embraces me, swirls around, then passes, a voice slips through my mind, leaving a phrase like dead leaves racing across a street. *Remember Athens.*

12.

Athens. What the hell does Athens have to do with any-thing? I've never been to Athens. Georgia or Greece. This could be some past life thing like the Nazi torture chamber. If I could remember Athens, maybe I could solve this whole thing. But if it was a past life experience, that was a damned long time ago and I'm lucky I can remember what I did last week.

Abigail said something about a cycle coming to an end. But what? If I'm Thomas, could Kat be Sarah? Is this some sort of eternal revenge because Thomas wouldn't fall in love with Abigail? I wish I had a regression therapist along, then I could remember what I'm supposed to about Athens. But until I find one, I've got to just go along and see what happens.

I guess when we meet up with Kat, I'll find out. I wish I had a plan, but I've got nothing except fear rushing through my veins and that phrase. Remember Athens.

It's late afternoon and we're on our way to Harriman State Park. Luckily, Meggan knows where she's going.

"Rick, what's happening?" Meggan sounds like she's ready to cry. "What just happened?"

"Somehow, Abigail has the power to move from one body to another. Her spirit must be in the house unless she needs to travel, and then she takes over a body—"

"Why is she doing this?"

"I don't know. Something from a past life maybe." I shrug. "Abigail is seeking revenge for her unrequited love."

Meggan glances at me. "Do you know how ridiculous that is? Someone dead for three centuries has come back to kill the two of you. Even if I believed in ghosts, that would be a real stretch. On top of that she can move from body to body?" She shakes her head. "What's happened the last two days—I don't know. Can you call it supernatural? I believe in an afterlife, that we go to Heaven and there's something more, but reincarnation isn't real. It's not. I suppose there are things beyond what we know and understand—what's happening in Kat's house—but ghosts of dead witches from the 1700's?"

"Then what is it? What's happening? Ariana wasn't acting. Something was making her hold a knife to Dallas's throat. All that shit at Kat's house and that thing that tore Ariana's friend apart were real. No matter what you believe, you can't discount anything that's happened."

"I'm not discounting anything, Rick," she says quietly. "I want to know what all of it means."

"It means we're in deep shit."

"Thank you for clarifying that. I feel much better. Well, hopefully when we meet up with them, everything'll be fine."

"Yeah, well, I'm not ... Them? Who's them?"

Meggan stares at the road ahead of us. The sun is just beginning to set in the west, casting long shadows across the street.

I sigh. "Nikki's with her, isn't she? Why didn't you tell me this before?" Because when Meggan told us that Kat suggested we all get together, some stupid part of me said, great! I should've remembered everything I've learned and made sure to find out the details of this little rendezvous. What's the saying? The Devil's in the details. For fuck's sake.

"She wants to see you," Meggan says.

"Kat or Nikki?" I ask.

"Katarina."

"I wish I had a cigarette."

Meggan shoots me a look that says, "You wouldn't be able to smoke it in here so don't even think about it".

It is too damned easy to forget five years of spirituality when you're back around those people who instigated your decision to get spiritual in the first place.

"Why didn't you tell me any of this before?" I wonder if Abigail knows Nikki's with Kat.

"I told you I was going to see Kat and she asked to see you.

I'm sorry about not telling you Nikki was going to be there. I
didn't think it was any big deal."

"No big deal?" I laugh. "Your lover can't get clean because of
Nikki, who's coming along, and you didn't think it was any big
deal enough to tell me?"

"I know she's keeping Kat from sobriety, but—"

"No. Wrong. Kat's keeping herself from sobriety. If Kat
wanted to get clean, all she has to do is say no to Nikki and tell
her to get lost."

"It's not that simple."

"Oh, it is that simple. Maybe not easy for Kat, but it doesn't
get any simpler than 'Just say no'."

Meggan frowns at me.

"Don't give me shit. I've been there."

"Don't act so fucking self-righteous. Just because it was easy
for you …"

I slam my fist against the car door and Meggan jumps. "I
never said it was easy. I said it was simple. It wasn't easy for me,
believe me. I was there. I know what I went through and it was
no picnic. I saw some people bottom out in NA and no matter
how much we let them open to us, they went back and shot up
or snorted or whatever and wound up dead. Don't pretend you
have any idea what it's like."

Her hands grip the steering wheel a little tighter and her
face is set in that angry façade that says, "one more thing and
she's gonna blow!" I turn the radio up, letting "One Step Closer"
by Linkin Park drown the car in a wave of noise.

She snaps the radio off. "This is all your fault. I want you to
tell me everything you know about Abigail."

"I'm in the dark as much as you are. Why do you think I
know what's going on? Because Dallas used to do this sort of
thing? All that means is that *he* may have a grasp on what's
happening. But I don't. I hope when we meet up with Kat that
nothing bad happens."

"What are you expecting?"

"I don't know." But I do. Abigail's going to be waiting there
and when Kat and I are together she'll explain everything
right before she kills us. I should just tell Meggan to drop me

off anywhere, but I also know that Abigail has ways of seeing and if she's still around Dallas and Ariana, I don't want to be responsible for their deaths. Whatever we're driving to is very important for Abigail. I just pray I live to tell Dallas about it over a few beers. "What's with Ariana?" Changing topics is the only way to get Abigail's evil grin out of my head.

Meggan frowns.

"What?" She knows something.

"Maybe Ari should tell you herself," Meggan says. "It's none of my business."

"What's none of your business?"

"The way … there's Nikki's car."

"Meggan, what did she say?"

"Later."

Ahead of us, Nikki's Mitsubishi 3000GT hunkers at the side of the road exactly where Ariana/Abigail said it would be. As Meggan pulls up behind the other car, I wonder if Nikki bought it with drug money.

Meggan slides the car into "Park" but leaves it running and gets out. I'm a little more hesitant. This isn't how I thought I'd meet Katarina again and certainly not with Nikki tagging along.

Kat gets out on the passenger side of the car. Her hair is longer, almost down to her ass. Otherwise, she hasn't changed which pisses me off because I remember how my hands felt touching every inch of her body and that's the last thing I want to remember right now. But she is really beautiful. I'd rather leave Meggan with Nikki and take a ride with Kat, reminisce, find some shadowy spot and fuck 'til the sun comes up. My heart kicks in my chest like it's kicking an old fool and saying, "Look what you gave up. Look what you're missing".

Well, Rick, no time like the present. I get out of the car. Kat and I stare at each other for a long time and though I want to say something, my throat has closed off and no words come out.

"It's good to see you, Rick." Kat comes around and leans against the back of Nikki's car.

"You, too, Kat." I stop by the front of the Corolla. I'm not sure I want to get too close to her.

"I'm glad you're safe." Meggan comes over and hugs Kat,

giving her a quick kiss. "I was worried about you, hon."

"It's okay." Kat gives Meggan's arm a reassuring squeeze. "I've been hanging with Nikki."

"Why didn't you call me?"

"It's kinda strange. Nikki was afraid that our father was after me and she didn't want me calling anyone in case he was there."

"You could've called me."

"I'm sorry." She glances at me and frowns. "What were you doing at my house?"

"It's a long story."

"It's always a long story, isn't it?"

It's good to see she's bitter and not ambivalent. I'd hate to think she didn't care.

"How about it's a crazy story and—"

"Crazy as someone just disappearing out of someone's life?"

Nikki gets out of her car and walks around to stand in front of the taillights. She's got that smug "I know better than you" look on her face; a standard look when she's around me. "Long time, no see, you bastard."

"A pleasure, as always." I stare at her with as much disgust as humanly possible.

"So, you're a long, crazy story away from whatever hole you crawled out of, huh, Rick?" Nikki asks. "And what are you here for? Decided to see if Kat would be happy to see you again?" She laughs. "Might as well get in a taxi and go home."

"Are you afraid I might take Kat away from you and your drugs? Who would you have to get high with?"

"Kat's doing just fine and has been fine without you." Nikki comes by her sister and gives her a hug. "Aren't you?"

"I'm fine," Kat says with hesitation.

"Well, good." I look from Kat to Nikki. "I'm glad everyone's real fucking fine. I'm not here because I want to be and I'm not here to see Kat or do anything. Someone's stalking Kat. You all know it and when Meggan told me, I felt like I should do something to help."

"How fucking noble," Nikki says. "Kat hasn't needed your help since you ran away from her and—"

"I didn't run away."

"Oh, yes, you did," Nikki says. "She was hurting, and you couldn't deal with her pain, or her need, and you ran away. You were too weak to help her and instead of admitting it, you turned tail and ran."

"You don't know what you're talking about." My chest tightens and I have to forcibly keep my jaw from clenching. My heart beats just a little faster and adrenaline seeps into my blood. I've never hit a woman before, but I'm coming close.

"I don't? Okay, Rick, let's pretend you didn't run away. What did you do? Wait. I know." She nods, looks at Kat, then back at me. "While Kat was fighting to get clean after Margo killed herself and Mitch overdosed, while she was in such pain because she wanted to get clean, but needed you to help her, you started fucking that slut, Kerri. You decided that it was more fun fucking Kerri than helping the woman who loved you more than life itself. What were you thinking, Rick, while you were fucking Kerri? Did you give a shit about Kat, now that you found someone who spread her legs for you any old time you needed to get off?"

I shake my head. "We've never slept together. What are you talking about?" *Walk away, Rick, before you launch yourself at her and do something real stupid!*

"Truth hurts, doesn't it?"

"What the fuck do you know about truth? Where were you when Kat was trying to get clean? Giving her more shit to get her high? What kind of sister were you?"

"At least I was always there for her."

"There for her? You call what you did being there for her? Jesus, Nikki, open your fucking eyes. Giving your sister drugs, whenever she wants, is not helping her. I left because I couldn't get through to Kat. She thought she was indestructible, that she could do whatever she wanted, and nothing would happen. No matter what I said and what I did, you were always there to make sure she had her high when she needed it. Don't lecture me about what's right. If you gave a damn about Kat, you'd get yourself clean and bring her with you. But that's too hard for you, isn't it? It's easier to keep drugging, and why do it alone when you can drag your sister down as well, right?"

"She does it because she wants to."

I laugh. "Any old time she wants she can stop, and you'll do nothing to get in the way of her recovery? I doubt it. You don't want to be alone, do you, Nikki? It frightens the shit out of you to imagine being alone. That's why you keep your sister wasted, this way you don't have to be alone."

"You don't know what you're talking about."

"One more question for you, Nikki. While you're flying, how many guys have you spread your legs for?"

She takes two steps and slaps me as hard as she can. Tears spring to my eyes and my cheek stings like hell.

"How dare you?" Nikki's eyes narrow and her mouth tightens. "Why don't you go home and fuck your little bitch, because there's nothing for you here." She turns away from me.

I grab her arm and turn her around to face me. Her eyes tremble for the briefest seconds. My whole body goes cold and my mouth opens to speak, but no words come out.

She yanks her arm out of my grasp. "Don't touch me." She walks back to Kat's side and hugs her again.

Meggan stares at me. "What's wrong with you?"

"Thanks for helping me." I shake my head, watching Nikki. "Meggan …"

"Why should I?"

Nikki moves near Meggan, scoops up a large rock and swings at Meggan's head, catching her right above her temple. Meggan crumples to the ground, unconscious.

"Nikki!" Kat screams. "What are you doing?"

"Abigail," I say.

In one quick step, she's in front of Kat. Her fingers tighten around Kat's throat and she looks back at me. "You're just too smart for me."

"How much of that was Nikki and how much of it was you?" I ask.

"Nikki's right here with me. I haven't crushed her, yet."

Kat struggles, but it's no use. "Nikki, what are you talking about?"

"Oh, Kat, Nikki's in here with me, but right now she can't

talk. I've mostly crushed her will and her soul. Right now, she's whimpering, unable to do much of anything. Nikki's insides have been, how shall I say, displaced for now. Her mind is almost gone, ripped apart, burned away to nothing." She laughs and it's Abigail's laugh.

"Rick," Kat says. "Help me!"

Abigail ignores her. "I hopped a ride in Meggan's psyche until we arrived and then jumped to Kat all with a couple of girl hugs. Then I came in to Nikki's mind, very quietly. Shh, be vewy quiet, I'm hunting weak souls! Hehehehe! She never knew I was coming, never saw it until it was too late. Her tiny mind couldn't comprehend what was happening to her. I tore her fragile psyche away like a spider web. I can pretty much destroy her at will. I'm not talking about death, soul moves on, I mean that I can crush her soul utterly that there's nothing left of her. But Nikki is a strong woman. She's not so easy to do away with."

"Nikki, what are you saying?" Kat asks.

"I'm not really Nikki," Abigail says.

"Who are you?" Kat asks.

"Your worst fucking nightmare." She grins, but the grin slips as if something interrupted her. "How do you feel, Rick, knowing that you lost again? Knowing that one more time, I am victorious, and your lives are mine."

"I don't understand," Kat says, trying to take a breath.

"Lost what?" I move closer her. "All you've said was something about a cycle coming to an end."

"It has," Nikki says, "and as always, I will enlighten you both. Long ago, there were two people who loved each other very much. Neither one of you remember, but I do." She glares at me. "Step back or I will choke the life out of her right now." Her fingers tighten around Kat's throat.

I step back and wait for her to relax her grip. When she does, I say, "Thomas and Sarah?"

"Why yes, as a matter of fact. And ..." She winces and gasps as her fingers drop from Kat's throat.

Kat throws her arms up and shoves her sister back.

While Nikki seems dazed, I charge her. But she's too quick

to recover and before I'm close enough, she backhands Kat and digs her nails into her throat. "You wanna play?" She turns to me and her gaze is withering. "Don't be stupid."

"You said we're both dead anyway. What difference does it make?"

She closes her eyes and her jaw muscles tighten.

"What's wrong?" I take another step in her direction.

"It's … it's nothing. Back off, Rick, or I'll rip her throat out!"

"You're gonna kill us anyway!" I grab her shoulder.

I never see her right hand slap me so hard that I stagger back, holding my cheek. My hand comes away bloody and I realize her nails scratched my skin.

"Now, where was I?" Abigail looks at me, then back at Kat. Her fingers loosen from around Kat's neck, but still hold her. "Oh, yes. These two people, Thomas and Sarah, loved each other very much. That would have been fine except that a young girl, recently moved from Salem, Massachusetts, happened to fall in love with the boy. But no matter what she did, this new girl couldn't get his affections away from his beloved. She did a spell and murdered her, hoping that once she was gone, he would notice this new girl.

"But it didn't quite work out. He was shocked and distraught so that no matter what this girl did, he never showed the slightest interest in her. As a matter of fact, he shunned her. She killed him then, and vowed that in …" She winces again. "Stop it," she mumbles. "God damned bitch! Keep it up and I'll destroy you. That's better." She takes a quick deep breath and smiles. "See, Nikki, I won't hurt you if you stop trying to resist. Be a good little girl and stop fighting me. There. That's good of you." She nods and looks up at us. "The girl vowed that for all time she would find the couple throughout their lifetimes and murder them together."

"That's insane," Kat says.

Now that I hear it from someone else it does sound like a great novel, but pretty nuts as a reality. I wonder what happened to Thomas. If he was to be executed, how did he live long enough for Abigail to pursue him?

"You expect us to believe that story?" Kat asks. "What are

you saying, that Rick and I were those two people and you were the girl from Massachusetts?" She laughs. "Give me a fucking break."

Abigail squeezes Kat's throat. "You're in no position to pass judgment on me, you fucking bitch. If it wasn't for you, Thomas and I would've been happy together. But no, you couldn't leave him alone, could you?"

"I don't know what you're talking about!" Kat screams. "You're insane!"

"Right now, Katarina, I have control of your pathetic sister's soul. Not just her weak mind, but her soul. Do you know what will happen if I choose to end her life? Her soul is destroyed, utterly and completely."

Kat shakes her head. "I don't believe you."

I turn to Abigail. "I believe you."

"Rick, don't play into her game."

"Kat, I've seen what she can do. She's not someone to be fucked with or laughed at."

"What are we supposed to do?" Kat asks.

"Simple," Abigail says. "Die."

Though I didn't think I was close enough, Abigail reaches out and wraps long fingers around my throat. I grab her arm, trying to pull her hand away, but she's too strong.

Katarina kicks out at her, but Abigail, in Nikki's skin, steps away from her. "Don't struggle, Katarina, or should I call you Sarah. There's nowhere to escape to." She gazes at me with disdain and her fingers tighten around my throat until I can barely breathe. She's stronger than I imagined. "Now, this is the fun part. Choosing the method of your demise. That's always the best part. It's where I get as creative as I can, notwithstanding the feeble mind I've got to deal with, to come up with a way to slaughter you and your beloved."

Meggan stirs on the ground.

"Meggan, help!" Kat struggles in Abigail's grasp to no avail. I figure to conserve my strength. If Abigail's as full of herself as I think she is, I've got time to do something.

Abigail laughs at Kat. "Elizabeth didn't help you the first time, Meggan isn't going to help you now! It's no use, my love.

Even if Meggan could help you, she'd just die before she could do anything." Abigail shrugs. "This is it. One more time around. How shall we do it this lifetime? Shall I reach into your chests and rip your hearts out? Then you can watch them stop beating seconds before you fall dead. How about like a couple of lifetimes ago when I tied the two of you naked and rammed a red-hot poker up her ass and right through you? Something original, something different. I could leave you tied spread-eagle to the ground and let the animals have at you. Nah, I don't want to wait around that long. But isn't this romantic? The two of you choked to death, side by side! The two of you dying together as you always have! But wait, this is too trite; this should be something more special, something wild. Let's draw Sarah out so we can look eye to eye. Sarah, come out, come out, wherever you are!"

Kat's eyes roll back in her head and her body shakes. Her mouth opens and she laughs. Fucking laughs at Abigail strangling her. "Wrong woman, bitch."

Abigail stares at Kat. Her eyes vibrate. "What the fuck?" She pulls Katarina closer to her and stares deep into her eyes. "Who the fuck are you? You're not Sarah!" She throws her to the ground and tosses me aside. She gasps in surprise and her eyes go wide. "You're the gutless bitch sister, aren't you! Oh, I'm going to enjoy slaughtering you. I'll start by ripping out your intestines and shoving them down your throat! You don't know how I've waited for this moment. I've happily slaughtered Thomas and Sarah life after life, but you … this is a real treat. I don't know when the last time was I ripped you to pieces!"

"Why don't you go hang yourself like you did after Thomas refused you?" Katarina/Elizabeth laughs.

"You bitch!" Nikki/Abigail screams.

Abigail hung herself? This is a new twist that I'm gonna have to find out about. But right now, she's distracted with Elizabeth. "Abigail."

"What?" She turns and looks at me.

I unleash all the anger I have for Nikki, for Kat, for everything that ever went wrong. I swing. My fist crushes the cartilage in Nikki's nose. Blood explodes from her face and for the second she's dazed, I punch her hard in the stomach. She may be a spirit or a demon, but she's in a human body that can be severely hurt.

Nikki/Abigail doubles over and falls to her knees. But I'm not finished. I pick up a good-sized branch, step toward Nikki and swing.

Meggan sees me and shouts, "No!"

The branch connects with Nikki's skull and there's a satisfying crack as the limb snaps in two.

"Oh my God!" Meggan screams.

Nikki/Abigail turns to me, blood pouring down her face and half grins. "Not over." She pitches forward, crumpling to the ground.

I throw the branch into the grass.

"What are you doing?" Meggan asks, trying to get to her feet. She staggers, then falls to one knee. "Stop it!"

I pop the trunk on Nikki's car. "Get Kat and get in your car. We'll be leaving soon." I walk back to where Nikki lies, pick her up and bring her to her car. She spits blood. "Never over."

"Right. Say good night, Gracie."

"Go fuck yourself."

"You, too, Nikki." I drop her unceremoniously into the trunk and shut it. A shiver runs through me. She'll be back and now she'll be pissed at me as well as Thomas, but hopefully in the meantime we can figure out a way of stopping her. I take the keys from the ignition and lock the doors. Let someone think it's abandoned. But if someone finds the car and gets Nikki out, she'll kill them, and I won't have anyone else die because of me.

The real problem is that Abigail won't hesitate to use someone else to find us. She won't stay in Nikki with her face all busted up, but she'll kill her and take someone else. Hopefully, Dallas will know what to do.

Meggan sits on the ground with Kat's head in her lap.

"I need your cell phone to call Dallas."

Meggan stares at me. "What happened? What did you do?"

"Abigail attacked us and planned to kill us. I had to stop her."

"You're insane. This is all because of what Nikki said to you, isn't it?"

"No. Now can I have your cell phone?"

"What happened to yours?"

"It died when we were in the tunnel."

"Only if you're calling the police and turning yourself in."

"Meggan, please, give me your cell phone. This is very important. I tell you what. Let me call Dallas and then I'll call the police. Okay?"

"Fine. It's in the car, in my pocketbook."

I head to the car.

"Thomas? Thomas, are you there?"

I glance back at Katarina.

"It's okay, Kat, I'm here." Meggan brushes hair out of Kat's face.

"Thomas, where are you?"

"I'm right here." I come back and kneel in front of them.

"I'm sorry," Kat, now Elizabeth, says.

"For what? You didn't know Abigail killed Sarah."

"But I did." Kat opens her eyes and stares at me. Her eyes aren't emerald, but soft blue, the color of Elizabeth's. "I knew. Abigail told me she loved you and was going to kill Sarah. She told me if I told anyone, she'd kill our whole family. I didn't know what to do. I stayed silent until the burden was too great for me and then I ..." She breaks down and sobs.

"Jesus." I close my eyes and see Elizabeth slowly turning at the end of a rope.

"What is she talking about?" Meggan looks from Kat to me. "I don't understand."

"The woman in that upstairs bedroom."

"The one ha ..." She stops herself before she says, 'hanging'.

"Thomas?" Kat/Elizabeth says. "Tell me you accept my apologies that I might find peace."

I take her hand. "I do, Elizabeth, I forgive you. It was a terrible burden for you to carry and I wish I could've helped. But you were courageous and brave to keep it to yourself."

"I was a fool. But I'm glad you forgive me. Now I can rest." Kat's eyes close and her body goes limp.

"You'll have to explain this to me," Meggan says.

I get Meggan's cell and dial Dallas's number and wait as it rings.

"Go."

"It's Rick. Are you guys all right?"

"Fine. Ariana came back to herself right after you guys left, and then we called a taxi for a ride to the hospital. Ariana refused an ambulance. We're almost done here and then we're going to a hotel."

I look at Meggan comforting Kat. "Turns out Abigail hitched a ride with Meggan until we got here and then jumped into Nikki. Do you think Abigail has to see the person she's jumping into?"

"In the rare cases of possession I've heard of, they have to at least see the person if not physically touch them."

"At least we know where Abigail is."

"Where?"

"Right now, Nikki is locked in the trunk of her car. I don't know what to do with her. If we leave the car, someone'll find her, and Abigail will just take another body over."

"Okay. Right. Let me think." Silence fills in until I hear Ariana in the background.

"What's wrong?" she asks.

"Something's come up," Dallas says. "And we need to deal with it."

"What is it?" Ariana asks.

"Don't worry yourself about it." To me, he says, "Bring her here."

"Are you insane?"

"No. Tie her up and tape her mouth closed."

"And if I'm tying her up and Abigail decides I'm her new ride, then what?"

"Okay, bad idea." Silence again. "Drive her over here. We'll meet in the parking lot and figure out something to do with her."

"As long as I don't have to touch her again." I am worried about her getting out of the trunk. But leaving the car here is just as bad an idea. At least this way, I can keep track of her. "All right. I'm going to give you to Meggan. Tell her where you guys wound up and I'll follow her."

"Sure."

I hand the phone to Meggan. She nods a few times, then hangs up. "You're serious about this?"

"I can't think of any other options right now. Come on. I'll help you get Kat in the car."

Meggan stands, but staggers and I hurry to her side to keep her from falling.

"Are you okay?" The shot she took from Abigail was pretty hard.

"Yeah. I'm okay. Just a wicked headache." Meggan smiles, as if trying to reassure me she's fine.

"If you're not up to driving …"

"No, I'll be fine. We'll just go slow."

"Let's get Kat in your car and we'll head to the hotel."

The two of us gently move Kat to the back seat of Meggan's car and lay her down. Meggan rummages through her pocketbook and pulls out a dozen business cards, and then hands me one. "Here. Her name is Cyndi. She's a friend of mine and a past life regression therapist."

"Why didn't you tell me about her before?"

"Maybe I didn't believe you. I told you I didn't believe in reincarnation. I sort of believe in the supernatural. More now after everything that's happened."

"Thank you." I walk back to Nikki's car and get in. Luckily, it's an automatic. Before I start the car, I listen for her. There's no sound from the trunk. That's a good thing.

Meggan pulls ahead of me and I follow. I really want to turn the radio on, but I need to hear when Nikki comes to because then I'm going to have to deal with two pissed off women.

"Where … oh, fuck."

Those are the first words from the trunk. We're coming off 287 onto Route 17 South. My fingers tighten on the steering wheel and my palms slip from sudden sweat. All I have to do is stay calm and look for the Comfort Inn on the right side.

"Hello?" Nikki calls.

"Hey, Abby, how's it going back there?"

Silence answers me.

"What's the matter Abigail, Nikki got your tongue?" Sometimes, I crack myself up.

"Go fuck yourself."

"Now that's not very nice, is it?"

"Let me out."

"Why? So you can kill me? That would be a pretty stupid thing for me to do. I think you're safer back there."

"Enjoy your peace while you can, Rick. I will find Sarah and then your life is mine."

"Tell me something, Abby, how come you didn't know Kat was Elizabeth? You were with her for how long that you didn't know?"

It's very quiet back there. It gives me time to ponder this new turn of events. Abigail didn't know Kat was Elizabeth. Why didn't she? Maybe she was so sure of herself that she never bothered checking. Maybe she's slipping.

"Abigail?"

"What?"

"How many lifetimes have you been doing this?"

"I don't know. Nine or ten. I've lost count."

Figuring each lifetime is thirty years or so, that would put us three hundred years ago, right around 1703. But she said she came from Salem, Massachusetts. If we make that the 1690's, it means she came to New Jersey around the time of the Salem witch trials. That's troubling. "Why are you doing this?"

"It's what you did to me."

"I didn't do anything to you. How can you hold me accountable for a life I don't even remember?"

"Each lifetime, right before I slaughter the two of you, I open your minds. This way you can remember."

"But in the meantime, neither one of us has any idea of what you're talking about. What can we do to end this?"

"You can die for me."

"Besides, dying, Abigail, what else can we do to exonerate ourselves and stop this?"

"Nothing. I swore you would never live long enough to know love and I plan to keep that promise now and forever."

"Don't you get tired of this game?"

"Never. It brings me great pleasure to watch the two of you die."

"And you've killed us every lifetime since, huh?"

"Yes, Rick. Every lifetime. There has never been one you escaped from me."

"How have you found us?"

"Sometimes it takes me a while, but I'm drawn to the two of you. You both seem to keep reincarnating near each other, so if I find one of you, the other usually isn't all that hard to find."

I don't believe that. When I call Cyndi, I'll find the lifetime we stopped her and do it again. Hopefully, this time it will be for good.

I don't feel any fear. Whatever Abigail is capable of, right now she's trapped in a woman's body locked in the trunk. When she didn't recognize Kat for who she was, she made a big mistake. She's slipping and for whatever reason she is, I plan on exploiting that. This meeting with Cyndi takes on a whole new meaning. Instead of just finding out basic truths about that lifetime, I can find out if we've ever stopped Abigail and how we did it. There has to be some way.

"Abigail, tell me about your life."

Silence again.

"Abby, you still back there?"

Silence. I glance in the rearview mirror and see a shape running across the highway into the brush.

"Shit." I pull over and sure enough, the trunk is open, and she's gone. "Son of a bitch." No one's going to be happy about this, but I'm not chasing after Nikki; I'll never catch her.

I slam the trunk and drive to the Comfort Inn, where Dallas meets me.

"Well? Did she say anything on the ride over?" He's a little too excited.

"She told me that she's been doing this for three-hundred years. Every lifetime, she opens our minds before she kills us and lets us remember. She claims we've never stopped her, but I think we have. And one more thing. She's gone. She somehow managed to get the trunk open and jumped out."

"She could be anywhere."

"We could call the police and give them Nikki's description, but with her ability to jump bodies, by the time they find Nikki she could be dead, and Abby moved into someone else. I don't think it's worth it."

"What do you think we should do?"

I close the car door and head to the hotel. "Get rest. Hopefully, it'll take some time before Abigail finds us. Meggan gave me the number of a friend of hers who is a regression therapist. I'll give her a call and make an appointment for tonight or tomorrow. Kerri's not going to be happy about me taking more time off, but we have to end this sooner than later.

Dallas nods. "We got a couple of rooms. Do you know what Meggan and Kat are going to do?"

"I've no idea." I follow Dallas into the lobby where the two women check in. "What a surprise to meet the two of you here."

Kat eyes me warily. "We seriously need to talk."

Meggan seems to blanche at that remark. I understand. God only knows what Kat's thinking.

"After you're checked in, meet us. We'll get something to eat and talk or whatever."

Meggan nods. Kat tries a smile on, but it slips away too fast.

I want to say something important, but I can't think of any-thing and Dallas says, "Let's go."

"What is it? Something wrong?" I follow Dallas to the eleva-tors. "Whatever happened with Ariana?" I ask. "Did she calm down? I'm really tired of fighting with women today."

He presses the "2" button. "She's fine. Everything's fine. I just wanted to fill you in on some things I learned. We had a long talk and I explained where you were coming from and she told me a bit about her life." He shakes his head and frowns. "She never mentioned Eddie or her parents, and I didn't push it. When and if she wants to tell you, then she will. Otherwise, try and stay away from being a bully. It turns her off."

"Thank you. Is that your official psychological opinion?"

"Yes." He grins. "I'll send you my bill."

"Great. Thanks." The elevator doors open and we head to our rooms.

"This way." Dallas points to the right. "There is one thing I'm concerned about and that is another one of those creatures showing up in the middle of the night and killing us."

"Good point. If Abby can send those things, we could be in a shitload of trouble. She was pretty upset when she found out Kat was really Elizabeth and not Sarah. If she finds Kat, she's gonna kill her. If Abigail heard where we were going, she could come here, switch bodies and find us. She could be anyone and we won't know it until it's too late."

"Why do you think Abigail didn't recognize Kat for who she is?"

I shrug. "Maybe it's more dumb luck that she found me, and she really doesn't know who's who."

He pulls a key card from his pocket and opens the door. "Welcome to home."

Ariana reclines on the bed, her back against the headboard and her legs stretched out, with a can of Sprite in her lap. "Are you all right?"

I don't answer, figuring she's asking Dallas.

"Rick? Are you all right?"

"It's been a very long day. I'm starving. When Meggan and Kat get here we'll order room service."

"Maybe we should go out?" Dallas asks. "Abby probably wouldn't attack us in a public place. It would be too obvious. But here with all of us in this room, it would be too easy."

As tired as I am, he's right. Not that going out is the answer, because eventually we have to come back here and sleep, and if Abigail really wants to kill us, that'll be her chance. Of course, that kind of thinking isn't going to help. Speaking of helping, I take Cyndi's business card out. "Can I borrow your cell?"

Dallas looks at his cell. "Almost dead. I have to charge it." He rummages through his bag, pulls out the charger and plugs it into the wall. "You can use it now." He hands me his phone. I dial Cyndi's number, and on the second ring, a warm voice answers the phone.

"Hello?"

"Hi. Is this Cyndi Tyler?"

"Yes. Can I help you?"

"My name is Rick Summers. I got your number from Meggan Reynolds. She said you might be able to help me with a … past life problem."

"A past life problem? That's the first time I've heard it phrased like that. Can you give me some idea of what your, um, problem is?"

"This is going to sound insane. Someone is trying to kill me and a friend of mine because of something that happened in a past life. It seems we—"

"Wait. Say that again. Someone is trying to kill you because of what?"

"This woman believes we did something to hurt her in a past life and she swore to kill us in every lifetime after that." I happen to glance at Ariana rolling her eyes. I shake my head. It's not worth arguing over this.

"Why don't you just call the police?" Cyndi asks.

"It's a little more complicated than that. This woman has the ability to jump bodies. It's like she's a spirit that can move from one body to the next and—"

"All right. Wait a minute. You're right, Mr. Summers, this does sound insane. People can't jump from body to body at will. It's impossible. As far as this having anything to do with rein-carnation, I don't know what to tell you. It sounds like someone who's mentally unstable, and maybe they believe what they told you, but I don't see how that's possible."

"Please, call me Rick. What if they had undergone some kind of regression and this issue arose for them and instead of dealing with it, they kept it to themselves until it became an obsession they had to live out."

"I suppose that's possible, but I doubt they'd ever be able to find the people responsible because that would mean the other people involved would remember, and in some way they'd all have to find each other. That's too far-fetched."

"Okay, Ms. Tyler, let's—"

"Oh, I'm not that old. Call me Cyndi."

"Sure, Cyndi. Let's forget all this for a moment. What if I'd like you to do a regression on me because I'm curious about something?"

"Sure. I can do that."

"Do you have any appointments available for tomorrow?"

"If you'd like to come by tonight, that would be fine. I'm only doing this because you're a friend of Meggan's. I don't do this for anyone. Besides, you sound like a fascinating person. I live in Upper Saddle River off of Lake Street. How soon can you be here?"

"I haven't eaten dinner. How about a half hour from now?"

"Okay, sure." She gives me her address, tells me how to get there, Next, I dial Kerri's number.

"Hi."

"It's Rick. I'm surprised to find you home. I thought you'd be out with Tina."

She takes a deep shaky breath. "We got in a big fight earlier and … we're no more."

"I'm sorry."

"I just wish it hadn't ended so ugly. We both said things we shouldn't have." She sniffs. "What's up? How're things in Jersey?"

I tell her everything that's happened since the last time we spoke up until now. When I finish, Kerri's silent.

"I really wish you were here." Something in her tone tells me this isn't one of our moments of innuendo. She's genuinely serious. "Then at least I'd know you were safe."

"I wish I was there, too." I suddenly have that empty feeling that comes when you're far from the one person who could make everything better with a simple smile. I get choked up and tears well in my eyes, threatening to break free. I take a deep breath. "Have you had any more dreams?"

"Yes. The same. I can't see the face of the third person, but there are more details. We're in a stone chamber and the third person is about to kill you. I'm holding some kind of necklace with a gem at the end. It doesn't make any sense."

Tears race down my face because I'm afraid I'm going to die, and I'll never see her again. I want to tell her everything's going to be fine, but I can't lie to her, so I say nothing.

"You're not coming back, are you?" Her voice trembles.

The dam breaks. I turn away from Dallas and Ariana as tears chase each other down my face. "Of course I'm coming back."

"When?"

I wipe the tears away and dig for strength. "In a day or so; probably not tomorrow."

She sighs, most likely collecting herself. "I'll cover for you, but you owe me." She's trying to be all business, but her sadness creeps in anyway.

"I owe you a lot."

"I collect big, you know."

"I hope so."

I expect her to laugh but she's silent. "When we're ready to hang up do me a favor."

"What's that?"

"Tell me you love me."

The tears come again. The truth—the truth I won't tell her—is that I may never see her again if we fail to stop Abigail. But I can't tell her. All I say is, "Okay. I've got to go, Kerri."

"I know."

"I love you."

"I love you." She hangs up without saying goodbye. It's probably better that way.

I hold the phone until I wipe my tears away. "Okay." I hang up and look at Dallas and Ariana.

"You okay?" Dallas asks.

"Yeah. Just fine."

"What's the plan?"

Someone knocks on the door and I jump. *No more caffeine for you, Mr. Summers.* I open the door. Meggan and Kat stand there, neither looking happy. I wonder what they talked about on their way up.

"Enter." I step out of the way and Meggan comes in. Kat, a bit hesitant, follows behind her.

"Where's dinner?" Meggan sits down on the bed. "Here or out?"

"I've got plans," I announce. "I'm seeing Cyndi tonight."

"The regression therapist?" Kat joins Meggan on the bed, sitting close enough to let me know who she wants.

"Yes."

Ariana rolls her eyes.

"Do you think she can help?" Meggan looks skeptical.

"I hope so."

"Why are you going to a regression therapist?" Kat asks.

"Because I believe she can help me understand what's happening. Abigail said that she's chased us down lifetime after lifetime because I wouldn't love her. Well, I want to know if that's true."

Ariana chuckles. "And this regression therapist is going to give you all the answers?"

"I hope so."

Ariana shrugs.

"Good luck," Meggan says.

"Thanks. I'm taking Nikki's car." I look over at Kat. "We'll talk when I get back. I need a phone, though in case I get in trouble."

Meggan hesitates, but then holds her phone out. "Take mine. You need it more than I do. If you need to reach us, call Dallas."

Kat grabs my arm as I walk past her. "I don't understand any of this. Who's Abigail and Sarah?"

I look into her dark eyes and brace myself to keep from falling in. "I promise, when I get back, I'll explain the whole thing to you, and you can decide if you believe it or not. All right?"

She shrugs and puts her hand on my cheek. "I've missed you."

I don't want to look at Meggan or know what she's thinking. "All right, people. Get something to eat and I'll call you when I'm done at Cyndi's." I leave the hotel room and head out to the parking lot. It's well-lit at 8:30, though there's no one out here.

I get in the car and pull out onto Route 17 South. Cyndi's house isn't far from here, so after I grab a couple of slices of pizza somewhere, we can get this over with. In the meantime, I decide this is the perfect opportunity to talk to God. "Okay, God, here's the deal. I don't know why this has happened in the past, why you've let this woman do this, but it stops here, with or without your help. I don't know your grand scheme and I'm not supposed to. I'm asking for a little guidance and some divine assistance here. Think you can swing that?" I turn on the radio to AC/DC's "Highway to Hell."

Nope. I hit the "Seek" button and find Aerosmith's "Janie's

Got A Gun."

No. "You're not working with me. These aren't good signs for a hopeful future. If I'm supposed to be your vessel, here to spread your word and do the most good, why is there some lunatic chick trying to off me? Now, we're gonna try the radio thing one more time, okay? Play along."

I touch the "seek" button again and the chorus of Rush's "Freewill" streams through the speakers, filling the car.

"Much better," I tell God. "Now we're getting somewhere." I sing along to Rush. Then Godsmack. After that I press the "Seek" button a couple of times and find Frank Sinatra singing "My way". How appropriate.

13.

I pull up in front of a sprawling, tan brick estate, a beautiful, damned expensive house. It probably has half a dozen bedrooms and half as many bathrooms. Why does one family need three bathrooms? Well, I guess if they've got a lot of women living under the roof, then they'd need more than one.

This is definitely an estate, though not one of those McMansions I've heard about. This one was built when houses were original pieces of art, not cut from a pre-fab model and snapped together in weeks. I can't wait to see the inside.

The two-car wide drive way is at the left end of the house and makes a right turn at the garage. A silver Jaguar sedan sits in the driveway and I pull in behind it. The license plate says "9 Lives" and I wonder if that's how many she's discovered of her own, or how many she thinks she's got in this lifetime. I get out of the car and close the door as quietly as possible because I suddenly feel like I'm walking on sacred ground.

The two slices of pizza sit heavy in my stomach; it's probably just nerves. What am I doing here? Is this really going to prove anything? What if I discover that Abigail never killed us and it's all bullshit? At this point I'm not sure what to believe. Cyndi suggested that Abigail is just some lunatic. I'd accept that more if I hadn't seen the things Abigail did. That shivering eye thing really disturbs me, but at least it's a way of knowing where she is. I pray, as I head up the front walk—laid out in slate stones—that I don't see Cyndi's eyes do that shift thing. I need to be somewhere Abigail isn't for a while.

At the front door, with its stained-glass diamonds, I stare at the doorbell. What if everything that Abigail said is true? I refuse to believe that we have no choice other than to die.

I'm reluctant to knock. I've heard about regression and all the debates on its authenticity as a means of discovering past lives. Is it merely the therapist's suggestions or does the person really go back to the lives they've lived before? *Just knock and tell Cyndi your apprehension about this and I'm sure she'll calm you down and everything'll be just …*

The front door swings open.

"Hi. You must be Rick." The woman standing at the door dressed in tight black jeans and dark blue blouse steps aside. "Come in." She might be forty, maybe a year or two older. The foyer light silhouettes her delicate, absolutely feminine frame, and dark straight hair that falls over her shoulders.

I take a hesitant step in and she closes the door behind me. Her eyes are the color of expensive dark chocolate and her hair is a few shades lighter. "I'm Cyndi." She smiles warmly and extends her hand.

"Rick Summers." I take her hand, not expecting the firm grip she's got.

The marble-floored foyer is spacious and rises up two floors. A huge chandelier hangs down and lights the entryway with a hundred tiny sparkling lights. A wide stairway curves up to the left and it's not difficult to imagine this woman coming down dressed in an elegant evening gown, ready to entertain her and her husband's rich friends. The living room to the right—as big as my whole apartment—is decorated in beautiful furniture that looks like it came from Italy. One long, leather couch, an ornately carved coffee table and several leather chairs fill the room, and classic impressionist paintings hang on the wall. Could they be anything but the originals? In the far corner is a baby grand piano next to a harp, and next to that is a cello.

"Do you play all of them?" I ask.

"The piano, mostly. I toy around with the harp and cello. A few friends play and we get together and just have fun."

To the left is a dining room that's also bigger than my apartment.

"This is some place you have."

"Yeah, thanks. I got to keep it after the divorce. It's been my

home for almost twenty years." She smiles warmly. "Come in."
She spins around, her long dark hair flowing after her. "How's
Meggan? I haven't seen her in months."

"She's good." Central air is working just fine, and I shiver
from the cool. Somewhere, a television is on. I follow her as she
walks to the back of the house.

"I really should give her a call."

The rooms are huge and richly decorated. The thing that
strikes me the most is that there's nothing masculine; everything has a distinctly feminine touch to it. Whoever her decora-
tor is, they have excellent taste. I may not know one designer
from the next, but I know class and I have taste and this woman
has some real pricey taste.

The deeper into the house we go, the louder the television
gets. We walk through a large room which in any other house
would be a living room, but this room's pretty sparse with a
couple of leather couches and one wall that's a bookcase.

"This place is amazing."

Adjacent to the living room is what I assume to be a breakfast nook. There's a small table with two chairs. A vase with a
small bouquet of purple flowers sits in the middle of the table
surrounded by books.

"Thanks. Like I said, I'm lucky to still be living here. The
divorce wasn't pretty, but that was two years ago and I'm a lot
happier now." She steps down two stairs into the sunken family room. A large TV, probably a 64-inch model, sits on the floor
against the right-hand wall and a black leather couch curves
around three walls on the left side of the room. The walls are
light wood paneling, with several impressionist paintings on
each wall. The floor is wall-to-wall thick blue carpet.

Cyndi stops in the middle of the room, turns and grins.
"Come into my parlor."

I shiver from nothing I can put a finger on.

She sits down on the couch and presses the "Off" button on
the television's remote. "Sit down and tell me about yourself
and what's going on that you want to be regressed."

I join her on the couch and her delicate perfume floats
around me. *Obsession*? I'm terrible with naming perfumes. I

know what I like and, of course, Cyndi's wearing it. Sweet and gentle without being sharp or cloying.

"Can I get you something to drink? Water, Coke, orange juice, coffee, tea? I would offer you wine, but after hearing your story, I'd rather we both be clear-headed."

"Nothing. I just want to get this started."

"Fine. Talk."

"It's all insane. I'm not sure where to start."

"You told me this woman claims to be trying to kill you because of something that happened in a past life. I asked why you don't call the police and you said it's because she can jump bodies. Tell me more about this. What makes you think she can jump from person to person?"

I tell her about the cemetery visit and the cab ride to Fair Lawn. "As I'm leaving the cemetery, I realize the driver is dead on the ground and this dead woman is driving."

"Dead?"

Looking down at my hands lying in my lap, I take a deep breath. "Dead. Shot in the head. She drove me to my ex-girl-friend's house—"

"Rick, are you sure she was dead?"

I laugh. "Sounds ridiculous, doesn't it? It gets much better." I fill her in on everything's that happened at Katarina's house.

"Were you alone when this happened?" She looks at me as if she thinks I'm crazy and I have to say, if someone was telling me that this happened to them, I'd think they were off their rocker.

"No. Meggan was there. She saw everything." Next, I tell her about Uncle William and Abigail.

"You realize how insane this sounds?"

I nod.

"Was Meggan with you through all this?"

"No. She got locked out of the room after Abigail called her Aunt."

"Go on."

"I woke up in Nazi Germany. I know what you're thinking. I thought it was a dream, but it felt real. Let's say it was a dream. Fine. At the end of it all, a woman saved me and the last thing

she said was 'Remember Athens'. I wouldn't think anything of
it, except I've heard that phrase whispered two or three times
since then."

"By who?"

"My mother."

Cyndi's eyes go wide. "But you said she's—"

"She is." I tell her what I remember about Thomas, Elizabeth,
Sarah and Abigail, including Sarah's murder and Abigail's sui-
cide. "Abigail hangs herself vowing to murder Thomas and
Sarah through every lifetime."

"Do you think you're Thomas?"

I look at the Impressionist paintings around the room.
Monet, Degas, Renoir and Cassatt. When I glance back at Cyndi,
that look of uncertainty is gone, replaced by something kind
and curious. "I don't know. That's why I came here. If all of this
is true, which is real hard to believe, then I need to know what
'Remember Athens' means. I think it's some clue as to how to
stop Abigail. How can someone remember their past lives like
that?"

"You suggested before that maybe she underwent a regression of her own and discovered that life where she was in love
with Thomas. But I think she's making up the part about killing the two of you every lifetime. People can be regressed, and
they may remember pieces of other lives, but nothing like what
you're telling me, that she remembers every lifetime she's had.
I've never, in all my experience, met someone who can remember *every* lifetime. She may be a disturbed woman and she's
transferring the spurned love that she discovered through the
regression onto you. Why? I don't know."

"How many lives do we have?"

"It depends. Some older souls have been around for centuries, while others just a few years."

"What do you mean by older souls?"

"Souls are like energy, but they encompass all we are. I
believe we, all of us, are part of a great consciousness that
some call God. God cannot manifest on Earth. It is beyond
Its capability because God is everything. We, the souls, leave
this Unmanifested Divinity and come to Earth to learn and

experience. A soul has lessons to learn and each lifetime it learns something different and new. At the end of a lifetime, the soul returns to God to share what it's learned and experienced. If there are more lessons to learn, the soul returns to Earth to continue. Imagine this is like college. At the end of the semester you go home to think on what you've learned, and in September you return until you've completed your studies.

"A friend of mine believes we all carry an inner flame inside ourselves."

"Right. It's like the God in all of us. There's a word: Namaste. It's a greeting that honors the God in each person.

She takes a sip from a bottle of Pellegrino. "Getting back to old souls. There are people alive now whose souls have been coming to Earth for centuries because they have many lessons to learn, or they didn't learn them the last lifetime, as if they're being held back from graduating to the next grade. Perhaps they're here to help other souls learn their lessons. One soul may be coming back for their twentieth lifetime while another may return for their second or third; they've just started learning."

"What do you think of all this?"

"I think we should do a regression and see what comes up for you. We can focus on the event when Abigail killed herself and then try to go back and discover what 'Remember Athens' means."

"Okay. What do I do?"

"You're going to lie down on the couch and relax." She indicates the couch next to her. "You're going to take deep breaths and clear your mind. I'm going to bring you to a place where we can visit past lives, but it's going to be like watching a movie. You'll be completely safe, and you will be in control of what you see. If you're not ready to experience something, you won't. I can't make you experience pain or your own death. I would never do that to anyone."

I lie down on the couch, close my eyes and take several deep breaths.

"Let yourself relax, let your mind drift. With each breath you become more relaxed. Imagine a wide, gold stairway that leads up to two magnificent doors. You walk up the nine stairs and a brilliant white light shines through the doors as they part for you. Allow yourself to be completely relaxed and see them opening for you, as the white light embraces you and you sink deeper into a relaxed state. This is a safe place. The light is warm and friendly, and you move inside, into a white fog that obscures everything. You are sinking deeper into a state of peace and the doors are opening wider.

"Inside the room, within the swirling fog, you sense time clearing as if your sight is clearing and you can see through time. You feel completely relaxed and safe here. You know nothing bad will happen to you and you will not see anything you do not wish to.

"The fog begins to dissipate. This is the 18th century and you're standing by a farmhouse with Abigail. This is the last day you will see her. Tell me what is happening."

I'm standing in a yard. I look around. Behind me is the house I live in with my mother; father; brother, William; and my sister, Elizabeth. Two girls sit near me. Both are beautiful and I'm in love with one of them, Sarah, the one with the honey-colored hair that seems to sparkle in the sunlight.

The other girl, Abigail, dark-haired and shy, is from New England. She's come here to be with her uncle, her step-father's brother. Something bad happened to her when she moved in, but she's never told me what it was.

The day is warm and fine and more wonderful than a sixteen-year-old boy from New Jersey could ask for.

"Thomas?"

I turn to my sister standing in the doorway.

"It's time for supper," Elizabeth says and disappears.

I turn back to the two girls. "I am sorry, but supper is ready. You may stay if you wish, but—"

"Will I see you tonight?" the dark-haired girl asks.

I shake my head. She likes me very much and I like her, but not as much as I like Sarah. "I'm sorry Abigail, but Sarah and I are …"

"Never mind." She runs out of the yard, very upset.

Sarah and I watch after her until she disappears over the hill.

"She frightens me, Thomas," Sarah says.

I take her hand. "There's nothing to be frightened of. She's real shy and seems scared of everything."

Sarah shrugs. "I will see you later on tonight." She kisses me on the cheek and skips away.

I watch her with my heart skipping along with her.

The scene dims like a play and when the world lightens, Abigail and I are older and sitting on the porch of my family's house.

"I have something I want to tell you." She turns her gaze away from me. "It's … it's something terrible that happened to me."

"You don't have to tell me, Abigail, if it hurts too much."

She glances at me, then looks down at her fingers tumbling over each other. "I want to open myself to you, so you know who I am."

"I know who you are."

She places a fingertip on my lips. Her finger is warm and soft. I almost kiss it, but Sarah's face comes to my mind and I do nothing.

"I told you I'm from New England. Salem, Massachusetts to be precise. I was accused of witchcraft. I frightened them very badly. I even told them that Satan wanted to destroy their Puritanical works. They put me in jail, but in 1693 they let me go." She giggles. "I had to leave, and I came here to live with my uncle. But he abused me whenever he wanted. Uncle William was a mean man and when he made me do things, I silently wished him dead and I knew soon he would die. One day, he had me strapped to a bed and I called my best friend and she came and took care of Uncle William. Slit him from his waist to his neck." She giggles. "All his guts came spilling out. I was so happy!"

"You should not talk that way."

"Why? Because it's the Devil's talk?" She laughs. "Puritans don't realize the freedom they could have if they just under-stood Satan."

"Abigail, that's not right to say."

"I am sorry. I don't mean to frighten you." She leans into me, and against my better judgment I take her in my arms. She cries like a babe, lost and frightened.

It is at that moment that I look up to see Sarah staring at us. She doesn't know, but all the same, she runs off, scared at what she thinks she sees. I can't leave Abigail, so I sit holding her until her cries fade and she presses against me. I never see her smile. Much later someone (my brother?) says he did, after Sarah ran off.

At Cyndi's prompting, the scene fades and returns to the barn behind the house my family lived in. Sarah's dead. Elizabeth's hung herself. Will has taken a bride and moved south. I have never fallen in love again, even with Abigail's constant attempts to seduce me.

I stare up at the hay loft. A rope is tied to some kind of bolt right under the roof's overhang and trails into the loft. Abigail comes to the edge and leans out.

"You've come," she says. Tears streak her face and her clothes are in a terrible state of disarray. "After all these years you've finally answered my notes." Her smile is one of sheer insanity. "But it's too late, Thomas. Too late for you, Sarah, and her gutless bitch-sister!" She crawls to the edge and laughs, perched like a bird. "This is only the beginning, Thomas! You will never know love and you will never know peace, for I shall find you and Sarah every lifetime and slaughter you both! You will know the pain I have felt, the longing I have for you! And there's nothing you can do to stop me!" She crouches on the ledge.

"You don't have to do this, Abigail!" I shout. "Abigail! Don't!" My cries attract passers-by and they come running. But it's too late.

Abigail launches herself from the loft. She smiles blissfully as she floats in the air. She is beautiful. She opens her dark eyes and stares at me with pity, rage, and love.

She starts to fall like a leaf on the wind, arms outspread as if to fly, but her wings fail her.

"Good-bye," she says, the instant before the slack of the rope runs out and her graceful flight abruptly ends. The rope cuts into her neck and she's jerked back, slamming against the wall of the house. Her breath goes out of her and she can't take another; the rope's too tight.

She doesn't flail. But stares accusingly at me instead. "Forever will I remember. Forever will you suffer." She spreads her arms, closes her eyes, and dies.

More people have gathered, and I push through them, sobbing hysterically. For who? For the people Abigail has murdered? For Abigail? Or for Sarah and I and all the lifetimes Abigail promises to hunt us?

"Oh my God. What have I done?"

"You're safe," Cyndi says. "This is a picture. You aren't there. Instead, you're watching this unfold before you. You are perfectly safe. Nothing can happen to you."

Abigail's grinning. Her eyes stare at me. I collapse to my knees and cry. God save me, what have I done? My friend, Jim, tries to comfort me, but I know that Abigail will do as she said and kill us until she tires of murdering us. Will she ever tire?

Cyndi says, "The scene fades, fog rises up, surrounding you. A deep sense of peace comes over you as you rest in the warmth of the mist. You know you are safe and that nothing can harm you here. Move forward so that as you do, the mist swirls around and past you. You are moving back in time. Rick, remember Athens."

A chill passes through me as I move within the thick, gray fog that curls around me. I don't know what's an inch in front of me.

"Remember Athens."

The fog shrinks down into the ground and I'm standing with four men and three women in an alleyway. Though their faces are unfamiliar, I recognize Meggan, Dallas, Ariana, Katarina, my mother, Allison, and Abigail from their eyes and their mannerisms. We are members of the Elusinian mystery, a religion that honors Demeter, the goddess of grain, and her daughter, Persephone. Unlike the Greek religions, the mysteries promise life after death and that promise brought me to become a member. The others felt the Greek gods were too impersonal and did little to offer us consolation upon our deaths.

"Euryanassa, what have you done?" Camirus (Dallas) stares wide-eyed at the woman who will be Abigail, a bloody dagger in her hand. She kneels next to Cyllene's (Katarina) body, lying in a pool of her blood.

The woman who will be Abigail stares at each of us. Camirus, Moreta (Mom), Peirasus (Meggan (a man)), Tenerus (Allison (also a man)) and myself. She gazes at us with madness in her eyes and a wicked grin upon her lips. "I ... I have eased Cyllene beyond this life into the next."

"You've murdered her!" Camirus shouts at her. "Do not seek to mock this scene by using the words of the initiation as a means of defending yourself. You must be tried as a murderess!"

Euryanassa throws her head back and laughs. She rises and drops the dagger at Cyllene's side. "You are all fools! Do you realize what potential we have? If you are immortal, we can rule Greece for all time!" She looks at each of us, and seeing our faces set in sad disapproval, she says, "You are nothing! You have this gift of Demeter and yet you'd squander it for ... For what? Tell me why you will not use this gift to rule those lesser people. The knowledge we could amass after centuries of life—"

"Is not for us," Tenerus says. "There will always be mysteries to this world, Euryanassa, and we cannot unravel them. The stars, the gods, all mysteries beyond our grasp."

"Death is for mortals, Euryanassa," I say. "It is a blessing. Not something to be shunned or feared."

"But if we only took the chance to walk with the gods, we would see it is good!" Euryanassa frowns at us, like children who won't learn. "But you will never see, buried in your politics and arts and sciences, you will never see the opportunity we have been given. Why spend your entire life gaining knowledge, only to lose it upon dying? Instead, leave the body before death and join with another, living body."

"That is against everything we know," Camirus says. "We live so that we may experience life a certain way. Death gives us a chance to review what we've learned and then move on to another life, to experience new things and pay any unsettled debt."

Moreta steps forward. "We cannot let this go unpunished, Euryanassa. You shall be brought before a jury in this life for what you have done, and we must come to terms with laws governing future lives."

"How do you mean?" I ask.

She turns to me. "Hadrian, you are a speaker of the people. You need make a law governing us. We shall certainly meet in the next life; we cannot allow vengeance and childish behavior to govern us. Here we are friends, seeking the same truths, but there may come a time when we do not seek the same path and may instead be rivals."

"Or enemies," Euryanassa says.

"There is too great a potential for the misuse of this gift. Though Euryanassa feels it is ours to use as we wish, there must be rules to govern to prevent this misuse."

"You do not know what you say, Moreta," Euryanassa says. "Though you may be named for a goddess, you are naught but a child!"

"Do not raise your voice to me."

"You think because you are an important woman in Athens that you have the right to do as you please and order people around? I will not bow to you, Moreta, whore of Athens!" She spits at the other woman.

"Spartan witch!" Moreta advances on Euryanassa.

I grab her arm as Euryanassa scoops up the dagger, still dripping with Cyllene's blood.

"Come, then," Euryanassa taunts. "Come meet your bloody fate that you may depart this life and we will find you well met in the next!"

"Moreta," I say, "Do not do this. Enough blood has been spilled this day."

Moreta shakes herself free of my grasp. "She is not worth my attention, anyway."

Euryanassa flees down the alleyway and disappears.

"She is Spartan?" Peirasus asks. "How is it that she has come to Athens?"

"She rode with merchants," Moreta says. "Most likely selling her body to gain a ride." She storms out of the alley and without another word, we disperse. We will report the murder to the proper individuals who will have Cyllene's body cremated. As I walk away, I debate Moreta's words. What kind of law would govern us through the ages? We are spirits using bodies to wrap ourselves in to experience life.

"You're moving ahead," Cyndi says. "Moving to a time when a solution is near."

"Have you come up with a solution to our problem?" Moreta asks.

"I have, but it isn't pleasant. I fear I have come up with the only solution to this situation."

Moreta puts a hand on my shoulder. "I cannot know the burden you suffer under. What we have asked of you is great. But if we allow ourselves to go unchecked ..."

"What would be the harm?"

She glances at me as if I have gone mad. "What are you saying? Do you agree with Euryanassa?"

I laugh. "Hardly. But if this punishment must be instilled and it comes from my hand, I would know what is wrong with moving from body to body."

She thinks for a moment. "We are all mortals, not gods. If the gods wish to travel in human form that is their choice. We do not have the right to do such a thing. Each body is accorded one soul to transport about and that is the way the gods would have us live. Anything else is to bring down their wrath."

I nod. "I agree."

"Then it shall be done as Demeter decrees." She bows slightly and leaves my study.

I pace around the room, staring at scrolls stacked neatly on shelves, and debate how to proceed. I sit at my desk and begin writing. Though I have come up with a solution, there has to be another answer. I will continue writing my thoughts until the one lurking just under my consciousness surfaces and offers a solution to me. Even if I must write through the night, I will burn candles to see by.

It seems like hours later that I hear a woman's groan as if in sudden pain. I glance around, but no one's there. I stand up, stretching my aching limbs and walk into the hallway and through my house. No one is awake but me. I return to my writings, looking through the last few pages I've written in case I've missed something. But there is nothing to offer even a hint of a different solution. I rub my temple and drop the papers on my desk, continuing to write whatever comes to mind.

"Hadrian?"

I look around the room, but I'm alone. Was that the wind? No. It was a woman whispering my name. I continue writing, deciding that the voice was my own exhausted imagination.

"Hadrian, there is a box that you must open."

I look around the small room and out into the hall, but no one is there. "Who calls my name?"

"Turn and see the box waiting for you to open. There you will find your answer."

"What? Who speaks to me?" The room is empty, but a slight chill has entered and wrapped itself around me. I stand to get my cloak and almost trip over a wooden box decorated with symbols of Demeter. "What is this?" I kneel before it and run my fingers over its smooth wood.

"It is the answer to all your questions." A woman stands in the shadows of the hall. "Open it and you shall know all you seek."

I shiver from the cool air suddenly sweeping into the room. "Open it."

My trembling hands touch the box, and before I can stop myself, I slowly lift the cover.

"Everything you ever wanted to know is yours." Laughter echoes through the house.

Gooseflesh breaks out on my skin and a light, shot through with blackness, radiates from the box.

"What is this?" I drop it and it opens, revealing its contents. Hundreds, thousands of images and memories swarm up from the box and surround me, racing around the room. "What … ?"

They press down on me, slithering over my skin and then, as if they were needles, pierce my eyes, blinding me. The pain sends me to my knees. I scream in agony as hundreds of images force themselves into my skull, crashing like immense waves over my brain. Memories claw into my mind's eye, filling my head with scenes of Athenian orgies, mystical ceremonies in the woods, slavery in the Roman Empire, fleeing the Black Plague as it stormed across Europe, murdering millions.

The Nazi interrogators executed my family and friends, taking my limbs and my life. More images that I can't identify—slaughters, orgies, family, love lost, the witch, Abigail, death and more death—explode in my vision until I collapse to the ground, writhing in blind agony.

The names I've had are whispered by a million voices until I'm deaf with their calling. A hundred voices ask me who I am.

A life as a woodcutter drifts past me. Another life as a centurion in the legions of Caligula shimmers around me. My life as Thomas Corwin and the one after it as a … wait. She's never succeeded! She swore she would find and destroy us. But she never has. She's either only found one of us or killed the wrong person. That's why she didn't know Katarina was Elizabeth.

The life of a farmer blossoms out of nothing, wiping out the previous lives and there she is, even in this other body I still recognize her and again she's a witch and … there! Now I understand what happened in the tunnel. Men come after her, chanting, and the scene replays itself, but she runs and like a leaf on the wind I'm carried along to watch this whole scene unfold. Down under the house is the tunnel, but deeper is another passage that leads to a chamber and an altar and … Abigail's body! No, not Abigail, but Euryanassa's body! Caligula told me to …

A barrage of memories assails me. I can't hold on to what I must to stop Abigail. I'm pulled apart, remade as infinite people from centuries of life and all the previous memories are wiped out, replaced in seconds and demolished again. I cry out, pleading for silence and darkness. The voices and images drown the person I am, leaving me suffocated by my own history. Pieces of me drift in the room and I desperately grab for them so I can complete myself. No! I have to remember! Who am I? What was I supposed to remember?

"You will never find what you're looking for, Hadrian, Thomas, Rick." The woman's voice drifts to me like mist. "You will never know peace and I will know vengeance once again." She laughs. "How do you like seeing your lives flash before your eyes? Every life, every minute drowning out the last. Do you remember your name? Who you are?"

Thousands of people call hundreds of names. I'm coming

apart. Senator is transposed over peacenik over philosopher over chemist over resistance fighter over musician over assassin over ... "Who am I?"

"You are everyone and no one!" the woman says. "How does it feel?"

Tears stream down my face. Abigail's there, always laughing at me.

"I'm going to count backward from ten," Abigail says. "When I reach one and snap my fingers you will wake up with all the memories from all your lives so that you won't be able to decipher who you are from the memories." She counts backward and snaps her fingers. "Wake up."

I open my eyes and look at this strange, beautiful woman I've never met, though there's something familiar about her.

"Welcome back to the present. Do you know who I am? Do you know who you are?"

"No." I stare at her. "No." I grasp for a name, a place, but I've been too many people to remember just one. The last name I remember was ... I don't remember. "Tell me who I am."

She giggles. "Seems that little box of lifetimes really shook you up."

I sit up and at first it seems someone took a can of red paint and flung it everywhere. But a little voice in my mind says it's not paint. That realization seeps into my brain like a cold chill. *Not paint.*

The thick smell of copper suffocates me. I choke to breathe.

"Can't stand the smell? You shouldn't mind it. Remember the life where a bunch of us had an orgy at Miller's Meat House? We weren't in our right minds, but I can't remember anything like that since."

"Why are you doing this?" My eyes come to rest on the dead woman sprawled on the floor. I should know her, but I can't place her. What am I doing here?

The stench overwhelms me, and I choke back bile. I cover my mouth and breath slowly, staring at the half-naked dead woman and the pool of blood she lies in. "Holy fuck," I mumble. She lays on her stomach with her head turned facing me. Her body is ripped open from the back of her head to her waist and her glassy doll eyes stare across the floor. I'm fascinated and repulsed by this carnage.

The other woman glances down at the dead woman. "That's Cyndi. Or it was. Shame about her. No spine. See?" She shows me Cyndi's spine, dripping blood and whatever other fluids were in her body. I turn and retch. "Don't have the stomach for this? Should've thought of that years ago." She drops the spine and it clatters wetly on the carpet. "What a mess. Planning to clean that up? Wouldn't want anyone knowing you've got no guts."

"Just like the slaughterhouse."

"Mm, yes. But too easy. She was so involved in showing you the sights of the past, she never heard me come in or sneak into her head and tear her pretty psyche to shreds. She never had a chance." She frowns down at the dead woman. "Turns out she really did have a spine." She looks up at me. "My name is Abigail."

I can't focus to remember where I know that name. I try concentrating on the images swirling around me, but they twist and break, shattering like glass. Scenes flash by, passing too quickly to see, but I'm left with residual emotions of joy, sadness, peace, pain. "I can't remember anything."

"Not a thing?" She stands and smiles down at me. She's tall and muscular, yet very feminine, dressed in a tight black corset and matching lace miniskirt, bare legs and black heels. Very stylish. "Like what you see?" Abigail offers several poses, some regal, most seductive, a couple outwardly sluttish. "We were lovers once, but things didn't work out. I've been lonely since then and you know what, Thomas?"

My name's Thomas. It is? No, it's not. That's wrong, but I can't remember what the hell my name is.

"Now we have to go." She saunters over and helps me to my feet. I almost collapse from the dizziness that crashes in on me. "We have an appointment to keep." She pulls me around Cyndi and leads me out of the house.

"Shouldn't we call the police?"

"Someone'll find her when she starts rotting." She lets the door close behind her and pulls me to the car in the driveway. "Ah, Nikki's car. How apropos."

"Who's Nikki?" Hundreds of memories continue to flood my brain, making it impossible for me to think clearly or remember one moment to the next. "What's happening to me?" I try pulling away from … from … this woman. What's her name?

"You're having memory overload, Hadrian. Don't worry, it won't end any time soon."

"I thought you called me Thomas."

"I did? Oops. Sorry, Jeffrey."

"You just…" Tears stream down my face. "Tell me my name!"

She yanks me close to her. Her breath reeks of mint. "Stop screaming, Rick, and stop being such a fucking baby about who you are. It doesn't matter because very soon you will be dead. But don't worry. Right before I tear you apart, you'll remember who you are and why I'm doing this." She drags me to the car and opens the trunk. "Consider this friendly payback." She throws me against the car, sweeps my legs out from under me, then lifts me into the trunk, and slams the door closed.

"Hey!" I bang on the inside of the trunk and kick the seats, but nothing happens. The woman gets in the car and drives off. In the darkness, I try to make sense of any of this. Who is this woman and why is she doing this to me? If only I could remember anything and hold onto it for more than a few seconds. But my mind's like a sieve, all thoughts racing and slipping through.

14.

Where am I?
Images come at me like a swarm of bees, trying to decipher any of them. Pieces of ancient Greece, ancient Rome, France, England, Africa, and America all gel together, creating bubbles of scenes that make no sense. Was I all these people? When the hell was I an aboriginal warrior? And when was I ever in Imperial China?

I kick at the back wall of the trunk and something sharp jabs my side. Probably a God-damned tire iron. It's not worth trying to escape if this woman can help me. She's mean. But something about her is kind and loving. Who is she?

The car stops several times, accelerates very fast and finally comes to a stop.

The trunk pops open and then the woman smiles wickedly at me. "We're home."

"Where?"

"One of your favorite places that you won't remember." She helps me out of the trunk and lets me lean on her when I almost fall over. "This is the house of your ex-lover, Katarina, and where, some three hundred years ago, all your troubles began. Let's go inside, shall we?" She pushes me toward the front door.

"I don't understand." The truth is, I don't remember.

"Don't worry, Thomas, it'll all be clear soon." She walks up to the porch and pushes the front door open without using a key.

I grab her shoulder. "What the hell's my name?"

She laughs but doesn't look at me. "Your name is whatever I call you."

Bitch.

"Come in." She takes me by the arm and pulls me in to the house. "Ah, home at last. Can you feel it? The Gateway is open and the veils between here and there are disappearing." She smiles warmly.

"What are you talking about?"

She glances at me and frowns. "Maybe I should fix your head. At least then you'll appreciate the magnitude of what's happening." She closes the door and leads me into the living room. "But first, there's something we should've done ages ago." She tangles our legs and pushes me down to the floor.

I stare up at her with trepidation and not a small amount of lust. She said we were lovers once and I wouldn't mind that experience again.

She slips a black thong down her long legs, kicks it off, and straddles me. She grins like a jackal and leans down so our faces are inches apart. "I know you want me."

Her closeness is intoxicating. My body reacts to her near-ness as she rubs her crotch against mine. I stare into her eyes that tremble every now and again. Why do they do that?

She kisses me, at first gently, with passion, then with the ferocity of years of denied desire and longing. Biting my lip hard, she draws blood, then sits up and undoes my shorts. "I'm really not who I am."

"You said—"

"I know."

I try stopping her, but she pushes my hands away.

"You see, Thomas, over the years I've had to … adapt, shall we say, to the newness of things. To do that, I have to move around through human bodies, and this is the newest one I found. Isn't she beautiful? We could've been something, you and I, once, but you shunned me. Remember that?"

I try grasping on to the memory that I know is there, but it's too elusive and crashes into hundreds of other memories so that I can't pull any one of them apart.

"You probably can't remember much of anything, so I'll tell you. I loved you, but you would never return my love. I made a vow to make sure you never knew love ever again. But now,

I've got you here, and I still love you even after all these years. I'm going to use this body—her name's Lora—and I will carry part of you inside me so even after you're dead, I will have you with me." She jerks my jean shorts down, my underwear down and presses herself against me.

"What you're doing is leaving Lora with a part of me inside her." I struggle under her, but Lora's a strong woman. "It's not you." I desperately want to remember who she is and what she's talking about, but too many lives rush at me and I want to scream. I'm losing myself and I wonder what will happen if I can't stop this flood of lives.

"Watch this." She closes her eyes for a moment and winces.

"What are you—"

"Quiet." Her neck muscles tense and her jaw tightens for several seconds and then goes slack. When she gazes at me, brown eyes stare back. The pupils dilate, almost growing to the size of the entire eyeball. Abruptly they shrink to half their size, then smaller as if a bright light was suddenly shined in her eyes. Her long, haunted moan grows louder, with staccato pauses, until the woman shrieks and her whole body grows slack. Her fingers that had clawed at my chest, relax. She stares glassy-eyed at me, the pupils returning to normal size, but taking on a bluish tint. Drool forms at her lips and spills in a big gob, splattering on the carpet. "There. She's all gone." She unbuttons the corset and starts rocking on me until I'm hard. "See, Thomas, it's just you and me. Lora's all gone." She quickly slips me inside her and moans. "Very nice."

"Abigail, I don't remember who you are and—"

She jerks her body hard against me, twisting so that a lightning bolt of pain shoots up from my groin. "Let me tell you a story." She slowly rocks back and forth on me. "There was this man who was on his back and a whore was on him, rocking just like I am. She got carried away and started going crazy, rocking too hard, lifting her body up and dropping down on him. But one time she came up a bit too high and when she came down hard on him...well." She holds up her index finger bent at a right angle. "I was real upset that he wouldn't finish and honestly, Hadrian, I don't want to do that to you. So just hold still, Thomas, and I won't hurt you."

"What's my name?"

She laughs and keeps rocking. Our sex brings memories of passion, boiling up from my depths. Strings of images crash into my mind's vision. Cyllene, Cleasastra, Mariana, Dorothy, and hundreds of other women (and men) move in like a movie sped up way too fast. Scenes stretch out before me of orgies and parties and illicit rendezvous and Nicole in France before I left Europe, and Sarah deep in the woods where no one would find us, and Katarina everywhere we could and—Katarina. That name stops me, almost grounds me. Katarina. I repeat it over and over, but her face fades until she's just another woman's body, naked and sweaty under me.

"Thomas, look at me."

I open my eyes and stare at Abigail, riding me.

"Touch me, Thomas."

Warmness spreads inside my head and I gently lay my fingertips on her breasts. She covers my hands and presses them against her cool skin. "See, love, I can even get in your head and make you do what I want. There's no escaping me. You're not strong enough." She laughs. "That's it." She rocks with more urgency, sending me straight to the edge of restraint.

Abigail's fingernails draw circles on my skin, pressing down until it hurts.

"Abigail—"

"Oh, no, not yet." She presses her fingertips against my forehead and searing heat spreads through my mind. "You're gonna love this."

The heat burns away the chaos of memories until Rick Summers is all that's left. The other memories fade, but never disappear, leaving echoes of themselves all over my mind. Somehow, I'm going to have to straighten them all out. I wonder if she realizes she's done this.

Before I can be thankful that I'm me again, something pulls at my mind and a part of me is yanked up through Abigail's fingers into her head. Suddenly I'm looking down at myself looking back at me. The sensation is so disorienting, that I feel the urge to puke, but Abigail calms me enough that the sensation passes.

"How does it feel to fuck yourself?" She laughs. "I'm inside you as well. Can't get any more intimate than this, can you?"

The Rick on the floor tries shoving Abigail off, but she clamps her legs tight to my sides.

"I wouldn't do that if I were you. If we're separated, we're gonna be stuck inside each other. Just relax and enjoy the ride."

Our minds are separate, but she can control me. I watch through Abigail's eyes as I run my hands over her and thrust up to meet her body. The sensation of being on both ends is nauseating. It's not bad enough I'm fucking the woman who's trying to kill me, but I get to feel myself thrusting inside her. I don't want to give Abigail what she wants, but she's controlling both of us. I try shutting her eyes and I succeed. Maybe she doesn't have as much control as I thought.

"Don't want to watch yourself?" she asks into her mind. "I love watching."

"Good for you."

She overpowers me and opens her eyes. I turn away and peer into her mind. Wait. I'm in her mind! I make my body grab her hips and buck up as hard as I can to distract her while I look for her memories. It's nearly impossible to focus, as I experience every sensation from both bodies.

A huge stone door rises before me, and with all my strength, I pull it open and gasp—an odd concept when one's got nothing but mental will. I'm at the entrance to a great hall in her memory palace, and I wonder how the hell am I ever going to find what I'm looking for. Maybe I'm not. Maybe I can't change fate and—bullshit. I head down the long corridor lined with gilded doors on both sides, wondering if there's a door I should open. What the hell? I open the second door on the left and stare at a man being dismembered by a woman in a bloody cooking apron. Wrong door.

All the doors look the same; finding the right one before Abigail is finished with me is going to be more difficult than I imagined. I run, hoping I'll catch a sign on a door—as if it's that simple—that'll give me a clue as to what's behind it.

I pick a door on the right side and push it open, revealing three naked men and one naked woman writhing on the floor, moving as one. She takes them into her, one at a time until she's sitting up on one with another behind her and one kneeling in front of her. The three men groan, "Sophia", moving with her like she's the ocean and they're waves. As they simultaneously approach oblivion, she pulls her bracelet from her wrist and unravels it, gently slipping it around the throat of the man under her. She suddenly tightens it and then bites down hard on the man in front of her. Screaming, he falls back, and Sophia spits half his penis out on to the floor.

Under her, the guy jerks around as she tightens the garrote until it sinks into his skin. Blood sprays everywhere. His screams are strangled off and his body stops moving.

Sophia turns and grins at the man behind her who has just enough time to register what's happening before she takes a long metal pin from her hair and jabs it straight through his throat. Without looking, she takes another pin from her hair, leans forward and drives it into the right eye of the guy with the bloody crotch, forcing it up into his brain.

Then Sophia turns and sees me, cocks her head and smiles, then pulls the needles free and stands. Her body, as feminine as I've seen, is spattered with blood. "Can I help you?"

I shake my head, staring at the bloody needles. "I don't think so."

"Not a thing I can do for you? A little pain, a little pleasure?" She clicks the needles together and brain matter drops to the floor.

"Can you tell me how you've killed Sarah and I in every lifetime?"

"Why don't you come in and I'll tell you?" She comes to the doorway, but hesitates at the threshold.

I instinctually take a step back from her and her dripping needles, afraid that she can reach me, even out here. "I'll just stand here."

"I think you should come in and then we'll talk. Or maybe we'll have a little fun first." She licks one needle then the other.

My stomach turns and if I don't walk away, I'm going to throw up. "That is fucking gross." I shiver. "Never mind. I'll just keep looking." I turn to go, keeping an eye on Sophia and her needles.

"Do you know how many memories are here?" she asks.

"Millions. Do you know how long it'll take you to find what you're looking for? Lifetimes. But if you come in here, I'll tell you what you want to know."

"I don't need to know anything that badly."

She giggles. "Of course you do." She winks seductively. "I am the only answer you'll find."

I feel a stirring sensation in my groin and for a second, I think I'm reacting to this twisted creature, but then I realize it's my link to my own body out there and the link to Abigail's body in here. I stare at the needles. *It's not worth it.* Besides, I don't know what the consequences of being stabbed with needles from someone's memory are. I decide on another tactic. "Aren't you pleased?"

"With what?" Her grin is still in place and her eyes look at me from under thick eyelashes.

"Aren't you proud at how many times you've beaten me?"

"Of course." She curls back into the room and indicates for me to follow her, waving a bloody needle at me. "I'm very proud and I will be again very soon."

"Who's Sarah?"

She frowns, scowls at me.

"How many times have you killed us? Once? Twice? Have you ever succeeded?"

"Of course I have." But she's not as cocky as she had been a few minutes ago.

"How many?"

"Come in here and I'll tell you."

"Go fuck yourself."

"Wanna watch me?" She takes the needles in one hand and guides them between her legs.

"I bet that's gonna hurt."

"Not as much as it will when we find Sarah and slaughter the two of you!"

"If you ever do."

She screams a guttural sound and throws the needles, dart-like, at me. I duck away, but they disintegrate at the doorway, reappearing on the floor.

"Nice try." I head back, letting myself float up from Abigail's memories into her mind.

"How's it feel, Rick?"

I know she's been asking this question over and over.

"Oh, it feels great." If I were any more physically disoriented, I'd puke. The sensation of sliding into her and being slid into at the same time is wickedly arousing and when I find fleeting moments of clarity, it's repulsively erotic. I'll never admit to anyone that I find the tiniest bit of pleasure in experiencing this, but, in some twisted way, I do.

I try dropping back into my body, away from Abigail and her dark, seductive will.

"Not quite yet, Rick." Abigail yanks me back inside her psyche and grinds her crotch hard against mine. "Not until we've consummated our little tryst."

The first sensations of my climax ripple through my body, and I know I don't have much longer. It's unsettling to have my masculinity ripped away like this. In forcing me into her psyche, moving a bit of herself into me, she's dominating me in the most intimate way possible.

My soul is drawn into Lora's body, poured like soup away from myself until I have only the barest strand back into me. She takes control, pulling Lora down to the floor. I attempt to keep her body upright but Abigail, in my body, has better control and she shoves me over.

She grabs my wrists, holds me down to the floor and uses my body to assault Lora. I scream in protest, but Abigail laughs with my voice.

"How do you like it?" She drops all her weight on me, rises, does it again.

I follow the thin silver strand back into myself, hoping to get out of her, away from the pain and utter humiliation. But Abigail's done this before, and I haven't, and as I climb the thread her will slams me back into Lora's body. She smothers me with my own body's weight. I shove her, trying to fight back, not wanting to hurt myself, but desperately wanting to escape.

Trembling with exhaustion from her relentless assault, I drop my arms to the floor and let her have her way. I flee, trying to find memories to hide in, thoughts to lose myself in, until Abigail is finished. But Lora is completely gone and where her memories used to be is a void so vast and deep that I imagine this is what it's like to stand on the rim of a black hole. And I scream into the infinite darkness, the torture of non-existence rising up to swallow me.

I force myself away from the horrific emptiness and become aware of Abigail. The humiliation is welcome compared to the utter blankness where Lora's soul used to be. Then I feel the barest hint of my orgasm through the thin strand holding my soul to my own body. Thank God, it'll be over soon.

Abigail thrusts hard into me and lets out a groan, my own voice, of pleasure. From what seems a huge distance, I feel her throbbing inside me, and I scream, cursing her to Hell.

"I can leave you in there," she whispers in my ear. "Maybe I'll just sever the thread and let you stay in that body. How'd you like that? Growing fat with your own seed." She laughs. "But I have better plans for you." She yanks me back into my own body, streaming past me, back into hers.

My head spins and vertigo clenches my stomach as I reorient to being alone in my body.

She rolls me off her and leans up on one elbow. "Rick," she whispers, "that was really wild. Maybe I'll keep you around just to pleasure me. How did you like watching yourself, feeling my ecstasy? How'd you like being in my body?" She goes to stand and almost falls over. "Shaky legs." She puts her corset back on, then smoothes her dress. "Thank you, Rick." She drops on the couch, grinning. "I know you're wondering, so I'll tell you what happened after I escaped from Nikki's car.

"I got out of the trunk and I ran over to a place called the Mason Jar. I waited until a woman came out by herself, one of the waitresses, and took her over. I like this body. I'm impressed. She's in much better shape than Nikki was. As far as Nikki goes, I would've killed her, but she's got cancer and doesn't have much longer to live. I figured why bother. I left her in the parking lot. Someone will find her and bring her to the hospital."

"She's got cancer?" I can barely think straight. Flashes of being raped and raping explode like fireworks and though I know exactly what happened—I think—it doesn't make it any easier to cope. Am I still a man? Or is there some part of Abigail left in me and some part of me in that woman? "Cancer?"

"Breast cancer. Poor thing. I almost thought to put her out of her misery, but for some reason, I decided to let her make her own decision. I didn't have the right to take that away from her. Now if you'll excuse me, I have some things to do in the basement." She stands up and slowly walks out of the room. "Don't go away."

Once she leaves, I get dressed and crawl over to the couch. Nausea twists my stomach and my head aches like a slow explosion. I feel violated and disgusted with myself for taking part in such an act, even though I had little say in what happened. She thinks that no matter what, she's in control. Fine. Let her keep thinking that; it'll be her undoing. She's never succeeded killing Sarah and me, even though Sophia never said so. The look on her face gave it away.

Climbing onto the couch, I lie there, closing my eyes, and swallowing the bile rising in my throat; I can still feel her in me, me in her. A shower would do me a world of good to clean her off me. I don't need this shit.

Behind my eyes, memories blossom out of nothing, filling my mind with images of the past, of Thomas, Hadrian, Herr Schwartz and a dozen other lives in between. Women I've loved and lost, friends come and gone and—

"Thomas?"

Not again.

"Thomas, I have something for you."

I slowly open my eyes and stare at Elizabeth. She's on her knees, her face close to mine. "I have drawn a picture for you!"

"What are you talking about?"

"I have drawn a picture for you to have. I believe you want to see it."

"I'm really fucking tired and I'm not in the mood for this." I close my eyes, hoping to pass out.

"Please, Thomas. This is very important."

Something in her voice makes me look at her. She's very pretty. I shouldn't have such thoughts for my sister, but then again, that was centuries ago and I'm someone else now. So is she. "What are you? You can't be the soul of Elizabeth; she's in Katarina. Are you a ghost?"

"An echo. A longing. A part of Elizabeth that wanders the earth, bound by sin."

"Can I free you?" This is way bizarre.

"Absolve my guilt by putting to rest the evil that caused me to take my life."

"Sure. I was planning to do that anyway."

"Here." She hands me the drawing and fades to nothing. Gossamer wisps curl and dissipate, leaving a cool spot where she knelt.

"Damn." I glance at the drawing, not knowing what to expect, but certainly not expecting what I see. It's Sarah and me holding hands, sitting on the front porch of the old house. I smile at the feelings that come up, remembering that day as if it were part of my life as Rick Summers. The day was warm and the smell of my father cooking out in the—

Holy shit.

Faces swim across the drawing. Two other faces appear from under Sarah and Thomas. One's mine, Rick Summers, and the other is—

Oh, fuck. Abigail's screwed up again.

Meggan's cell rings. "Hello?"

"Where the hell are you?" Meggan shouts. "We've been worried about you!"

"Listen to me—"

"Are you okay? What happened at Cyndi's? Kerri called and—"

"Meggan?"

"Are you ... what?"

"Shut up. I'm at Kat's house with Abigail."

"You're at Kat's house? How did you get there?"

"Abigail drove me here in the trunk of Nikki's car. Did you say Kerri called?"

"Yes. She said she needed to talk to you about a dream she had. I didn't know what to tell her because I couldn't reach you at Cyndi's house. What happened?"

"Cyndi ... Abigail killed her. Listen to me. I want you,

Dallas, and Ariana to stay at the hotel."

"What? We're coming to Kat's house to help you."

"No, you're not. I won't have any more deaths on my conscience."

"You're going to take her on by yourself?"

If only I had a plan so I could tell Meggan I've got this, but I don't, and I have no idea what I'm going to do, but at least if the four of them stay away, I'll be the only one in harm's way.

"We're coming over." Meggan clicks the phone off.

"Meggan? Meggan?" I redial, and the phone rings until Dallas's voicemail kicks in. I don't leave a message. She knows who it is and she's not going to answer it. "Shit." I lie back on the couch and close my eyes. Odd sensations from our sex scratch at my nerves. What I'd really like to do is go downstairs and kick the shit out of Abigail, but I don't have the strength and I'm still dizzy. I know Meggan's going to ignore me and the four of them are coming. So, the plan is to get to Abigail before the cavalry arrives.

The question is, does Abigail know about Sarah? If she doesn't, there's still time to come up with a plan. But if she knows, we're all as good as dead.

And then there's Kerri and her dream. I dial her number.

"Where are you?" No hello.

"Hey, Kerri. I—"

"Where the hell are you?"

"Kat's house."

"When are you coming back to New York?"

I don't answer. Right now, I have no answer.

"Okay. You do what you have to do and come home. All right?"

"Sure. Hey, about those—"

She clicks off. I redial, but it's my night to be hung up on and ignored. I pocket the phone. I have to know what Abigail's doing. Steadying myself, I climb off the couch. I am so fucked up, I'm lucky if I make it down the stairs without falling and breaking my neck.

The door to the basement is open but I don't hear any noise. Of course, she's probably gone down into the tunnel and wherever from there, so I wouldn't hear anything. I take the stairs slowly, gripping the banister for all that my life's worth. It won't do me any good to hurt myself before the epic battle that's to come.

Pausing on the stairs, I think about that. Epic battle? Me? Though I don't have the centuries of rage Abigail carries with her, I am sufficiently pissed off at having my current life messed, screwed with, and generally fucked up.

But am I ready for death? That shouldn't really enter into the equation. Yet it does because Abigail can do things that I can't and that puts me at a disadvantage. Even if Dallas, Meggan, Kat, and Ariana show up in time, what can they do? We're only mortal with one lifetime's worth of knowledge. Sure, Dallas knows about ghosts and the paranormal, but Abigail is more than just a paranormal experience. She's got centuries of knowledge and abilities far beyond the five of us.

At the bottom of the stairs, I head to the laundry room. I have no doubts about where she is and as I suspected, the rug's moved away and the trap door's open. Before I'm halfway across the room, I hear her voice, chanting or something. This end of the room is unnaturally cold. Is it only the cold or is it the chilling sound of her chanting, as if she's summoning something, that makes me shiver. For fuck's sake. I've seen too many horror movies for my own good. I should have a stake or a hammer, something to use as a weapon.

It happens that I'm standing in Kat's father's tool zone and I take a look around for something to match Abigail's rage. Hammers, screwdrivers, and pliers hang on the wall, but none of them have that special something that says, "Kill Abigail". The nail gun, on the other hand, and the drill with the big bit still in its mouth say, "Bye bye."

The nail gun is almost empty, but I refill it with the biggest nails I can find that'll fit the cartridge. The drill still has batteries in it, but I find new ones and replace them—don't want to aim and fire and have nothing happen. I'll take it, but it may not do much good.

I grab a flashlight and head down the ladder. It's a bit awkward with two power tools in my hand and a flashlight in my mouth, but there's no one else here to help me. The drill has a little hand strap and I leave that around my wrist as I climb down.

At the bottom of the ladder it is fucking cold enough that I see my breath in little plumes of white. I shine the flashlight to the far end of the tunnel, but the light dies way before I see anything. I turn to the wall that used to be there. When Ariana and I were down here, this ladder was inches from a brick wall that seems to have disappeared. Now there's a tunnel that goes off into the darkness. Go figure.

I take a deep breath, convincing myself that this is it, that I can do this. Abigail hasn't won before and she's not going to win this time. Unlike the past, though, I want this to end here and not go on for another lifetime or two. Hopefully, I can pull this off and keep my life intact.

Okay, Rick. This is as good a time as any to kick Abigail's ass for everything she's done to you and those you love. Take no prisoners. I hear Metallica's *St. Anger* blasting in my head as I grip the flashlight and the nail gun and walk off into the dark, chilling tunnel.

Abigail's voice grows louder, and I know I'm heading in the right direction. I was wrong; she's not chanting but singing to someone in a language that might be Greek. Some of the words sound familiar, but I can't make sense of them. It doesn't matter. I'm not here to listen to Abigail's song. I'm here to put an end to her insanity.

Ahead of me, candlelight flickers on the wall of the tunnel and the chamber Abigail's in. Twin shadows detach from the flames and approach me. They're two of those brown men, sinuous and tall and they growl and come at me. Nail gun, don't fail me now. My hand trembles as I pull the trigger. Nothing happens. Fucking safety. The first brown man is on me, baring its teeth, trying to rip my arm off. The second brown man grabs the drill from me and yanks it, almost snapping my wrist.

"He needs to be alive!" Abigail shouts from the chamber. "Don't kill him."

The brown men pause. Time enough at last. Snapping the safety off the nail gun, I fire point blank into one of their heads.

The thing falls back, hissing, bleeding black from his nailed skull. I whip the gun around to the second and fire twice, nailing it in the eyes. It backs off, scratching at its face, and in that moment, I put a couple of nails through its throat. It chokes as black liquid spills from the wounds.

"Very good, Rick." Abigail, still dressed in Lora's body, steps out of the chamber and smiles politely. "I can summon more of them. They're the slaves of demons and such and Hell is full of them."

"That's wonderful." I point the nail gun at Abigail. "Why shouldn't I kill you?"

"Because I'll flee this body. She's dead anyway." She shrugs. "Come in here. I have something to show you."

I keep the nail gun pointed ahead of me and cautiously follow her into a ten-by-ten-foot chamber that reeks of death and rot. I cover my nose with my shirt, so it cuts down on the stink. Candelabra stand in the corners with five burning candles on each sending flames dancing across the earthen walls. Body parts, that I can only assume belong to Dave Dawson and his son, litter the floor. A huge waist-high, stone slab sits in the center of the room, leaving little space around it. On the slab is a body in a state of horrible decay and around it the stench is almost unbearable.

"What the fuck?"

"Meet Euryanassa."

The blood drains from my body. I'm sure of it. This is the body of the woman who decided immortality was more important than following the natural order of things, who decided the gods' way would not be her own.

"How dare you?" I turn my gaze away from the corpse and stare at Abigail's smiling face. "This is a mockery of life itself."

"Ah, Hadrian. You've come back. How sweet of you." She walks around the altar, gazing with love at the rotting body and then she looks at me. "You never could understand, could you? No, you and the rest of those fools were too interested in the way Nature intended life to be. Oh, I'm sorry. It was Demeter, right? Demeter dictates that we live one life and then move on to the next, never retaining any knowledge from the previous life and then fumble through the next and the next life. We should be blind to the veil and never wish to see through it to what we've learned in lives past. How utterly foolish! Do you have any idea what I've done with all that I've learned? I can leave this body and take over another. I can move through the planes of existence. I have visited the underworld, Hadrian, and come back the wiser!" She laughs. "But you who would hold me in contempt will never understand the gift we've been given. None of you will." She touches the wasted body. "I brought this body from Greece to the New World and with the help of the local Indians, buried it here. Little did I know that my body held the seeds of such evil that everyone who lived in the house built on this ground would eventually commit some heinous crime, be it murder, or incest, or worse."

"Like what you did to William?"

She laughs and the sound is immediately drawn into the earthen walls.

"Who is Auntie Jean?"

"My special friend. A spirit of great power that I met long ago. She served me well, but in the end, I had to extinguish her before she became too powerful." She picks up a ceremonial knife that must be at least a thousand years old. "Do you know what my mistake was?" She laughs without humor. "I succumbed to a single emotion. While the Dutch were settling this state and dealing with the Lenapi Indians, I fell in love with you. We had agreed back in Greece that we would meet in each lifetime and if love developed, then we would allow it to grow and blossom. But not me. I had seen what true love was like; I had felt it, and I desperately wanted to feel it again. When I fled Salem and came to New Jersey, I never expected to find the two of you. But I did and, well, you know the rest."

"What now? I know that you've never been able to keep the promise you made to me that day you hung yourself."

"Oh, a couple of times I killed the two of you, but for the most part I always came close. Do you have any idea how pissed off I was each time I thought I had you both, but didn't? When I looked in Kat's eyes and saw Elizabeth, I wanted to rip her to pieces." She gazes down at the knife. "Truth is, I still do."

Somewhere far above us a door closes.

"Company?" Her hand flashes out and her fingers brush my face. "Ah, Meggan, Dallas, and Ariana and—" She gasps. "And Katarina. Oh, I'm going to enjoy this more than you could imagine!"

"Abigail, they've done nothing to hurt you. Let them be. You want me, fine, I'm here. But don't—"

"Wait." She steps closer and presses her fingers against my forehead. I try pulling her hand away, but she pushes me back, up against the wall. "You know who Sarah is. Tell me. Tell me who she is so I can—" Her eyes go wide. "No." She backs away. "No. Not again." She looks wildly around the room as if she's following a buzzing fly. "I cannot have failed again." She shakes her head. "No." Her eyes come to rest on me and her lips curl into a snarling grin. "Let's go see who's here." She places the dagger on the altar and comes at me. "Shall we say hello?" She presses her hand against my forehead and slams my head into the earthen wall, that gives way, and as I start falling, she throws me to the floor and presses her hot fingers as hard as she can against my forehead.

"No!"

But it's too late. She swarms into my brain with the force of a hurricane, wiping me away from myself. Black winds whip around the inside of my skull as she forces her insane will over mine. I fall away, battered by the force of her dominating ego, until I'm lost in the blackness of sweeping chaos that bears me along like a mad river.

"I will crush you," she screams in my head. "Sarah is gone and I have no further use for you! But wait! I do!" Her laugh crashes down over me, drowns me, and washes me away from myself. "Watch, Rick, and see how powerful I am and how utterly useless it is to fight me." We leave the room in my body, Lora's body unmoving on the floor, and head back to the ladder.

"Abigail, please don't do this." My voice is like a whisper in a gale. The blackness crushes down on me and I hold onto memories to keep from disappearing into oblivion. If I give into the chaotic shadows I will be utterly destroyed with no chance for another life. I have to hold on to who I am as the dark storm tries to rip away my essence. Through it all, I see out of my eyes, though I'm very far away from my mind I can't do anything but watch.

We climb the ladder and meet the four of them in the laundry room.

Dallas comes forward first. "Rick, are you okay?"

Abigail clears my throat. "Just fine. I … I killed Abigail. Let's all go upstairs."

"How did you do that?" Dallas asks.

"She was still getting used to her new body. There was a knife and I stabbed her over and over."

"How did you keep her from shifting bodies?"

Abigail shrugs. "I guess I caught her by surprise. It was some kind of ceremonial knife, so maybe that had something to do with it."

Dallas nods and stares at me. "Good job."

"I'm glad you're safe," Kat says.

"Me, too," Meggan says.

Then she and Meggan head up first, mumbling to each other.

"We were really worried about you, dude," Dallas says next to me. "I'm glad you're all right."

Abigail nods and looks back at Ariana.

"I'm glad to see you, too," Ariana says. "I'm glad it's all over with."

Abigail smiles kindly. It's the kind of smile you give someone right before you slide the knife in their back.

Once in the living room the four of them sit down, but Abigail stands by the entrance way and looks at each of them, her gaze coming to rest on Katarina. Sharp pain jolts through my essence as Abigail summons my memories. "Kat, remember you wanted to talk before?"

"Sure." She nervously looks at Meggan. "Sure."

"Why don't we relax for now?" Meggan says. "There'll be plenty of time later to talk."

Abigail bristles. Her rage stirs the black shadows. If she could, she'd murder Meggan right here and now. "I'd rather talk now, Meg. It'll only take a moment. We could go upstairs."

Kat tries concealing a grin, but does a poor job. What is she thinking? She gets up and Abigail follows her up. I've got to do something to warn Kat, but Abigail's too strong. Any time I try moving close to my mind, the black winds sweep me away, tossing me like a piece of paper.

Abigail chuckles in my head. "It'll be worse for you if you try anything. Not that you can do anything to stop me. You are, Rick, a few hairs away from being annihilated and I wouldn't want to have to do that to you. We still have much more to do together!"

"Abigail, you win. All right? I concede that you are the stronger of all of us. The council was wrong to treat you the way they did. Maybe you had the right idea about retaining knowledge throughout time."

"No, Hadrian, or whoever you fancy yourself as at the moment, you don't believe a word of it. Remember, I'm in here with you, too, and I know what you think, believe, and even what you feel. Don't lay that shit on me."

At the top of the stairs, Abigail, in my body, follows Kat to her room and looks around.

"It's been a long time, Rick, since we've been together in this room." Kat sits on the bed and pats the space next to her.

"I'm going to enjoy this," Abigail whispers to me as she goes to Kat's dresser and picks up a guitar-shaped letter opener.

"Please, Abby," I say. "I'll do whatever you want."

"Oh, yes, you will do whatever I want. I'm in complete control. You don't have a choice!" She holds the sharp metal opener behind her back and sits down next to Kat.

"So, what's up?" Kat asks.

"Run!" I scream.

Abigail's laugh echoes in my brain until I'm deafened.

"She can't hear you." Then she says to Kat, "I've been thinking about what a fool I've been since I left you. I still love you more than you'll ever know. You know, it's funny. Usually I'm not very straightforward, but I wanted you to get the point."

"You've always been straightforward, Rick, you've never—"

Abigail whips the letter opener out from behind her back and drives it into Kat's throat, twisting the knife-like piece of metal in and up.

"No!" I scream with all my being.

Kat's eyes go wide, and her fingers claw at my hands that force the letter opener deeper.

"Look into my eyes, Elizabeth," Abigail says. She climbs to her knees and drives it deeper. Katarina collapses on the bed and Abigail straddles her. "It's me, Abigail, you bitch. You ruined everything. I know you told Thomas the truth, and I promised I'd get you for it. Well, here I am."

Katarina's hot, thick blood spills over the letter opener, covering my fingers.

Kat's hands feebly try fighting off the metal dagger buried in her neck as she chokes on her own blood spilling from the wound and drooling from her mouth. Tears run down her face as she stares at me, her eyes pleading with me.

"Stop it!" I scream, sobbing. "Stop it!" I rise up out of the dark to try reclaiming my will, but Abigail's too strong and forces the blackness down on me. I feel myself splintering apart, losing myself; the strands that keep me anchored begin snapping one by one. "No! No!" Several more and I'm gone. "Stop it!" Four. Three. Two. I reach out and grasp on to the last two strands.

"Rick." Katarina spits blood. Her body convulses and then she's still.

"Abigail?" I say.

"Yes, my love?"

"I'm going to kill you."

"I doubt it." She climbs off the bed, leaving the letter opener buried in Katarina's throat.

"I'm going to kill you," I say.

She stares at Kat's body. "I may not be able to take Sarah from you, but I will take everyone you care about. Look long and hard, Rick. I want to feel your emptiness and loneliness and pain. Oh, yes, that feels good."

I throw it all at her. My rage, my pain, my hatred for her, and she takes it and laughs. "Very nice. Let's see who's next." She leaves the room, licking the blood from her/my fingers. The house has changed again. It looks like it hasn't been lived in for years. Doors hang off their hinges. The walls are spotted with mold and huge cracks and holes zig-zag from one wall to the next. The slats on the linen closet door are broken out as if someone punched them out from within the closet. The rug at the top of the stairs is filthy and threadbare. Dark stains cover most of the floor and I don't want to even hazard a guess as to what made them. The whole place smells of rot and decay. And in front of me, Meggan screams.

Abigail looks at her. "Come to save your lover? Too late."

"Rick, what did you do?" Meggan peers over my shoulder and her eyes go wide with fear, hate, shock, and the crush of reality. "Oh my God! No!" She tries pushing past me, but Abigail grabs her by the throat and slams her against the linen closet door. "Please, Rick, let me save her!" She fights against me, clawing at my hands and, scratching my skin until blood ribbons across my arms. "Let me go!"

"She's already dead." Abigail's words, my voice.

I'd cry if she'd let me, but all I can do is scream in pain for Katarina's senseless death.

"Why?" Tears stream down Meggan's face.

Abigail twists my mouth into a smile. "What are you doing up here? I thought you'd wait for me downstairs."

"I … I … Dallas said you weren't yourself. I wanted to be sure Kat was okay. He thought Abigail—"

Abigail tightens my fingers around Meggan's throat, cutting off her air. "So, Dallas is the smart one. I wonder who he is." She lifts Meggan up by her throat, pressing her against the broken door. "No matter. When I rip him open and expose his insides, I'll know who he is this lifetime."

Meggan winces from the knife-like broken slats poking her in the back. "Please." She sobs, her face red and bloated.

Abigail tightens her grip and places her other hand on Meggan's waist.

"What are you doing?" Meggan asks.

"Human serration."

"No!" I force my will at Abigail's, trying to keep my hands still. "Abigail, don't!"

She presses Meggan against the broken door.

"Abigail, there's no reason to do this!" I shout at her. The

winds kick up, violently slamming against my psyche. My grip
on the last two strands of my being starts sliding. The winds
buffet me. I wind the two chords around my wrist. "You can't
get rid of me that easily!"

"If I wanted to, I could destroy you like a fly!" Her voice
booms at me like wicked thunder. "I play with you because you
keep me amused, and I want you to watch how easy it is for me
to kill your friends before I take your pathetic life!"

I scream.

Abigail presses Meggan as hard as she can up against the
door, almost lets her go, and then presses her up again.

Meggan screams as rivulets of blood race down the door.
She flails wildly and Abigail turns her head to avoid getting
my eyes scratched out. "One more time, what do you say?" She
laughs as she draws Meggan away from the door and slams her
back, raising her up against the broken slats. Meggan thrashes
wildly as thick blood pours down the door.

"Kill her!" Meggan shouts.

Abigail freezes. "What?" She backs up, dropping Meggan on
the floor. The back of her shirt is torn and soaked in blood. Her
skin is flayed, ripped, exposing muscle and tissue. Absolutely
fucking gross.

It's only then I see the open cell phone and the blinking
green light. Dallas has heard all of this.

Abigail lifts her head as if listening. "Fuck! My body!" She
shoves herself out of me and for a brief instant no one is in control. I collapse to the floor, inches away from Meggan. At least I
didn't fall on her; that would've been much worse.

Meggan's still alive, breathing heavily and sobbing.

I stretch myself back into my body, asserting my will to take
control of my fingers and toes, my arms—bloody from Meggan's
fingernails—and legs. I've never been so happy to wiggle my
fingers and toes before in my life. I'll never take that for granted.

I sit up slowly, getting used to being in myself again.

Metal nails spill across the attic floor and suddenly the ceiling caves in. Plaster showers down on the far side of the stairs
and one of those nasty brown men stretches itself to its full
seven-foot height. Another jumps down through the hole and

the two of them stare at us with hatred. I guess Abigail's ready to end this.

I grab Meggan under her arms and try pulling her into Kat's room. Not that I really want to go back in there, but it's the closest room with a door that locks.

She groans, trying to pull away from me, away from the person she thinks I am.

"Meggan, it's me, Rick. Stop struggling, I'm trying to save you!"

She fights me, screaming and crying.

One of the brown men launches at me. I've no time to defend myself. It slams into me, knocking me back in Kat's room. But this isn't Kat's room anymore. It's Elizabeth's room, complete with framed drawings and my sister slowly spinning from the ceiling. Kat is on the bed that's now a cot and my heart aches as I stare at her.

The brown man stalks into the room and I swing wildly, trying to connect with any part of the creature, but it shoves me away from the cot. It leans over and pulls the letter opener from Kat's throat, brings it to its lips and licks the blood off it with a blackened, swollen tongue. Then, dropping it, the thing turns to me. "Hadrian." Its voice is gruff and deep.

"How do you—"

"I was Taelus. A friend of your family's. You will help us escape Euryanassa's control?"

"What are you talking about?" My head reels with this new revelation. The brown men were human.

"We were all human once, but thought Euryanassa or whoever she was through time, would give us power, so we joined her. She poisoned us, twisting our souls until we became what you see before you. We hunger, but she will not feed us except human flesh. We thirst, so we must drink blood. I was the one outside the house last night, offering you memories, trying to help you."

"You ..."

"Destroy her. Set us free." He turns toward Meggan lying in the hall. "Remember Athens, Hadrian."

"No!" I get up, stumbling over my shaky legs. I fall hard,

slamming my head against the wall, shooting little silver fireworks off in my vision. The two brown men move in on Meggan. I look for anything to use as a weapon, but all I can find are the jagged pieces of wood sticking out of the closet door. I climb to my feet and rush to it. I hesitate; scraps of Meggan's flesh stick to the broken slats.

The brown men kneel by Meggan. She screams.

I look over my shoulder and freeze in terror. Blood in my veins, once hot and moving, turns to ice and my heart stops. They are digging into her back, ripping chunks of her out and eating them. Blood and gore cover their faces. One of them bends over her and starts ripping pieces of her with its teeth, swallowing the hunks of meat like a ravenous pit bull.

The scream builds in my throat, raw and merciless, until it rips from me, fills the house and echoes. Something between a sob and an insane laugh catches in my throat. A voice inside me says I have to get out of here before I'm next.

But Meggan—

Meggan is dead.

But Katarina—

Katarina's dead.

What the fuck good am I doing? Everyone around me is dying.

Dallas and Ariana are still alive. I'll save them and kill Abigail.

Kill her? How? She's a millennia old spirit who jumps bodies at will. How do you stop that?

I drop the pieces of the door and sprint down the stairs heedless of the danger of the stairs collapsing under me. I've got to get to the basement and there's no time to worry about falling, breaking bones, or killing myself. Which is good, because right at the bottom stair, I twist my ankle and go down hard. "Mother fucker." Rolling over, I rub my ankle and it hurts bad. I hope I didn't break it. Judging by the looks of the house, there probably aren't any ambulances nearby.

I stand slowly, stepping gingerly on my foot. Oh, yeah, it fucking hurts. I'm the only one here. I assume the others are in the basement. Good old Dallas figured out I wasn't myself and took Ariana downstairs. Smart move. I'm sure he tried convincing Meggan to go with them, but Meggan needed to rescue her lover. What a shame.

The house has changed, but not to any I've been in before. This could be Abigail's own creation, though for the life of me I don't know how she's doing this. The walls are dark, rotting wood with ragged holes in some spots. The furniture is very simple, but mostly broken. This could be the first house built on this spot, where everything started. Cobwebs, so large they resemble chunks of gossamer wallpaper, hang down in the corners and even down to the furniture. This is not a place I want to spend a lot of time in. I only pray that when and if we stop Abigail, we get back to our own time.

"We have to save them!"

I turn and stare at the man I know to be Thomas Corwin. "How did you ... I thought we were—"

"We have to stop Euryanassa." Hadrian, dressed in a toga, steps from behind me and comes up next to Thomas. "She has caused too much death and she must be stopped at any cost."

"Even the cost of my friends?" Thomas asks.

"Excuse me," I say. "How did you—?"

"She has never won." Herr Schwartz comes in from another room. "She has only murdered innocent people, friends of ours." He's dressed in filthy, loose trousers and a frayed white dress shirt that's seen better days.

"How do I kill her?" I ask the gathering crowd of people I've been.

"Caligula knew."

I look over my shoulder at a Roman centurion coming down the stairs, hand on his sword hilt. "But before he could tell me, I was sent off to lead several legions against barbarians." He shakes his head. "I never found out."

"Well, who would know?" I ask.

"I heard rumor," the centurion says, "that he often spoke of these things to his closest friends during his nightly orgies."

"Orgies?" A woman comes in from another hallway. "Really? Tell me more." She's got a European accent and is dressed like a peasant, perhaps from the middle ages.

Okay. This is going way too far. I can accept all the men in the room, but a woman who's fascinated by orgies? I wasn't her. Well, I probably was, but it's too weird to contemplate. "Who are you?"

"My name is Greta." She glances at the centurion. "I knew love like that until the Black Plague came and took first my lovers, and then me and my family."

I shake my head. "Thank you very much for coming everyone, but this isn't helping me any. Abigail's here now, and I've got to get to her before she kills two of my friends."

"They are lost." Herr Schwartz shakes his head and frowns.

"They're not lost," I say. "But I need to know how to stop her."

My selves look at each other, but no one speaks.

"I have to go." I realize I don't know the layout of this house. "Anyone know where the basement is?"

"This way." Herr Schwartz leads me back in the direction he came.

I take one last look at the other people standing around in the room. "You know, I could use your help. She has killed some, if not all of you. I would think you'd all want some kind of revenge against her."

"But we can't kill her," Schwartz says. "How many of us have tried to stop her, and in doing so, sealed our own fates and those we love?"

"Wait." I turn to the centurion. "You said Caligula knew how to stop her?"

"Yes."

"Do any of you know who Caligula is now?" I almost figure Dallas is Caligula. But even if it is, short of a regression, he wouldn't remember anything.

They all shake their heads and mumble, "No."

"Do any if you know how to stop this spirit?"

"I do." A man off to my right barely raises his hand and nods.

"Who are you?" I ask.

"Jakob Walter. Foot soldier in the army of Napoleon."

"Okay." I've been more people than I ever could've imagined. "How?"

He steps forward, into the thick of my selves. "It's really quite simple. Just bind her in one body and destroy it. If she's allowed to move to another body, she'll escape, but if you hold her within that dying body, she can't escape."

"Okay. How do I—?"

"Hey Summers!" Someone pushes through the crowd, shoving my incarnations aside. "You fucking bastard!" Chuck Petrovska stands in front of me, a gun in his hand and a wicked grin on his face. "Thought you left me for dead, didn't you?" He waves the gun at me.

"A guy can hope."

He laughs. "No such luck, Summers. After you and that lesbian bitch left, a little girl came down and took me upstairs to her room."

"Abigail?"

"Oh, yes, Rick, Abigail. And she told me things you wouldn't believe."

"I think I would, Chuck."

"She told me you broke her heart a long time ago. It seems you have a habit of breaking hearts. First Abigail and then my Katarina."

"You know something? She probably didn't tell you the whole story. Did she tell you I was already in love with someone and that she killed her because she didn't like the fact that I was in love with someone else? Bet she didn't."

"You're a poor liar, Rick." He gazes around. "You throwing a costume party for freaks in here?"

I look at the gun, then at that insane look in his eyes. He's a step off from reality. As if standing in a decrepit version of the first house in New Jersey with a gang of people I've been throughout history is a good example of reality. Why doesn't anyone do something? We're like ten against one. He's got a gun and some of these people have never seen one, but surely, we can overwhelm him by sheer numbers.

"Have you noticed the house is a little different than the one you lived in?"

He looks up at the ceiling, then the walls. "Abigail told me how she opened time so that she controls where in time this house is. We're back in history. You know, if you go outside and the house shifts back, you're shit out of luck."

"I believe it."

"Who are all these people?" He waves the gun around him.

"They're me. I'm sure if Abigail told you how she could move the house around, she told you how easy it is for past lives to congregate here."

"Past lives?"

Other people start coming into the room and I can only guess they're Chuck's former selves. Then again, they could be more of me from other times. How many lives have I lived?

"Reincarnation."

He shakes his head and laughs. "No such thing."

"What Abigail told you is from the 1700s, Chuck, back when the Dutch were just settling New Jersey."

"Bullshit!" He points the gun at me. "Truth. Now."

"Fuck yourself. You don't want to believe the truth? Screw you." I shove past him, but he grabs my arm. There's no longer any sanity in his eyes.

"I'll shoot you, you bastard. You've hurt my daughter. You hurt Abigail. I should put a bullet in your fucking brain before you break another woman's heart."

"Let him go," the centurion says.

"Fuck you!" He shoots him. The armor takes some of the force, but there's no way, no matter how good Roman armor was, that it could stand up to a bullet fired point blank.

The centurion stumbles back in amazement. He looks down at the hole in his armor and winces. "How—?" He falls backward.

How can you kill someone who's already dead for millennia? Maybe I'm still at Cyndi's house trying to figure out who I am. Yeah, that has to be it because none of this can be real. Kat, Meggan, Dallas, and Ariana are back at the hotel waiting for me. Abigail, dressed as Lora, is somewhere in between. Didn't she say she had to go out somewhere? Maybe not.

"Look, Summers," Chuck says, pointing the gun at my face. "I don't care who these fucks are. You and I have a little trip to make." He giggles and it's very unpleasant. "I promised Abigail that if I found you, I'd bring you to her and let her have her revenge first and then I'd finish you off."

"That's very kind of you." I stare down the barrel of the gun, wondering how many bullets he's got in there. It doesn't matter. All he needs is one.

He glances around. "Where's the fucking basement?"

Thomas Corwin appears in the crowd, makes his way through to Chuck. "It's this way." He wrinkles his nose.

"What's wrong with you?" Chuck asks.

"This place smells of death," Herr Schwartz says. "I know the stench of death too well."

"As do I," the Union soldier announces. He's somewhere to my left, but every time I look, he looks away. "I laid in a field for days, waiting for death. It was all around me, but He would never come to claim me, not for almost a week. Then a man came. He reminded me of the pictures of Abraham Lincoln. He came to me and took my hand. Then he lifted me up and bore me away across the field. I saw all my buddies and we walked off the battlefield together, reunited in death."

"You actually saw death?" the Middle Eastern man asks.

If I wasn't terrified to be in this house, this would be funny. I can imagine Woody Allen turning this into one of his schticks.

"Yes," the soldier says.

"You're about to see death!" Chuck shouts, waving the gun at the soldier, but keeps his eyes on me. He knows better than to look away. I'll punch his face in.

"Weren't you frightened?" Greta asks.

The soldier shakes his head. "I thought I would be, but after being in the field and praying for Him to come, I was more relieved and grateful than scared."

"Shut up!" Chuck shouts.

I wish Chuck wasn't here fucking this up. This is the greatest opportunity I've ever had to learn about history, especially mine. If all these shades retain their memories, I can learn all about my lives.

But Chuck is his usual jackass self. I should just take him down and shoot him, but I don't want to chance him getting loose and killing me. I have to play along until I'm face to face with Abigail. Of course, then it'll be two on one and my odds will suck even more, but I can't afford to lose track of this freak with a gun.

"Come on, Chuck. Let's go downstairs."

"You." He points the gun at Corwin. "Where's the basement?"

"This way."

We follow my former self to the back door. He opens it and steps outside. I hesitate at the threshold.

"What's wrong?" Chuck asks.

"This isn't our time and I'm afraid if we step out of the house, we won't be able to get back in."

"Don't be such a pussy, Summers." Chuck shoves me forward, but I hold on to the doorframe.

"But this is the only way to the basement," Corwin says. "Through the cellar doors." He points to two metal doors set at an angle against the back of the house.

"Of course." I take a deep breath, close my eyes and step outside. Nothing untoward happens except the warm breeze on my face. Somewhere in the distance, to the west, I think, a plume of smoke rises.

"Indians," Thomas Corwin says behind me. "Lenapi Indians. Their tribe is only a day's ride away."

I stare at the rising smoke, trying to imagine the original Americans only a days' horse ride away. What it could be like to stay here and live among these people. I'm not ready for that adventure.

"Let's go." Chuck jams the gun in my back. "We don't have all freakin' day."

We walk over to the large, rusted doors. One of them stands ajar, a slice of darkness leaking out and dripping down the single step. I take a deep breath and pull the door open. It creaks badly, sending a shiver down my spine. "So much for surprise."

"Good luck," Corwin says, extending his hand. "Somehow I believe I know you."

I smile at him, his kind, blue eyes sparkling. "We've met before, long ago."

"Like the others in there?" He nods in the direction of the living room.

"Yeah."

He pats me on the back. "Well, good luck."

"Enough with the bullshit," Chuck shouts. "Downstairs!"

"Thanks." The desire to flee this place is immediate. *Run away! Get out of here as fast as you can! We'll deal with Abigail some other time when it doesn't feel so damned ... funereal!* Death lives here and has cast a pall over the house, bringing gloom and despair. I want to start down the stairs, but my feet are protesting.

Someone screams. A woman. I shiver, now more reluctant to go down there. It's nothing. Ariana probably just saw a rat and she's afraid of rodents. Sure, that's all it is, just one single—

Deformed homicidal maniac with a butcher knife and sharp teeth who isn't stopped by bullets or two-by-fours and loves the taste of human flesh and prefers their meals tartar if not still breathing.

—rat or maybe even a mouse! So, why can't I take the first step down into the basement? Remember the basement? Sure. But not this basement. The one I remember is where we had band practice, where Kat I made wild love too many times for me to count, where we planned our dreams of being a national act, touring with other eighties bands, where the Dawsons were ripped apart, where Abigail turned into something less than human, and tried killing us.

But this isn't that basement. This is Abigail's world and I don't know a damned thing about it, other than people are dying. Dallas and Ariana are down there, and I've got nothing but a maniac with a gun behind me, overjoyed to turn me over to Abigail. Fucking great.

Daylight streams down to another doorway and the rest is dark. I wish I had a flashlight, but they didn't have them back here. I suppose I could've grabbed a candle but, inevitably, that would get blown out at a very crucial moment. I go down in the dark and pray my eyes adjust quick enough before one of those brown monstrosities attacks me.

"It's about time." Chuck follows me down, staying a couple of feet behind me.

"Did Abby tell you what her plan is for me?"

"She loves you, Rick. She just wants to make you feel the way you left her feeling. Empty-hearted and broken."

"Why do you believe her?"

"Because I know you, Summers. I know what you did to my Katarina."

"Which is worse than you raping your daughter? They call that incest, Chuck."

He slams me on the back of my head with his fist and I go stumbling forward, falling to my knees. When I look back at him, his teeth are pressed together in a snarl and his eyes show no sensibility.

"You know, Summers, Abigail said she wanted you alive. She didn't say I couldn't kick the living shit out of you."

My heart stops and I shudder. This could be very bad. "You know, Chuck, there's no reason for hostilities."

He runs at me and punts me in the stomach. I grunt and collapse. I can't get a breath and the pain is bad. I hope he didn't trash anything important.

"Get up, you fuck." Chuck stands over me. "I thought you were tough. You're nothing but a pussy piece of shit."

Sometimes I can put shit like that out of my head and laugh it off. But I've always hated this asshole. I take short breaths, trying to let the pain go. Sure. Nice and easy. 'Cause nice and easy does it every time. I throw a punch to the back of his knee and he goes down with a grunt.

Before he can react, I grab him by the back of his head and shove him into the wall of dirt. I give him a kidney punch, pull him away from the wall and hit him in the face. His head snaps back and he falls over. He's still got the gun, but I hope he's too dazed to use it.

"Did Abigail say anything about you showing up at all?" I stand up and kick the gun out of his hand. "Did she, Chuck? Tell me something. Did you fuck her, too?"

"I'm gonna kill you, Summers." He rolls over and gets to his hands and knees. Perfect.

I come at him and nail him in the stomach the same way he

did to me. He falls over on his back, holding his guts and gri-
macing in pain. "Sucks, doesn't it?"

Just … wait … I'm … fuckin' … gonna … hurt … you."

"I have a better idea." I grab him and drag him to his knees.
Blood drools from his mouth. "This is for what you did to Kat."
I kick him in the stomach. He doubles over and coughs and
groans. He grabs my leg and I step away from him. "That felt
good, didn't it, Chuck? How long have you been raping your
daughter? Maybe I should do it again." I come at him and his
fist shoots out, nailing me in the groin. I go spinning to the floor
holding myself, the pain blinding me, wiping out all ability to
think.

He crawls to me, hauls me to my knees and hits me in the
face. My head slams against the earth wall, sending clumps of
dirt everywhere, including in my mouth. While I'm spitting dirt
out, trying to find my balls, he lunges at me, slamming me into
the unforgiving wall. I hit it hard, losing my breath. He brings
his head up hard, under my chin and snaps my head back. He
moves away, letting me fall face down on the floor. The proverbial stars spin around, shooting little points of white light
through my vision.

"Should I drag you to Abigail now?" Chuck asks. "Or really
hurt you first so that there's just enough of you left for Abigail
to have. Tell me, Summers, what do you want?"

I spit blood, running my tongue over my teeth. They're all
still there. Luckily, I didn't bite my tongue off; that would've
sucked big time. It takes me a second to catch my breath and
focus on a thought. "Why don't we go see Abigail now?"

"Wrong answer."

I was afraid of that. I stay on the floor, trying to get ready for
his next assault. Why give him any openings to hit me?

"Get up."

"I'd rather stay right here. Why don't you go on ahead?"

"If only Kat was here to see what a fucking pussy you are."

I speak before thinking. "Kat's dead. Abigail killed her."

"What?" he screams. "What did you do to her?" He drags
me up and throws me against the wall. "You tell me where she

is and what you did to her!" Something clicks at waist level and then a very sharp point digs into my stomach. "Tell me!"

I swallow thick, coppery blood and I want to retch. "Abigail killed her."

"I don't believe you." He presses the switchblade in harder.

"Chuck, believe me." Darkness slips over my eyes for a brief second and I start falling, but Chuck props me up. I see his leering face again. "I didn't do anything. Abigail—"

"Abigail wouldn't … wouldn't do anything to Katarina."

"Why wouldn't she?"

"Because."

"Because isn't an answer."

"Because I told her not to harm her. Abigail's after you, not Katarina."

"Actually, she was after both of us until she realized Kat wasn't the person she thought she was."

"Rick, listen very carefully. If you don't tell me the truth, I'm going to take this switchblade and impale your balls on it. Do you understand me?"

"Clear."

"Now, tell me what you did to my daughter."

No matter what I say, I'm fucked. If I tell him Abigail did it, he won't believe me, and if I tell him I did it then he'll surely skewer me. I need another plan. "Why don't you put the knife down? I'm not going anywhere. You're right here. We can talk, right?"

He laughs. Bad sign. "How stupid do you think I am?"

"You're a pretty smart guy."

"That's right and I'm not going to move an inch. If I don't hear what I want, I'm going to make sure you can't have children ever."

"What do you want to hear?"

"Tell me what you did, then get down on your hands and knees and beg for my forgiveness. If I believe you, then we go see Abigail. If I don't believe you, I don't know what I'll do, but I'm sure I'll think of something to make you suffer."

I really wish I could kill him now. Our history has never been a friendly one and it wasn't until I learned he was sleeping with his daughter that I realized why. I'm competition for him. I should kill him just for that, let alone the grief he's caused me since. The truth is, nothing I can say will make any difference. But I can distract him. "What do you know about Abigail?"

"What?" He presses the blade against the inside of my thigh. "I don't want to slip, Rick, so why don't you tell me what you did to my daughter."

"I didn't do anything to her."

He shakes his head. "One more time and that's it for you and your balls. What did you do to Katarina?"

I have to time this just right. "I killed her."

He freezes.

I shove him back.

He drives the blade forward and I try ducking away from him. The blade slices my thigh open and sticks into the wall.

I wish I had the time to get away from him, but the pain in my leg drives me to my knees.

"You God-damned son of a bitch, motherfucker!" He pulls the switchblade from the wall and thrusts again, almost taking my eye out. Instead, he grazes the side of my head, opening another bloody cut. "I'm going to kill you, you fuck!" He pulls the blade back out of the wall.

I stumble away from him, up into the darkness of the hallway. If he can't see me, he can't kill me. Good plan. The pain in my thigh is excruciating, but nothing like what I'd be feeling if he'd hit his target.

"Come back here, Summers!"

I lunge into the pitch blackness of the tunnel and slam against a dirt wall. End of the hallway. I take a second to orient myself and that's when Chuck slams into the wall to my right.

"I know you're here."

I throw myself to the left, keeping along the wall. If this is the same tunnel I was in before, it should lead to Abigail's little chamber. If not, I'll have to face an insane man with a switchblade in the dark. What more could I ask for?

"I hear you, Summers. I'm going to catch you, and then I'm going to cut you apart!"

Weren't there torches here last time? The wall curves slightly to the left, and I abruptly stumble as the floor disappears from under me. I crash down stone stairs, the pain in my leg exploding every time my thigh hits stone. Brilliant dots blossom in my vision each time my skull connects with the stairs.

"Fuck!"

Chuck's coming down after me. I hope I hit bottom and get out of the way before he and his switchblade land on top of me.

The stairs end and I roll to a stop against a hard dirt wall. I quickly lunge to the right, praying that's where the hallway goes. I don't hit any walls, but as I climb to my feet, I slam against a hard body standing in the middle of the corridor.

It hisses and snarls at me. It's probably one of those brown men. I have little time to react before it grabs me by the shirt and hauls me up the passageway. I suddenly don't care what happens to Chuck. After what I saw one of these things do to Meggan, my own future has quickly come into question.

"Where are you, Summers? I'm gonna kill you, you God-damned fuck!"

"Charming, isn't he?" I mumble, but the brown man isn't interested in conversation, only in dragging me to whatever hell it calls home.

I close my eyes and choke from the stench of the thing. It reeks worse than some of the homeless people I pass in the city who haven't bathed in months.

I try standing, but the pain in my thigh lightning bolts up my leg and I stumble. Luckily, the brown man has a good grasp on me, otherwise I'd fall and have a chance of getting away.

I desperately need a plan. Whatever became of Dallas and Ariana is beyond my control. I hope they're still alive, but the chances that they are, if they met up with Abigail, are slim and none.

The brown man stops, and I anticipate him dropping me. Which he does. Down another flight of stone stairs. These seem to be longer and harder and by the time I hit bottom, my entire body aches. I think the cut on my thigh has ripped open more and the one on my head is dripping blood in my eye. What more can go—?

"Ah, Rick. Nice of you to join us," Abigail says somewhere in front of me.

"Thought I'd drop in." I wince when I try standing. My ankle's sprained, or worse. Certainly a few fingers on my hand need to be snapped back in place, but they'll have to wait. I think I pass out from the pain because the next thing I know, the room is lit by hundreds of candles and I'm held up against the wall by two of the brown men. On the far wall, Chuck is in a similar position. Beyond the candlelight, the chamber is in total darkness and I wish she had left the entire room that way.

The creature on the altar looks hideous in the flickering light. It may've been a woman once a long time ago, but now the skin is rotting off and parts of the skull are visible under the clumps of black wire that used to be long, luxurious hair. The body is wrapped in a filthy, decrepit black shawl and a flowing skirt that once was vivid, but is now stained and matted to the gray, flaking flesh. The stink that rises from the dead thing is unbearable and far worse than Ex-Judith. I remember Abigail saying the name, Euryanassa. Could this really be the body of the woman from Greece? No fucking way.

"Recognize her?" Abigail asks.

"No." I do. But refuse to believe that this is the body of Euryanassa. When I was with Cyndi, I saw her with the rest of us in Athens. *Remember Athens.* If only I could. Then maybe I'd remember how to stop Abigail.

"Yes, you do. I can see it in your eyes. It's my body from when I lived in Greece two and a half millennia ago."

"Why is she here? She should be buried or cremated in Greece where she belongs."

"What the hell is going on?" Chuck says. "Who are you?"

Abigail saunters over to him and runs her fingers under his chin. "Don't you recognize me? I'm your Abigail all grown up."

"You're ..." He's got that look of hungry lust on his face.

"Yes, dear Charles, except in another body. This is someone else's. Unfortunately, the Abigail that you met grew up and hung herself because of him." She points at me.

Chuck shakes his head. "Let me at him. He hurt you, he hurt my Katarina."

"He killed her," Abigail says. "I was there."

I chuckle. "Sure you were. You were in my head, making me kill her."

"Oh, please, Rick, don't be so melodramatic." Abigail giggles and comes back near the altar.

"Why is she here?" I try not to look at her ancient body, but I'm fascinated that it hasn't disintegrated yet.

"Long ago, toward the end of Euryanassa's life, I sought out an Egyptian magi who knew the secrets to eternal life. He taught me how to preserve a body for as long as I wanted. After he taught me what I wanted to know, I killed him and performed the rituals over this body. Buried deep within the chest is a vessel made of spider webs and the essence of dead things, and that is where I go to rest when I'm weary from moving from body to body."

"You're insane," Chuck says.

I have to laugh. He's calling her insane. Two peas in a pod and all that. "You brought this dead body with you wherever you went? Didn't people get suspicious of a lone woman lugging something that resembled a coffin and probably stank?"

"I wasn't always a woman. I've kept her in numerous trunks and told people it was my personal belongings. No one bothered me. Those who got curious wound up like the proverbial curious cat. Once I came to New Jersey, I buried my body here so it would no longer be a burden to me. The world grew up and houses were built on this land. First a farm house, and then more houses and soon the passageways were lost, and I had to find another way to get to my body. But then I learned how to remove this house from the present and move it back through time. I also learned how to access the Veils between worlds."

"The Veils?"

"That separate the living from the dead."

"You turned Kat's house into a haunted house?"

"When I brought you here, I gently parted the Veils so that the dead could move into the world of the living."

"What for?"

"To be my servants."

I look at the two brown men holding me, softly hissing. "Why are you telling me this?"

"Because you're as good as dead. Why not? But before the grand finale, I want to show you something." She takes several candles and moves deeper into the chamber. "When I came down here, I found your friend Dallas and Ariana snooping around and I couldn't let that happen. It seems your friend came with some sort of mystical protection against the undead and evil spirits. Luckily, once I took over Ariana and crushed her soul, it was easy to attack Dallas."

She puts the candles up to torches on the walls, illuminating the rest of the chamber. Dallas sits in the far corner of the room, slumped over. A brown man crouches over what remains of Ariana, its maw bloody from its meal.

I close my eyes and shudder, praying my death is a lot faster. My stomach twists and dizziness washes through my head. I throw myself forward, hoping to catch my captors off guard, but it's like fighting a wall. All that happens is my stomach gives up what little it has.

"You always know how to make such a mess." Abigail sighs. "Why can't you be more like Chuck? See? He's not vomiting all over the place." She glances over at him and smiles, then looks back at me. "Don't bother trying to get away, Rick, they're quite strong and in your condition you'll never break free."

"You said we would be together," Chuck says. "Why are you doing this to me?" He looks at the two brown men holding him, glaring at him with hunger.

Abigail smiles. "We will be together. Just not the way you understand together."

"What are you talking about?" Chuck's voice cracks with fear.

"Watch this." Abigail moves to the altar and I wonder if she's going to take her ceremonial dagger and cut Chuck open.

My palms grow hot and sweat breaks out on my forehead. My heart thumps in my chest, growing louder until I imagine I hear my blood rushing through my ears.

"Watch closely, kids, I don't do this very often." She steps up to the altar and gazes lovingly on the prone creature. She touches its face and brings her face closer to the thing. I'm fascinated and repulsed at the same time and I really want to close my eyes before Abigail does whatever it is she's planning. But I don't. I watch with disgust as she kisses the thing on the lips and then slides her tongue in the dead thing's mouth and groans. She climbs on the altar and straddles the creature that used to be a woman.

"What in God's name are you doing?" Chuck asks.

Abigail takes the dead thing's face in her hands and kisses it again. Lora's body convulses, spasms, jerks around, sits up and slips to the floor. I stare at the dead woman, another victim of Abigail's insanity.

"What's going on?" Chuck demands. "What's she doing?"

"You wouldn't believe it if I told you."

"Rick, we've got to get out of here."

"Oh, really, Chuck? You were the one who was gung-ho to bring me down here. What happened? Change your mind about being together with Abigail?"

"I ... I ..."

The body on the altar shivers and a huge cloud billows out, filling the room. The dust of ages fills my lungs and I start choking, coughing, trying to clear my throat to breathe.

Chuck coughs and chokes and I hope he chokes to death. If it weren't for him, I wouldn't be trapped here, watching Frankenstein come to life on the slab.

The arm twitches and lifts slightly. The lips move and it wheezes, making a dry whispery sound as if it's expiring. The brown man by Ariana's body stands and lurches to the altar, its arms cradling something. It's not until it's next to the stone slab that I realize it's pulled organs from Ariana's body. It places them down on the altar, chooses one, and slips it between Euryanassa's desiccated lips. A wet chewing sound comes from the woman's mouth. "Another."

"Oh, shit." A sob chokes my voice. My breath shudders in my lungs and tears stream down my face. Goosebumps race up my arms and I feel faint. I close my eyes from the nightmare and pray for a swift end to this horror.

"Yes," the ancient woman says. Her voice is quiet and rough. When was the last time she spoke?

I open my eyes because it's just instinctual to want to know what's happening. I really wish I could wipe those instincts out right now.

The brown man places another organ in Euryanassa's mouth, letting gore drip between the dead woman's lips. "Another." The brown man obliges and the dead, ancient woman chews each one, until her gray skin takes on a white hue, as if it's returning to the way it was in Greece.

With tremendous effort, takes the Ariana's heart in her hands. "Thank you." She chews on it, making terrible noises that make my skin crawl, until her face is covered in gore. "Delicious. I feel much better now." She takes a slow deep breath and smiles. "It's been too long since I've moved in this body. For centuries I've just come here to rest. Now I will live again as I did long ago." Her words come slowly as if she's remembering how to form the sounds needed to speak.

"Why?" I ask. "Why not just leave the body alone and stay in Lora's?" I wrinkle my nose and breathe through my mouth. "Certainly smelled better."

She laughs. "Because this lifetime, I want to kill you as I was when you sentenced me for my desires."

"Living forever goes against nature. We're created to live a life, sit in judgment and review that life, and then move on."

She barks a laugh. "And who should sit in judgment of us? Who has the right to tell us if we lived right or not?"

"We judge our lives and determine if there's anything else we needed to learn."

"And if we never go through that judgment and retain what we've learned through lifetimes? Why is that bad?"

"How will we know if we are bettering ourselves? If we are learning what we must?"

"Who decides what we are to learn?" Euryanassa blinks and takes a deep breath. "Are you going to tell me it's God, Hadrian? Is it one of the Greek gods who decides what we are to learn?"

Thoughts come into my head as memories born from another lifetime. "We come from the manifestation, Euryanassa. We leave the Godhead to experience life because God cannot manifest on this plane. We go forth and—"

"Blah, blah, blah." With great effort and difficulty, Euryanassa sits up. "Too fucking long since I've moved." She winces and her fingers claw at the stone. "This hurts."

"Poor baby."

"Hadrian, you are so blind. We have the greatest gift and the gods gave it to us. Why should we squander it?"

"Because it serves only our selfish needs, not what God desires."

"Who gives a fuck what the gods desire? Open your eyes, Hadrian, people die every day. They have since the beginning of time. Greece was no different. Cyllene found that out."

"What the fuck are you two babbling about?" Chuck asks, forgotten.

We both look at him.

"I don't know what you are," Chuck shouts, "but a girl named Abigail promised that if I brought her Rick, we would be together, and I'd have a daughter that respected me. Well, Rick is here, and if you're that little girl grown up, you know you made me a promise and I—"

Euryanassa puts a decaying finger to her lips. "Shh." She pushes herself to the edge of the slab. "Attend me." The brown man at the altar comes to Euryanassa and waits while she pulls herself with great effort to the edge of the rock altar. She winces and has to pause every few inches to take a deep breath.

"Not as young as you used to be, eh 'Nassa?" I smile, wondering how powerful she's going to be in a body that's twenty-five-hundred years old. "When was the last time you went for a stroll?"

"Do not mock me, Hadrian. I will make you suffer like you've never suffered before!" The filthy rags that used to be her dress scrape along the stone like dead leaves. Her body trembles from age and her flesh is dried parchment. She is the living dead.

With the help of the brown man, Euryanassa slowly stands, leaning heavily on the creature's shoulder.

"Let me go!" Chuck shouts, trying to break free from the

two brown men holding him. "Please, we had a deal!"

"What are you afraid of?" Euryanassa asks. "A little old lady?"

Chuck cries like a child. "This isn't happening!"

"Oh, but it is!" She laughs and it echoes around the room as if it is a living thing. "Have you never heard how foolish it is to make deals with the Devil?"

Chucks start sobbing and a dark stain soaks through the front of his pants. "Please, let me go! I don't want to die."

How pathetic.

Euryanassa slowly turns her head, wincing from stiff neck muscles. Her eyes are gone, eaten away over the centuries. Fierce, yellow pinpoints of cold light stare at me with fierce malice. "Do you see, Hadrian, why my way is preferable? I would never fall prey to such fears as he has. I know too much. I've experienced too much." She turns back to Chuck. "I told you we would be together, and I did not lie. Unfortunately for you, 'together' as you know it is sexual. 'Together' as I meant it is a lot more than that. It is, in a way, a devouring of your very essence."

"Why? Why? Why?" He's panting, fear forcing his breath.

She slowly hobbles over to him, her tattered rags flowing out behind her, leaving a trail of dust, filth, and stink. "You do not know the truth, Charles. I have been alive for millennia. I have seen the rise and fall of the Roman Empire, the Third Reich, and I'll be around to see the fall of the American Empire. But that's another story." She cocks her head and smiles kindly, showing black teeth. "But right now, it is you and I and I have much to show you before I rip your soul apart."

"Why are you doing this? I don't even know who you are!" Chuck puts up a mighty struggle, but it's no use. The brown men have him, and in a moment Euryanassa will have him as well.

"Because I can." Her fingers graze his face. "So much fear and ignorance. I'm going to set you free, Charles, then you can spend your last moments illuminated."

"Please, don't." He flinches away from her.

"You don't even understand what I'm talking about." She sighs and brushes his face with the backs of her fingers. "Now you will see." She jams her fingers into his eyes, piercing his eyeballs.

He screams and thrashes around, held tight by the two dead creatures.

"In blindness will you find sight." She presses her fingers in deeper until her knuckles brush his eye sockets. "Ah." She twists her fingers and his body jerks like a marionette on drunken strings. "That's it." She draws her fingers out covered in ...

I double over as much as I can and retch. Again.

I look up at her and turn away, but in that brief instant, she has her mouth pressed against his eye socket.

"Stop it!" I scream. "Stop it!"

"Hadrian, are you coming unhinged?" Her laugh is a hideous noise that rips at my mind. "After all these years you'd think I'm the one who would be insane. But it looks like you're cracking."

My heart skips and my breath comes in ragged gulps.

"Are you cracking?" Her voice is kind. Her skirts scrape on the floor and draw razor blades across my nerves. "Are you losing your mind? All your friends are dead, Rick. You are completely alone. Of all the people you've known, I am the only one left." She shuffles closer and the stench of death and rotten meat suffocates me.

I cough against the tide of bile rising in my throat. "Why did you kill Allison and my mother?"

"I wanted to hurt you by taking your family away. How was I to know your sister was Sarah? Next time, I'll be more careful to make sure I save her until I can get the two of you together." The reek of her ancient flesh rotting off her bones slams down my throat and fills my nose.

I clench my teeth, but I won't look up into her malicious yellow eyes. "You've failed before. You'll fail again."

She chuckles; it's like dry leaves over cold cement. "I may have failed this time, but you will die slowly and painfully and there's no one to save you."

"What will you do?" I have to keep her talking until I can think of a way out of this.

"What will I do when?"

"Once I'm dead. You won't have anything else to live for."
I try putting weight on the leg with the cut and when I do, I
barely support myself. There goes one plan out the window.

"I will wait, learn more, and when the time is right, I will
be drawn to you and Sarah and this time I will not fail." She
comes closer to me. "I have learned much in the eons that I've
lived. Some things I have forgotten, while others I never forget.
One of the things I've learned is how to make blood boil. Not all
at once. Just in certain places of your body. I just have to touch
you and—"

I take a deep breath and lash out with my foot, kicking her
as hard as I can. The blow isn't as strong as I want it to be, but I
connect with her thigh. Bones crack and she staggers backward,
screaming in some foreign language.

She turns her rage-filled gaze on me. "What will I do when
you are dead? That will be a long time from now! I will torture
you, heal you, break you, and you will beg me for death. But I
will refuse you!" She looks at one of the brown men holding me.
"Break his leg."

"Wait!"

With the force of a stone wrecking ball, the thing punches
my leg, cracking my femur. Pain explodes in my thigh. Fresh
blood runs from the enlarged cut.

"Let him go," Euryanassa says.

The brown men do as she asks, and I fall to the floor.

"You dare strike me!" Spit flies from her lipless mouth. "You
will know pain like you've never known in all your lives!" She
reaches for the ceremonial dagger on the altar. "This has been
used to sacrifice virgins throughout time." When she turns back
to me, her mouth is pulled in a wicked grin. She limps toward
me, closing the distance until she's mere feet from me. "First I
will take your eyes and then your tongue."

A shadow comes into the room behind Euryanassa, but I
can't tell who or what it is. Probably another brown man, ready
to inflict more pain. In the flickering torch light, the shadow
is small and moves with stealth. Then it's behind the ancient
witch, and she's pulled backward. Euryanassa trips over her

feet and falls to her knees. Kerri is behind her with a black cord wrapped around her throat. A glowing pendant hangs against her gray, withered flesh, burning its symbol into her skin.

"You're not doing anything," Kerri says.

"Who—?"

"Your mistake was forgetting about me, and you've been very careless, Euryanassa … or should I call you Clealeta. That was your name in Rome, wasn't it? When you were my whore."

"Caligula?" Euryanassa gasps.

"Apparently, once upon a time. You're trying to kill someone who means the world to me and I will not let that happen." She yanks on the cord, pulling Euryanassa away from me.

Tears fall and I stay doubled over in pain. I watch the blood running from my leg, wondering if I'll die here in the—how did Kerri get here? She wasn't here when the house shifted. How did she even know to come here?

Euryanassa laughs. "Kill her!"

The brown men close in on the ancient witch and Kerri.

But Kerri tightens the cord around her neck. "I have protections. They can't see me."

Euryanassa chuckles. "You can't kill me. I'll just move to another body and live on as I've always done."

"This is a charm of binding. Turns out I've been having these really weird dreams and when I told a friend about them, she sent me to a very interesting individual who had amulets and spells and was more than happy to help. You're not going anywhere."

The yellow eyes flare brightly, and she snarls. "I will kill you!" She grits her teeth, straining against the black cord. "I will rip your eyes out, chew your tongue from your mouth, claw symbols of eternal torture on your flesh until your soul burns, you fucking bitch!" Euryanassa claws at her throat as Kerri pulls her back. The dagger drops from her hand, kicking up a tiny cloud from the dirt floor. If only I could do more than crawl. By the time I reached for the dagger, Euryanassa would have her brown men break my other leg. I'm truly a one-legged man in an ass-kicking festival. Except it's my ass that's about to be kicked. *What the fuck*, I think and pull myself nearer to the dagger. The white-hot lightning bolt of pain blast from my broken leg, but I need to do something to help Kerri.

Euryanassa throws herself back, slamming her skull into Kerri's chest. Kerri falls backward, crashing against the far wall. She gasps, and the black cord slips from her hand, but the pendant is seared to Euryanassa's withered flesh.

The ancient woman turns and grabs her arm. "You would use your hand against me?" She twists Kerri's arm, snapping it at the elbow. Kerri screams, crying in agony. "I will teach you to ..." She glances over her shoulder at me, still crawling toward the dagger. "You are quite foolish, Rick, Hadrian, Thomas. There is no escape for you." She lunges across the room, faster than I could've imagined.

Just as I reach for the dagger, she takes it in her skeletal fingers, turns it blade down and drives it through my outstretched hand into the dirt floor.

"Stay put!"

This new pain is sharper, brighter than the dull agony in my leg and I cry out. I grasp the hilt and try to pull, but I have very little strength left.

Euryanassa faces Kerri. "And as for you, my little whore. I have something special for you." She mumbles several words I don't understand and the skin on her hand changes until the entire palm and her bony fingers are covered with flesh-colored spikes. "Are you still with us? I'm going flay your chest open, break your ribs apart, and rip your heart out. It has been a long time since I ate the heart of the young and I miss it ..."

Kerri mumbles something, but I don't catch the words. I'm too busy trying to get the dagger out of my hand.

Euryanassa hisses, and then says, "How dare you!"

But Kerri doesn't stop. Her mumblings grow louder; she's chanting. I close my eyes and yank the dagger free. I know what Kerri's singing. It's the same chant I heard in the tunnel under Kat's house, but I hadn't recognized it. Maybe after Abigail opened the past to me, it became clear. I know it and join in. Centuries ago, monks had created a chant of exorcism that destroyed the host body when it was decided that there was no hope in rescuing the poor soul who was possessed. Here, along with the charm of binding, it has the same effect.

Euryanassa cries out. The spikes on her hand sink back into her palm. The chanting opens small holes on her skin that bleed black blood. I wonder if that amulet will really bind her to her old body. I hope so.

I clutch the dagger in my left hand, praying I can still use it with as much force as I'll need to. Against the dull pain in my leg and the burning agony in my hand, I keep chanting and crawl closer to the ancient abomination.

The creature that should've died in ancient Greece falls to her knees, covers her ears, but it's no use. Just like in the tunnel, our chanting opens wounds on her arms, her legs, and her face.

I pull myself closer, close enough to smell her roadkill reek. "Euryanassa, Abigail, Clealeta, by the power of the gods, I deny you life." I reach up and plunge the dagger into her chest where her spirit resides.

She jerks away from me, the dagger embedded to the hilt. Her hands flail wildly, but each time she reaches for the dagger, she pulls her hand away as if burned. Her scream fills the chamber, deafening me. Black blood pours from the wounds, spilling down her tattered Greek tunic and skirts. The pendant blazes white, sealing her spirit in the twenty-five-hundred-year old body.

Her head turns. She looks at me with something like hatred and pity in those yellow eyes. Her hand comes up as if she's reaching for me. "I loved you, Thomas." And then she collapses, the yellow fire in her eye sockets dimming until there's nothing but a black tar-like substance drooling down her face, as if she's crying. Then nothing.

I crawl over to Kerri.

"Did we win?" she asks. "God my arm hurts so much." She reaches out to me with her good arm.

"We did." I take her hand

Kerri cries.

I'm fall in and out of consciousness. We're both going to die down here. No one knows we're here.

"Oh, shit." Dallas stirs, stretches, and looks around. "Anyone get the license plate of that truck? I'm gonna have one fucking headache." He sees us. "I … oh shit! Oh, shit!" He crawls over to me and as the darkness of unconsciousness washes over me, the last thing I hear is Dallas telling me everything's going to be fine.

15.

A week later and Kerri and I sit in her apartment, drinking Bacardi Silvers. I'd been in the hospital for close to a week for the cracked femur and the other injuries, but I'm free now. She would hear no arguments about where I would stay, so she and Dallas rummaged through my apartment and collected a variety of necessities.

The doctors said I should stay off it as much as possible, which Kerri has stuck to, unless I have to go to the bathroom. Then it's crutches and a rolling office chair.

"I can't believe it's only been a week since ..." Kerri frowns and takes a long, slow drink of her Bacardi Silver.

"I know." I stare out the kitchen window at a back alley. We're waiting for Dallas to show up with answers, like how he plans to keep the three of us out of jail or mental institutions for the rest of our lives. Not that we did anything wrong, but the police found us in a house with five dead bodies, a three-thousand-year old woman and a number of piles of human remains that had been the brown men. This was a very tall order.

"I just hope Dallas knows what he's doing," Kerri says. "I mean it's bad enough, but it could be worse."

"Worse?" I laugh. "We're the prime suspects in five murders. The police don't believe us, but why should they? Would you buy something supernatural killed those people?" I glance at Kerri, beautiful, even with the troubled look on her face. "Dallas said he had connections."

She touches my arm. "But Rick, murder is murder."

"I know. But there are a lot of extenuating circumstances."

"We've talked about them already. Pieces of brown men in

Kat's blood and Meggan's body and Ariana's body. Traces of
Euryanassa in Chuck's brain—"

"What more do you want? That should absolve us if only
the police weren't so gung-ho to nail us with the murders."

Someone knocks on the door and we both jump. She lets
Dallas in, and he joins us at the dinette table, sitting across from
me.

"How's the leg?" he asks.

"Getting better all the time," I answer with a smirk.

"A few more days and you'll be up dancing!" He laughs.

"Probably more like a month or two, if not more," I say.

"Really?" Dallas asks.

"That's what the doctors are saying." Kerri shrugs.

"Well?" I ask, hoping for a miracle.

He grins. He did it. "I contacted my friend, Nate Johnson.
He's a field supervisor for the FBI out in Kansas. He was my
contact back when I was doing investigations and I brought him
in on a lot of cases. I wanted him to see what I saw, hoping
that they set up a real X-files department to help us handle all
the calls. The group I worked with was small and we couldn't
get everywhere. Some of the cases were real and others hoaxes.
I thought if I could get the FBI involved, maybe we could get
help."

"What happened?" Kerri asks.

"Nate joined us off the record, saw a lot of unbelievable
shit, but couldn't do much with all the bureaucracy going on.
Nevertheless, he still helps me out when he can." Dallas smiles.
"Here's the deal. The FBI is taking over the case because of
the magnitude of the situation. I mean they've got a number
of dead, that unidentified body in the sub-basement, and the
remains of the brown men. So, this is what they're going to do.
They're going to reconstruct the old woman and use her face as
the mastermind behind a cult plot that Chuck was involved in.

"They looked into Chuck's background and discovered
numerous run-ins with the police. Seems he's an alcoholic
pedophile with a fondness for teenage girls. So they're coming
up with a story that involves drugs, the five dead people, and a
cult with Euryanassa as the leader. Nate's good with this shit."

He glances around the bar. "I've gotta go, but it looks like we're off the hook. They'll use Euryanassa's face as the murderess who convinced people to kill for her. I'll be in touch." He rises and heads to the door. "You guys take care." He gives me the thumbs up and leaves, closing the door behind him.

That day comes back to me in vivid color. Kerri told me later that after we spoke, she took the amulet and came to New Jersey by taxi. The house had returned to its 2004 self and Kerri just followed the stench down into the sub-basement.

"Let's go somewhere." She rests her hand on my arm and grins that sweet elfin grin that makes my heart beat faster. "When you *can* get up and dance."

"Kerri—"

She kisses me and when we break she says, "Even better than I imagined."

"Really?"

"Isa and Todd can run the store. Maybe somewhere where we can be alone without worrying about anything but being together. That's if you're interested."

I nod and take her face in my hands. "I did say I love you and I mean it." I kiss her.

She pulls away from me with a sigh. "I know you have a lot to deal with after everything that happened. I'm here for you if you need me. Okay?"

"Yeah. Thanks."

"I love you, Rick." She squeezes my hand and grins like a little girl with a big crush.

"I love you, too."

16.

THREE YEARS LATER...

The baby girl, hours old, stares at the ceiling. *How did I ... oh no! No, this can't be. They trapped me in a body and killed it and now I'm trapped in this ...* She raises short, stubby arms and waves them in the air. *No!* she cries.

"Oh, sweetheart, it's okay."

Suddenly, the smell of baby powder assaults the girl's nostrils and she cries louder. But when the woman picks her up with soft, gentle hands, she relaxes. *It'll be okay. Everything's going to be—*

Her tiny heart stops. She knows the two people standing at the window waving at her. She knows them by many names. Kerri and Rick. Anna and Thomas. Motela and Hadrian. Many other names come to mind, but it doesn't matter. These are the two people that stopped her after centuries of freedom, and they would pay. She would see to it that their lives were a living ...

The woman bends down and scoops up another baby. She holds one in each arm and turns to the two people at the window.

The baby girl turns and looks at this new baby. *Fucking great. A twin sister.* She stares into the other girl's eyes and she smiles with recognition. *Sarah. How nice to see you again.* She grins. *Oh, this life will be worth it. Finally, I'll have my revenge against Sarah and Thomas. I'll know exactly where they are at all times. Daddy and Sister.* She grins and chuckles. The other girl looks at her and frowns.

Maybe a fire, she thinks. That'll kill all of them. *Or a car accident.* She laughs to herself. *Maybe this isn't so bad after all. All I have to do is remember. Remember. Remember that they ... who? Wait. What's happening? I have to remember them, Thomas and ... and ... what was her name? Who's name? Remember, dammit! Hold on to those names, those faces of the people that ... that what? Did someone do something to me? Why's it slipping away? No! All my memories! Everything I've learned! I can't forget! Remember! Euryanassa, Abigail, come on, girl, hold on to the hatred and remember them.*

Remember.

Remember what?

What?

Re—

"Gaa ..."

ABOUT THE AUTHOR

Gary is the self-employed author of Forever Will You Suffer, a supernatural, time-shifting tale of unrequited love gone horribly wrong and Institutional Memory, a story of cosmic terror in the corporate workplace. He, with Mary Sangiovanni, co-edited Dark Territories, the anthology from the Garden State Horror Writers. Several of his short works have been published, including "Stay Here", "The Fine Art of Madness", and "He Loves Me, He Loves Me Not".

A member of the Horror Writers Association since 2005, Gary has also been a member of the Garden State Horror Writers since 2003, where he spent two years as president.

When he's not spilling his imagination on the page, he plays house-husband, and sometimes plays guitar. He's currently at work on his next novel or three, but that's another story.

NOVELS:
Forever Will You Suffer
Institutional Memory

SHORT STORIES:
"The Fine Art of Madness" (Now I Lay Me Down to Sleep (Necon eBooks))
"He Loves Me, He Loves Me Not" (Space & Time Magazine)
"Stay Here" (GSHW anthology: Dark Notes From New Jersey – 2005)
"You Just Can't Win" (Horrorworld – 2005)

OTHER BITS:
On Writing Horror (WD Press): Roundtable discussion on new horror authors

Curious about other Crossroad Press books?
Stop by our site:
http://store.crossroadpress.com
We offer quality writing
in digital, audio, and print formats.